ALABAMA

LOUISIANA

GULF OF MEXICO

owes
ERS
xxx

813.54
Si6h

DATE DUE			

D1067890

WITHDRAWN
L R COLLEGE LIBRARY

The Horse Soldiers

By the same author:

JOURNEY HOME

AMERICAN YEARS

THE YEARS OF GROWTH

WESTWARD THE TIDE

YEARS OF ILLUSION

THE PORT OF NEW ORLEANS

MUSIC OUT OF DIXIE

HAROLD SINCLAIR

The Horse Soldiers

Harper & Brothers: New York

CARL A. RUDISILL LIBRARY
LENOIR RHYNE COLLEGE

813.54
Si 6h
14 3982
cyn. 1988

THE HORSE SOLDIERS

Copyright © 1956 by Harold Augustus Sinclair

Printed in the United States of America. All rights in this book are reserved. No part of the book may be used or reproduced in any manner whatsoever without written permission except in the case of brief quotations embodied in critical articles and reviews. For information address Harper & Brothers, 49 East 33rd Street, New York 16, N. Y.

FIRST EDITION

A-F

Library of Congress catalog card number: 55-11296

Once more for Ward, another good soldier . . .

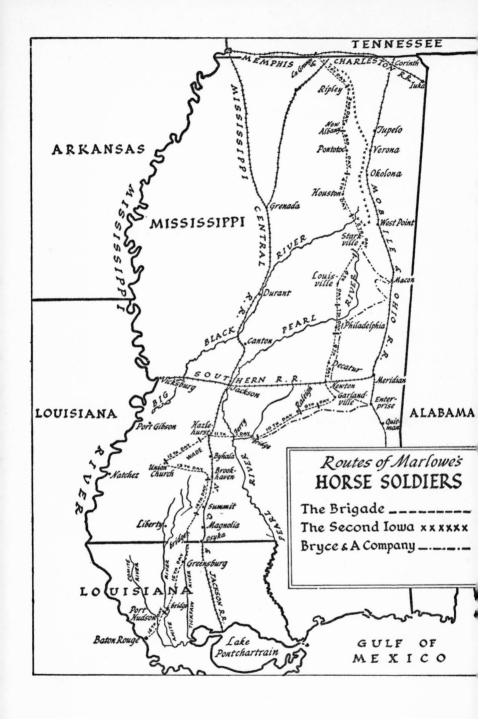

Routes of Marlowe's
HORSE SOLDIERS

The Brigade ----------
The Second Iowa ×××××
Bryce & A Company -·--·--·-

Contents

A Note About The Horse Soldiers

An honest historian would be the first to admit that historical writing at best never more than approximates truth, that it is impossible to reconstruct the true past from documents. One can only select representative facets of the past—names, places, actions. Historical fact can be stark reality, as real as a Brady photograph of the Civil War, but factual history seldom reaches into the hearts and minds of the characters who made it. The historian may use his imagination only in the selection and arrangement of such facts as may have been recorded by persons who lived in the time and place of which he writes. He can never invent; he shies away even from conjecture.

The novelist, however, creating a story around a historical event is free to develop character, to invent speech and thought that reveal character. Because of this, a novelist who knows humanity often reproduces in his work a picture of the past that is more believable to us than the bare bones of history.

Such a book is Harold Sinclair's *The Horse Soldiers*, a masterful re-creation of one of the Civil War's most dramatic adventures—Grierson's Raid. Through the art of fiction, new dimensions have been brought to the factual account, yet nowhere has the author departed from essential truth in telling his version of the story. This is a first-rate example of art turned upon recorded history so that evocation of past time is made more meaningful to the reader.

Colonel Jack Marlowe, Captain Asa Bryce, Major Dick Gray and their horse soldiers, working their way deeper behind Confederate lines than any Union cavalry force had ever ventured, are no mere ghosts of Grierson's Raiders. Their speech is true; their reactions to events and to each other are true. Everything that happens to them could have happened. In fact, it is more than likely that their richly developed characters and their remarkable adventures will be better remembered than the names of most battles and leaders of the Civil War.

> D. Alexander Brown.
> (*historian, author of* GRIERSON'S RAID)

Author's Note

This book is fiction, not history, but students of the American Civil War will recognize that it is based on the episode in that conflict generally known as Grierson's Raid. The original brigade, some 1,700 men, was composed of the Sixth and Seventh Illinois and the Second Iowa Volunteer Cavalry, all under the command of Colonel Benjamin H. Grierson, himself sometime colonel of the Sixth, together with mounted Battery K of the First Illinois Artillery. (In this tale the battery has been abandoned, because the part it played was not significant to this story.) At the time, and according to the army table of organization, a standard cavalry regiment numbered about 1,200 men and three regiments in a brigade would consequently include around 3,600 men. In actual practice, especially by 1863, no brigade commander ever had anything like that many men at his disposal. Through the various erosions of war, regimental strength was more likely to run anywhere from two to five hundred men, and brigade strength added up accordingly. So much for the basic situation.

In the main body of the story the characters and their names are fictional, although their actions are based on historical records. In those parenthetical chapters generally titled "The Pursuit," the names of those Confederate officers who pursued the real Colonel Grierson so fruitlessly—Pemberton, Richardson, Wirt Adams, Ruggles, Loring, Barteau, De Baun, etc.—are taken from the official records of the original exploit.

Place names, elapsed time, the route of the brigade—and its several offshoots—are in general faithful to the original. The newspaper excerpt from the Columbus, Mississippi, *Republic*, on page 150, is taken verbatim from the real journal of that time and place —it is representative of many of the contemporary Mississippi newspaper accounts of Grierson's Raid.

Finally, it is not represented that anything in or of the original adventure occurred exactly as this novel would have it.

HAROLD SINCLAIR

June, 1955

The Horse Soldiers

Beware
Of entrance to a quarrel; but being in,
Bear't that th' opposed may beware of thee.

<small>POLONIUS TO LAERTES, *Hamlet*, Act I, Scene 3</small>

1

Night Talk

The cold nicotine taste suddenly sour in his mouth, Marlowe flung the remains of his tattered cigar through the open window. The gesture was vaguely savage, a physical reflection of his current state of mind.

He thought, with detached bitterness: What a hell of a way to run a war—a notion that had occurred to him at least a thousand times during the past two years. Yet he no longer found any real intellectual solace in this military heresy; the thought had become threadbare from overuse, a sort of wry and certainly not too orginal personal cliché. Lately he had played with the notion that this was an entirely wrong approach to military criticism—perhaps war could only be understood by assuming in the beginning that utter confusion was its normal state. Once you accepted that point of view then the irrational became rational, the . . .

1

Behind him Smith's chair creaked as the general moved irritably. He said, "By God, Marlowe! I had hoped this would be one time when Hurlbut would put his proposition without going back to Genesis and working up through Fort Sumter. But oh, no! He—"

Marlowe turned from the window and with the impersonal military courtesy which by now had become ingrained habit said, "Beg pardon, sir?" Of course he had been aware of General Smith's voice but had in truth missed the sense of the words.

"I was just saying—"

Hurlbut re-entered the room and resumed his seat at the big paper-cluttered table which served him as desk. Major General Stephen A. Hurlbut was a long way from being the youngest general officer in the Union Army, but at forty-eight he was commander of the Sixteenth Army Corps and the Memphis Military District, outranked by only a handful of men in the West, a figure of authority to be reckoned with if not loved or admired.

With the heartiness of the natural bore Hurlbut said once again, "Well, now, gentlemen, where were we? Oh, yes—" and Marlowe had a violent desire to kick something—hard. It was now ten o'clock and except for the supper interval (Hurlbut had had a personal eating engagement) they had been here since around three in the afternoon—that is Smith and Marlowe had. Hurlbut had been up and out and back again so many times they had lost all count. He was one of those executives who can leave no detail to its own or someone else's devices. There was no knowing which of these departures, if any, concerned a perhaps fateful military decision, a routine check on a sidetracked car of mule feed, or a personal visit to the necessary.

They were here to reach a decision of importance, yes—or at any rate to listen to one. In fact, for this Smith and Marlowe had been summoned in person from Smith's First Division Headquarters at La Grange, fifty miles to the east on the Memphis & Charleston Railroad, which they were nominally engaged in guarding against Confederate forays which seldom occurred in

any real force. In spite of General Hurlbut's diversions and cir-
cumlocutions they had disposed of the real meat of the matter in a
relatively short time. If it was important in the military sense—and
it was—it was also reasonably uncomplicated.

Hurlbut had taken his stance before the big wall map of Mississippi and given them the full picture as of this time, April 3, 1863,
including a lecture on the state's geography and topography, most
of which they already knew or they wouldn't have been here in
the first place.

Union forces held the Mississippi itself from Memphis south and
from the Gulf north to the general area between Port Hudson and
Vicksburg, the last great Confederate bastion in the west, and
about which Grant and Sherman even now were slowly massing
all the strength they could bring to bear effectively; they held the
Tennessee–Mississippi border east to the Alabama line and beyond,
paralleling the Memphis & Charleston Railroad. Beyond the picket
points inside this huge right angle they held nothing, but, as Hurlbut put it:

"Right now we don't care. There's nothing much in interior
Mississippi that's worth a damn militarily—or any other way to my
way of thinking—and what there is will eventually die on the vine.
But there is one thing down there that's a lot of bother."

Again Hurlbut was at the map—Marlowe could see it almost as
well with his eyes closed. He had nothing against maps as such
—two-dimensional diagrams of unimportant towns and meandering
lines representing rivers and railroads. All very well as far as they
went but neatly omitting the thousand-and-one details of consequence to a cavalryman. With a finger Hurlbut traced the elementary railroad system of the state. From Memphis southeastward
near the center of the state ran the Mississippi Central, at Jackson
becoming the New Orleans & Jackson and extending on to the
Crescent City; from the Tennessee border south, and holding close
to the Alabama line, the Mobile & Ohio, ending at Mobile on the
Gulf; running almost straight east out of Vicksburg and bisecting

the north-south lines of the two former, respectively, at Jackson and Meridian, was the Southern.

"The damned nuisance," Hurlbut said, "is the Southern—*here*. Ninety per cent of the supplies for Pemberton at Vicksburg are getting to him that way, either from Alabama and Georgia, from interior Mississippi itself, or up from Mobile by way of the transfer point at Meridian. That's the problem and the proposition, gentlemen, to damage and tear up the line and equipment of the Southern as much as possible. Your First Brigade, Marlowe, is the right force in the right place at the right time."

Hurlbut had plowed on, determined to get it all framed in words. A force of infantry with some artillery would move southward from Corinth, staying close to the M. & O. and the Alabama line. Similar forces would march southeast from Memphis and slightly southwest from La Grange, both angling toward the Mississippi Central where it crossed the Tallahatchie River. All three of these movements would be nothing more than diversions, intended only to draw Rebel strength to the eastern and western sides of the state, leaving the center open and undefended—the planners hoped. These three columns would move far enough south to draw the maximum possible amount of Rebel attention, far enough to make their intentions appear serious—and then withdraw. Giving these others a couple of days to accomplish their diversions and draw fire, Marlowe's First Cavalry Brigade of Smith's First Division of the Sixteenth Corps would then go straight down through the open center.

Well, it was not too improbable a scheme. With any luck it was quite possible, even probable, that Marlowe would get to and work his pleasure on the Southern Railroad. Getting back, of course, would be another matter entirely. So far so good, even though it had taken Hurlbut more than four hours of actual talking time to expound the proposition.

Smith himself would handle the feint southwestward from La Grange, although he was here now more specifically as Marlowe's immediate superior, military protocol—it was proper to deal with

Marlowe as the principal in the plan, but also proper to have General Smith in on the details. Actually Marlowe had heard rumors of some such scheme for months, though not that he was to head it. The plan itself was not original with any one source. Grant himself had had some such notion in February, but had abandoned it because of bad weather and equally bad roads. Hurlbut had pondered a similar scheme; so had General Smith himself. None of the three ideas had been precisely alike and now this final, actual plan was something of a synthesis of all of them.

Smith grinned with sardonic relish. "I wouldn't mind trading places with you, Colonel, though to tell the truth it doesn't look to me as though you'd even get a choice between being shot and hung."

"I appreciate that, sir," Marlowe said dryly, "though it's a point that's never worried me much—too academic. I might say, General Hurlbut, that it's a hell of a long ways from La Grange to the nearest point on the Southern—two hundred miles through territory as thick with Rebels as hair on a dog. I'm not thinking so much of the military as of civilians only too willing to carry news."

"Everyone concerned is well aware of that," Hurlbut said a little stiffly. He hesitated, as though searching for precisely the words he wanted. "I don't believe you know this," he said somewhat elliptically, "but at one time we considered asking for volunteers for this thing. But the notion was discarded as impractical. You can ask for one volunteer, ten, maybe even fifty; you can't ask for a thousand without having the story all over the country. In this thing there must be a big enough force to handle any nominal opposition, yet not so big as to be unwieldy. This is essentially a raid, not a campaign."

"Oh, I understand that perfectly," Marlowe agreed.

Hurlbut made a steeple of his fingertips. "In all honesty, Colonel Marlowe, there's a little more that could, perhaps even should, be said. You commented on the distance. Did you intend that as an official objection?"

"Certainly not, sir!" Marlowe almost barked. Then he checked himself. "Probably the remark was uncalled for. Say I was calculating out loud. Obviously we're all aware of the distance involved."

"Yes. Well, if you go strictly by the book you might, I say *might*, raise the point that even top authority might not have the right to order such a force into a situation that—er, such a situation. Let's not fool ourselves. I'd be a double damned fool if I deliberately ordered an officer into a thing like this, when and if I knew personally that he had no stomach for it—and no written orders have been issued on it."

It was a delicate and somewhat devious point but it was out in the open now. This was something planned in advance, with deliberate calculation, and if the whole thing turned into a bloody debacle with perhaps nothing accomplished, and the field officer commanding could or would maintain that he had been personally opposed from the beginning—well, the ensuing hell might reach all the way to Washington City. Marlowe couldn't merely acquiesce by silence, not now. He had to speak up and be counted, one way or another.

"Oh, I'm absolutely all in favor, sir!" he said quickly. "I'd hate to miss the chance to handle it. Frankly, an officer in my spot doesn't too often get a chance at really independent command. On the other hand, it seems only common sense to weigh the pros and cons."

"Certainly—in fact, the only thing to do. I might say, gentlemen, that while General Grant didn't originate this idea, this precise plan that is, he is interested personally and has made several specific suggestions. Vicksburg is proving to be considerably more of a problem than was thought at first, and—well, every bit of extra pressure will be useful. I might also add, Colonel, that several officers were considered for this operation, but I insisted you were the only logical choice."

"Why, thanks, General," Marlowe said, his voice again dry and noncommittal. "I appreciate that." He didn't necessarily believe the general entirely but of course it might be so. The general hadn't said that Grant had personally suggested others but the inference was there—in fact, no one else was ever considered. A dubious honor perhaps, as Smith had so plainly suggested, but then this too was war.

"You understand, Marlowe," Hurlbut went on, taking up the slack, "your one and only objective is the Southern Railway, and you are not to engage if it can possibly be avoided. You can't hope to gain by battle, other than to perhaps shake off minor forces. And trouble attracts trouble, you know."

"I'm aware of that, sir. But the meat of it's in that phrase, 'If it can be avoided.' That's partly what I had in mind when I spoke of two hundred miles being a long way. We can propose; they may dispose."

"There's always that," Hurlbut conceded.

"With your permission, I'd like to have a couple of matters definitely understood, sir."

"Well?"

"I know my men, at any rate those in my own First Illinois. Every last one is a volunteer and with few exceptions they're all veterans. A few have already done some time in Rebel prison camps and they don't care for any more of that. If we should get in a hole I wouldn't deny them the chance to save their own necks. I doubt very much that I could."

"Well, no," Hurlbut agreed. "It's a thing we don't dwell on too much, but when you get down close enough to fundamentals it's the individual soldier who finally makes his decision as to whether to fight or quit. He may be influenced by orders or the example of others, but he finally comes to the final split second where he has to decide whether to throw away his rifle or keep on using it. These are imponderables. You'll undoubtedly run into some trouble; that, I suppose, we can take for granted. The thing is not to go looking for it en masse. Nobody requires miracles of you, Colonel, but above all you're not going down there with the primary intention of fighting. You'd be more useful doing that at Vicksburg."

"I appreciate that, though I'll probably need a miracle in the personal sense, General."

With time out for supper at the Gayoso House, plus the other innumerable interruptions, all this had brought them finally to around nine o'clock. It had taken far too long but still they were were in general agreement. . . .

This neat brick building on the Memphis levee, once the business premises of Messrs. Mayhew & Company, Cotton Factors, now by due process of civil war—Marlowe rather relished that phrase— was headquarters for the Sixteenth Army Corps. Even at this latish hour there was considerable activity belowstairs. Up here they could hear the coming and going of hurried footsteps, occasional hoofbeats in the street outside, the intermittent droning talk of bored duty clerks, the staccato hammering of telegraph sounders.

Thus Hurlbut one more time: "Well, gentlemen, where were . . . ?"

"This further question occurs to me," Marlowe said, with a masterly patience which escaped Hurlbut entirely. "I've always figured that a man shouldn't deliberately gamble unless he could afford to lose—or at any rate was prepared to, and there's no denying that this is a long gamble. Is Army Headquarters prepared to stand the loss of a full cavalry brigade? Maybe I should say the possible loss?"

Hurlbut looked out the window toward the dark flowing river. Near the midstream channel a fully lighted gunboat churned its cumbrous way north—this was Union water and there was little need for caution these days.

"I wouldn't say they're quite prepared to take it for granted in advance," Hurlbut said a little obliquely, again seeming to choose his words one at a time. "But once on your way there won't be any choice—I mean from this end, and any military move is a gamble up to a point. That's the best answer I can give you, Colonel."

"Then I reckon it'll have to do, sir."

Hurlbut moved heavily in his chair, fumbled in a table drawer, and came up with a fresh cigar. "There is one other little point we haven't touched on, gentlemen. Assuming that you make it to the line of the Southern, Marlowe, then you should swing to your left and plan to make your way back generally by way of western Alabama."

Marlowe came erect like a suddenly uncoiled spring and erupted an almost explosive "No!" His mind had been ranging far ahead of their talk and now a sense of outrage, the outrage of plain common sense, welled in him. Hurlbut's remark had been offhand-edly casual but had struck Marlowe as being utterly preposterous.

Hurlbut's heavy brows went up and he leaned slightly forward on the table. Coldly he said, "How was that again?"

"As I see it, General, if we manage to get that far we will have stirred up all of Central Mississippi in the process. There'll be nothing to do but go on. I just don't see any other possible way, sir!"

"Go on?" Hurlbut looked at the colonel as though the latter had taken leave of his senses and suggested returning by way of Atlanta and Richmond. "Go on where, sir?"

"To wherever I can, or have to—there'll be no knowing until I get there. Even if these feints up here work—and I think they will in the beginning—how long is it going to take the Johnnies to find out—guess—what I'm really up to? Four days? Five or six? Good God, General! If I can even manage to move a thousand men two hundred miles in *seven* days, if I don't have to fire a gun, it will be a near miracle. And once the word is out every Reb in Mississippi will be out to get us. No, I don't dare try to come back. All I *can* do is try to keep ahead of 'em."

"I don't see it," Hurlbut said stubbornly.

Marlowe glared hard at the floor. He held himself to be no tactical genius, but a ten-year-old could see that with a minimum of luck anybody could get himself into this bear trap; the trick would lie in getting out. Of course Hurlbut was no cavalry specialist, but he was a general officer, one, furthermore, anointed with the special unguents of West Point, and he ought to know. . . .

"I've given this a lot of thought, Marlowe, believe me, and I know Alabama's your best bet. You'll be doing the unexpected, throw 'em off balance—double back. That'll do it."

"Head into Alabama, yes, maybe, if I have to. But as I see it, it will be near suicide to try and double back—"

Smith, with a minimum of motion, finally got up and drifted unobtrusively to one of the windows, almost directly behind Hurlbut.

. . . It had been this sudden apparent stubbornness of Marlowe on which the whole thing came near foundering. Hurlbut's mind was made up. Smith was being as publicly neutral as possible; if he had backed Hurlbut with words then Marlowe would have been sunk under sheer weight of numbers; but he wasn't giving Marlowe any open encouragement either. The latter could expound his case up to a point, but he couldn't make a corps commander swallow a judgment he was determined *not* to swallow. A corps commander's judgment is, according to the book, presumed to be sound because of what *he* is, not what the judgment is.

Very coldly Hurlbut said, "Are you deliberately questioning my judgment in this, Colonel Marlowe?"

At the window Smith nodded at Hurlbut's broad back and shook his head violently.

Marlowe felt the rising tide of futility. "Oh, certainly not, sir. It's only that—" He hesitated, momentarily hunting for the right phrase.

"Only what, Colonel?"

With an effort Marlowe rearranged his face and took in a deep breath. "Obviously we both recognize the problem, General. Possibly it's just that we're approaching it from opposite points of view." It sounded as though it made some sort of sense but for the life of him Marlowe at the moment couldn't have explained just what the sense was.

"Hmm. Possibly. Once you're on your way," Hurlbut said a bit more warmly, "you will of course have to use a good deal of discretion, but I must insist on this point. You'll find I'm right, Colonel."

Marlowe wondered if the general actually believed a word of that, or whether he was just acting like a general, but he said, "You'll put these details in writing, sir?"

"Oh, yes, certainly, when we reach that stage. I wanted this talk to iron out these trivial details it shouldn't be necessary to put on paper."

"Begging your pardon, sir," Marlowe said with what he hoped was proper deference, "I wouldn't consider the possible return route to be a small matter."

Hurlbut waved a hand. "Well, I was speaking in generalities, Colonel. The official orders will of course be sent through General Smith here."

"Of course, sir," Marlowe said woodenly.

Hurlbut rose abruptly—he could reach a stopping point when he put his mind to it. "I don't think it will be necessary to have you and General Smith here again in person. You, or at any rate General Smith, will hear from me. I'll wish you all the luck, Colonel."

"Thanks, General. We can use any there is to spare."

At the entrance downstairs they acknowledged the salute of a rather slovenly sentry and passed on into the semidarkness of the street. Beyond earshot of the sentry Smith chuckled and said, "You strike me as a man with maybe a good deal on his mind, Marlowe. You might as well unload some of it on me—within reason, of course."

"Ah, the God-damned desk army! It's no wonder we haven't wiped up this whole stinking business long ago."

"Mmm—maybe. But have you ever heard of a war that wasn't run this way, more or less? I mean, the confusion is never absent, it just takes different forms. I've often thought that the field officers of Hannibal and Alexander probably had the same kind of complaints."

"At least not the same amount of paper and red tape."

"Who knows? But if not that, probably something just as aggravating. As for Hurlbut—well, rank always has its privileges and that covers a lot of territory."

"We're all human enough, if that's what you mean."

"Oh, partly—and in a war of politicians and amateurs you sure have to allow for that. But I'll tell you something else. In this deal Hurlbut is just acting as intermediary—we happen to be in his department. If this thing happens to work out, why, he can claim a certain amount of credit; if it doesn't, then he was just passing on the orders. Very neat. One way he may gain a little but in neither case can he lose. Incidentally, are you really in favor of this thing or merely going along for want of a real choice? I know what you told Hurlbut but now I'm asking you myself."

"Oh, hell yes, I'm all in favor, General. Of course it's a long gamble but I personally don't have too much to lose. And with some luck I may even get away with it, or enough to make it worth the effort. Personally, I'm a little sick of this business of wait, wait, wait."

"Keep your pants on," Smith said calmly. "You know what I said about rank having its privileges. That's why I warned you off Hurlbut—in a full-dress wrangle you'd only lose. He was obliged to leave his own mark on this somewhere and that was it. You can forget that part of it."

"Well—I'm not so sure. As far as I could see and hear he was plain enough." Fishing a little, Marlowe was aware that Smith was pointing toward something.

"Sure he was clear enough—as to what he thinks, or anyway believes he thinks, and once he'd made his pitch he didn't see any way to back down. But the nub of the matter is this—the official orders, as he said, will come to me, and just exactly how those orders read is, technically, none of your business. You will be concerned solely with the orders you in turn get from me."

"I take it then that you don't altogether agree with General Hurlbut?"

"Well, now, Colonel," Smith said with deceptive mildness, "I didn't say *exactly* that. Let's say that on this particular point I'm a little more inclined to agree with you. There's a difference. God knows, Marlowe, I froth at the mouth over some of the things the gold braid does—and doesn't do. But all the same the Hurlbuts have their function—they provide a point of departure if nothing else. Frankly, Marlowe, for my money you happen to be one of the best field officers I know—no, no especial compliment, hear me out—but just as frankly, I'm not sure it would be all net gain if every field officer was a twin to you. Mind you, all this is just a private theory of mine—I wouldn't particularly want it advertised in the papers."

Marlowe grinned in the darkness. "I think I know exactly what you mean, sir." More than a few people didn't care a great deal for General Sooy Smith but Marlowe had never had cause to complain. Smith was not a man to carry his innermost feelings on display, and yet on occasion—as of now—Marlowe had been able to get past the barrier—or allowed past it. He felt easier with Smith than with a good many others of like rank, but all the same Smith was still "General." He might (on occasion) be slightly heretical on general issues but one couldn't count on it. It was supposed to be fairly common knowledge, for instance, that there was little love lost between Smith and Hurlbut, but Smith wouldn't remark on that here—whatever the truth involved it was not the business of a mere colonel, regardless of how good an officer he might be.

They walked a way farther in silence and then Marlowe laughed softly, as though at some private joke.

"What?" Smith asked.

"Purely a personal matter. After two years I'm still a regimental colonel, which in one sense is perfectly all right with me. I have no ambition to run the war personally—the headaches Grant has would have foundered me long ago. Yet for the past six months I've had a brigade to manage and now I've been handed this hot potato—and still on the brigade level. If there's such a shortage of brigadiers, then why not make a few? In some ways I don't really give a damn, but there's a matter of principle involved too. If I'm to have the responsibility indefinitely I'd just as soon have the permanent rank to go with it. To me that seems like elementary justice."

Smith chuckled sourly. "There's no shortage of brigadiers as such, Marlowe. In fact, one thing this army needs is fewer brigadiers and more good sergeants. The President can make brigadiers by the dozen—and by God! he does—but even he can't make a first-class sergeant. Seriously, I know how you feel and—well, I've sent your name up twice but I can only propose." Apparently Smith didn't choose to linger on the almost always delicate matter of promotion, at any rate he abruptly changed the subject. "Incidentally, where are you bound for?"

"Right now? I suppose the M. & C. yards—back to La Grange. The last passenger went at eight o'clock and of course Hurlbut fixed that. I'll have to see if I can manage a ride in a frieght caboose or on a flatcar."

"Well, in that case the Gayoso Bar isn't much out of your way —have a couple for the road. I'm staying over at the Gayoso until tomorrow myself, now that I'm here. A little personal business."

They turned left into relatively brighter lighted Gayoso Street and a pair of slightly drunken infantrymen hastily made way for their braid.

"Time enough for a couple," Marlowe agreed. "No telling when I can get a ride."

Somewhere on the dark river behind them a steamboat whistle bellowed mournfully. For an instant Marlowe felt that loneliness of spirit which is the occupational disease of the nonprofessional soldier who fights a war far from the place he thinks of as home.

2

Horse Soldiers

One of the things a field army produces in quantity is rumor. Even in the most sanguinary of wars an army does more waiting than fighting, and speculation serves to pass the time, provide a fresh topic for talk, and somewhat alleviate the universal boredom. And sometimes, of course, the rumors actually have a basis in truth.

The present flutter in the First Brigade was set afoot by several minor but apparently related occurrences. To begin with Colonel Marlowe had gone to Memphis, Corps Headquarters, with General Smith, on official business it was said, and stayed overnight—or at least Marlowe didn't return until the next morning; and this was considered portentous if only because it was so unusual. Then shortly after his return the colonel had issued orders that the shoeing of every mount in the brigade was to be checked, and to be repaired or replaced as warranted. In addition all equipment, with special reference to arms and leather accouterments, was to be put in first-rate order, subject to a general inspection to follow.

15

The brigade nodded its collective head and agreed that it all added up to something more than the usual monotonous routine of the past winter.

Sergeant Nate Brown sat with his back propped comfortably against the trunk of a live-oak tree, a hundred yards or so from the tent lines which housed the First Illinois Cavalry. He chewed his wad of cut plug industriously and from time to time cocked an eye at the stringy private working the bellows of the portable forge. At this exact moment the sergeant felt good. Spring comes early here where Tennessee drifts into Mississippi, a full month earlier than in Dexter County, Illinois; actually right now it felt more like early summer than spring, and it was pleasant to sit here in the dappled shade and do nothing but exercise his jaws. Pretty soon he would have to go to work—damned if a man could ever escape that, even in a war. But one thing about being a noncom, you had a certain limited amount of leeway.

Brown watched the youth at the bellows almost paternally—he was really fond of him. A farm boy, Private Ed Stumm had hardly been ten miles from home when, shortly after that hell on earth at Shiloh, he had enlisted in Company A of the First. With innocent and grave composure he told Captain Bryce that he had come to take the place of his brother Harry, killed in the first Rebel onslaught that peaceful (up to then) Sunday morning. Nobody doubted his good intentions for a moment—these solemn recruits were often that way in the beginning. Captain Bryce, equally straight-faced, said, "Any more of you Stumms at home in case we need 'em?" Ed said, "Yes, sir—two, except they ain't as old as I am an' Paw didn't want to send 'em just yet." And nobody doubted that that was the truth either. He'd made a good soldier, in the estimation of his fellows and that was what counted.

At the bellows Private Stumm gradually eased off and finally came to a complete stop. He removed his battered and dusty hat and raked sweat from his brow with a finger.

Without moving a fraction of an inch the sergeant said, "God damn it, kid, I told you to keep that fire jumpin'!"

"I know, Sarge, I know, but what in hell for? You ain't gonna hot up any shoes till Murphy and Pete get here with 'em. Don't get in an uproar—the heat'll hold awhile."

But having delivered his order the sergeant made no effort to follow it up, nor had he intended to. "Yeah, an' that reminds me —where in hell are they?" It was really a rhetorical question, the sergeant not being vitally interested in an answer at the moment. "They been gone long enough to haul a load o' shoes clean from Memphis. Well, we don't have to work till they git here. Maybe it ain't such a bad idea at that."

Being thus reprieved, if only by omission, Private Stumm pulled a fresh blade of grass and chewed it softly, thoughtfully, country-man fashion. "Nice weather, Sarge. It kinda gets you thinkin'. Back up home my old man'll be plowin' about now if it ain't too wet. I never figgered to see the day when I'd downright hanker to watch the hind end of a span o' mules on a plow. But I dunno—"

"Homesick, kid?"

"Naah. I was maybe a little at first but I got over it. It ain't any-thing like that. It's just that—well, seems like a man ought to work if he's able. Anyhow, I was raised that way."

"Great jumpin' Christ! You mean to tell me you ain't gittin' enough work to suit you?" The sergeant's eyes suddenly glowed with sinister interest.

"Oh, there ain't no shortage o' work. I reckon I mean a man ought to be doin' somethin' *useful*."

On that one the sergeant shifted his cud to the other jaw and for once didn't come back with the instantaneous retort. In a fumbling kind of way the boy had, you might say, made a fair commentary on the whole business of war.

But having gotten the sergeant off the all-important subject of work in hand, Stumm said, "Whatta you reckon the Old Man's up to, Sarge?"

Colonel Jack Marlowe, a venerable thirty-six years of age, was of course and inevitably the Old Man.

"Well, he ain't consulted me about it yet. Course he will—the same time he tells the rest of whoever's goin'. But jokin' to one side, it'll probably be Vicksburg; anyway, that's the smart guess, way things are. I sure hope to hell it ain't middle or east Tennessee. People in that Godforsaken country're born with one leg shorter'n the other an' they plant corn on them sidehills with a shotgun. Me, I'll take my ground on the flattish side if I got any druthers. But the word is that Grant's havin' his troubles down there an' we might be elected—we sure ain't doin' any good here. The God-damn' horse calvary," Sergeant Brown added reflectively, and re-lieved his mouth.

It was, logically enough in the circumstances, the collective opinion of the brigade that it would be going to Vicksburg, cur-rently the most important place in Mississippi.

"What's the matter with the calvary?" Stumm persisted. Having gotten off the subject of work, he intended to keep it that way. "You enlisted in it, didn't you?"

"Yeah," Brown drawled, "but you might say it was sorta under false pretenses—I mean the calvary was under false pretenses." Sometimes he wasn't sure whether Stumm was all or only a small part green country boy.

"As how?"

"Well, it's a sad an' pitiful story, bub. There I was, black-smithin' for more'n fifteen years—hell, I've even took prizes at fairs for some o' the shoes I've made. It ain't a bad trade an' I made my two, three, four dollars a day whenever I wanted to work at it. But a man can get tired o' the best deal on earth—I dunno, maybe bankers git tired o' foolin' with money. So when the John-nies started this dingfod I was gittin' tired of burnin' holes in my pants, to say nothin' o' fresh manure down my neck on the average o' once a day. Abe asked for volunteers—couple times I did a little work for him personal when I was in Springfield—an' I bit. Back there it looked to be a nice little outin'. Bein' associated with horses, why, I had a natural turn for the God-damn' calvary. Be-sides, if you're goin' to war you might as well ride as walk "

"So then what you kickin' about?"

"Hold on—I'm comin' to that. Well, the braid comes around an' asks what every man's trade is, an' like a God-damn' dummy I come right out an' admit I'm a farrier. Jesus Lover! Imagine— admittin' you're a farrier right in the middle of a damn' calvary outfit!" The sergeant spat in vast self-disgust. "So for two years more I'm still horseshoein'—but for a stinkin' sergeant's pay an' rotten rations. Next time they ask, I'm gonna be a clerk or a sampler in a wholesale liquor house."

"Yeah," Stumm nodded soberly, "I see how it is."

An open wagon behind a team of mules pulled to stop a few yards away. Corporal Murphy climbed back over the seat into the wagon bed and kicked one of a half-dozen kegs of new horseshoes. "Hey, Sarge," he called cheerfully, "where you want this load o' hardware put at?"

Sergeant Brown rose and picked up the leather apron he'd been sitting on all this time. Ignoring the corporal's question on principle, he roared, "Where in hell you soldiers been all mornin'?"

"Now, Sarge, it's a good three mile over there to that warehouse an' you know how them bastard quartermaster—"

"Don't gimme no back talk, Murphy! Unload them shoes over there in the shade an' then get that wagon the hell outta the road!"

"All right! All right! I was only sayin'—"

"Stumm, you hump yourself on that forge. You shoulda been doin' that instead o' waggin' your jaws!"

Nate tied on the heavy leather apron and rolled up his sleeves. He wasn't at all what would be called a big man—many blacksmiths are not—but after years at the anvil his forearms were thick as fence posts. He walked to the anvil, which stood on a heavy oak block, picked up the four-pound hammer, and struck the anvil a sort of practice blow that rang like a cathedral bell.

"All right, you Pete! Get the hell over there an' get 'em movin'. First platoon of A Company first, the rest of 'em in order. Jump now!"

They jumped—and Sergeant Brown, farrier to the horse cavalry, was back in business again.

3

Marlowe

Marlowe crumpled the brief note brought by the orderly, tossed it on the ground and mangled it still further under a boot-heel. The note had read:

> Sorry, but still no official orders. Have been prodding Hurlbut as much as prudent but so far without result. Will let you know instant when there is anything. Regards.
>
> Smith.

Marlowe disliked to push General Smith, even in the most polite manner—it was poor general procedure, for one thing. And Smith too in this was only an intermediary and obviously couldn't pass on something he didn't have. But to Marlowe the waiting was becoming most intolerable and he felt he had to do something, anything. Even a knowingly futile gesture gave him a feeling of movement of a kind; there was a certain relief in trying. For his own present peace of mind he ocassionally wished he'd never heard of the Mississippi project.

In a somewhat different way this feeling also operated in the brigade itself. After what seemed to the men an almost wasted winter—and who could say they weren't right?—it had become obvious that they were now to do something, they were as eager and ready as they would ever be—and nothing happened. They would, of course, do whatever was required if and when the time ever came, but each extra day of delay (after a certain point had been passed) dulled the edge of eagerness just a little more. Perhaps in the long run it wouldn't make any measurable difference. Morale was a difficult thing to isolate and weigh of itself. Marlowe was perfectly aware of these things and the knowledge added to his own feeling of helpless frustration.

From a field locker at the foot of his cot he took a half-empty bottle of whisky and poured himself a long drink. He started to put the bottle back, changed his mind, shrugged, and poured a second round as hefty as the first.

John Francis Marlowe was not, at bottom, what was commonly known as a drinking man. He was more aware than most that life consists of a great many things besides the passing solace to be found in a bottle, but certainly he was no stranger to it.

In the sprawling Union Army of 1863 almost any kind of human equation could be found, but even so Marlowe was perhaps a somewhat unique variation. For most men (aside from the relative handful of Regulars) the war was an interruption of their normal lives, something for which they momentarily turned aside, as though to put out a fire in the house of a neighbor. But for Marlowe the beginning of the war coincided almost exactly with the ending of a special period in his own life. All the ten years of his marriage he had been in love with Elaine, both romantically and realistically, but during the last three years of it she had obviously been ailing, and seriously. Of course she made light of it at first, belittled it as something unimportant that would presently pass away, and later tried gallantly to conceal it, until that too had become physically impossible. The doctors—he'd had a whole bevy of the best available—had been baffled, and a couple of them had gone so far as to admit it—well, almost. In the end it was agreed that the only thing which *might* help—and they stressed the might —was a complete change of climate and surroundings. That, Marlowe had reflected privately, was at any rate one way of removing the patient from their own area of medical responsibility. He had also doubted, again in private of course, that such treatment, if such it could be called, would help, yet he could see no alternative and was at a point where he would have tried anything short of sheer witchcraft. Accordingly he had liquidated a very prosperous grain-handling business, had sold his house and other property, most of their less personal household goods, and his horses—and then Elaine had died. One night they had been dicussing train and steamer arrangements. The next morning he had gone to her room as usual and found her dead.

It was as starkly simple as that—and as emotionally stunning.

Quite aside from the emotional turbulence, Marlowe overnight was set almost completely adrift as a man can be; he didn't have even the mundane things to which men turn for relief in times of great personal stress. He no longer had business affairs to occupy part of his time with routine chores. There were no children to make necessary paternal demands on him. He no longer had even the right to occupy the very house where she had lived and died —the deed had been turned over to the purchaser and they had used the place a little longer merely as a matter of courtesy. Thus overnight he had become a man with no present goal and no fore-seeable future. From what he would always think of as the best ten years of his life, he had left only himself and an impressive but impersonal row of figures in a bankbook.

So for John Marlowe, the outbreak of the war, in the limited personal sense, had been providential. It was possible, indeed even probable, that he would have been drawn into it anyway—many another man with an invalid wife was, but in his case that was beside the point. Of course he was hardly so unrealistic as to see the war, even to the smallest degree, as something arranged for his private benefit, and more than most he was aware of the war's larger implications. Certainly the war was not of his personal making or even choice—he had always felt that the North-South dissension should have been settled long since by means of the intelligence nature had provided. But since the war was an inescapable fact, and his own circumstances were what the spin of the wheel had decreed, he had entered the war somewhat in the way a man might emigrate to a new country to make a fresh start.

Being who and what he was he very likely would have come to command eventually in any case. But through his acquaintance in state political circles, his former business associates, and his financial standing, he had received his colonelcy with a minimum of effort. As he had told Sooy Smith quite honestly, he hadn't the slightest desire to run the war personally. On the other hand, he could see no especial virtue, public or private, in deliberately relegating himself to the anonymity of the ranks.

All these things being true, he devoted himself to making war with a singleness of purpose unmatched by most of his colleagues in arms. He didn't consider this, even privately, as any great patriotic virtue—he simply had little else to occupy him. This was anything but a professional army, in fact it was probably the greatest *non*professional army ever assembled, and the majority of its members, regardless of rank, figuratively had one foot in the army and the other at home. Wives, children, sweethearts, the prosperity of the family farm, business matters back home, occupied a part of almost every soldier's mind. But not Colonel Jack Marlowe's. He was dedicated to the prosecution of the war simply because he had no other more urgent personal purpose.

With this motivation, and his rank—a colonel being the highest field grade commanding men in the strictly personal sense—another man might have become a military martinet, a Fourth of July patriot, or one of those civilians-cum-soldiers infatuated with the surface trappings of war but singularly unconcerned with its vital prosecution. To the good fortune of the First Illinois Volunteer Cavalry, and later Smith's First Cavalry Brigade of the First Division, Marlowe was none of these things. He had a direct sort of mind, the faculty of separating immediate issues and treating them according to their relative importance. There were more than a few officers who, while using every stratagem to preserve their own individuality and personal status, operated on the curious theory that a man who volunteers to defend and preserve his country in the ranks somehow has fewer rights than those others who choose to remain aloof. A peculiar theory if there ever was one, yet somehow a part of the gospel according to Mars. This was done, of course, in the name of discipline and winning the war, though in sober fact it hadn't won the war yet and apparently wasn't going to in the foreseeable future. But this theory was not Marlowe's. To him the sole purpose of an army in wartime was to win with the greatest possible dispatch, and within his own personal area of control he acted accordingly and with as little foofaraw as possible.

The men of the First might slouch in their saddles, in fact they usually did, and they often wore and transported astonishingly nonregulation equipment. Against a formal backdrop such as Buckingham Palace they would have looked like a bewhiskered barbarian rabble. But they ate the best that was available, their pay was on time as often as Marlowe could manage it, their horses were shod and shabby equipment replaced, they had never yet given a foot of ground except by specific order, and any man who believed he had a grievance could take his case directly to the colonel. There he could expect to get justice, although not necessarily always the sort he had in mind.

In common with hundreds of his amateur colleagues Marlowe had read that Bible of the Union Army, Hardee's *Tactics*—but he had promptly given his away. Hardee's theories, as far as he could see and according to his growing experience, had little relationship to a war, catch-as-catch-can, collar-and-eyebrow style, being fought in this sixth decade of the nineteenth century through the middle and lower South. Whether in spite of this or because of it the First would cheerfully have followed him to hell if the orders read that way—or even to West Texas. They would have groused and cussed the day they enlisted in the con-demned cavalry, which they did all the time anyway, but they would have gone.

It was only during long periods of inaction, of doing absolutely nothing of discernible value, of waiting, waiting on some distant decision, that Marlowe was seized with this feeling of literally sickening futility—these agonizing periods when apparently nothing could be done to further the main stream of the war, and circumstances prohibited doing anything for one's self. It was at times like these that he was stricken with an almost savage depression of spirit. To him the philosophy of the average soldier, "Well, at least you ain't bein' shot at," was altogether irrelevant. (He assured himself that these moments of black melancholy had nothing whatever to do with the loss of Elaine, but he was not really certain of this.) Now that he was a brigadier—"acting" but nevertheless actual to all practical purposes—he didn't even have the company reports to fiddle with. And perhaps there was a certain physical loneliness involved.

It was only at times like this that Marlowe turned to the dubious satisfaction of the bottle. He was fully aware of its flaws but—well, there it was and at the moment there seemed to be nothing better. His juniors could have sworn they had never seen him even slightly under the influence, and they would have been dead right, but he drank for all that, sometimes, steadily and with grim concentration . . .

He leaned against the pole in his open tent doorway and fumbled absently in an inner pocket for a fresh cigar. The sharp edge of futility was gone, momentarily floated away on the three drinks. The glow of the whisky spread through him like wavelets from a stone dropped in a still pool, and the terrible inner tension eased a little.

Beyond the end of the long company street he could see the

small cloud of dust and smoke, the orderly confusion, of Sergeant Brown's temporary horseshoeing establishment. By now Brown would probably have just about finished with the First. He smiled with faint grimness. At least they'd be ready, even if they never had any place to go.

4

Orders

General Smith's headquarters were in a not very pretentious two-story frame house in La Grange proper. It had been the home and office of a certain ferociously patriotic Dr. K. When it appeared that the Yankees were going to settle more or less permanently, the doctor had denounced them in a letter to the local press (weekly), then struck a powerful blow for the Confederacy by removing himself and his family to Montgomery, Alabama. Which was all right with the Yankees, since it saved them the bother of ousting Dr. K. Now the doctor's old consultation room was the headquarters of Smith's First Division of the Sixteenth Army Corps.

The thin yellow light from the hanging lamp threw Smith's craggy features into shadowy relief. The doors and windows were open against the very warm spring night and a circle of frantic moths alternately advanced on and retreated from the hot lamp chimney.

The general wore a regulation tunic, unbuttoned down the front and frosted with shattered cigar ashes. Occasionally he brushed absently at the ashes, as though irritably aware of them but not really interested in removing them.

"Gabe!" Smith roared, and a fat orderly private materialized from another room on the double.

With a blunt finger Smith indicated a handsome majolica pitcher on the table. "Take that and bring us some fresh water—that stuff tastes like something out of a swamp."

"Yes sir—right away."

Marlowe waited, relaxed. He didn't so much mind waiting now. Something must have moved somewhere or Smith wouldn't have so hurriedly summoned him into La Grange.

The general fumbled at his steel-rimmed spectacles and indicated the confusion of papers before him.

"They say even mountains move, Marlowe. General Hurlbut finally did too. I suppose you've guessed?"

"More or less," Marlowe agreed. "But you never know."

Over the spectacles Smith eyed him shrewdly. "You've been in a swivet." It was a statement, not a question.

Marlowe shrugged. "All right, so I have. You have to be congenitally lazy to enjoy doing nothing at all. I figured if it was worth doing it ought to be done at once. And it's been eleven days since we were first handed this—"

"What the hell's eleven days in a big war?"

"Time enough to lose one. Waterloo happened in a lot less and so did Shiloh. The men have been jumpy—naturally. Specifically they don't—can't—know a thing. But the brigade was overhauled from stem to stern quite a while ago—not knowing, I didn't dare put it off. So the men took for granted something was afoot; why wouldn't they? Now the edge is gone. The delay wasn't very smart, even if only on that account."

"There'd be hell to pay if news of this got out, and you'd be right in the middle of it."

"No doubt," Marlowe agreed dryly. "But if anything at all got out it came from Memphis, not from me. I haven't even said a word to the regimental officers, which might have been keeping things almost too quiet. Naturally most of them have done a little probing—after all, they have a certain right to know. But as I get it the grapevine has it that we are going to Vicksburg. That's the logical supposition. Personally, I haven't disabused the notion—or encouraged it."

"Hmm. Might even have been a good idea to have planted a notion something like that."

"Maybe." Marlowe shrugged again. "My thought is that you'd better not try to get too fancy in these things. Better to let them alone."

"All right, let's get down to cases. I'll give it to you exactly as I see it. Ordinarily, I wouldn't mind showing you Hurlbut's orders, in fact I'd certainly rather—save me repeating it all. My God! There's enough detail here to finish the war—if it was pertinent. You complain about the delay—damned if I don't think maybe Hurlbut has been using all this time to compose the orders. But I'll spare you. This way you can swear, if you ever have to—which I hope you won't—that your instructions came solely from me and naturally that's all you know. Officially, that's all you have to know."

"I know, General, and as I've said, I appreciate that."

"Well, keep it in the back of your head then," Smith said gruffly. "So—there's been no change in the general plan, that's all here in the orders I have written out for you, but there's a point or two it still may pay to discuss—"

The orderly put the pitcher of fresh water on the table and Smith, after Marlowe had declined, poured and drank off a tumblerful.

"Aaaah! A fair drink but it sure don't have much body. Where? —Oh yes. Now as to this business of coming back, assuming you do—" Smith hesitated, grinned. "We might as well get it straight between us. To me the point is that you get back, or out, and I personally don't give a damn how you do it or where you have to go—go by way of Texas if you have to. Once you're gone from here you're strictly on your own and no man can guess what kind of a mess you may wind up in. Hurlbut may think he can risk the loss of a full brigade for the sake of a pet notion—of course he doesn't think of it that way— but I'm damned if I'm going to help him do it."

"Fair enough. I simply can't see it except as playing it the way the cards fall."

"Neither can I. If you manage to get through and out you'll be a genius and nobody will question how you did it. If you don't— well, you'll sure be out of reach of criticism for a while. If they have to blame somebody—and by God! as usual they will—they can have me. Let's leave it at that." Smith picked up papers from a pile and glanced over them. "Well, here's another one you may not care too much for, but don't go off half-cocked. You're to take rations for five days—"

"Oh, now wait a minute—begging your pardon, General, but somebody can't count. Why, if I do better than thirty miles a day, which you know is one hell of an average for that distance, without any opposition and with good weather, it will still take me better than six full days even to reach the Southern. I can graze horses, if I have the time and place, but not men."

Smith leaned back in his chair, removed his glasses, and rubbed his eyes. "Keep your shirt on, Marlowe. I know what's in your mind well enough but let's take another look at it. To begin with, cavalry rations means men *and* horses. Right? So put it like this— suppose you double that, make it ten days, but you end up being gone fifteen days, or longer. You still have to eat off the country a third of the time because you haven't any choice."

"I know, General, but—"

Smith rode over the attempted interruption. "Damn it, Jack"— he rarely used the familiar like this—"let me tell you in this case.

You take rations for five days but you're still gone twelve or fifteen, you still wind up eating off the country but you've saved the original weight at the time when it's probably the most important. How long *will* you be gone anyway, Marlowe?" he added craftily.

"Why, nobody," Marlowe said, taken by surprise, "could answer that. You know, sir—"

"Certainly I know—that's just the point. It comes down to this. You're going to have to live off the country sooner or later, so make it sooner and save yourself the load."

Marlowe hesitated, then said, "I see. Well, maybe I did jump to conclusions a mite too fast." Right or wrong in this, Smith was on his side in general and there was no sense in antagonizing him over a relatively minor point. "But—it's been army policy to *buy* local supplies—and I'll undoubtedly have to have a lot of 'em. Has that policy been changed?"

"No-o-o, I wouldn't put it quite like that," Smith said with a mock-judicial air. "It's like this—just give your juniors authority to issue bills on the quartermaster general at Memphis. You don't ask people if they'll accept the bills, you understand, you just give them to 'em whether they like it or not. That way you eat, and the bills will be honored, if and when the holders can get them to Memphis and they think it's worth the effort. Don't go hungry, Marlowe—not as long as there's anything at all to be had."

"In other words, we're not to pay any attention to any—er, ordinary objections?"

"That's my understanding exactly. And here's something else along that line. You'll be traveling so damned fast I don't see how there'll be time for the point to arise, but this comes from Grant himself so you'd better bear it in mind." The general again glanced at the papers in his hand. "To quote, 'These troops are to keep well together, and to let marauding alone for once.' "

Marlowe grinned a little crookedly. "Well, I'll be damned. What's that mean—marauding?"

"I'm just repeating exactly what it says here, Colonel. I suppose it means something either more or less than looting, but just which?"

"I suppose it's up to me to make the distinction?"

"Why, yes, I suppose so." Smith suddenly banged the table with a hard fist. "Damn it all, Marlowe, I've got no personal taste for being hard on these people down here—not just as people. But by any known and recognized rules of government anywhere they are in insurrection. They knew that, or they should have, when they started the shooting. Now if they don't want people to get hurt, in one way and another, then the people and the politicians—yes, all of 'em on both sides—can stop their war. They've had two full years to see what a shooting war's like—and they always get worse instead of better."

"There's one other important thing, important to me anyway. When do we go?"

"Oh, Lord, yes—that. Well, it's like this . . ."

The feinting columns, including that of Smith himself from here at La Grange, would leave the next day. Being mostly infantry with a scattering of artillery, they would be slow. The First Brigade would leave two days later, the morning of the seventeenth. The others would need a good running start to be effective.

"Well, anything I've left out you'll have to make up as you go along," Smith said finally, "and I imagine there'll be a lot of it. Have a drink before we end this, Colonel?"

Marlowe said, more or less automatically, "Why yes sir, thanks," although he didn't really care whether he had a drink or not. Now that the proposition had been resolved the tension had abated and he felt fine. Still, there were the amenities. One drink then led almost inevitably to another (it was excellent whisky; Smith said it had come down the river from the Planters House in St. Louis), and they talked a little, mostly for the sake of talk, with neither saying what was perhaps foremost in his mind. There is always an inescapable reticence, along with the loneliness, in the very nature of command.

Smith said, "What did you do before the war, Marlowe? I don't believe I ever heard."

The colonel told him, and added, "Why?"

"No great reason beyond simple curiosity. I'm interested in the amazing answers you sometimes get to that in this army." The general chuckled. "I asked one field officer that—a good one too but never mind his name, and the sonofabitch told me with a straight face that he'd been a bank robber. It made me about two-thirds mad at the time—you know, I thought he was trying to make an ass out of me. But I found out later it was the simple truth!"

Marlowe laughed as he said, "There's a sergeant in the First who used to run a whorehouse for a Chicago politician."

"Oh, I don't doubt. An amateur war's the damnedest thing, as of course has been said *ad nauseam*, but it's amazing what chance can turn up—or down. Do you happen to know Giles Smith?"

"Only by name and reputation, sir."

"Well, I always think of him as a kind of prime example. Incidentally, he's no relation of mine except in so far as I suppose all Smiths go back to the same original source, whatever that may be. But even men who don't care too much for him personally agree that he's one of the best general officers in the army—no reflection on present company, of course. Well, anyway, when this war started he was running a small hotel in some downstate Illinois town—just another fair-sized civilian duck in his own puddle—I thought maybe you'd known him up there. He raised a local company on his own but the governor turned it down because the state quota was full at the time. About the same time Giles's brother Morgan, a steamboat captain, I believe, organized the nucleus of the Eighth Missouri Infantry—mostly a bunch of rough monkeys off the St. Louis river front. So not to be put off, Giles took his orphan company to St. Louis and threw it in as part of Morgan's Eighth. Now Giles is a division commander and a damned good one, which must go to show something or other. I wonder what the Prussian professionals, or for that matter the fancy British, would think of a fellow who in less than two years went from obscure country hotelkeeper to major general—and I happen to know that Giles has no political friends to speak of either. It's a kind of minor miracle—or one hell of a note, depending on how you look at it."

"Well, it wouldn't be too hard to find a parallel in the fact that Mr. Lincoln's president."

"Oh, that," Smith said almost contemptuously, "but Smith earned his." He rose abruptly and held out a hand. "I'll say good-by, Colonel. I'll be getting out early in the morning myself. If you bring this off you'll be one of the biggest men in the army, temporarily anyway. If you don't . . . well . . . I'll wish you luck, Jack."

"I'll see you later, General, somewhere—as you say, with luck."

5

Staff Meeting

Since there was hardly room in Marlowe's tent the staff meeting was held outside in the shade of a gnarled and ancient water oak. He always tried to keep these things as simple as possible, but even so it was quite a gathering.

The list included Major Dick Gray, presently commanding the First Illinois Cavalry in Marlowe's place; Colonel Secord of the Second Illinois; Colonel Blaney of the Second Iowa; their respective juniors who had a right to be there; Majors Keller and Wells, surgeons respectively of the First and Second Illinois, whom Marlowe had on hand for an especial reason; and a Captain Harris, an aide from General Smith's staff who had been left behind—after all, Smith's feinting column would be back in a few days—there was no reason to suppose they would be involved in any action of consequence.

These things had to be done but Marlowe never relished them, for their own sake as it were, as so many general officers seemed to—those who confused talking about action with the action itself. He believed in the chain of command, or rather in the realistic delegation of authority and responsibility, and of course information had to be imparted, but he didn't fancy himself in the role of lecturer or lawgiver. He supposed he didn't cut too bad a figure at it, that his juniors didn't resent his efforts or laugh at them, but he still didn't care for the role. Like so many of these men whose military status was temporary (though many of these amateurs had seen, or would see, more action than many professionals would experience in a lifetime) he disliked the system while admitting its necessity—or the necessity for something like it.

"If you gentlemen will bear with me in our usual manner," he began, "I'll try to cover the situation as completely as I can. No interruptions, please. When I've finished, then as many questions or comments as you please—well, within reason."

He knew these people, in the sense of their command ability and past performance—he considered that the only part of their lives which really concerned him. He knew the shortcomings of each one, which on the whole were minor—no more than to be expected in a generally imperfect world. None was brilliant in the military sense, or at least the brilliance hadn't shown up yet; all were competent. In general he would not have exchanged them for any similar group he knew of—better, in his view, to have a junior whose faults were known than one with a surface brilliance but hidden flaws to show up in a time of crisis.

He knew in advance what their individual reactions would be when he had outlined the situation and what was to be done. Major Gray would contribute a flippant remark, harmless enough in itself, to show his own nonchalance and cover what remained of his own unsureness. As long as Gray had been second in the regiment (Lieutenant Colonel Kelsey, the nominal second, had gone home on sick leave and never returned) his had been a sort of what-the-hell, I-only-take-orders-here attitude. But when he was given acting command of the First a good deal of this attitude had vanished, or at least been sublimated, and he had tried hard to live up to his larger responsibility.

Blaney of the Second Iowa would ask a question or two which would be really more of a statement, framed to demonstrate publicly that he had the situation thoroughly in mind. Blaney was ten years older than Marlowe, a reasonably good colonel of regiment who neither merited higher command nor wanted it, the kind of man who actually enjoyed the median position he knew he could manage without too much strain.

Secord would say little or nothing—whatever he might say would be terse and to the point. A good officer, a little overcautious at times, perhaps, but solidly dependable, one of those whom Marlowe, in his role as brigadier, seldom thought about; he didn't have to. He had learned from experience that, as long as it was humanly and militarily possible, Secord would have the Second Illinois in the right place at the right time.

So it would be with the others, each according to his particular personality bent. . . .

Fifty yards away, in each of several directions, beyond earshot and there to keep others still farther away, sentries moved with lazy slowness in the hot spring sun. Even as he talked now Marlowe himself inwardly damned the regulations which decreed these blistering wool uniforms. Of course they did wear like so much sheet iron.

"So there you have it, gentlemen," the colonel said finally. "As I said in the beginning, you're entitled as usual to any reasonable and pertinent questions or comments. Only one thing—we're not going to gain much by irrelevant discussion as such. Your guesses as to what happens when we leave here, for instance, are just as good as mine, maybe better, and speculation on that will be largely a waste of our time. Well?"

"No particular questions, at least not now," Major Gray said, running more or less true to form, "but I've been thinking while you gave us this—maybe this is better than playing the role of stalking horse for General Grant at Vicksburg."

Marlowe shrugged indifferently. "A matter of opinion, I suppose. Have there been rumors to that effect?"

"Well, certainly some that I've heard personally—or been asked about. You know how the talk goes when the men know that something is up but not exactly what—like the old maid on her wedding night—you know."

"Yes, I daresay. You, Secord?"

Colonel Frank Secord waved a big hairy hand. "No question as to procedure, Colonel, but I wonder—technically, of course, this isn't any of my business, I'm just curious—does Memphis understand what kind of a bear trap they're shoving us into down there?"

"They know," Marlowe said a little grimly, "and they've weighed the chances—or so they say. But once we're on our way that'll be all up to us. What about you, Colonel Blaney?"

Blaney had just finished mopping his almost entirely bald head and now he fingered his wispy beard nervously—at least a stranger might have thought it was nervousness. You couldn't—and Marlowe knew this—always be sure about Blaney. "Just one thing in particular," Blaney drawled disarmingly. "You've got the Second Iowa—me—picked as the regiment to pull out and double back . . .

In his discourse Marlowe had explained that, somewhere along the line, probably four or five days out—at any rate at his discretion, one of the brigade's three regiments would turn back. This was intended to lighten and speed up the remainder of the column and at the same time provide a screen to hold off and confuse possible pursuit. The Second Iowa had been named specifically.

". . . Is there some special reason for that? By God! I'd hate to have it suggested that the Second can't stand up alongside anybody—!"

"Nonsense, Colonel," Marlowe said blandly. "There's no such inference. Personally, I'm glad I didn't have to make the choice—

I'd have had to flip a coin. Actually, it was a matter of orders I had nothing to do with."

"Well—in that case. I wanted to know."

"As a matter of fact, Colonel," Marlowe went on, "I think you're looking at it in the wrong way. The regiment that comes back will in effect be an independent command, a matter of considerable responsibility."

"All right," Blaney said. "That's good enough—we don't hanker to be heroes either."

Sometimes Blaney for some reason struck Marlowe as being slightly ridiculous, and at the same time he was a little ashamed of the feeling, for certainly there was nothing inherently ridiculous about a man defending his country. All the same he occasionally reminded Marlowe of a worried mother hen and he couldn't resist prodding him harmlessly. "Surely, Colonel," Marlowe said, still bland—he glanced at and past the others—"You're not suggesting that your Second Iowa is superior to the other brigade regiments. Or are you?"

Blaney cocked an eye at him. "There's no use trying to bait me, Colonel," he said coolly. "It ain't hardly worth the trouble. I know what I meant and so do you." And with that Blaney helped himself to a fresh chew of fine-cut.

Marlowe wished now that he hadn't bothered. "Anybody else?"

There was a little more, of course, but nothing important.

Finally Marlowe turned to Captain Harris, Smith's youthful aide, and said, "We've neglected you a little, I'm afraid, Captain. Is there anything you'd like to add, or maybe are supposed to, before we finish this up?"

Captain Harris seemed a little startled at the sound of his name, as though his mind had been anywhere but here under a water oak in Tennessee on an April morning. "Why, no, not a thing, Colonel. I'm here mostly as a matter of courtesy, you might say. This is all your funer—" He caught his tongue and shut it off abruptly.

Marlowe smiled faintly. "Don't remind us so pungently, Captain. We'll find it out soon enough for ourselves, I expect."

"I should have wished you luck, and I do," Harris said in some embarrassment.

"Thanks. We can use it. As a matter of fact," Marlowe went on, "I'm already getting a little tired of that phrase. Whether any of us lives through the day is, in a way, a matter of luck—and I suspect that in this case we'll make a good deal of our own.

"There is one other thing I've left until now. That concerns the presence here of Majors Keller and Wells. I needn't remind you that as a rule we don't bother the medics with the details of brigade procedure."

Wells and Keller, brothers in the private fraternity of medicine, glanced briefly at each other and away. "I wondered," Keller drawled, "just why we were being so honored."

"I wouldn't put it quite in that way," Marlowe said. He tossed away his dead cigar, took his time about getting out a fresh one and setting it alight. Let them wait. They had all morning. Like a great many medical men in this army, they were in it but not too much of it. Necessarily of officer status, they held no direct command responsibility. Theoretically, and according to regulations, they were as much subject to discipline as anyone else, but practice was another matter. It's a little hard to censure a man for being drunk on the post when tomorrow or the next day he may have to decide whether or not to deprive you of a limb. These regimental doctor-surgeons as a group—of course there were exceptions—were inclined to be aloof, cynical, and ungodly, something of a law unto themselves, and they were apt to have little regard for rank as such. A great many officers—and of course there were exceptions on this side too—regarded surgeons, in one sense, as being somewhat like sutlers, a necessary evil. Excess baggage and general nuisances 95 per cent of the time—and the other 5 per cent the only useful men in the army. They also enjoyed a certain amount of respect because of their command of the supposed mysteries—but they didn't get any of it from Colonel Marlowe.

He said, "Would either of you gentlemen, Keller or Wells, care to make a general statement about the physical condition of the men? I'll explain what I'm getting at directly."

"The sick report is made up every day—" Keller began.

"If I'd wanted that," Marlowe interrupted icily, "I'd have said so. I asked for a general statement."

Keller started to say something, then shrugged and apparently changed his mind. "Very well—if I understand you correctly, Colonel. On the whole, the health of the men is about what you'd expect in any similar group—probably a bit higher than the average. I'm speaking of the First, of course, my own charge, but I'm surmising the others would run about the same. You have no ailing youngsters or oldsters to begin with—they either didn't come or have already gone. This outdoorish life is generally healthful —aside from stopping a bullet, and while the grub is a little monotonous, it's all right and not too much different from what most of 'em would be getting at home. On the other hand, in a group as large as a regiment you find the usual quota of aches and pains, some mildly serious, some imaginary, about what you'd expect in a similar civilian group. Always barring pregnancy, Colonel—we don't have that to contend with."

Marlowe went along with the general laughter as far as a thin smile—but no further. There wasn't much to be done about Keller—not that he especially wanted to do anything—and he seemed to be as competent as most of these butchers.

"Is that what you had in mind, Colonel?" Keller said.

"More or less, I suppose." Marlowe rather wished now he had approached this a little differently. "Anyhow, the principal point is this. If this were a routine move of the whole brigade every man would go and we'd make allowances for the ailing, if any. But this is in no way a routine move and there will be allowances for no one—above all we can't be bothered with nursing cripples or sick men. I want you surgeons to strike from the duty roster every man who is ailing in the slightest now, and every last one who in your judgment is likely to become so in the near future. You don't have to make a thorough individual examination, but you've treated these men before. You ought to know them in that sense. And I'm putting that as an order!"

"I think we get the general idea, Colonel," Keller said almost disinterestedly, "but we're doctors, not fortunetellers or prophets."

"By God! How well I know that!" Marlowe's hitherto calm voice crackled with sudden incisive bitterness. For an instant the memory of Elaine was there in his mind like a searing pain. "But you're also supposed to have what you people call medical insight. I've heard the God-damned phrase so often it gives me a personal pain in the rump, but it's your phrase, not mine!"

Keller's lips set in a straight line and the others appeared a little embarrassed. Of course there was really nothing sacred about the surgeons. There was no reason why a general officer couldn't tell them anything he saw fit, but the fact was they were seldom, if ever, put over the jumps in public—it just wasn't done.

"I don't want a wholesale release from duty, we can't stand it for one thing. But a week from now, when we may be trying to stand off a couple of Rebel divisions, I damned well don't want to be nursing sick men who'll claim they've had it coming on for *two* weeks. That's the point I'm making and I'm putting it up to you two. I haven't included Blaney's Second Iowa because they'll be coming back in a few days anyway."

"Very well," Keller said stiffly, "but in that case you'll have to accept our opinions. That's a matter of professional judgment and also something which can't be measured by army regulations."

"I thought that's what I said," Marlowe said more mildly, "and technically I have to accept your judgment every time you put a man on the roster with a bellyache. Well, that's all for the present, gentlemen, if there are no more questions. Major Keller, will you stay for just a minute when the others have gone?"

Keller looked up in quick surprise but said nothing, only raised his brows slightly in the direction of his fellow surgeon, Wells.

When they were presently alone Marlowe said, as pleasantly as he could, "I wasn't being personal, Major. I hope you understand that."

"I know," Keller said, but not as though he especially believed that. "But none of this military claptrap, even the so-called impersonal business, bothers me, Colonel. A doctor can always resign whenever he doesn't like what he gets in—or from—the service."

"But you're still in uniform prescribing salts and quinine." There was a hint of curiosity in Marlowe's voice.

Keller shrugged. "So I am—but medicine is wherever you find it. But was that what you had on your mind, Colonel?"

"Well, not quite. I wanted a professional opinion of a sort from you and I didn't see any point in detaining the others with it."

Keller's brows went up in mild surprise. "Surely you don't mean yourself?"

"No, I don't." Marlowe grinned. "Sorry if that disappoints you. But this is a matter strictly in your field and I wanted a professional opinion. I'm perfectly serious, believe me. Well, anyway— this will be what the textbooks delight in calling a flying column —we hope. Meaning, in plain English, that we take only the supplies and equipment each man totes for himself, according to his job. In your capacity as surgeon, precisely what would that mean?"

"Well, not being a so-called fighting man, I *don't* carry such hardware as carbine, pistol, or that clumsy hedge knife you people call a saber. I do personally carry my own kit of medicines and instruments. In the first place, I wouldn't chance getting caught without the tools of my profession, not in these highly uncertain circumstances. In the second place, my instrument kit happens to be the finest Sheffield steel money can buy, and I don't choose to have them banged around in the hind end of an ambulance. Is that what you had in mind?"

"More or less—yes, I think so. In other words, with your own personal equipment you could take care of most of the injuries we might expect? I mean in your own regiment, of course."

"Now wait a minute—I didn't say quite that. Up to a point, Colonel, only up to a point. One man, three or four or maybe a half dozen, yes. But if we run into some real hell and I had forty or fifty men laid out on the ground at once, I'd probably be out of drugs and bandages before I even got a good start—barring some other supply."

"That's what I'm driving at. Within a few days the column will be cut to about a thousand men. There will be only two of you—you and Wells. That's still quite a force and I suppose a couple of led horses wouldn't make too much difference. The question is, do you want them and will they be worth the effort?"

Keller hesitated in thought. Then, "Even I'm enough of a cavalryman to know that led horses can be a holy nuisance when you're in a hurry, Colonel."

"I appreciate that only too well," Marlowe said dryly, "but it's hardly what could be called a medical opinion, Major. That's what I wanted from you."

This time Keller hesitated longer but finally he said, "Then no, I think no extra horses, Colonel. Do you want to know why?"

"Not necessarily in detail. I probably wouldn't follow your statistics."

"Nothing like that involved—it's a lot simpler. Everybody concerned knows that this whole business is a gamble. I'm no soldier but even I know that. Let's just say this is a small gamble to go along with the big one. Taking only five days' rations there is also, statistically, the possibility that we might starve. Same principle."

"I see. Well, I hope you're right—the ultimate responsibility would—will be mine."

"I don't know that it's exactly a question of being 'right.' It's possible that the whole brigade will go through without a scratch. It's also a possibility that we could walk into a smallpox epidemic. All medicine is a gamble of a sort and you always, war or no war, have to do what you believe to be best all around. I have a professional conscience to think about, Colonel."

"Does that imply that I haven't?" Marlowe was mildly amused—but only mildly. Somehow he simply didn't follow Keller's turns of thought, if that was the right phrase.

Keller shrugged—Marlowe wondered what the gesture meant. "The choice of language is yours, Colonel. I don't care to split hairs, but put it this way—you're not a professional here; you're in for the duration but I'm in for life. In uniform or out, a sick or wounded man is all the same to me."

"I see," Marlowe said slowly, "I think. Well, thanks, Major. I think we've covered the point."

"You're welcome."

As Keller walked away, stiff-backed even in the hot morning sun, he was thinking, with certain personal variations: who of his own free will would want to be a general officer? He had never liked Marlowe particularly—he didn't now; yet neither did he actively dislike him. Certainly the man was fair, as he saw fairness. Perhaps it was Marlowe's apparently God-almighty cocksureness that irked him as much as anything. Still, and in all truth, if Marlowe couldn't (and moreover wouldn't) be sure of himself and make it stick, then who in the brigade could? Sometimes, Keller thought—and not with special regard to what they had just been discussing—a man had better make a wrong decision than none at all. His mind instinctively rebelled at this unscientific proposition, yet there it was.

Back at his tent Marlowe threw aside the heavy blouse and opened his collar. Once more, for the umpteenth time, he studied his battered map of Mississippi, so worn now it was starting to come apart at the folds. He could never know it too well.

Yet his mind wasn't really on it this morning and his thoughts moved elsewhere. Oddly enough, and both would have been surprised had they been aware of the coincidence, he and Keller were thinking of different facets of the same general problem. He would have denied that he disliked medical men as a class, yet he certainly didn't share the general awe of them. He supposed this came about because of the belief—if not abetted by the medics then certainly not denied—that doctors were closer than ordinary men to the ultimate mysteries of birth and death. This Marlowe simply did not believe. In his opinion they were skilled mechanics, some more so than others. Still, interesting as this might be in the speculative sense, it had nothing to do with the problem presently in hand.

It was characteristic of Marlowe that, once involved in this gigantic war mechanism, he should, unlike so many of his fellow officers, try to understand it. He knew that an army, at any rate this one, was held together by the Official Army Regulations plus faith—and of these two, faith was not the lesser. The private's faith in the sergeant, the sergeant's in the company commander, and so on up the line, the chain of command in reverse. This chain of faith can skip a notch or two without harm—the sergeant may despise his captain and still believe in the colonel, but always somewhere there has to be that solid anchor point. Perhaps, Marlowe thought, that was the chief importance of command, that at each point it believe implicitly in itself. He himself, so far as he was aware, had never had a signal failure. (He knocked on wood.) He was also acutely aware that any man could and most men at some time did fail, and he occasionally wondered if, and in what circumstances, disaster would lay *him* by the heels. . . .

6

Private Schwartz

The solitaire was hardly all-absorbing but it served to pass the time—that was what most of the brigade was doing, marking time until day after tomorrow. Marlowe had been asked to a poker session by some of his juniors, and while he would have relished the company he lately had declined all these invitations. For one thing he came away winner four times out of five because he played that kind of poker, but he didn't relish winning money he well knew his juniors couldn't afford to lose, and it went against his grain to lose by deliberate choice.

He missed game again, swept up the cards, and using them as a fan, brushed irritably at the infernal bugs swarming around the lantern on the field desk. Pushing the cards together deftly, he started to reshuffle. Then he recognized the footsteps of the approaching sentry but let the man come ahead and rap on the tent pole.

"Well?"

"A Private Schwartz from A Company of the First asks permission to speak to the colonel, sir."

"What th— All right, Macey. Let him come on in."

The youth came into the light, blinking a little, started to remove his hat, remembered in time and transformed the movement into a salute of sorts. "I got a note for you, sir—from Major Keller, please."

Wondering a little at the hint of odd accent, Marlowe held the note to the light:

Colonel Marlowe:—

This man (the army's description, not mine) has just recovered from an attack of fever (malaria) which in his case I am certain is chronic. According to my understanding of your order, I have removed him from the duty list. He insists, however, on taking the matter to you, and I suppose that is his privilege.

Keller,
Surgeon Major.

"What's your first name?" Marlowe demanded sharply. Now he looked closely at the youth for the first time. A chunky, solidly built lad, blond, typical Saxon complexion, seventeen, maybe eighteen, hardly more, and now more than somewhat nervous in the presence of authority. From boots to hat his uniform fitted him about like a saddle on a hog. He seemed faintly familiar to Marlowe—or maybe it was just that he was so familiar with the general type.

"Bernhard, sir."

"Well, what's the story?"

"My father is Johann—John Schwartz. We have that farm next to your place on Salt Creek, near Eddyville—"

Oh, yes, John Schwartz—now Marlowe knew, of course, one of the hard-working, stalwart German emigrants of the wave of

1848. The Schwartz crew had often helped out his own farm tenant during busy seasons. The familiarity was family resemblance, of course, though it was quite possible he had seen the boy himself without paying any particular attention to him.

"I see—up to a point. Yes, I recall your father, to be sure. But then what?"

"Yes sir. Well, I've only been in the regiment since January and this is my first chance to be in anything important. I don't want to miss it if there's any chance, sir."

"Why didn't you come around then and make yourself known?"

"Well, I ain't one to push, Colonel, sir, an' I'm just a plain private."

Mmmm. Probably just as well, at that. Still Marlowe knew something of this breed—sometimes a little on the slow side mentally, but stubborn, and proud as the devil himself.

"Is what Major Keller said about the fever correct?"

"I dunno exactly what he wrote, sir, but it's true I've had it off an' on. Don't hurt nothin'. But I'm all right now an' I won't have another spell for a long time. That doctor up at Springfield knowed about it an' he passed me."

"Did Major Keller tell you *why* you were pulled off duty?"

"Yes sir—some, that is."

Marlowe considered. Having been so emphatic with Keller in the beginning, he naturally disliked overriding him now. Yet the boy had wanted this enough to face up to Keller—and yet what was the use of having authority if you didn't use it? Deciding instantly, he reached for pen and paper and wrote rapidly:

Major Keller:—
You will please restore the bearer to duty as before. Sorry if I appear to be invading your province but I believe there are mitigating circumstances in this case and the responsibility is mine. Regards.

   Marlowe,
   Commanding 1st Cavalry Brigade.

"All right, there you are, bub," he said. This was one of these things it wasn't really worth wasting much time on, one way or another. "Seeing you're so damned anxious to tangle with the Johnnies I'm rescinding Major Keller's order. But you'd better understand this thoroughly—if you get sick or for any reason can't hold up your end, then God help you because you won't get any from anybody else! I mean that. You'll be left to take on the Confederate army by yourself and you won't like Andersonville worth a damn! All clear?"

"Yes sir," Private Schwartz said woodenly.

"Then that's all, except remember what I told you."

"Yes sir—and I'm obliged to you, Colonel."

Marlowe waved him out with a gesture of dismissal and again picked up the cards.

Macey was back again, his carbine carefully at port. "Beg pardon, Colonel. Major Gray would like a word."

"Very well." Marlowe sighed and pushed the cards aside. "And Macey, ask the guard corporal to see if he can find Sergeant King and run him over here—"

7

The Raiders

The colonel leaned on the saddle pommel and watched as the loose column evolved out of apparent chaos and moved off down the road toward Ripley. Good men, these, he thought. Perhaps not the best in the army—though what really is "best" in that sense?—but good enough, not flamboyant but solid and dependable. Their very regimental numbers indicated their volunteer and veteran status—the bounty men and the conscripts hadn't started to come in yet. They were no longer innocently enthusiastic—which was really no bad thing, but the one-time eagerness had been replaced by a largely silent determination to see this business through to the bitter end, whatever it might prove to be. Few relished the job to be done but still fewer denied its necessity. Most of them had been ninety-day men originally, and almost to a man they had re-enlisted at the three-year call—and they had learned one thing in particular the hard way, that an Enfield in the hands of the other man, no matter who he is or what he calls himself, is a great and potent equalizer.

The spring morning was all anyone could ask—even as Marlowe watched the day came to full light. The air was fresh and fragrant as thought it had been washed, and where it hadn't been beaten into hardpan by hoofs the earth could actually be smelled from atop a horse. Marlowe had a live sense of well being. He had enjoyed his breakfast, the first cigar of the day was drawing well, and now that they were actually moving the nervous tension was completely gone. He felt consciously relaxed, both mentally and physically, and confident. From here on, until it finally ended, all he had to do was concentrate on the direction of this maneuver. It was a game of chess with a presently invisible opponent, in which he would make one move at a time, with due allowance for the one expected to follow.

With him now were his own aide, Lieutenant Jay Davis, who enjoyed a fairly soft job because Marlowe chose to attend to so many chores himself; Surgeon Major Keller, who had no specific place in the column; and the orderly, Sergeant King. The latter, being of lowly rank, maintained a discreet distance, within call but out of casual earshot. Keller too was some distance from Marlowe, probably because he seemed to have a determined preference for his own company.

This First Brigade of some 1,500 men was not large as cavalry strength was counted in this army, yet at the same time 1,500 is a considerable lot of men and horseflesh anywhere. In files of three, which was about all this narrow country road would accommodate comfortably, the column extended for a minimum of a mile and a quarter. When men and animals began to slacken off a little the column would lengthen still more. The effective and orderly manipulation of a column this size, just in the physical sense, is no job for an amateur. Marlowe had more than once seen the disastrous results of mishandling cavalry—some of the chaos at Shiloh had been one shining example—which could create more havoc than the enemy.

He watched the column now with an eye at once that of a merely interested spectator and a professional cavalryman—in two years these men too had moved from amateur to professional status. Legend grew slowly in this western army but it did grow—and Marlowe was proud of the fact that this (technically) First Cavalry Brigade of General Smith's First Division of the Sixteenth Army Corps was known in this whole area simply as Marlowe's Cavalry. Even if he didn't have the star he had the brigade. Yesterday they had stood a final full-scale inspection—Marlowe had gone down the lines himself with the regimental officers—and he knew they were ready for what he would have to ask of them—it would be a great deal. They were fit—the surgeons had weeded out perhaps two dozen doubtful cases. They were carrying forty rounds of ammunition per man and five days' rations—the soldier's standard fare of bacon, hardrock Uncle Sam hardtack, the army's desiccated vegetables (potatoes and shredded carrots and turnips pressed hard and intended to be made edible by boiling), coffee, sugar, and an extra supply of salt—even now, in 1863, salt was becoming ever harder to find in the Confederacy. Like every good officer, Marlowe knew that the men, not taken into the confidence of the high command in advance, usually guessed where or how far they were going by the amount of rations issued before a movement. They had orders now to make the rations do double duty, that is rations for five days were supposed to last ten. Enough, say, to make a round trip to Columbus, Mississippi, from which point the Confederate General Dan Ruggles now and then raided the Union positions along the Memphis & Charleston Railroad. On the face of it it was a good enough guess—they would be deep in the heart of Mississippi before they discovered how wrong it was. The knowledge already hung on Marlowe's mind like a great weight, one that he would have to carry alone.

He had few illusions concerning the proper military role of cavalry, not now that is, though he'd had his share when he entered the service. Like most people he had passively assumed, without really thinking about it because there was no reason to, that in combat the man on horseback is naturally superior to the infantryman. It was a folk belief as old as the horse-man relationship itself. The myth, whatever truth might have been in it once, had been shattered in fact by the British archers at Agincourt, although the orthodox military mind had been almost the last to discover it. But the myth had persisted passively in America, largely because there had so seldom been occasion to really test it. God knew America had done its share of bloodletting and more, but it had mostly occurred in a wilderness where there were no horses to be had and no roads to maneuver them on had they been available.

Even now, North as well as South—though in the latter it might have been more expected—the myth still persisted, fostered in part by newspaper stories running heavily to poetic license. Such men as Turner Ashby, John Mosby, and particularly Jeb Stuart and his "dashing, gray-clad legions," had achieved the status of popular legend even in the supposedly cold-blooded North. Stuart with his oversized black whiskers and plumed hat, his silk-lined comic-opera cloak, and his personal jongleur and court jester, Banjoist Sweeny. When the Stuart legions took to the warpath it was popularly supposed that everything quailed before them—which, if true, should have enabled them to win the war. There was, also and for instance, the famous joyride around McClellan. It was an effective piece of high theater but in the military sense it accomplished nothing whatever. It was also popularly supposed that Stuart was General Lee's "eyes," and possibly that accounted for even the canny Lee's occasional blindness. Out here in the uncouth and unlettered West, where the Federals were doing a slow but eventually certain job of winning their war, the Confederate General Nathan Bedford Forrest had neither fancy cloak nor personal banjoist, but a great many Federals could testify that Forrest knew what the horse soldiers were for—and furthermore used that knowledge much too often for Federal comfort.

Unlike Sergeant Brown, Marlowe hadn't entered the cavalry in order to ride to war rather than walk—as an officer he could have ridden in any case. But under the hammer of reality the myth quickly became evident for what it was—in fact, it never had much validity except in so far as the man on foot had been conditioned to believe in the horseman's natural superiority.

The myth had melted under the harsh reality of Confederate gunfire and Yankee common sense. There were, to be sure, still corps commanders who did not understand the real function of cavalry, but the horse soldiers themselves had learned their limitations. There had been that mental concept in which horsemen automatically rode down cringing and helpless infantryman—maybe on the plains of the Low Countries before the day of the rifled barrel, but not often on the snarled landscape of Kentucky and Tennessee and Mississippi. It depended in part on the battle experience of the infantry concerned, but experience being equal, after two years of bitter trial the wise cavalry commander shuddered a little at the notion of openly attacking a comparable force of infantry. It was a matter of elemental common sense and arithmetic. Horse and man together presented a far larger target than a man alone, and killing or wounding the horse was as damaging and disrupting as killing the rider. And while a horse might be much faster it was not one tenth so maneuverable as a man—nobody ever saw a horse taking shelter behind a tree or a fallen log or a rail fence. Moreover, even for a sharpshooter, a saddle is about the worst possible firing platform.

Then there was the never-ending drudgery of merely maintaining a cavalry outfit, which can be one of the most hellish aggravations known to man and has no end. Horses, like men, have to be fed and watered, and they require ten times as much in sheer bulk. Unless it has been experienced it is hard to understand what a hell of a chore the seemingly simple matter of watering a brigade of horse can be. Like men, horses become sick and lame for God only knows what mysterious reasons, and are far less able to care for themselves. They have to be shod and their gear endlessly looked after. No, Marlowe had few illusions about the cavalry as such—he had long since learned that a cavalryman is simply a soldier mounted on a horse in order to move him faster from here to there.

Nevertheless—yes, nevertheless—on a shining new morning such as this a smart cavalry column, viewed from Marlowe's vantage point, can be a sight to lift the heart. And the knowledge, the confidence, that he could wield these men and animals as a single weapon gave him a sense of personal power that had nothing to do with the larger issues of the war. Brassy-throated bugles sounded with imperious and ancient compulsion, broken cadenced hoofs shuffled, shuffled in the dust of this southern earth, and one felt an involuntary shiver along the spine.

Marlowe was no great or even mildly ardent biblical scholar but he was well aware that men had gone to war with trumpets and horses ever since Joshua had gotten himself involved in the Jericho campaign, and no doubt long before that. He smiled inwardly at the thought but remembered that the outward similarity to his own situation ended there. For one thing, Joshua had had the avowed help of the Lord. For another, Joshua had two spies out in advance of his army, and the spies, setting a lasting precedent (literary at any rate) in such matters, had taken refuge in the establishment of a prostitute, where they had been tracked down by the provost—no doubt a man of experience in such things. The record sets forth that they escaped the provost but does not say whether they did Joshua any good in the military sense. Probably not, Marlowe surmised. Certainly the spies and espionage agents in this war, strangely enough, both military and civilian, had scarcely been worth their expense money—at least not in any instance Marlowe knew about.

He kneed his mount over beside the taciturn Keller.

"I feel I owe you an apology of sorts, or at any rate an explanation, in the matter of the Schwartz lad," Marlowe said.

"It turned out that I knew him in a kind of secondhand way and I suppose that weakened me."

Keller glanced briefly, almost indifferently, at the colonel and then back to the moving column—as though he was quite aware that Marlowe was sincere only up to a point. "Why, no explanation necessary, Colonel, as far as I'm concerned. They were your orders, and my understanding is that the man with the authority to give them has the authority to change them."

"Well, strictly speaking, yes—but I try not to make a habit of reversing myself over trivial matters."

Keller shrugged with one shoulder. "I'm not one of those who make an elaborate point of principle in such minor matters either, Colonel. Life's too short."

"That's not a common point of view in this army," Marlowe said dryly. "You should know the first unwritten general order—maintain your own position first and at all costs."

Keller shrugged again. "I daresay, Colonel, but that has never particularly interested me either."

Marlowe always found him a hard man either to agree or disagree with—there seemed to be no place to get hold of him. He had occasionally thought it might be profitable, or at any rate mildly interesting, to know Keller better, but nothing had ever come of the notion. Keller seemed to have an ingrained indifference, perhaps aloofness was a better word, in regard to the world in general and the officer corps in particular, and it seemed to have no especial reference to Marlowe—possibly not toward his fellow medics, though Marlowe of course had no way of knowing that. On the other hand, again so far as the colonel knew, it had never once been suggested or even hinted that Keller was remiss in his professional duties, and that was not a thing which could be said of all army surgeons.

"Ever read much history, Colonel?" Keller said suddenly and without preamble.

"Why, quite a lot," Marlowe said in some surprise. "But not in any particular field and mostly for my own amusement. I don't consider myself any kind of authority on any period or place."

Keller removed his cigar from his teeth and with it pointed toward the moving column. "Consider how we cling to the useless precedent of the past, Colonel, even when we make war—or especially in war. Look at those men of yours, every last one of 'em with a saber banging around his legs and getting in his way. We somehow assume that a military horseman and a sword of some kind go together. I suppose it goes back to the time when all warriors were horsemen, or perhaps vice versa, and the sword was the most lethal weapon available."

"Oh, I agree—at least up to a point. For instance, the Scottish clans gave the British and each other hell with the claymore, and they were not a race of horsemen—but perhaps that's the kind of exception that proves the rule. It just happened to occur to me."

"Has it ever occurred to you, also, that a surgeon who treats battle wounds might be a better judge of weapon effectiveness than the Ordnance Department?"

"Well"—Marlowe smiled in appreciation, it was the kind of unorthodoxy he relished—"I hadn't thought of that exact point, I must admit, but maybe you have something there. But think of the uproar that would ensue if a surgeon were actually called in to advise Ordnance on such a point. It'd never do. Armies are run by precedent and the book, Major, not logic and reason. I'm impressed with that fact each day that passes—it comes at me from all directions."

"I suppose I got to thinking about this saber business because I'm a part of the First myself, but as a surgeon I have a natural clinical interest in what weapons do and don't do. When I first came into the cavalry service and saw the troopers sporting these frog stickers, I had visions of men being chopped all to hell. What else were these knives for? Well, I've handled men hurt in half the major battles here in the West, to say nothing of the minor ones, and I give you my word, Colonel, I have yet to see my first authentic saber wound that wasn't gotten in connection with a grindstone! Yet your boys go on lugging that hardware around their legs and the generals talk solemnly about the science of war!"

"Well, yes, but it wasn't me you heard talking about the science of war." He had never before heard Keller make a speech this long on any subject—he could have hardly imagined him doing so. "But again you're only right up to a point, Major. I've never seen a saber wound either, much less inflicted one, but all the same those knives are useful in all sorts of ways not specified in the manual of arms. A handy cavalryman can use one to pry with, to cut firewood, chop brush and horse fodder, dig a garbage hole—"

The last company of the Second Iowa moved into the column formation and Colonel Blaney trotted over to the spot where Marlowe sat with Keller.

"'Morning, Colonel, Major Keller," Blaney said cheerfully. "Fine morning to start our business. Everything in order and on schedule, I take it."

Marlowe raised a hand to Blaney while he winced at the cheerful clichés, but at the same time he also thought, Why do I always belittle the man in my mind? He had no really valid reason for disliking Blaney, and if he wasn't brilliant he was still a better all-round officer than any number of others Marlowe could name offhand. He spoke to Blaney then, glanced away without allowing his distaste to show. Perhaps that was it. Blaney not only wore a straggly beard that never seemed to grow beyond a certain point but he was also an inveterate tobacco chewer—though this last was certainly no distinction in this army, rather the opposite. But it takes an expert to spit past a beard, especially in any kind of breeze, and Blaney had never bothered to become expert; it nearly always showed.

"Well, men"—Marlowe gathered in bridle leather—"we'd best get on our way or the rest of the column will think we've decided not to go." He nodded to Keller as he shook out the reins. "I hope we can find time to continue our discussion another time, Major."

The long column vanished into the forest to the south like a gigantic blue serpent, though hardly with serpent stealth. Six thousand-odd shod hoofs, together with the casual talk of the riders, can make a powerful lot of noise in rural stillness. These same 6,000 hoofs, even at a walk, churn any dry dirt road into a cloud of thick dust (in fact, the road was already a full inch deep with the yellow-red dust) moving in unison with the column. From Marlowe on down this didn't annoy anyone too much at the moment. The important thing was that they were on the move, just where didn't matter a lot. If the delay had hurt the brigade's spirit it certainly didn't show now. Oh, none of them were eager in the ordinary sense—since Shiloh few veterans were eager; it just didn't pay. But the drive was there; Marlowe knew; he could feel it; he would have been a poorer officer if he hadn't been able to.

8

Column South

.

The brigade was stretched out, more or less at rest, for three quarters of a mile and drawn back into the scattered pine growth for a distance of fifty yards or so. He couldn't see them, but Marlowe knew sentries patrolled the dark, narrow road at regular intervals, and a mile or so farther on the village of Ripley, whether its inhabitants knew it or not, was also surrounded by moving pickets.

This was the first full day the colonel himself had spent in the saddle for months, and while he was tired and very aware of his bottom fatigue he was hardly exhausted. Now he half-reclined on the ground, supporting himself with one elbow on the folded saddle blanket, which in turn was draped over the saddle seat. Unconsciously, of their own accord, his nostrils sorted out the night camp odors: the thick new grass where he lay, the ingrained horsy flavor of the blanket, the occasional fleeting smell of bacon in a hot pan, the wood-smoke taste of the small fire now dying into embers, and the pungent Havana aroma of his own cigar.

They had this day covered about twenty actual miles, in some ways not too bad but also not good—in fact, much less than good. As a rule one had to make certain allowances for the first shake-down day of a long march, but even so regulations decreed that a cavalry movement of this size should average three miles per hour, allowing for the regular short break in each hour. How much better a column could do depended on many factors, but here they could not afford to do less. He thought a little grimly of General Hurlbut and his five days' rations. At this rate it would take ten days merely to reach the line of the Southern—and that was far, far too long.

He sat upright and said sharply, "Davis!"

"Yes sir," the lieutenant answered immediately.

"A little business here for you to attend. You can manage the first part directly—I mean it won't be necessary for you to go through Major Gray—I'll explain to him. Now this is for Captain Landry, D Company of the First. Tomorrow morning I want three men out in front of the column as a point—about a quarter mile out. And I want them in an approximation of civilian clothes—where and how they get 'em is up to them and Landry. They ought to manage something around this village up ahead. Now Landry is to put this strictly on a volunteer basis—he'll still get plenty of men. But tell him for God's sake to pick some with their wits about them. Is that clear enough?"

"Well, yes sir, only—" Davis hesitated.

"Only what?" Marlowe said sharply.

"I was only going to mention that—well, if they should get taken in civilian clothes it could be their necks, literally. Of course, sir—"

"When I want you to explain the so-called rules of war," Marlowe interrupted wearily, "I'll ask you, Lieutenant! Landry knows that as well as I do—maybe even as well as you do—and he is to explain it to his volunteers. I was getting around to that when you undertook to advise me. But before you see Landry ask Major Gray to report here to me. I'll send King after the others but you'll be up there by Gray at the head of the line anyway. *Now* is it clear?"

"Yes sir," Davis said woodenly. He was a solemn young man and his feelings weren't really hurt at this more than implied rebuke. He was aware, often to his own private discomfiture, that he had never yet, in all his twenty-two years, learned when properly to keep his mouth shut.

"On your way then!"

When Davis had gone it was Sergeant King's turn. "You through with your supper stuff, Sergeant?"

"Yes sir. Nothin' to clean except the skillet and our coffee cans, Colonel."

"All right. Then my compliments to Colonel Blaney and Colonel Secord, and ask them to see me here as soon as convenient."

In something like twenty minutes the regimental commanders were on hand—Major Dick Gray was the last to arrive, he had farther to come. Marlowe didn't waste time on any amenities.

"Sorry to bother you with this, gentlemen," he said, amiable enough in the beginning. "I know you need your sleep, we all do. But this had to be said and I thought now was the time and place to do it. The point is this—today we made a bit over twenty miles and that's simply not good enough, not by more than 50 per cent. I'm not especially complaining now as such, you understand, I'm simply stating a fact. Well, we can't change what we did today but from now on we'll damned well have to do better as well as making up for today. I'm putting those things as other facts."

He let it rest there for a moment and for long seconds none of them said anything in answer. The fire had almost fallen into ashes now but there was still enough light to illuminate, or highlight, their faces, alike only in their momentary quiet.

"Oh, I don't know, Jack—you always have to make allowances

for a first day," Blaney said. His voice was bland, unexcited, yes, perhaps even a little fatherly—he was enough older than Marlowe to make the difference.

Marlow's voice also was calm but harsher now. "I said we'd have to do better, a lot better, and that stands. You know what regulation procedure is—three miles an hour even allowing men and animals a breather. You know what I think of some regulations, but there's nothing wrong with that one. We were out of La Grange at six this morning and on the road for something over twelve hours. It adds up to thirty-six miles and we actually made a little over twenty. You have to understand, and make the men understand, that speed is the only thing that can keep us out of trouble. You've got no baggage wagons or extra equipment to fool with, no ambulances. If we're ever going to make time it's got to be now, while men and horses are fresh and we're not slowed down by foraging. I'll listen to anything you have to say but . . ."

"Jack," Secord interrupted, "I know what regulation movement time is, and so does everybody else here—but it happens you're the one who ordered the two-hour halt at Hazel Creek this afternoon and that—"

"And that still wouldn't account for the difference," Marlowe said harshly. "You know why I held them there—or if you don't you have to assume that I had good enough reason in my opinion."

Blaney looked thoughtful—though thoughtful about what was hard to say. Major Gray made a little grimace but said not a word. Secord stood with his hands in his pants pockets, kicking gently at the earth with one worn boot toe.

"All right, Jack," Secord said presently—glanced quickly at Gray and then away again. "I reckon nobody can argue with your arithmetic, but there's something else here. There's nothing personal in this, you understand, nothing at all, and I'm not complaining. But the fact remains that my regiment's the one in the middle and I'll be damned if I can move any faster than the one in front of me."

Gray's head came up with a snap—he hadn't said a word up

to now, but Marlowe had anticipated that one also and his right
hand moved gently as he said, "Hold it, Dick. I'll grant you that's
a fact, Secord, but it's only one of several and doesn't affect the
over-all situation. There wasn't anything personal in what I said
in the beginning either. You know— well, Christ knows, and more
important, you know, how little I enjoy riding any of you and
I shouldn't have to, but in the last analysis the responsibility is
mine and I have to make the most of it. Before we started on this
thing I made up my mind that it wasn't going to fail because of
anything I knew I had to do but didn't. I'm no genius and I
can't foresee anything—in fact, the million things I don't see are
what scare me, but you're going to hear plenty about what I *do*
see."

Naturally it didn't end quite there. Marlowe let them chew on
it for a few minutes just to clear the air, but then he did stop it.
He raised a hand, gentle as a fluttering dove, and said, "Thanks
to all of you. I said I wasn't going to prolong this and I've said
what I had to say. Save your energy for the road tomorrow—you'll
need it. That's all."

When they had gone the colonel again lay down with his head
on the saddle and tried to relax. He managed with his body but
the mind was a different thing—it never stopped. Somehow he had
a feeling, vague but still there, of frustration. You talked, you
explained, you put the basic facts in their hands—or heads
(which?) and ended up wondering what if anything you had
accomplished. Moreover, there was the further personal truth
that if they had really pinned him down he could not have said
exactly, in any detail, how he expected them to speed up the
column. But, he asked himself, should he have to? After all, they
were in direct personal command of the troops—it was their
problem. It could be also, he admitted wryly— just how Olympian
was he?—that his own feeling of personal importance might be
a little overblown—it just could be.

He turned over on his side and for a long distance through the
pines he could see the crooked lines of fires, now dying away

rapidly. He wasn't worried about any kind of surprise attack here—they weren't far enough south yet and the distribution of Confederate force in this area (always barring the unexpected) was very well known. The brigade might have been spotted by a roving patrol but he even doubted that—there was little reason why a patrol should be here.

He recognized Davis's footsteps as the lieutenant approached the fire after again staking his horse. Davis said softly, "You awake, Colonel?"

"Quite. Everything arranged, Davis?"

"Yes sir. Landry got fifteen volunteers and could have had more except he cut them off. That's a tough—Well, I mean, that outfit doesn't give a damn for anything much, sir."

Marlowe chuckled—Davis himself did not come from the First —as he answered dryly, "I know. Neither does any other company in the First. That's why I sent you there. Better bed down, Lieutenant. Four o'clock comes early."

All about them were the unending sounds of horse movement, for even at night a close-packed cavalry camp is never completely silent. Tired men can be reasoned, cajoled, or even ordered into silence, but not horses. Marlowe was acutely aware of the endless chorus of hoof stamping, shuffling, breaking of wind, sneezes, snorts, coughs, and occasional short neighs, and he didn't like it in the security sense. But all he could do was hope it wouldn't be heard by the wrong ears.

Somewhere not far off a trooper breathed the notes of *Lorena* into a mouth harp. The sound was cut off sharply in midphrase, probably by an unsentimental sergeant interested in sleep, but Marlowe drifted off musing on the strangeness of a war in which fighting men happily adopted and cherished the most personal music of the other side. . . .

The truth was that, for reasons trivial in themselves and therefore the more exasperating, they didn't make measurably better time. The colonel's order to move faster was, taken by itself, so simple and reasonable that the regimental commanders couldn't

very well take issue with it; for one of them to maintain cate-
gorically that he couldn't move a notch faster, when they had
been on the road only one day, would have been an admission of
incompetence. They had done better, far better, before. Nevertheless, they did not seem to move noticeably faster. It was one
of those things nobody seemed able to explain.

Marlowe himself was up and down the full length of the
column several times, and while he gave orders here and there
he didn't seem to change the situation. There were evident
reasons why they didn't move more rapidly. First there was the
elemental fact that, in general, the larger a cavalry unit the less
able it is to move fast and still maintain order. The horseflesh of the
brigade was, on the whole, no better or worse than similar Federal
units. In it were animals with traces of some of the best bloodlines
in the country, and there was a corresponding number of just plain
plugs. The net result was an average of stamina and speed. Men
and horses could feed, or be fed, in the organized sense only
morning and evening, but horses simply had to be watered oftener
than that. In the nature of things a brigade could be watered
efficiently only at creeks and rivers—1,500 horses (and men)
could quickly drink dry any well in these parts, and it was the
Lord who had arranged the intervals between these water supplies.
Sometimes they watered sooner than they would have liked,
simply because the water was there and there was no knowing
how far it was to the next supply. The process would start off in
orderly fashion at a ford or crossing, then the water would begin
to roil and muddy underfoot and men and horses would start
edging slowly upstream in search of something more palatable.
Presently men and horses, regardless of orders and fuming officers,
would be scattered the hell and gone along the bank. Then
troopers stretching their legs on the ground would be suddenly
overtaken by imperious calls of nature and 20 per cent of the
brigade would be scattered in the bushes with its pants down. It
was all harmless enough in itself, and no doubt necessary, but it
took time, time, time.

Near noon Marlowe rode out in front to have a look at the three-man point. He recognized the sergeant in charge and said, "It's Bullen, isn't that right, Sergeant?"

"Yes sir! Andy Bullen, sir."

Dressed variously in civilian clothing, they looked much like countrymen anywhere, which two of them were in fact. Marlowe looked them over carefully. Carbines were still in the saddle boots. They still carried their pistols but the belts were slacked, non-military fashion, and the sabers were gone. That they were armed was not in itself suspicious. Men did not always go armed in this country but when they did the fact was seldom remarked on.

Marlowe grinned and said, "What became of the sabers, Sergeant?"

"Oh, Cap'n Landry's got 'em tied on his blanket roll."

"Have any trouble getting the clothes?"

"Well—" Bullen paused and spat in the road dust. "No *trouble* exactly, Colonel. Fella there in Ripley had a general store, such as it was. Didn't amount to nothin' but he had what we needed. Cap'n Landry—uh, persuaded him."

"I see." Marlowe didn't pursue the point further. "Well, I wanted to tell you boys—I don't expect you to stay out here on this limb indefinitely. I'll see that somebody else gets a whack at it."

Bullen shrugged and again spat a brown stream. "S'all right with me, Colonel, speakin' personal. Just as soon be here as any place else. More elbow room out here."

"Well, we'll see. Don't run into any bear traps. If you see anything that looks like Rebel force don't start a war on your own. Just get the hell out of there with the information."

Dropping back, he fell in beside Major Gray, in the vanguard of the First Illinois.

Between Marlowe and the other senior officers of the First Brigade there was a relationship odd in the objective military sense but commonplace in this army, where a man's actual rank often bore little relationship to the size of his command. Marlowe was an acting brigadier and was actually in command of the First Brigade, and nobody questioned either his authority or his fitness to exercise it, yet on the official rolls he was a colonel, no more. Likewise no one questioned Dick Gray's command of the First Illinois Volunteer Cavalry although he was in fact a major. Moreover, he had been Marlowe's second when the latter was still in direct command of the First, and that created a degree of intimacy that couldn't be simply discarded like a soiled shirt. Still further, the colonelcy of Blaney of the Second Iowa antedated that of Marlowe by two weeks, so that strictly by the book Blaney was actually senior officer in the brigade and, again according to the book, should have been acting brigadier. But nobody, least of all Blaney, gave a damn about that either. This kind of confusion, bearing out at least one of Marlowe's contentions, was more or less normal here in the West. (They hadn't heard the tale of the beardless second lieutenant who, after certain particular hell in the valley of Virginia, showed up as senior surviving officer of all that remained of the Sixty-sixth New York—and got a rough going over from a regulation-bound general, on the ground that the regiment had been mishandled. But they wouldn't have been surprised.) One result of all this was that, without it being in any way planned, between Marlowe and the others there was a certain military formality in public but practically none in private.

Gray was still more than a little salty from the night before. "God damn it, Jack," he said, "if Secord thinks he can boot this outfit along any faster let him get the Second up here and try it! If I lope 'em a mile I have to walk 'em another mile in order to even it up. If I—"

"Don't get excited," Marlowe said calmly. "Of course Secord was right in that he can't move any faster than you do, but that's only part of it. If he was up here he wouldn't be doing any better than you are—if I didn't think so I'd damned sure have him up here. I'm not satisfied, no, but I'm not blaming anybody either. I've got no choice but to keep pushing, Dick."

"Oh, sure, but you know how I feel about it. Hell, if I had my way I'd have the whole damned outfit in Meridian tomorrow morning, but I'm no wizard."

"Don't let it throw you," Marlowe said calmly. "We'll make out. Just keep shoving 'em as much as you can."

Munching cold beef wrapped in a chunk of bread, he moved back again and rode a while with Secord. The latter waved a hand at the general landscape and said, "You wouldn't guess there's a war going on, would you? If you ask me, if I wasn't in uniform and under orders I wouldn't raise a hand to take this country down here. And if it was mine, I wouldn't fire a gun to keep the Godforsaken place." Secord was from that overgrown and brawling but still infant metropolis, Chicago. Secord hadn't thought much of southern Illinois either, Marlowe remembered, although it had been the cradle of his home state.

"Oh, I don't know, Frank. The point seems to be that they *are* fighting for it, whatever their reasons." Marlowe raised his eyes to a cutbank where the dogwood bloomed in a pristine riot of beauty. He sighed faintly. "Even the most ignorant savage seems to have some spot of earth he holds as his own. I don't know— maybe he fights for it simply because he hasn't got anything better. Ever been down here in this country before?"

"No, and that's only the half of it, Jack—when this mess is over I won't ever, God willing, be back again. Jesus, take a good look at it." Secord pointed to a story-and-a-half house set back a little way from the winding road; they had just come in sight of it as they rounded a bend. A violently rutted lane wriggled toward the house in front of which new spring weeds were already growing luxuriantly. Behind the house and a little to one side stood a half-dozen ramshackle Negro shanties. A couple of thin hogs rooted aimlessly before what was known in some locations as the manor house or the big house—in this case it could only be called either in comparison with the "quarters." From a privy a paunchy white man emerged, still in the act of hoisting a gallus over one shoulder. At sight of the seemingly (from his point of view) endless blue column he stopped suddenly and even at this distance they could see the look of utter unbelief settle on his face and stay there. Then as they watched the man broke for the house at an awkward run. Secord laughed sardonically. "Seemed a little surprised, wasn't he? —the damned Yankees tramping on the sacred soil. Take a good look at the civilization their politicians yawp about. Great Christ! They must feel a compulsion to brag big because they have so little to brag about in fact. If it was up to me I'd let 'em choke to death in their own hog wallows—yes, niggers and all!"

"Well"—Marlowe tossed away the remaining bread crust and a piece of gristle and wiped his hands on an already filthy handkerchief—"I won't argue it with you, Frank. After all, we're on the same side. But as usual there's another side to the story, certainly from their point of view, and that's what makes horse-races—"

He wouldn't even quarrel too much with Secord's not too brilliant generalizations, except in so far as they were not all the truth or even the most important part of it. A civilization is more than land and physical structures which for the most part were much less than magnificent; yes, even more than people; the whole, in short, was more than the sum of its parts. Unlike Secord, Marlowe had been here before, at a time when even the most violent of the local patriots would not have prophesied, or for that matter advocated, this present fratricide. Of course he hadn't been on this particular road or even in this county, but all the same he was no stranger to this delta country of Mississippi and Louisiana. In fact, he felt a curious personal affinity with that larger entity called The South. Not with its peculiar fault of Negro servitude, to be sure, which in truth many of the best minds in the South had long since known for what it was in fact; not for the fantastic bombast of the politicians, drunk on their own words, who when the chips were really down had proved to have little more capacity than children playing at make-believe. Not for these and similar things, but for something else larger and better which the South itself had never been able to define in a way its enemies could understand. He didn't advertise it, but toward this South he sometimes felt as a man may feel toward a fine friend who on occasion is unaccountably taken with insane drunkenness. A man, a friend, who is kind and gentle, generous and honorable and perhaps even wise—save when the narcotic madness seized mind and body and spirit. It was probable, he thought wryly, that few of his opposite numbers in the Confederate ranks would appreciate his nice—and wholly gratuitous—distinctions.

He came back to the present with a start and gathered up the bridle leather he had allowed to go slack. "Keep pushing 'em, Frank," he said shortly. "Tonight we'll ride right up to the edge of dark, depending a little on when we find water for a camp."

9

Reconnaissance

So passed the second day and part of the third, but their pace did not accelerate. Marlowe fumed inwardly. He knew why they lost ground, or rather failed to gain any, on the third day, but there was no general fault which accounted for their slowness.

They passed through the county-seat towns of New Albany and Pontotoc, hardly more than unpainted villages, with their shabby, pitifully imitative little Greek Revival courthouses, the paint peeling—the courthouses usually were painted, once, when built—and the wood of their disguised marble columns and cornices already starting to decay, where justice of some kind was meted out.

They had worked out a technique for getting through these places—naturally most roads led to and through them. Marlowe didn't expect real trouble in these towns but then there was no way to be sure in advance. So they would send forward a company of the Second Iowa and it would police the place. This usually amounted to nothing more than resting their horses until the balance of the column passed. Curiously, they would frequently be welcomed as friends—until the surprised inhabitants learned the truth. Possibly this wasn't so extraordinary in itself— there were always Confederate units that wore blue, or at least something more blue than gray. No considerable body of troops from either side, certainly none this size, had ever passed this way. Except for the railway line Marlowe was after there was nothing of military value hereabouts, and these people, still believing in what they thought was a powerful and all-protecting government, at first simply couldn't believe these troops weren't their own. They learned differently in a hurry, though in all truth not a single bona-fide noncombatant suffered personal injury at the hands of the brigade. In fact, it hadn't even started to requisition horses and rations—not yet.

In the physical sense this country here hadn't suffered from the war, and it would never experience the hammering devastation that was even now being conjured up for Vicksburg. It was neither the richest nor the most populous part of Mississippi but it had a virile agriculture and so was important in the larger southern scheme of things. Along this road now traveled by the brigade spring planting was briskly under way—there seemed to be no lack of labor here and it wasn't all Negro by any means. The orators, still in their world of fantasy, spoke reverently of the southern male leaping to the defense of hearth and home as one man, but while the percentage was very high indeed it was also a very long way from total. There were able-bodied white men hereabouts in considerable quantity—the brigade could see them plainly as it passed by.

And that was one of the things which worried Marlowe a little. Not, of course, in the sense of the brigade itself being attacked. To be sure some bushwhacker might be tempted to a little target practice; it happened occasionally; that would be an aggravation but hardly a catastrophe. But there was always the possibility that some local patriot, unwilling to wear a uniform but not averse to putting in his bit as long as little risk was involved, might carry word of the brigade's passing to the nearest Confederate force —in which case the fat might well be in the fire. Since they were off the railroad line there was no telegraph available, but Marlowe knew very well how fast and mysteriously news can travel. In two and a half days they hadn't seen a single Rebel in uniform, nor heard of any, but that didn't mean there might not be an infantry brigade dug in around the next bend or on the next riverbank. Marlowe did not believe this likely but neither did he dare operate much farther solely on a basis of self-communion. So he halted the column, dispatched King to hold up Sergeant Bullen and his civilian-clad cohorts, then sent Lieutenant Davis to summon the captains of A, B, and C companies of the First.

Word went down the line that they would be here for a while and it was all right to relax. Within minutes horse gear had been pulled off, animals were staked out, and long ranks of men were fast asleep by the roadside. As veterans they looked upon any chance to sleep as so much extra profit.

Besides Davis there were present Captains Bryce and Harwood of A and B companies, and First Lieutenant Burns of C. They listened and watched attentively as Marlowe talked and drew a diagram in the dust with a long, sharp willow stick.

"I'm not worried," he said, "at least no more than normal. But the fact is that we're moving blind and that's not good if it can be helped. Now I'm not concerned—much—with what's ahead of us. I am concerned with any force that may be coming up behind us or moving in on our flanks. In those respects a big enough force could give us one hell of a surprise. Now there's no logical reason why there should be any Rebel force on our right, to the west, but still, there could be.

"So you, Burns, will backtrack here till you come to that road we crossed about a half-hour ago and head west. Then swing south and back east and pick us up again."

"Beg pardon, sir," Burns said a little nervously—as a relatively new company commander he wasn't accustomed to getting his orders directly from the acting brigadier. "I'm afraid I don't understand just how far I'm supposed to go."

Marlowe gestured mildly. "Not so fast, Burns, I'm coming to that—and this applies to you others as well. It's right at ten o'clock now and I'm going to hold the column here until two, but not one minute longer. You are all to guide yourselves by that interval. In other words, give yourselves roughly two hours out and two back. But we'll move at two whether *any* of you are back. It'll be up to you to catch us then."

"I understand, sir," Burns said with controlled eagerness. "Any special instructions?"

"This is to be just a general reconnaissance—I want to know what Rebel force is around, if any. The less you turn up the better I'll like it, but if there is any I damn' well want to know it. Another thing—stay out of trouble and for God's sake don't pick any fights. I don't want any dead Rebels—I want information and I want you fellows back in the column. Clear enough now?"

"Yes sir."

"Then get moving, Burns—you needn't wait for the others."

"Now Bryce, and you, Harwood. As we sit here we're roughly fifteen miles west of the line of the M. & O. Now we know Ruggles has always had a certain amount of force along the railroad and he must still have. The point is, how much and where is it as of now? Ruggles has been running things on the north end of the M. & O., and while he's no genius he's nobody's damned fool either. It may be—it was supposed to and I hope it worked—that when Dodge moved down from Corinth, east of the M. & O., he pulled Ruggles off base—which, of course, was the main idea. But maybe he didn't either. Maybe Ruggles smelled a rat and is moving down to head us off; he could easily enough. We're moving almost exactly parallel with the M. & O.; he could bring his outfit down by rail—he'd be moving a damned sight faster than we are—go on past us, detrain, and move in ahead of us. Unless he's got far more strength than I think, we could probably whip him. But the collision wouldn't do us any good and I don't want to waste the time anyway."

The colonel tossed aside the stick and dusted his hands.

"I'm afraid that as usual I'm talking too much for what I'm getting said," he commented wryly. "But what I told Burns applies to you fellows—except that I think you're a little more likely to run into some Johnnies. Bryce, you will head east and north, toward the M. & O. Harwood the same except to the south. That should give us a good spread in relation to the railroad. Don't overlook anything—and don't tamper with the M. & O. even if you have a good chance. I repeat, we stay here until two, not a minute longer."

Marlowe watched them thoughtfully as they remounted—particularly Asa Bryce. He knew something about Bryce, not too much, but the man interested him more than a little. He knew personally a great many men in the First Illinois, yet he was also acutely aware of how little he knew of them as individuals, as distinct from the military pattern. Knowing a man—or a woman—takes time, time a wartime colonel of regiment doesn't always have. He recalled the discussion he'd had with General Smith about the sometimes peculiar civilian pursuits of men now submerged in the vast anonymity of the army. In a way Bryce was a case in point—though wasn't every other man when you isolated him? Anyway, Bryce had been a professor of Greek and Roman history at Aberdeen College, and, if you accepted the popular concept, few pursuits were less warlike. The professor as a type was supposed to be impractical, visionary, unaffected by and unable to manage affairs outside his own world, worthy perhaps but hardly to be trusted with the world's workaday business. Not a particle of all this nonsense applied in Bryce's case.

Marlowe regarded him as unquestionably the ablest company commander in the First. He was almost too much inclined to call on Bryce and A Company whenever an especially ticklish job turned up. And yet Bryce too on occasion had displayed some— well, rather surprising personal quirks. He was, for instance, the regiment's senior company commander, and when the majority was open it was offered to him as a matter of course. Marlowe had been pleased at the idea of removing him from company routine and bringing him closer to himself. And Bryce had refused the majority point-blank. More than surprised, Marlowe had said, "Any special reason you'd care to go into, Captain?" Bryce had said, politely but firmly, "No sir, none that I'd care to go into—at least not here and now," and that was that. (It was thus that Dick Gray came into the majority and eventually the acting colonelcy of the First. In time, with the uncertainties of war, Gray might very possibly receive the general officer's berth that otherwise would have gone to Bryce. For want of a nail . . .) Marlowe had too much respect for Bryce's integrity as an individual to argue with him—and there was nothing in regulations which said a man had to accept promotion. To refuse was not the common re- action, to be sure, but still there were many men to whom pro- motion as such was not the most important part of soldiering— they provided a sort of counterbalance to those who regarded personal advancement as the *only* good reason for being here. Besides regarding Bryce as an exceptionally competent officer Marlowe liked him very much personally, which was not at all the same thing. He would have hated to lose him for any reason.

Sergeant King saluted vaguely and said, "I put your gear under that paw-paw tree yonder, Colonel, case you figure on a little rest."

"All right," Marlowe said briefly. "But if you let me sleep past one-thirty I'll break you down to private."

"Yes *sir!*" the sergeant acknowledged. He had now survived these threats of being broken for a full year and a half—in fact, he had survived when he had fully deserved to be broken and knew it.

What the reconnaissance parties learned, even in the negative sense, would in part determine when the Second Iowa would be detached and sent back to La Grange, or at any rate *started* for La Grange. Marlowe had a notion, of course still unsupported by evidence, that the Second was apt to encounter some first-class hell before it got back to La Grange—again, if it did get back.

10

Report

Ravenously hungry, Marlowe had almost enjoyed his supper. It was the same old coarse, monotonous fare but with an added fillip. In some way Marlowe didn't bother inquiring into how Sergeant King had produced a pound or so of fresh butter—if he'd paid for it he would have promptly asked to be reimbursed, but he hadn't.

The colonel kept telling himself it was still too soon to worry but all the same he was nervous. Actually, he had not expected any of the three recon companies back by two o'clock on the dot —you couldn't run these things on schedule and two had been only a target time. Burns had made it near three and Harwood around four. Neither had found anything except natives surprised into momentary paralysis at the strange sight of Federal cavalry, though Harwood had gone clear to the M. & O. line. He had followed the line for five miles, encountering one six-car freight train, and passed through one village too small to warrant a telegraph operator at the one-room depot.

No, the problem now was the continued absence of Company A. Bryce could be trusted to do nothing foolhardy or reckless but that didn't mean he couldn't have stumbled into something beyond his capacity to handle—and by all logic it was Bryce who would have been most likely to encounter trouble. There had always been Confederate force along the upper thirty or forty miles of the M. & O., there to provide a deterrent to Dodge at Corinth. The force Ruggles was supposed to have there would have been no match for the brigade but it could have swallowed A Company whole.

Marlowe was nursing a tin cup of bitter black coffee, well laced with whisky, when Bryce rode out of the darkness. Out of sight on the road the colonel could hear horses moving in a bunch, the rest of A Company. Bryce slid to the ground rather than dismounted, and Marlowe saw the captain's legs almost give way as they made contact with the earth.

Marlowe nearly sighed with relief. "Trouble, Asa?"

Bryce half-reclined on the grass and rubbed his legs, a rueful expression on his filthy, stubbled face—ordinarily he was clean-shaven. "Legs half-paralyzed—and so's my rump. Trouble? No, nothing really in that category. Just one damned thing and another and it all took time. Any coffee to spare, Colonel?"

"Sergeant!"

"Yes sir! Comin' right up. You like a stick o' somethin' in it, Cap'n?"

"No—yes, I believe I will. My brains, what there are of 'em, feel like a busted cotton bale. The others all back?"

Marlowe nodded. "Not on time—I didn't expect that—but back. They didn't see anything but landscape."

"Un-hunh." Bryce blew on the coffee, took a long swallow, and said, "Aaaah! That's what you'd call a drink with authority. We did run into a couple of things, Colonel, but nothing to change the course of the war." Bryce began a low chuckle that ended in a short laugh.

"What's so damned funny?" Marlowe said a little irritably. Another officer he might have brusquely ordered to get on with his report, but not Bryce.

"Sorry. I'll get to it in a minute. I couldn't help the laugh— funniest damn' thing I've seen in months." Bryce chuckled again and finished the charged coffee. "We found a pretty good road but until past noon didn't see anything but rundown shacks. I kept going—I wanted to get to the railroad, and came to this place called Tupelo or something like that. Anyway, it didn't amount to a damn as a town, and ran into this company of home guards—"

"Good Lord!"

"No, no trouble, Colonel. Bear with me. I sent in a couple of men to scout the place, and they reported these home guards were having a shindig. There was a place near the center of town—you know, a little grove, a well, and a watering trough. There were about forty in this bunch, not counting the Negroes doing the work. They were about to pitch into a barbecue the Negroes had been fixing—a nice hog and about a dozen chickens. My God! We could smell it a couple miles away."

Marlowe impatiently said, "Well?" but right now he could almost smell it himself.

"They were armed, of course, but the guns were stacked about a hundred feet from the barbecue. They were so busy getting ready to work on the barbecue that nobody paid any attention to us. We came tearing in like a young cyclone, surrounded 'em like a bunch of cattle, they had no place to go, and that was that. One lad shot off his mouth—somebody always has to show how brave he is—and got the butt end of a quirt across the jaw a couple of times. That pretty well discouraged the argument."

"Hmm. Home guards," Marlowe said reflectively. He busied himself with a fresh cigar.

"Oh, you know, Colonel. It's Sunday and they're supposed to drill. What it works out to is, they pitch horseshoes, chew tobacco and drink a little whisky on the sly, brag, swap news and argue—then eat the barbecue and go home. You know—defending their country. This time there were a few variations."

"Like what?"

Bryce laughed again, though this time a little wearily. "We stood the whole bunch against and around a nice big shade tree, took a couple of picket ropes and cinched them around good and tight, like a corn shock. There was some complaint that the boys on the inside, next to the tree, were a little short of breath, but I didn't have time to check. Then we put four guards on them while the rest of us ate the barbecue—it was just ready. You know, Colonel, I couldn't have kept the boys away from that grub."

"I daresay," Marlowe commented dryly. "So what then?"

"Well, there were the guns—damnedest batch of hardware you ever laid eyes on. There was everything from muzzle-loading shotguns to banged-up muskets the British must have left at the Battle of New Orleans. The boys busted every last one of 'em on the ground and then competed in seeing how far they could throw and scatter the pieces. They had a nice time and the whole thing took only about an hour."

"All very well," Marlowe grunted, "but I don't know that it contributes much to our over-all information."

"Well, what the hell were we supposed to do," Bryce said imperturbably, "hand 'em back the guns and give 'em a free shot? Anyway, there's a little more to it. I don't know whether you know it, Colonel, but I've got two ex-telegraphers in A—Corporal Stanley and Hoblit. Both of 'em used to work on the I.C. I don't understand that stuff myself. But we went over to the M. & O. depot, kicked in the door, and the boys worked on the wire. They raised somebody up the line—Stanley says these operators chew the rag back and forth all the time. So anyway, Ruggles has about a thousand men up around Baldwyn—"

"Damn!" Marlowe sat up like a suddenly jerked puppet. "Doing what? Christ, all last night and at sunup we weren't twenty miles from there!"

"Sure," Bryce drawled, "but we're not there now and he still is. He must think he knows something we know damned well ain't so. He's supposed to be digging in to hold off an attack on the M. & O. up there."

Marlowe frowned. "You're sure, Bryce?"

"No sir," Bryce said patiently, "I'm not *sure*—I didn't see him myself. I'm telling you what Stanley said he got off the wire and I don't think he made it up. The wire sure said a lot of *something*. Hell's fire, Colonel, if I'd gone up there myself I never would have caught up with you, and then what would I have done with the information?"

"I know, I know," Marlowe said hastily. "That was a damn' fool question. But you know our situation as well as I do. Damn it! I feel like the blind man in blindman's buff."

"I know. But whether Ruggles is digging or not, we're a good forty miles ahead of him now."

"There's that," Marlowe conceded. "It's reasonable."

"Stanley couldn't ask the other fellow what *kind* of troops were up there, he didn't think it would sound natural. The other fellow did ask him if *he'd* heard of any Federals loose down here and of course Stanley said no."

"They'll be disabused of that notion as soon as the regular Tupelo operator got back on the job."

Bryce shrugged. His fatigue showed plainly in his homely features now. "Sorry, Colonel, but you can't have everything, though it's not my business to remind you of that."

"Oh, hell, Bryce, I'm sorry if I sounded critical—I didn't mean to be. You did a neat job, as usual. I was a little jumpy when you didn't show up, though I should have known better."

"Not necessarily," Bryce said with sudden somberness. "Everybody's luck runs out sometime and I figure I'm quite a bit past due now. My Christ, Colonel! I'm tired. It happens that we rode something like thirty-odd miles farther than the rest of the brigade did today. I'm not complaining, but all the same it leaves a mark."

"Sure, sure," Marlowe said absently. "Hard on the horses."

Bryce smiled sourly. "But not on the men, Colonel?" He hadn't been able to resist that one.

"What? Oh, sure, I know what you mean, Captain, and I agree that I'm a heartless sonofabitch and a slave driver. But let's be real nasty while we're at it. Tired men can manage on fresh horses but spanking fresh men won't go anywhere on fagged horses. We're only three days out of La Grange, but how'd you like to have A Company down here afoot?"

"All right." Bryce rubbed a dirty forehead with an equally dirty hand. "I just couldn't pass that one up."

"Damn it, Bryce!" Marlowe glanced around, saw that Sergeant King was apparently asleep and Lieutenant Davis nowhere in sight. "I still wish you'd taken the majority. It was your affair if you didn't want it but I still wish you had."

"Thanks," Bryce said, "but I don't." He got slowly, wearily to his feet, unfolding one limb at a time. "Me, right now I'm at least through for the day—but you're not. You're never through, Colonel. No, Gray's welcome as far as I'm concerned."

"The hell with it." Marlowe waved a hand. "Go on and get your sleep. You'll need it. Don't worry—I'll have more chores for A Company."

"No doubt," Bryce said without feeling. "At least it keeps things from getting dull. Good night, Colonel."

Marlowe lay down again and for a while before closing his eyes watched a huge orange moon edge upward into the darkness. For the time being at least, he reflected, the hounds had not found the true scent, but he didn't doubt that they would. The question was, when?

Of course Bryce was right—*he* would be through when the war was over.

11

The Point

Of course Sergeant Andy Bullen heard the talk between Privates Dorsey and Moore; he couldn't very well help himself. But unless one of them addressed him directly he paid them as little heed as possible. They weren't talking *about* anything, just talking to pass the time and relieve the boredom. There wasn't much else they could do while they rode, although yesterday they had, for a while, hit upon one variation. The day being Sunday (it was near noon before either of them remembered), they took turns singing every hymn they could together dredge up from memory—beginning with "Blessed Assurance" and working through "Safely Through Another Week" to "What Will You Do with Jesus?" Critical objection to all this was that neither of them could sing worth a damn and whenever they forgot the precise lyrics, which was often, they invented new ones which were anything but worshipful. Still, it was Sunday and the sergeant bore with it as a matter of principle.

Actually the great gap in their sympathetic rapport lay in the fact that Sergeant Andrew Jackson Bullen was thirty-two years old, whereas Privates Dorsey and Moore were, respectively, twenty and twenty-one, and between twenty and thirty-two there is an almost unbridgeable gulf. They considered the sergeant an old fogy while he in turn had never heard either of them say a single thing he considered interesting or intelligent in itself.

So Private Dorsey was starting to say "Whatta you think, Sarge?" for the third time when Bullen came out of his brown study and said, "What the devil are you talkin' about?"

"Why, I was just sayin', Sarge," Dorsey resumed apologetically, "when d'you reckon the Old Man will relieve us?"

"Relieve us?" Bullen spoke the words in wonder, almost as though he'd never heard them before. "What the hell you mean, relieve?"

"Why, just that, you know, relieve us."

"Do you want to be relieved? Do you have to be?"

"Why, I dunno," Dorsey said in sudden mild confusion. "It's just that the colonel said we'd get relieved and—"

"That wasn't what I asked you, Dorsey. I said, do you *want* to be relieved?"

"Well, I wasn't talkin' about that, Sarge. It's just that the Colonel said we wouldn't have to stay out here all the time. He said he'd—"

"Oh, horse manure! I know what he said, but it's all right with me if he never relieves us. What's the difference whether you ride up here or back in the line? It's just as far and takes just as long either way. Me, I like it up here. Up here I only have to listen to you two yammer, but back there I have to listen to the whole damn' company. But I'll tell you what I'll do. If you've got cold feet I'll run you back to Cap'n Landry with a note an' tell him to send me up another man."

"Aw, now, Sarge, you know I never said no such thing. With

me an' Archie here it's just the principle of the thing, an' you know dang well the Old Man—"

"Oh, horse manure!" Bullen snorted again. "Neither one of you'd recognize a principle if you found one in the road. Say, hold on—" Bullen came out of his lazy saddle slouch with a sudden snap. Up ahead they could see a buggy approaching, the horse at a trot which threatened to lapse into a walk at the slightest provocation. "Easy now!" Bullen said, his voice suddenly taut. "You two keep your big mouths shut and out of the way. I'll do the talkin'."

Bullen waved his boys to the side of the road so it was obvious they were not blocking the buggy's passage—yet his own stance made it plain that he expected the buggy to stop. As the rig came closer almost anyone could have made a proper guess as to the character of its occupants. The tired-faced elderly man in the rusty black frock coat and equally rusty plug hat had a worn bag between his feet—a typical and obvious country M.D. The girl—she might have been seventeen—kept her eyes down with proper modesty, but Bullen could see she was the spitting image of the man. The girl was anything but pretty, but there was a youthful freshness about her which made the matter of looks unimportant. Privates Dorsey and Moore eyed the girl—she kept her eyes on the hands twisting a handkerchief in her lap—with looks half-bashful and half-hungry. The ancient horse racked to a stop when the man barely lifted the reins.

"Beg pardon, suh an' ma'am," Bullen said in his best Below-the-Line accent. "We're a patrol from the Twentieth Alabama Horse, Colonel Gordon." Andy wondered if there was any such outfit—not that the man was likely to know for certain there *wasn't*. "I'm Sergeant Bullen."

"Why, pleased to know you, suh," the man said with grave courtesy. "Dr. Abernathy—and this is my daughter, Miss Cynthia."

"A real pleasure, Doctor an' ma'am." Bullen raised his dusty hat courteously—and suddenly remembering something else, he clamped his other hand over the broad brass belt buckle stamped USA.

"On my regular trip to see a couple of my regular country patients," the doctor said affably. "Old people, you know."

"Why, sure 'nough. I'm sorry to keep y'all even a minute but I hoped you might help us out. I reckon you've heard about that mess o'Yankees under General Marlowe?"

Abernathy frowned and pursed his thin lips. "Why, yes, some, though frankly I haven't known how much to believe. I've heard there are as many as five thousand of them and that they have been burning and pillaging like savages. I didn't quite believe that, but Yankee soldiers, I don't know—We haven't had any personal experience with them hereabouts."

"Well, we ain't heard about 'em burning anything—yet, but a man just can't tell," Bullen said solemnly. "But we're after 'em, Doctor, depend on that. Which brings me to the point. This town up here ahead is Houston, ain't that right?"

"Why, yes suh, that's correct. Mighty fine little town."

"Un-hunh. Well," Bullen said blandly, "we're supposed to rejoin Colonel—er, Gordon and the rest of the regiment there. I just wondered if you'd seen any of 'em come in there yet?"

"Why, no, no suh, can't say that I have. Haven't seen hide nor hair of any troops, Sergeant. Now let's see." The doctor consulted a huge silver watch. "We've been on the road just about three quarters of an hour and of course they could have arrived after we left. I must say, though, that I haven't heard of any troops in the neighborhood."

"Well, I'm sure obliged to you, suh," Bullen said heartily. "They'll be there eventually. I reckon we'll just have to wait. Sorry if we've held you up, suh."

"Not at all, Sergeant, not at all. Sorry I couldn't be of more help to you. A pleasure to meet you. Good luck, my boy."

The three dusty horse soldiers lifted their hats as the doctor clucked the unwilling nag under reluctant way again.

"Come on, you damned Yankees," the sergeant rasped. "By God! Anybody'd think you never saw a skirt before."

"Well," Moore said, "I ain't seen any close enough to suit me lately, not even any Rebel skirts."

Sergeant Bullen rid himself of his cud and bit off a fresh piece of plug. He chuckled and then laughed aloud. "By damn! I'd like to see the old goat's face in about twenty minutes when him an' that nag an' buggy tangle with three regiments of Federals. There sure ain't room in this road for both of 'em goin' in opposite directions. He's gonna be a mighty surprised and disillusioned man."

"You ought to be ashamed—lyin' to a nice innocent old man like that, right straight into his face."

"Hell," Andy said cheerfully, "I'd lie to my grandmother—if I had one and I was on point under the Old Man's orders."

"You wouldn't be likely to meet up with her down here, would you, Sarge?"

"I ain't so sure," Bullen said, suddenly sober. He eyed the private appraisingly. "You know, you ain't as damn' funny as you may think, Dorsey. I had one grandmother who lived all her life in Dallum County—and that's about thirty miles straight west o' here. Come on, God damn it! Get yourselves down the road before the advance runs over us!"

12

Blaney's Orders

In the faint glow from the fire Marlowe opened the face of the finely made hunter in his hand, made a mental note of the hour, and then carefully wound the watch. Not that the time mattered in the least—they were moving according to sunrise and sunset. This was a minor personal ritual which had nothing to do with time as measured in hours or days. The watch had been a first anniversary gift from his wife, the only physical thing of hers that he now retained about his person. He reminded himself on occasion that regard for these personal icons was pointless, a rather silly sentiment. These things of the spirit, if they were really valid, should have no need for physical reminders. And yet—his fingers moved lightly, caressingly, perhaps a little hungrily over the smooth yellow gold before he returned it to an inner pocket.

The lanky figure of Colonel Blaney materialized out of the gloom and Blaney said without preamble, "Well, Jack?"

"Oh, hello, Colonel. Find something to sit on. Sergeant!" Marlowe's voice rose a little peremptorily. "Where the hell are you?"

"Comin', Colonel, comin'."

"Hustle some fresh wood for this fire. I need some light."

"Wood it is, Colonel!"

With his usual directness Marlowe dismissed the shades of the past from his mind and concentrated on the moment. As he set afire a fresh cigar he suddenly thought, I wonder if I really trust Blaney? And just as quickly he dismissed the notion as utterly irrelevant—it was not the question at issue. Again he wondered if he wasn't simply continuing to be unfair to Blaney. Well, in any event he hadn't chosen Colonel Blaney—he had been chosen for him. He, Marlowe, was charged with giving the orders, and from there on it would be up to the Second Iowa. He wished, fleetingly, that he had also called in Blaney's second but it was too late for that now. He looked at the older man as the fire flared with new fuel. He said, "You look a little pooped, Colonel."

Blaney shrugged indifferently. "Well, why not? This is no dress parade. I'm not an old man yet, Jack, but neither does the juice lubricate like it did once." He looked tired. Oh, not to the point of exhaustion, just tired, like a man who has already done a good day's work, looks forward to his rest, but accepts the forced overtime as a matter of course. He kicked an ember back into the fire impatiently, massaged his forehead with a palm. "I don't reckon you know it, Jack—no reason why you should, or give a damn about it if you do—but I've done almost my share of soldierin'. You don't know what I mean? Well, I was with Scott in the shindigs at Cerro Gordo, Molino del Rey, and Chapultepec in '47," he said calmly, impersonally, as though speaking of someone else. "Not that many another man in this army wasn't there too, including nobody less than Grant—also including those Rebel sonsabitches, Floyd and Twiggs. Well, none of those shindigs stacked up to Shiloh but they had their points. It was June and July and August, mostly. I was a sergeant in the foot and I walked, not rode, hell's own blistering way from Vera Cruz to Mexico City. We lived, those of us that did, on bad beef, enchiladas, and worse water. Well, that was a long time ago, Jack, or seems like it now. When you survive all you think of at the time is that you're lucky. It's only after that it catches up with you. Hell, what am I talking about anyway?"

"I didn't know all that," Marlowe said. Suddenly his feeling about Blaney was entirely different from what it had ever been before, though he couldn't have said in exactly what way.

Blaney chuckled as the sergeant added a little more fat pine to the fire. "Hell, how do you think I got elected colonel of the Second? Out there in that corn-and-hog country I was the only blooded soldier, the only gen-u-ine old soldier—or anyway one of the few—who knew the difference between squads right and port arms—hell, one of the few who knew there *were* such things, let alone what the difference was. But never mind that. Like I said, what's on your mind, Jack?"

"Of course you've known you and the Second would be pulling out. I'm the one who has to decide, and in my judgment tomorrow morning's the time."

For a moment Blaney didn't say anything but his face, if anything, appeared a little more weary. "All right," he said shortly. "So let's have the rest of it, Colonel."

Marlowe couldn't help but note the shift in his address. He unfolded his tattered map.

"So far we've let the line of the M. & O. alone—it isn't what we mainly came after. But I've decided now that something ought to be done about it. In all logic, it's just too damned easy for Ruggles—or somebody—to move his forces up and down that line as he pleases. Captain Bryce of the First made contact with it about noon yesterday."

"I heard something about that. I'd like to have seen it."

"I believe now I should have had him tear hell out of the telegraph line as long as he was right there, but he had orders to let it alone, and if the omission causes trouble the fault is mine."

Blaney spat thoughtfully. "Tearing up the line would at least have give 'em a little bother. But we've been on the road four days now. It don't stand to reason they don't know somebody's down here anyway."

"Oh, we know now that they know—Bryce proved that for sure. I'd be amazed if somebody's not on our tail right now. It's going to be up to you to block off or slow up whatever's behind. That was figured originally."

"You know, Jack," Blaney chuckled sourly, "sometimes I'm not extra smart, I mean in some ways. I had to spout off my big mouth about being picked as the one to go back to La Grange. I still think I had a reasonable complaint—except that then it was for the wrong reasons. We build a fire for eighty, ninety miles down here and then I'm supposed to turn around and put it out. Well—"

Perhaps Blaney had a point but, again, in the circumstances it was irrelevant—and Marlowe was determined not to get involved in even the mildest kind of argument, one nobody could win. He said, a little stiffly, "You know as much about what's behind us as I know what's ahead."

"All right, Jack," Blaney said quietly. "There's still twice as many of you as us. But have it your way—even if it ain't so."

"You know I didn't write the orders." Even against his will there was an edge in Marlowe's voice; he was trying to argue a case that didn't require argument. "You have to pick up the chips from where they fall."

"All right, Jack. Let it go at that. So what else?"

"Well, as long as you're going back, I've got a couple of small chores for you on the way. Here, take a look—"

At the moment they were bivouacked about midway between Houston and Starkville. In the morning the Second Iowa would take the first road to the left, in the direction of the M. & O. and West Point. Here there was a railroad bridge, ripe for burning.

Having done that they would cross the rail line, turn north and, the Lord willing, also take out the bridge at Okolona, the next town above.

"Is that all?" Blaney didn't try to conceal the sarcasm.

"It's a big order, maybe," Marlowe agreed, "but you can always try. Who knows? With luck you may walk through without a sign of trouble—"

"Let us now render 'Praise God, from Whom All Blessings Flow.'"

"All right, damn it! As you said, this is no dress parade, but there's not a Rebel behind every bush either."

"I'll do what the orders say, Jack—within the limits of what *can* be done, but just don't take too much for granted." Blaney got stiffly to his feet. "I'm not strong on this hunch business but this is more than that. I got a feeling. Mostly I'm a practical man and take it as it comes. But this time I'm thinking luck's about run out for the Second."

"Nonsense!" Marlowe said, with a heartiness he couldn't feel. "You're overworking your imagination, Colonel."

"Am I?" Blaney smiled as though at some secret thought. "I'm the goat in this deal, Jack. Oh, it's like everything else in a God-damned war—it's nobody's fault. But it's true all the same. You turn a regiment loose inside enemy territory, a good ninety miles from base in all directions, and what do you expect to happen? No, don't tell me."

"You knew it was this way all the time." Marlowe, in spite of himself and for reasons he couldn't quite fathom, was somehow on the defensive, and he didn't like it.

"I told you I'm a little slow sometimes. Well, I'll say so long and good luck, Jack."

"It ought to be the other way around."

"I reckon maybe we'd just better call it a Mexican standoff. I'll be seeing you—maybe."

Marlowe watched Blaney disappear in the darkness. Then he reached for a saddlebag and extracted a bottle—right now he felt he really needed a drink, perhaps deserved one. He had few illusions concerning what—probably—was in store for the Second Iowa. That was one of the prices command exacted. Still, there was such a thing as luck and it didn't necessarily have to be all bad.

13

Rain

Anyone thinking about it at all—and Marlowe for one thought about it because it was part of his business—knew it had to happen sooner or later. This was East Mississippi hill country and this was the time of year. By all the laws of nature it had to come, and the longer it was postponed the more violent it would be and the longer it was likely to last.

Rain—drenching, hammering, blinding, semi-tropical rain.

Marlowe had the record perfectly in mind. It had rained for two hours, not heavily, on the afternoon of the thirteenth, four days before they left La Grange. Since then there had been occasional cloudy periods, when the air was heavy and threatening, but not a drop had fallen on the First Brigade or in its vicinity. It had also clouded over occasionally since they had been on the road, but either Nature had changed her mind or they had outrun the actual precipitation. Marlowe knew it would come sooner or later. He didn't fear rain, any amount of it—that would have been preposterous, but certainly it was a military factor of consequence. Neither did he think of it in terms of physical discomfort —after two years the brigade had learned well that it didn't suspend operations because of mere weather, as a farmer is forced to stop plowing. And yet there was that too. No man functions quite normally with rain running down his spine inside his shirt, filling his eyes and dripping from his soaked beard, slowly overflowing his boots.

The sunrise this morning was no more than a crimson band at the base of the overcast in the eastern sky, and even that disappeared when the sun climbed invisibly upward and vanished in the leaden mist overhead.

Near eight o'clock, when the rain had been falling for perhaps ten minutes, the last company—actually the rear guard—of the Second had turned off into the West Point road. Marlowe did not see Colonel Blaney this morning—not directly, that is. There was no solid reason why he should. Everything it was necessary to say (officially) had been said last night. Actually Marlowe felt a little angered—no, irritated was the better word—at his mixed feelings about Blaney. What, if anything, happened to Blaney (and by extension all of the Second Iowa), it could be no worse than what was potentially in store for the First and Second Illinois. It had happened that the Second Iowa's number had come up in a certain way. It was more than foolish to feel in any way sorry for Blaney. In fact, he was mistakenly aggrandizing himself by assuming that Blaney would be better off by remaining with the brigade and hence under his, Marlowe's, all-protecting guidance. Hell, you could play draughts only by setting the blacks against the reds. There were no other colors.

As Colonel Blaney himself turned into the side road he raised a hand in a farewell gesture, but it didn't seem directed to anyone in particular.

Marlowe swung his mount and moved to order Secord to shift

his last company back five hundred yards, to assume the rear-guard position vacated by the Second.

Secord passed the word to an orderly and then jerked a thumb skyward. "We're going to catch it." It was already raining but not hard.

Marlowe shrugged. "It's one of the facts of life."

"If it amounts to much—and it looks like it was going to—it'll slow us down even more, Colonel."

"So—it will slow everybody else down accordingly. Rebel horses aren't any better in the mud than ours."

Twenty yards farther on Secord said casually, "Somehow I don't envy Blaney."

"Why?" Marlowe almost barked, and was surprised at his own unwarranted vehemence.

Secord's brows went up as he glanced briefly at Marlowe and away again. "Why, I don't know—Well, hell, Jack, if there's Rebs around, and there's bound to be, stands to reason they're likely to be thicker along the M. & O. That's all."

For answer Marlowe kicked his mount with spurred heels and moved toward the head of the column. Secord watched his retreating back and shrugged in his own turn. The privileges of rank—of course the Old Man had a right to be salty now and then if that's the way he felt.

Marlowe was only halfway to the head of the line, riding around the files of the First, when the rain seemed to reach its maximum rate of fall and stayed there. The sky opened and water fell with a force that stung bare hands on bridle reins. The road was dusty and of course uncared for—there were ruts left over from the last rain, whenever that was, and the combination of dust, pouring rain, and 4,000 churning hoofs turned the road into a fearsome quagmire within minutes. Only the men and animals in the very lead files of the First even slightly escaped the showers of mud flung by the shod hoofs.

Even as Marlowe moved in beside Major Gray a mounted man came flogging toward them, making better time than the column.

The road ahead was of course wet and slippery but it hadn't yet been churned into a loblolly. The rider reined in and swung his horse at an angle across the lead file, backing the animal sidewise as the file kept coming. His salute degenerated into a movement that cascaded water out of his hatbrim.

"Excuse me, Major, but—" The rider looked about him a little uncertainly, having just recognized the colonel.

"What the hell's the matter up there?" Gray demanded before the man could go on.

Marlowe's barely smoked cigar was sodden and dead and he flung it irritably into the mud.

"Well, Major, sir, it's like this. I mean, Sergeant Bullen wants to know, considerin' this rain an' all, if we should keep goin'—"

Marlowe raised a staying hand in Gray's direction and snapped, "What's your name, soldier?"

"Why, er—Private Dorsey, sir, D Company," said the startled trooper.

"You're breathing, aren't you? You're alive and all in one piece?"

"Yes sir!"

"And you're still mounted?"

"Er—yes sir!" Dorsey began to hate Sergeant Bullen.

"Then get yourself the hell back up there and tell Sergeant Bullen that when rain stops this column the God-damned water will be over his head! When I want it stopped for any other reason he'll be notified. Now move, Dorsey!"

"Yes *sir!*"

Dorsey stood not a second on the order of his going. But as he swung his horse the animal, raked suddenly with spurs, dug frantically with both hind feet. One great soft blob of mud caught Marlowe in the chest but the one from the other foot took Major Gray in his stubble-bearded face.

Dick cleaned his face—well, partly—with an already filthy handkerchief and then flung the cloth savagely into the road.

"God damn such a God-damned country!" he said with cold passion.

Nobody else said anything—but for a moment part of Company A had trouble with their facial control.

Here the road, though narrow and hedged closely with brush, was fairly straight; it rose and fell gently, with the natural contours of the land, and for the moment there were few hills of consequence. Marlowe could see quite a distance, both ahead and back down the line—always allowing for the rain. There was sudden confusion far down the files. Horses shied nervously and milled in the narrow roadway. As the colonel watched the column seemed to come apart like a rope breaking, the front half moving on after momentary hesitation, the rear section stalled, blocked by the confusion in the road.

Marlowe wheeled and smacked lightly with his quirt. He was no sentimentalist about horseflesh but he had never learned to use spurs instinctively.

It was plain to see what had happened. At the foot of a grade a small stream ran across the road, not worth bridging but now running knee-deep on the horses in this flood. A center horse in a file of B Company (Second Illinois) had stumbled in midstream, floundered its way out to comparatively higher and drier ground, and then really gone down, scattering horses on either side and front and back. The angry and hatless sergeant rider—his hat lay half-buried in the ditch—was mud from ears to boots. He was on his feet now as Marlowe came up, gathering in the slippery bridle reins, apparently about to try giving the animal an assist to its feet. Riders pressed back into the dripping brush as Secord came storming up.

"God damn it, Sergeant!" the colonel barked. "That right foreleg is broken!"

"Why, no, Colonel, I don't think—" The sergeant appeared suddenly bewildered, as though the possibility simply hadn't occurred to him.

CARL A. RUDISILL LIBRARY
LENOIR RHYNE COLLEGE

"Shoot the sonofabitch, get your gear off, and get the carcass out of the road!"

"But, Colonel, this here horse—"

"Shoot the sonofabitch!" Secord snarled savagely. "You've got one useless horse holding up the whole God-damned stinking regiment!"

The noncom unbuckled a holster flap. With the look of a man in pain, he closed his eyes as he put the pistol muzzle squarely between the animal's eyes and pulled the trigger. The great head, after one spasm, sank slowly down. Thick dark blood mingled with the muddy slop of the road and in a sudden final reflex the animal's lower bowel emptied with a great gush.

"Give him a hand, you men!" Secord barked. "Drag it into the ditch and split up the gear between you. Sergeant, you'll get the first loose mount we run into, whether it's in a pasture or a barn or on the road. You'll have to ride double till then."

Marlowe watched silently. This was Colonel Secord's affair, not his. He reached absently for a cigar but changed his mind— in this flood a cigar would neither light nor smoke.

"The best damn' horse I ever had," the sergeant said to no one in particular. Nobody tried to answer him.

Ah, yes! Marlowe thought sardonically. The dashing, romantic, panoplied horse dragoons. Come to think about it, just what *was* the difference between dragoons and plain horse soldiers?

They rode, shoulders hunched against the downpour, miserable and nearly silent in their misery. After the first fifteen minutes they could get no wetter but men and horses steadily became more heavily coated with mud. Men toughened by long months in the field found rumps and thighs galled and blistered by the constant friction between wet wool and wet saddle leather. They rode, becoming hungrier and thirstier—yes, thirstier in spite of this skyful of water. The streams were nauseating liquid mud and at the one lonely farmstead they encountered in two hours of riding the first three companies of the First completely emptied the shallow well.

Marlowe was morose, bitter, drawn into himself, willing his mind to temporary blankness. He was one of those people for whom this kind of weather, without any compensating stimulant, can be one of the most powerful depressants. He would have cheerfully given a week's pay for a couple of long drinks from the saddlebag bottle behind his left leg, but he could not favor himself in front of the men. Of course he could turn temporarily aside into the brush, ostensibly on a call of nature, yet a perverse kind of pride forbade that.

Hell, Marlowe, he chided himself, you're no worse off than anybody else!

Though it was becoming a more academic question with each hour that passed, as a dutiful afterthought Marlowe wondered how the Second Iowa was making out. Actually, once Blaney had disappeared down the West Point road he had passed from any effective brigade jurisdiction. But he hadn't passed from Marlowe's mind, and in his view Blaney was still a part of this operation.

THE PURSUIT

Nobody had ever imagined that Marlowe and the First Brigade could or would pass through Mississippi, even its wilder portions, invisible and unheard. As a matter of fact, his movement was known, or at any rate strongly rumored, within hours of his departure from La Grange. But there were two things which Confederate intelligence didn't know and, until it was a little late, wouldn't guess: Marlowe's real strength and where he intended ultimately to use it.

For better or worse, it was Captain Bryce's frolic of Sunday noon, particularly his diddling with the M. & O. telegraph, which gave the Rebels their first definite point of departure. The Tenth Alabama Cavalry, Colonel C. R. Barteau, had arrived to hear the harrowing tale, considerably inflated, of the abused home guard, within hours of the departure of A Company. And while no one ever held it against him, it was right there that Barteau made his first wrong guess. He could only believe that Bryce was merely a feeler, presaging a real attack on the M. & O. Accordingly, and using his best judgment, Colonel Barteau moved south and east to protect, so he thought, Okolona and Aberdeen. If he had merely followed A Company he would eventually have come up with a tired First Brigade. According to the percentages, Marlowe would very likely have made hash of the Tenth Alabama, but just as surely not without incurring casualties which very well could have unhinged the whole scheme. For while Colonel Barteau was no tactical genius he was a doggedly determined man with guts to spare, and he would have attacked the brigade on sight had he been outnumbered ten to one.

But he did not choose to follow A Company—not on that particular Sunday afternoon.

On the other hand, Barteau did not retire to Okolona to sit out the war. When whatever he expected didn't happen he put patrols to work and in due time learned definitely that the Federals had passed southward through Pontotoc, with apparent intention of attacking the M. & O. somewhere on farther south. By the time he received this information Barteau realized that Marlowe had already passed far south of his, Barteau's, position. Estimates of the column's strength varied from 500 to 5,000—civilian estimates of military numbers are notoriously inaccurate. Nevertheless, considering his lack of real data, Barteau made a fairly good guess at Marlowe's strength—he only missed by a few hundred and that on the short side. So he set out in pursuit, picking it up at the point where the brigade had last been seen by an actual eye-witness.

But here Barteau made still another decision which was both good and bad. Knowing he was badly outnumbered, he augmented his command with what other troops were available. The trouble was, these troops consisted of indifferently mounted and trained state militia, a partial battalion of even worse infantry, and three antiquated guns that likely couldn't have hit Lookout Mountain at point-blank range.

There was one thing (among many, of course) that Marlowe didn't know: if the First Brigade was slow, Barteau's droop-drawered outfit was even slower. Barteau's chief advantage, if such it could be called, was that he knew what he was after and approximately where it was.

On the night of April 20–21, Monday, Barteau, made increasingly eager by roadside reports, drove his backwoods outfit until nearly midnight, but there was a limit beyond which even Barteau couldn't drive them. After all, the majority of them were not too willing amateurs. When, nearly dead on their feet, they fell out by the roadside, they were only twelve miles behind the rear guard of the bivouacked First Brigade. In the morning, though not early, Barteau booted them on their reluctant way again.

That the Lord sends the rain on the just and unjust alike is indubitably true, and it was to Colonel Barteau's great credit that he kept his ill-assorted show on the road at all—though the men may have figured it was better to keep moving than sit still, for certainly there was no shelter where they were. If the First Brigade was miserable, Barteau's men were more so. More than half his force now was infantry, and walking in mud is even worse than riding in it, besides which they still insisted on dragging along the useless guns.

In due course Barteau came to the road junction where the Second Iowa had taken leave of the rest of the brigade. There Barteau stopped to consider and thereby added another error to his string. No single mistake he made was disastrous in itself, not one was the result of too hasty judgment, and each was understandable. But no matter how good a field officer's judgment may be he must also have luck—and this was one of the weeks Barteau simply didn't have it.

In this mud the trail, or rather trails, of the First Brigade would have been plain to a blind man. The question was, which one? Because it seemed to be the logical thing Barteau couldn't rid him-

self of the belief that Marlowe was gunning for the M. & O. Railroad. He weighed the evidence, or thought he did, and accordingly veered off down the West Point road, in pursuit of what he firmly believed to be the largest portion of the brigade. It was, in fact, a very long time before he discovered his error, for as late as April 30, nine days later, when he had a little breathing spell, he wrote in an official report:

"The enemy divided here at this point, about 200 going on to Starkville and 700 continuing their march on the West Point road."

Again all credit to Barteau: he unhesitatingly chose what he believed to be the hard way, but good intentions alone are seldom enough and the decision cost him any real chance he'd ever had of catching the elusive First Brigade.

To complicate matters still further, in far-off Jackson, some 140 miles to the southwest, Lieutenant General Pemberton himself decided to take a hand in the game. Since neither Ruggles nor Barteau knew the precise whereabouts of the raiders, though they were closest to them, it was hardly reasonable that General Pemberton, being much less than clairvoyant, should. Nevertheless, he promptly moved into this blind chess game. By telegraph he ordered all troops at Meridian, where the M. & O. crossed the Southern, to move north via the M. & O. and join forces with Ruggles. Pemberton too believed Marlowe's target was the M. & O. For a blind guess it could have been worse, except that it didn't catch Marlowe. As the 2,000 men moved north by train they were passed by the slower mounted First, a dozen miles to the west and still heading innocently southward.

As subsequent events proved only too well, General Pemberton's luck was even worse than Colonel Barteau's.

14

Colonel Blaney

Blaney was in no particular hurry. His orders didn't say *when* he had to do any particular thing. He had no illusions about his own position. At the moment the Second Iowa was bait—the baby tossed out of the fleeing sleigh in the hope of temporarily appeasing the pursuing wolves. Such being his opinion, Blaney presently was in a mood to let the Rebels find *him*, if that was their pleasure. As matters stood now, in this rain and with visibility almost nil, it didn't seem reasonable that anybody would be doing any hunting soon. So Blaney deliberately let the Second take its own sweet time.

The country here was broken. That is to say, the hills were gentle and the landscape alternated between pasture land, occasional cultivated fields, and timber patches of all sizes, scattered at random. But for the rain visibility would have been excellent, the chances of a surprise ambush almost nil, and even so the visibility was good enough for Blaney to know there was no immediate threat near. Of course he had out an advance and a rear guard as a matter of regulation procedure.

Regardless of the smashing rain and improbable as it might seem, Blaney—and he wasn't the only one by dozens—was doing a good job of sleeping in the saddle. For one thing he was tired, and with this rain and dampness he could feel the ghosts of rheumatism, arthritis, and other ancient aches and pains come slowly to life in his spare frame.

The first inkling he had that anything was amiss was when a nervous young courier lurched against him and then shook him respectfully by one arm.

"Colonel Blaney, sir!" The corporal's voice was urgent.

"Hunh?" Blaney said foggily. "Eh, what's that, son?"

"I'm from Cap'n Broder, Colonel—the rear guard. He says cavalry is movin' up from the rear an' he needs instructions right away!"

Blaney came suddenly awake—or very nearly. "Cavalry? Movin' up? In this God-damned muck—how the hell can they?"

"Well, they ain't comin' up very *fast*, that's a fact. The thing is, they must be movin' faster'n us or they wouldn't have come in sight."

"Hmm. I see. Johnnies, son?" It was, Blaney recognized instantly, a silly question on the face of it. They couldn't be from the brigade, that was certain, and he remembered a random quotation: He who is not with Me is against Me. Well, except for the long-gone brigade it was a lead-pipe cinch the Second Iowa had no friends in Mississippi.

"Who else, Colonel?" The corporal inclined his head and water cascaded from his hat into his lap. It didn't make him any wetter but he said, "God damn!"

"How many, would you say?"

The corporal shrugged. "Hard to tell exactly in this slop, sir, but there's a lot o' the sonsabitches—I seen some of 'em myself."

"God damn it," Blaney said thoughtfully, "why can't they wait till it's drier? I'll probably still be here." And then the colonel did what some people might have considered an odd thing. He reached inside his tunic, drew forth his watch, scrutinized it carefully and then replaced it. "It is now," he announced, "exactly eleven ten on the twenty-first of April."

"Yes sir," said the corporal in respectful astonishment.

"Well—go back and tell Broder to hold his position but not to engage unless he's forced into it. I'll have more orders for him directly. Hump yourself now, son!"

"On my way, Colonel!"

Blaney sighed and then winced as pain shot through his left hip. What the blue hell, he wondered, did this Rebel, whoever he was, think he was trying to do? On occasion he admitted cheerfully that he was no strategist—in fact, when allegedly brainier people explained the grand strategy of the generals Blaney usually remained just as unenlightened as before. But he had something which the theorist so often lacked: the capacity to deal instinctively and ably with a situation which he could see. Right now he wasn't worried in the least. He was perfectly confident that somehow he would make this ambitious fellow rue the day.

The rain, thank the Lord, was slackening some now.

When the orderly returned with his second, Major Dixon—the Second also did not support a lieutenant colonel—Blaney repeated what he knew so far.

"What do you figure to do?" Dixon asked.

"Well, now, I figure it's like this. The orders were to proceed to West Point an' tear up the bridges, an' that's what we're headin' for—looks like right now we couldn't go any other direction. If that map of Marlowe's is any good we ought to be about four, five miles from there now an' gettin' closer every step, slow as they are. So we keep goin'—because we want to an' because we can't help ourselves."

"What about this outfit behind us?"

"As I see it he's sort of got himself sewed up. One thing is for damn' sure—one column can't attack another as long as they're butted end to end. He can't hurt us unless he gets around us or at least up on a flank. I don't *think* he can do either one in this road an' this rain, and I *know* he can't without Cap'n Broder's rear guard knowin' about it."

"Sounds good enough, Colonel—anyway until something happens to change it. You got something for me?"

"Yeah, Dix. Go back there an' give Broder a little moral encouragement. I don't want him to get flighty. If there has to be some shootin', why, all right. Just make it count. If it looks like you might be run over, then of course fall back here and we'll do some more figurin'."

The regiment, maintaining only the roughest semblance of order, plowed doggedly ahead, still unaware that anything was amiss. Colonel Blaney moved his belt around and unbuckled his holster flap, the better to get at the Navy Colt in a hurry, then splashed his way toward the head of the column. In his passing he now and then whacked the rumps of horses that were far out of formation, and he kept calling, "Close up, men! Close up!" The order was more a matter of habit than any real intention of re-forming the line, and nothing much happened anyway. Here and there men glanced up, then relaxed again as the colonel showed no signs of stopping. They knew that only a fool would expect parade order in this weather and Colonel Blaney was no fool, at any rate not in that respect.

They emerged from a timber belt and the visibility, as the rain slackened almost to a drizzle, was suddenly much better.

Blaney realized, when the ragged firing broke out, that he had been wound up, waiting for it. The sound actually gave him release. He was as wide awake now as it was possible to be, and, he told himself grimly, he had better be!

For besides the danger signal inherent in the firing itself there was another thing badly wrong with it: it came not from behind but from straight ahead! This, Blaney told himself calmly, is the God-damned bear trap for sure.

He waited now as a courier from the advance came hurrying back.

"We sure tangled with something, Colonel," the man said a little breathlessly. "Looks like a couple companies. They stopped an' we stopped an' Lieutenant Allen's pulled the boys out of the road."

"Well," Blaney said absently, "there goes Marlowe's damn' bridges."

Another ragged flurry of shots ripped the silence and Blaney recognized the distinctive shots of the Second's Sharps carbines.

"Beg pardon, sir?"

"Hunh? Never mind, bub. Anybody hurt?"

"Not that I saw, but we got a couple."

"All right. Just tell Allen to fall back on the column, slow. Looks like we ain't goin' nowhere right now."

The men in the ranks might ignore or dog certain routine orders, the possible consequences were defined and limited by regulations anyway. But gunfire was something else. In the last analysis gunfire, the other side's, was apt to be the most personal and final thing a soldier had to do with. The files suddenly came awake and alert and when company commanders barked orders to close up they were obeyed with alacrity—doubly so when sporadic firing erupted in their rear.

The country was open, only dotted here and there with occasional clumps of trees and brush, not dead flat but gently undulating, an almost ideal spot for classic battle procedure—except that Blaney had no intention of engaging in any such damned foolishness. He could see pretty well now. In fact, he could see better than that, for the colonel possessed one piece of superfine equipment. The proud folk of Braintree, Iowa, instead of presenting their only colonel with the traditional fancy-dress sword, had given him the finest set of military glasses their money could buy. Now—he judged about two miles ahead—with the aid of the glasses he could see lines of infantry deploying to his right and left from some presently invisible center—this same road to West Point, undoubtedly.

He saw something else too, largely by chance. Far off to the left, beyond possible gunshot or pursuit, a lone man was riding hell for leather, obviously heading for these same deploying troops in front.

Well—

Blaney found himself beside his bugler. The files had slowed even more of their own accord, but he said, "Blow me a Halt, son. One'll be enough. And then a couple o' Recalls." Might as well get together what force he had. Obviously he was going to need all of it and then some.

. . . Once more Colonel Barteau had been both right and wrong. In his anxiety, and sure he was right behind the brigade, he had booted his Tenth Alabama along by sheer will power. In so doing he had finally made contact but he had also left a considerable gap between himself and his infantry. When he heard the firing up ahead he was jubilant, he was certain he knew what it was, and he suddenly felt like a man about to be handed first prize. For these could only be the troops sent up from Meridian, and whereas he had (so he assumed) been badly outnumbered and not really in a proper position to attack, the shoe was now on the other foot with a vengeance. Thus his courier had gone forward to advise his opposite number of the true situation. In another half-hour he would have these upstart and reckless Yankees by the short hairs. But there was still a lot of circle about General Marlowe to be closed. So, his cavalry obviously being much faster, he split his Tenth Alabama and sent it right and left to help complete the encirclement. He would hold the center with the infantry still coming up—when it got here. His own Tenth had orders to hold its fire unless it was directly attacked—no use frightening the quarry into action too soon. Colonel Barteau could have rubbed his hands in satisfaction except that he was too busy otherwise. . . .

Captain Broder and his rear guard came splashing up the road. "Any casualties, Cap'n?"

"No sir—not yet," Broder said. "They wasn't any too anxious to move in. I couldn't swear to it, Colonel—I had the impression that cavalry is up to a circling movement. That timber give 'em cover."

"What the hell else can he do?" Blaney snorted impatiently. "Where the devil is Major Dixon, Broder?"

"He didn't come back with us, sir. Said he'd stay a bit to get a better look."

Hmm. Blaney twisted his mouth and frowned. Damned fool, Dixon—and a good man. Blaney plied his glasses. The lines in his front were making slow progress. Still, they were perceptibly closer.

Well—Blaney was suddenly glad these people down here were either too poor or too lazy to fence off their roads—fences would play hell with what he was about to do. Then he was firing his orders, probably the only ones possible in the circumstances—

Like practically every other veteran Federal regiment in the West the Second was under strength. It comprised seven companies totaling something over 400 men. Now Blaney swung them athwart the road and facing their own rear, four companies in the first wave and three in the second, troopers riding knee to knee now. The files were quiet, tense, and wary—and the sudden cry of a mockingbird was almost shocking. The carbines were out of the boots now, holster flaps loose. The hard word had gone down the lines: when they came to—well, whatever they came to, they would go through and keep on going or the war would end right here for a lot of the Second Iowa Volunteer Cavalry.

Blaney rode near the center, on the comparatively less muddy margin of the road, a little behind the second rank. He had his bugler, Murphy, near at hand. Let it be not supposed that Colonel Blaney's position had to do with any concern for himself. It was a purely practical matter. This business of leading men rather than driving them was all very well for public consumption—Blaney had done his own foolish share. But these fancy heroics also had a way of getting colonels dead and leaving their regiments temporarily leaderless. Moreover, this "leading" left a man completely ignorant of what was happening behind him. No, Blaney was back here—and was damned well going to stay here—in order to know exactly what was going on and to take steps if need be.

He wondered where in God's name that ass Dixon was, and as though in answer the center files parted and let the major through.

Blaney eyed the foam-flecked horse and said critically, "You founder that nag, Dixon, you sure won't enjoy walkin'. Well?"

"Their cavalry aims to take us on the flanks," Dixon said shortly. "They've moved out that way and it's the logical thing. There's infantry here in front and the bastards have a couple of small-bore guns."

"Mmm. How far ahead now?"

"Oh—call it five hundred yards."

"Well," Blaney said thoughtfully, "I reckon we could surrender. That would simplify everything."

"Oh, for Christ's sake!" Dixon snorted disgustedly. He didn't even bother to look at Blaney. "Let's get on with the job!"

Blaney grinned, averted his head, and spat.

. . . They could see the scattered ranks of militiamen and home guards even before the first ragged volley let go. In the center of the road men worked frantically with a gun—and even as Blaney watched abandoned the piece and ran for the brush. Blaney grinned—thank God for wet-powder charges. From a corner of his eye he saw men and horses go down—C and D companies, he thought. He drew his pistol and laid it over a thigh, then turned and spoke calmly to the bugler.

"Murphy! All right, son. Give us a Charge—and see you blow the hell out of it!"

The Second surged forward in a compact blue wave, the front rank firing in steady rolling crashes. They were hurt, and grievously —it could have hardly been otherwise, but this simply wasn't Colonel Barteau's day, or even week.

15

Captain Bryce

The rain, heavy and unwelcome as it was, had been relatively local. For Colonel Blaney and the Second Iowa it had, to their good fortune, stopped a little after noon. Farther to the southwest, in the path of the brigade, it had slowly diminished in volume and finally quit altogether about three of the afternoon. In the heavy humid atmosphere it would be some time before the brigade, with its stiff wool uniforms, would be thoroughly dry, but by evening the process was well under way.

They bivouacked a few miles below Starkville. Marlowe, as befitted rank, was a little better off than the rest. Sergeant King had located a cattle shelter—no more than a makeshift roof mounted on posts. (The folk of this country didn't believe in pampering their ordinary stock—one reason so much of it was so poor in quality.) But it was shelter of a sort, and in the downpour the covered earth had remained drier than the surrounding ground. To give it a further air of luxury, the sergeant had provided some square footage of dry straw, "borrowed" from a nearby farmstead. In fact, the entire strawstack, together with a nearby haystack, had vanished under the onslaughts of the supply sergeants, first come first served. So also had all the oats, corn, and loose horses on the place. So also had the entire contents of smokehouse, root cellar, and hen roost.

The proprietors, an elderly man and his wife, protested bitterly —at first, and then gave up. What was the use? Camped practically in their back yard were more men than they had ever seen in one place before. And these Yankees were obviously in no mood for argument. In fact, these Yankees were not like these unsophisticated people had expected an army to be. They were neither polite nor impolite. They simply went about their thievery, confiscation, requisitioning, whatever it might be called, as though these owners weren't there. They ignored them, or looked at and through them as though they didn't exist. It was baffling—and more frightening than if these soldiers had snarled at the man's protests or abused him verbally. The man was the more afraid of what he did not understand and could not anticipate. In the end the man only watched and swallowed his silent bitterness. After a while a Lieutenant Colonel Fairlie (Colonel Secord's second) appeared and courteously asked the man's name.

"What difference does it make to you—you thieves?"

"To me," Fairlie said indifferently, "it makes no difference whatever. I haven't the slightest interest. But I'm about to draw you an order on the Federal quartermaster general in Memphis. If your name is on it and you can identify yourself properly it will be paid promptly on presentation. If I have to draw it to bearer, then I can't vouch for what view Memphis may take. It's entirely up to you, sir."

"I insist—well, John Carstairs, sir, Oktibbeha County, Mississippi, Confederate States of America."

Fairlie wrote rapidly and then handed the order to Carstairs.

"You might have a look at that, sir. I think you'll find it reasonable."

Carstairs took the order but didn't look at it. His hands shook with his wrath. "I protest this, sir! This is barefaced robbery—!"

"Not quite, I think." Fairlie smiled thinly—though not with the pure cynicism Carstairs imagined. "But that isn't my affair. If you have a complaint I suggest you take it up with what you call your government in Richmond."

"Sir, I—"

But Colonel Fairlie had already gone.

There was a good deal more to this "living off the country" than met the casual eye. The practical military point of view was, "Why should they complain? We could have, justifiably, *taken* what we needed. But no, we paid, and at a more than generous rate." All of which was indeed true—but only up to a point. In the case of this particular farmstead (and others like it) the supplies the First Brigade devoured in less than an hour would have, and were intended to, last these people more or less until the next harvest. It came down to the simple fact that, no matter how desirable they were in one sense, nobody could eat bills on a Union quartermaster general. Who on a desert island would exchange his food supply for pure gold?

There was another side to this from the requisitioners' point of view. "Living off the country" has a large, opulent sound; there is a picture of rollicking cavalrymen with hams and other fine provender dangling from their saddles. Well, it depends on the country—and Oktibbeha County, Mississippi, was by no means York or Lancaster County, Pennsylvania. Starkville, for instance. Two rather miserable general stores provided all the village's ordinary day-to-day needs. The supply sergeants ruthlessly stripped the shelves and got less than enough to furnish one hungry regiment one solid meal.

"Rations for X days" is a misleading phrase when the rations are carried by individual soldiers. In this respect the brigade behaved precisely as its individual members would have behaved civilianwise. Having been issued rations for five days, half of them would have something saved against the sixth and even the seventh day; as many had empty grub sacks at the end of the third day—for every ant a grasshopper. And besides, there was an axiom in this army which said that unconsumed rations did you no good when you were dead. So on this night of the fifth day the brigade was not only still wet but in spots it was hungry. . . .

Naked to the waist—his shirt and tunic were drying on a pole by the fire—Marlowe was engaged in the day's most complicated operation. Sergeant King had found him a tin basin and now, with razor and soap, he was working on the five-day beard and the coating of mud—ordinarily he affected only a thick mustache. Since the roof of the shelter was straw, the fire had to be placed a little distance outside. And to have the small mirror any use in the available light it was hung on one of the posts about three feet above the ground. Marlowe knelt on the straw, manipulating the razor and his neck like a contortionist at rehearsal.

Colonel Secord came into the ring of firelight, stopped short, and said, "Dress parade in the morning?"

Marlowe cleaned the blade of the razor again. "To tell the truth I'm scraping off mud. I'm not concerned so much with the whiskers." He glanced briefly at Secord's filthy, mud-streaked face. "It wouldn't hurt you either. Have a look at yourself."

Secord shook his head. "I'm afraid to. I'm also so God-damned tired I wouldn't shave if it would get me a permit to sleep with Aphrodite tonight. You got a spare drink?"

"Over there in the saddlebag. Your men eat tonight?" Marlowe himself had dined on part of a small ham and some hard bread, together with what King reminded him was the last of the coffee. He hadn't cared much for the way the ham was cured but it was edible. He stood up, rubbing his now tender face, reddened where the razor had pulled rather than sheared.

"If that's a shave then I'm a nigger preacher from Georgia," Secord observed. He smacked the cork back into the bottle with the heel of one hand. "Oh, the men? This is one night I'm not going to worry about it. God damn it—they knew the grub was for five days."

"Yes—well, you have to make a certain amount of allowance. What the devil was that fracas back there in Starkville?"

"Fracas?"

"Well, whatever it was. I understood somebody was yelling for the commanding officer but I didn't bother to stop and see what it was."

"Oh, that." Secord laughed shortly. "When the advance went in—my C Company—there was a Jew peddler trying to do business there in the street—he had a wagonload of these wool hats the yahoos down here seem to like. The damned fool actually tried to sell C Company some headgear. Well, one thing led to another and it ended up with the company taking his hats and giving 'em all away to the niggers and the kids on the street. Then they traded him a couple o' beat-out horses for the fair span o' mules he had on the wagon. Naturally he yelled bloody murder."

"I daresay." Marlowe got into his now nearly dry shirt—after the rain the night air was considerably chillier than usual. "What'd they trade him for the hats?"

"Several offers to kick his teeth in if he didn't shut up," Secord said indifferently. "Or so I heard. You know," he added thoughtfully, "on a jaunt like this a mule's no bad animal. Of course the men don't like the idea of mules, but a mule's got more guts and staying power than the average cavalry plug. But somehow a man feels like he's half jackass himself when he rides a mule. I dunno—funny thing."

"I know—man on a mule in this country feels like he's asking to be laughed at, like he was wearing a woman's hat or skirt. Besides, it's harder to produce mules. Coming my way?"

"Where?"

"Up toward the head of the line."

"I'm going the other way—to sleep."

"You're welcome to bed down here. It's drier."

"No, thanks. I'll feel better with the regiment. Old faithful

Secord, the Rock of Cook County and father of the regiment, that's me."

"Suit yourself, Frank."

Speaking of sleep had reminded him of the sergeant's suggestion that he use one of the beds at the farmhouse. "No," Marlowe had said snappishly. "Too much bother."

"Why, hell, Colonel, no bother atall. I'll just go over there an'—"

"No!" Marlowe said, ending it there.

To him there was something quite impersonal about requisitioning food and forage, aside from the fact that he wasn't required to manage it personally. Given their present situation, it was something he had to do. But somehow he would not add to their sense of bitter personal injury by invading the privacy of these people. He would have quartered sick or wounded men without hesitation. He would not indulge his personal comfort. Perhaps it was a meaningless distinction, but—well, there it was.

Marlowe, picking his way over the dark, sodden ground, felt a little foolish—or was that the word? By all rules of procedure he should have required Major Gray and Bryce to come to him. Instead, he was going to them, or more precisely to Bryce. This uncalled-for courtesy, this going out of his way—he had no exact words for it—wouldn't make the task of Bryce any easier. There was no reason to suppose Bryce would even notice this ultra-fine distinction, no reason why he should. Yet somehow it made *him* feel better. He was acutely aware of what he was asking—requiring—of Bryce and A Company. He was aware also—and that's where the fault lay—that Bryce would know. It was at once more than he, Marlowe, had a right (moral at least) to require and no less than he must in the circumstances. These things always got him back to the inherent paradoxes of this war business, one of which was that those who could least be spared must inevitably be most exposed to loss—those who in all logic could least be spared must be offered to preserve the less deserving.

But you are not God, Marlowe reminded himself, not even a

minor god as gods go, but merely an acting—not even brevet—brigadier, charged with an operation which was no more than a louse bite on the gross body of the war.

He skirted a knot of dedicated poker players, placing the minuscule wagers and the discards on a piece of salvaged plank. There was nothing unusual about the game—a certain number of soldiers gambled as naturally as they breathed. At least some of them, Marlowe thought, would gamble in the antechamber of hell while they waited for their preliminary interviews with the devil. But then what was wrong with that?

He paused, nodded amiably, and said, "What beats me is how you fellows can tell one card from another in this light."

A dirty corporal said disgustedly, "A nickel's too high for me. Oh, hell, Colonel, we been usin' these same pasteboards so damn' long we kin tell by the feel."

A trivial passage but not without its small meaning—if these men had their worries about tomorrow they were not pressing enough to turn them from ordinary habit, and that was all to the good.

When presently he got Gray and Bryce together, and aside in a spot of comparative privacy, he came directly to the point:

"I don't like to rob you, Major, but I have to borrow A Company again."

Gray and Bryce waited, curious but not too surprised.

"How many men on the A Company roster as of now, Asa?"

"Thirty-four, Colonel," Bryce answered promptly. "Major Keller cut out two at La Grange. He was probably right—anyway, I didn't complain."

Thirty-four men in an active service company! It was ridiculous but it was also commonplace. When the ranks of these western regiments were reduced by normal losses there was no regular method of replacing them. There were occasional enlistments in a regiment especially preferred for some personal reason, but that had little effect on the over-all situation. When a state's quota of men in the field fell below the norm it was more expedient politically to activate an entirely new regiment—more appointments to be made or approved under the political aegis of the state. Even General Sherman complained that only in the outfits from Wisconsin did the word "regiment" mean what it was supposed to—to indicate a specific number of fighting men. After two years of active service an Illinois regiment might muster anywhere from two to eight hundred men, and in this army there were brigades operating with fewer men than regulations established for a regiment. Well, you made do with what you had.

"I wish you had more strength," Marlowe said, "but it can't be helped. The point is, gentlemen, we've got to keep the minds of our friends focused on the M. & O. as long as possible. They'll soon know we're actually after the Southern, but I hope not until after we've gotten there. In the meantime, as long as we keep pecking at the M. & O. they can't be dead sure and they'll have to split themselves to a certain extent. We can't spare more than A Company for that now. That's about it."

Frowning slightly, Bryce said, "Just what do you expect me to do, Colonel?"

"Anything and everything you can to the M. & O., as far down as possible, and at the same time keep yourself in the clear."

They digested that for a moment and then Gray said, "That, if you don't mind my saying so, Jack, is one hell of a large order for one way under-strength company."

"I said at the beginning I didn't like it too well myself, Major. On the other hand, I don't know that two or even three companies would really be so much better. Regardless of that, we can't spare 'em anyway. What would you say, Bryce?" The colonel kept his voice almost casual though he knew Bryce was in no way taken in.

The captain shrugged and at the same time looked sardonically at Marlowe. "Say about what, Colonel?" Bryce's tone was innocent enough on the surface.

Irritated but determined to keep everything under control,

Marlowe said, "About anything, Captain. I know what's possibly involved here, and you know it."

"If it's an order, then what difference does it make what I think about it?" Bryce's tone was cool enough but seemed suddenly withdrawn, remote. "You know, we all know, how much chance we have once we are really separated from the column here. Sure, with luck we can probably dodge for a while. But in the long run —why fool ourselves?" Bryce let it go with a shrug.

"Very well then," Marlowe said impersonally. Since Bryce had chosen a certain attitude there was nothing he could do about it —nor could he blame him.

"And how long am I supposed to take on this picnic, Colonel?"

"Well." Marlowe didn't know the exact answer to that but he had to say something. He tried to pick his words carefully. "I see it purely as a matter of discretion and judgment, Captain—the principal reason I want you to handle this. If you're blocked off and can't reach the railroad at all, why, then pull out and rejoin as soon as you can. If you strike the road once but can't chance it again, then come on back—hell, we may be stopped dead ourselves in the next twenty, thirty miles."

Bryce smiled thinly. "Colonel, you know in all fairness, you know damned well, I can't operate on the basis of what *may* happen to the rest of you. Like I said, why fool ourselves? Right now my animals are as beat as the rest, yet if I do anything at all I'll have to cover at least two miles to your one. We can skip the details, but honestly, do you expect me to ever get back?"

"I have to proceed on that assumption," Marlowe said stiffly. With another junior officer some of this might have been close to insubordination, or at least implied insolence—but with Bryce, no, not here in these circumstances. This was a more personal thing and not putting it so didn't change it.

"All right, let's boil it down so we understand each other, Colonel. I strike the M. & O. as many times as I can—*if* I can. I rejoin the brigade when and *if* I can."

"You put it better than I did, I think."

"So—I'd like one further thing understood."

"Well?"

"It's this—and I want to say it with Major Gray here as witness—"

"That wouldn't make any difference," Marlowe said quickly. "You know that, Asa."

"Well, he's here in any case," Bryce said imperturbably. "I don't want to overdramatize this, but we all know A Company is being put right smack over a barrel. As of now we're out of grub for men and horses, so I'm going to have to forage from tomorrow morning on. Well, once I start on this I'm damned well not going to be stopped by anything or anybody I can handle. I do not give a damn if it's in uniform or not and I'm not going to worry about being polite to anybody. Is that plain enough, Colonel?"

"In the last analysis you have to depend on your own judgment."

"All right—but neither do I want it questioned after the fact by some sonofabitch in Memphis! We're not going on a routine patrol from a base we can fall back on. We— But hell, you know these things better than I do."

"I"—Marlowe had to say it though it deliberately put his own judgment in doubt—"I intended to give you a chance to refuse this on personal grounds, Asa." And the instant he said it he knew he'd made another mistake.

"No, by God!" Bryce flared, and there was obvious anger in his voice for the first time in the discussion. "I submit that you put this as an order, Colonel. You can countermand the order if you like but you have no right to put it up to me. I've never refused an order yet and I won't start here. Major Gray will bear me out."

"It wasn't precisely like that—"

"It is to me. This regiment has never operated strictly by the book and it's been the better for it, but I can stand on it if I have to!"

"Very well then," Marlowe said coldly. "Let the order stand."

"Yes sir," Bryce said woodenly. "I assume we go in the morning? After all, my men are entitled to a little sleep tonight."

"I suggest that you fall in at the rear of the column in the morning and take the first road to our left."

"Yes sir. Will that be all, Colonel?"

"Unless you think of something else I'd say that from here on it's up to you, Captain." Prolonging this could only make things —well, more complicated. "I—well, luck."

"Thanks. If you'll excuse me then." Bryce swung on his heel and walked away into the darkness.

Gray kicked at the soggy earth with a boot toe, waiting for Marlowe to say something.

"Well," Marlowe said heavily, "I expect almost anybody could have handled that better than I did, Dick. You always think of the right way afterward."

"Who doesn't, Jack? But—well, Bryce had his side of it. You couldn't—I wouldn't exactly feel like thanking anybody for a package like that myself."

"It has to be done, somebody has to do it." Am I, Marlowe thought, trying to convince myself of something? And if so, what?

Gray gave him an odd look before passing a hand over his tired eyes. "Christ, Jack, are you trying to sell me something? You don't have to, you know."

"It's not that—" Marlowe said half-angrily—and let it go at that. "I was just thinking as I walked over here—why is it that the best men always get the roughest go?"

"If they didn't," Gray said, "how would anything that amounts to a damn ever get done? A man does what he has to do, Jack."

"And in my place I have to give the orders, is that it?"

"I guess that's it. I didn't say you had to like it. Maybe Grant doesn't either—I wouldn't know about that. I know I don't. But if you don't know what you have to do when you accept the eagles you're too stupid to wear 'em. Nothing personal, you understand," Gray added hastily.

"You sure?" Marlowe summoned a fleeting grin. "You're right, of course."

"I said, nothing personal. It's not my business to—"

"Maybe it's a good thing somebody does once in a while. Nobody is cast iron, Dick. Well, I'll see you."

Marlowe took a step or two, then swung back abruptly.

"Oh, Dick—"

"Yes?"

"Somehow this slipped my mind. As long as Secord's in the rear he'll have to take care of it—I'll explain to him in the morning, but you need to know about it. Starting tomorrow morning we burn or otherwise tear out every bridge, no matter how small."

"Yes, sure. One thing—"

"Such as what?"

"Bryce'll be behind us too."

"Certainly—and he'll do like anybody else behind us, manage the best way he can."

"One other thing, as long as we're on this. We're not bad off for horseflesh yet but we will be. I'm wondering—"

"Yes, I agree. All right, starting tomorrow morning pick up every loose horse you see, exchange your worst ones in rotation. You'll have to figure out some kind of system. The only thing, don't go too far out of your way—I mean like to the end of a half-mile pasture. Take too much time. We'll have to eventually but we're not that bad off yet."

"I'll see to it."

Wherever he might have been temporarily, Gray reflected, the colonel was back in the saddle now.

The fires had died down and Marlowe picked his way carefully through rows of sleeping men. The sky had cleared with the sunset and the night was alive with the remote and impersonal stars. In a clear spot he stopped and for a moment looked up into the eternal immensity of space, gripped by an actual physical awareness of the vast emptiness. An owl hooted softly, was answered by another; and the night scurriers made small sounds in the grass; a horse sneezed and stomped; an invisible sleeper threshed restlessly in weariness, mumbled "A little longer." A little longer until what? Where? For which of ten million reasons? He shivered involuntarily. Command was a place where you must always be alone and lonely.

16

Blaney Again

Colonel Blaney sat on the ground, his weary back braced against a tree trunk. A passing observer might have thought him asleep except that he whittled steadily on a pine stick. Creamy shavings covered his knees and littered the ground. He worked his way completely around the stick, the blade peeling off exactly uniform chips, then moved up an inch or so and started a fresh pattern. Whittling, Blaney always said, was a fine stimulus to the thinking process, and right now he had considerable to think about. At the moment he couldn't recall everything that had oc-curred since yesterday noon. Too much of it had been a hurrying blur of confusion, and he hadn't seen it all personally anyway, but practically all of it had been bad.

In general the two waves of the Second had gone through Colonel Barteau's slipshod militiamen like an overdose of salts.

But not without cost. The Rebels had got in one respectable volley, a second not so solid, and then a ragged scattering of fire as they disintegrated. The Second went on through but left behind eighteen men, five of them officers. There was no way of knowing how they were divided as to killed or wounded, and certainly there was no going back after them, for of course they had actually gone between the then Rebel lines. Officially Blaney could only record them as missing and hope the dead would be buried and the wounded treated. In addition the Second had eleven wounded, their injuries ranging from incidental to severe, still with them—three even now were in makeshift litters slung between tandem horses, and at least two others should have been.

Fully aware of how badly outnumbered he was, Blaney had gone on, back the way he had come; there was no alternative. But he did not go all the way back to the road where he had parted company with the brigade. About halfway there he had come to an even narrower north-south crossroad—he had noticed it earlier in the day but it had been of no interest then. Now he took it to his own right—north again. Exactly why he could not have said but he did have a misty notion in the back of his tired mind.

In the meantime Barteau, now mad enough to bite nails, had gotten his Tenth Alabama back together and once more started in pursuit. In the general confusion the Second had gained about three miles, but the respite had given them scarcely more than enough time to wait on the attention of their riding wounded. By midafternoon Barteau was on their tail again and a desultory rearguard action continued right up to dark. With darkness the Rebels had temporarily desisted and again the Second had gained a little distance, but two hours after sunup the rear-guard skirmishing began again. To Blaney there was only one consolation, such as it was: both sides were about equally beat out. He remembered a hot-weather story from Texas, about the coyote chasing the jackrabbit with both of them walking. . . .

Now Blaney reversed his stick and began whittling on the fresh

end. As he'd told Marlowe, he was a practical man, but like everyone else he had more than one character trait—and at least one
other of Blaney's was plain stubbornness.

He lifted his head and yelled, "Orderly!"

Some yards away a weary sergeant got up off his back and
mumbled, "Yeah, Colonel?"

"Go get me Captain Prince, son!"

When Prince appeared Blaney said, "Rest your legs, Cap'n, an'
listen. Now I'm going to keep the regiment here for another
twenty minutes if the Rebels don't root us out. Take your company—you'll have some head start—an' keep goin' till you find
some place where you can lay hands on a couple wagons—I don't
give a hoot what kind they are as long as they'll carry the
wounded. Get teams for 'em too, or anyway team harness. We
can use the animals that belong to our own wounded if we have
to, but get the extra nags if you can. You don't need to be polite
and you don't need to take any argument."

Prince nodded. "Yes sir. What then, Colonel?"

"Stay on this road and wait until we show up. We'll be along
but it may take a little time. Now git!"

The colonel got up, tossed away his carving, and walked over
to a figure prone in the shade of some hazel brush. He reached
down and shook Dixon gently by one shoulder. "Dix?" he said
inquiringly. He thought the major's face was a little pale behind
its ordinary ruddiness.

Dixon sat up instantly and said, "What is it, Colonel?"

"How you feelin'?"

Dixon shook his head as though to clear it. "Hell, I'm all right.
Why the devil shouldn't I be?"

"Well," Blaney drawled, "a stranger lookin' at you sure
wouldn't think so. Not offhand." He regarded Dixon solemnly,
thoughtfully.

There was a two-foot rip in Major Dixon's left breeches leg
and the heavy blue fabric was soaked with blood clear down in-

side his boot. There was a wide bloody bandage, improvised from his shirttail, midway on his thigh.

"Damn it, Colonel, I told you it's only a long scratch. I know it looks like hell but I've lost more blood with a nosebleed!"

"All right, all right. Here's the thing. I've sent Cap'n Prince on ahead to lay hands on some wagons for the wounded. We're bound to strike another crossroads directly and I'm going to send the wagons back toward the La Grange pike on that. That'll give them a chance to get out of this and at the same time get 'em off our backs. We're not up to movin' very fast but they make us even slower. I'll send a company along as escort—that'll be you, Dix."

"Like hell it will!" Dixon snapped. "Not me. You got another think coming. What're you up to, anyway?"

"Well," Blaney explained, "we never did get to West Point, so I figure to tear up the M. & O. at this place farther north called Okolona. Long as these Rebels are bent on chasin' us we might as well have 'em chase us up there where we can do some good."

"And land us in another bear trap like the last one?"

"We got out of it, didn't we?" Blaney said reasonably. "I always hate to lose men but I hated especially to lose those yesterday. Generally you can get something in trade for your casualties, but back there we got nothing."

"We got out. But you're wrong about one thing."

"Shucks, that's a good average for me. But which one?"

"For one thing I damned well ain't going anywhere as one of a party of wounded. I could have got this bad a raking off some blackberry briars. Furthermore, there's no use sending an officer and a full company as escort—if you keep on lookin' for trouble we can't spare 'em, to start with. And they don't need it. Send a sergeant and a platoon. A small party will draw less attention and be just as much help to the wounded."

Blaney reflected for as long as it took him to locate and process a fresh chew. "Mmm. Could be you're right, Dix. Could be this

Rebel sonofabitch behind us won't waste time bothering with such a small party. But you're sure you're all right?"

"How many times do I have to tell you?" Dixon said irritably. "See?" He got to his feet and stood defiantly with most of his weight on the gruesome-looking leg. "What more do you want? Besides, I don't ride or shoot with that leg. By God! You act like you're getting soft!"

"Maybe I am," Blaney said thoughtfully. "But to tell you the simple truth, Dix, I think I'm just gettin' a little tired o' the damn' war."

The colonel looked at his watch, sighed tiredly, and told Bugler Murphy to blow him a Boots and Saddles.

Dixon rubbed his whiskered chin with a blood-streaked hand— there had been no opportunity to wash. "Judas! I may have been hungrier but I can't remember when."

"Who ain't?" Blaney answered him. "You never miss the water till the well runs dry. Come on, let's ride."

17

Small War

Bryce rode loosely, slouched in the saddle like most of A Company, aware of a half-dozen desultory dialogues all about him but paying little real attention to any of them.

". . . It was when I was workin' as a mud clerk on the old *Kate Depew*—she burned at the Quincy landing in the winter of '58—clerk ain't such a lowlike job as it sounds, not on a good packet like the *Kate*. Well, you may not believe this, but I swear it's the honest-to-God truth. This woman came aboard at Dunleith—that's what they used to call East Dubuque before the railroad crossed there—an' right away she started givin' me the come-on look . . ."

". . . Just because they ain't never figgered out this here perpetual-motion thing yet ain't no sign they ain't goin' to. Now this here's my own idea, see? You take one big wheel, it don't make no difference what exact size . . ."

It was true that Bryce had gone to sleep—when eventually he did sleep in spite of his weariness—in a mood near to bitterness. He would have been stupid indeed if he hadn't seen in an instant what Marlowe was letting him in for. Of course the Old Man wouldn't say so—how could he?—but his feeling had been plain enough. As a rule Marlowe was not a man to act reluctantly, once his mind was made up on an official matter. If a stick had a dirty end A Company got it, that was the point—and the unfairness was manifest.

But when reveille pulled him reluctantly from the well of sleep the feeling had gone, or rather changed. Fair was a word children used in their games; it had a very small place in the army. He did not question the necessity of the move, not in the circumstances. And if there was any fault it lay in the circumstances, not in the reasoning of Marlowe. To be sure the Old Man had been the focus of his anger, but that too was an accident. And the Old Man might have said a number of things which he obviously chose not to. He could, for one thing, have reminded Bryce that if he had taken the majority when it was offered him he would not now be personally leading a company liable to any and all necessary duty. Well, first things always first—and a man knew, or should know, that when he willingly (or even unwillingly) put on the uniform he resigned most of his rights to yea and nay.

Actually, in other circumstances, he would have enjoyed this freedom of command. Not because he derived any great pleasure from issuing orders, but because it freed him from the natural restraint of regimental and brigade operations. And even in the matter of this faring forth it was the principle of the thing rather than the thing itself. If someone else had drawn this assignment, and bungled it, old General Bryce would immediately have thought of a dozen ways *he* would have done it better. Well—

This morning he had done something which even Dick Gray would probably have raised hell about—except that he was and would remain unaware of it. In spite of the fact that they had slept all night as usual, he had deliberately taken them a quarter mile off the road into the timber and given men and horses three hours of extra rest. Nobody thanked him—he hadn't expected anyone to, but all the same he knew it was appreciated.

Unlike the straight section-line roads of Central Illinois, the "highways" in this benighted country wound like aimless snake tracks, apparently going nowhere in particular. Often enough they they did go nowhere except to join another equally winding road. Their very nature provided excellent cover except that it could work against as well as for you.

They started up a longish slope, not really steep except in the sense that from here they couldn't see what lay beyond the summit. One of the two men on point in front came back into view, raised and pushed a hand palm outward and forward in the signal to halt. Bryce rode forward and joined him.

"Something wrong, Charley?"

"Nothin' to get excited about right now, Cap'n, but you better have a look at the other side o' the ridge."

At the top they found the other man already dismounted and Bryce left him to hold the horses.

Ahead of them the timber thinned considerably and the ground fell away in a long, easy slope to the railroad line and a village Bryce assumed was Macon. But that wasn't all, or even the most important thing. Strung out for a quarter mile along the railroad were men, a great many men. At this distance—Bryce had no glasses—he couldn't see much detail but these couldn't be anything but troops. Sunlight glinted occasionally on rifle barrels. There was also a conglomerate train still standing by, a mixture of coaches, boxcars, and flats, whether just arrived or just going there was no way for Bryce to tell. But if the men were *going* somewhere they indicated no hurry to get aboard the cars.

Charley Dirks whistled softly and said, "Bro-*ther!*"

"Un-hunh," Bryce agreed. "I'd figured we might load up the grub sacks down there but this looks like the end of the line."

"Say, wait a second!" Dirks laid a quick hand on the captain's arm. "There, near that second bend."

They stayed long enough for Bryce to get a good look. There were three mounted men—obviously a routine patrol sent out from the town. Bryce guessed them not to be cavalrymen but infantrymen given horses for this chore. They carried neither sabers nor saddlebags. Two of them wore their muskets slung across their backs, the third rode with a leg flung across the saddle pommel and his rifle in turn lay carelessly across the leg. If they were particularly alert it didn't show. Probably, Bryce thought, they took for granted there was nothing here likely to concern them.

He jerked his head and in another moment they rode hurriedly back down the slope.

They could, Bryce reflected, simply take to their heels and the patrol, unless one of them was adept at reading road signs, might not even guess A Company had been within ten miles of here. But that was contrary to his instinct and training—and one of a cavalryman's primary jobs was to garner information. These three probably wouldn't have much, but then you never knew. More than that, A Company could use those three horses.

He simply dismounted the company, left every other man to hold two horses, in the cover away from the road, and put the others in concealment.

The three riders, all unsuspecting, moved casually down the hill. Then the one with the rifle on his leg suddenly exclaimed, "Hey, y'all! Hold on a minute. Somethin' funny—" He slid to the ground and stood looking at the place in the still-soft road where A Company had stopped, milled around, and then moved into the timber. "Say—!"

Then a horse nickered in the timber—it really didn't matter now, and Bryce said, "Damn it—get 'em, boys!"

That was about all there was to it—almost. The arms of the two mounted men went up—their rifles still slung uselessly behind them. But when the horse nickered the man on the ground had cocked his rifle in an instantaneous reaction. Now as his arms went up he let go the piece—it was obviously unintentional—and when it hit the ground it discharged. Sergeant Nate Brown's hat departed from his head as though snatched by an invisible hand.

"Why, you God-damn' awkward—!"

"Easy, Nate, easy," Bryce said. He waved at the two riders. "Down on the ground, you two. Make it fast and careful."

Troopers retrieved the muskets—none of the three had any other weapons—and shoved the three into line in the road.

"Some of you get those junk saddles off the horses," Bryce ordered, "and throw 'em in the brush somewhere. These peckerwoods won't need 'em. Leave the bridles to lead with."

The three stood there, arms still up but beginning to sag slightly already, looking variously sullen, angry, discomfited, uneasy. Their eyes shifted curiously, warily.

Bryce looked them over without emotion—he had seen ten thousand of their brothers. Then, "I need a little information, boys," he said pleasantly enough. "You'll make it easier on yourselves if I get it in a hurry and without any argument."

One of them, apparently the oldest of the three, muttered "Don't tell the gawdam bluebellies nothin'. Y'all ain't called on to. It ain't regalation."

"That's right," Bryce agreed, still pleasant. "But now and then we have to ignore the finer points. Is this town up ahead here Macon?"

Sullenly, "Why'n't y'll go on an' see?"

"Un-hunh. What troops are those there now?"

No answer at all now.

"Well, well," Bryce said conversationally, "have it your own way, but at least one of you could have saved yourself a little bother." He looked them over more carefully now, making a swift choice. Yes—the one in the middle, the one who'd dropped the cocked rifle. "Kelso"—this time the captain's voice crackled—"take your saber and apply it to the rump of that jackass in the middle so it'll do the most good!"

"Yes *sir!*"

The saber came out with a rusty, metallic rasping sound that almost put a man's teeth on edge and the middle man's sleepy eyes were suddenly wide.

"Now looky heah, Majuh, y'all cain't—"

"Don't tell the sombitches nothin', Dink—they pure bluffin'."

Bryce's mouth tightened. "I warned you men we didn't have time to fool around. Now, you, what troops are there in Macon? Encourage the man a little, Kelso."

Kelso nodded—and supplied encouragement.

The man winced visibly and sweat oozed suddenly on his forehead—but he was still silent.

"Ah, a real pure-quill patriot," Bryce observed. "Too bad all that will power has to go to waste. Nate," he said to the sergeant, still smarting over his narrow escape from the wild bullet, "Kelso needs a little help. Give this brave lad a little pleasure on the belly button. That'll help square that hole in your hat."

Sergeant Brown grinned in anticipation. "A pleasure, Cap'n!"

The saber point flicked out, came to rest on the butternut tunic, and pressed inward, making a measurable indented cone in the thick cloth. The prisoner opened his mouth, closed it again, and swallowed painfully. He flinched visibly but Kelso's blade was still there.

"What troops are those in Macon, soldier?"

"Answer the Cap'n, you sonofabitch!" the sergeant snapped suddenly, unexpectedly. "I don't have to be a gentleman like he does." The sergeant measured carefully, sprayed tobacco juice squarely in the center of the man's chest. The foul stuff settled, then ran slowly downward in a pattern like a river delta. The tunic cloth parted under the pressure and suddenly the saber point disappeared. The man had his share of guts and he stood rigid as a corpse, but this was too much.

"Part of—of the Thirty-third Alabama. Part of the Seventh Kentucky and Twelve Loosiana, Majuh. Gen'l Loring's in command."

"Well, now, that's better. They just get here?"

" 'Bout two hours ago."

"Un-hunh. Are they staying? How long?"

"I—I guess so. I don't know sure 'nough. They got to stay anyhow till we git back. An' I heard said they were diggin' emplacements for two six-pounders that come up with the Seventh from Meridian."

"Now that's what I call intelligent cooperation, friend."

There was more but it wasn't important, and Bryce finally said, "Well, when you get back—and that's going to take you a little time—give Loring General Marlowe's compliments and tell him we'll get to him directly."

Somebody said, "What about these junk guns, Cap'n?"

"Smash 'em and throw the pieces in the brush. Now, you three, start peeling off your duds!"

They stared at the captain in new astonishment but still stood silent, unmoving, possibly unbelieving.

"You heard me!" Bryce barked. "I said get 'em off—and fast."

"But, Cap'n, seh—" one of them began.

"Off—or I have them taken off you. You see, gentlemen, we can't take you with us and we don't want you to go anywhere else in too big a hurry. Of course we could tie you up, say about a hundred yards back in the brush, and in that case the buzzards would find you eventually. Besides, we wouldn't treat even a Rebel like *that*. Corporal, give 'em a hand, a lot of hands, if you think they need it."

They undressed because they had no choice, albeit in sullen anger, acutely embarrassed resentment, and a dawning realization of the reception they were bound to get on their return to Macon.

"Let 'em keep whatever junk they have in their pockets," Bryce said carelessly.

Ridicule is a bloodless but potent weapon and A Company didn't spare the whips. What one man didn't think of another promptly did. None of the three Confederate tunics were anywhere near alike and it turned out that only one of the three wore socks inside his crumbling boots. And when they were down to

nothing but soiled shirts there were ribald and shattering comments on spindly, hairy shanks and posteriors.

"Look there, I swear that ain't a man—looks like a bear."

"Bear—hell! That's pure skunk fur or I ain't never seen any!"

Shamed, ridiculed, and reduced to impotent speechless rage,
they stood there dumbly, almost like sheep huddled for protec-
tion.

"Please, Cap'n, if y'all'd jes' let us—"

"Get moving and don't even look back!" Bryce cracked. "And
tell your General Loring he'd better dig deep if he doesn't want
General Marlowe's division to run plumb over him. Now move!"
He doubted the remark would carry with any particular effect,
but you never could tell.

With the company mounted again they sat their horses and
watched the three dejected figures move slowly back up the rutted
road. On pale, tender, dirty feet they minced, frog-hopped at
each sharp stone, and generally progressed like chickens on a hot
griddle. Company A watched silently for a moment, then added
the final parting insult—a collective guffaw that echoed among the
trees.

You could say this of Cap'n Bryce—he thought of the damnedest
things sometimes.

Someone said, "What'll we do with these rags, Cap'n?"

"Tote 'em a mile or so and then put 'em in the road and set
fire to them. They might come back on the chance we left the
stuff here. Now let's get the hell out of here!"

Bryce led them back toward the west but only as far as the
first road, where he turned south again. This road was still only
four or five miles from the railroad but that didn't worry him at
the moment. With only infantry at Macon there was no chance of
effective pursuit from there. In fact, he saw the presence of the
troops at Macon as reassuring; as long as they were there they
couldn't be anywhere else. Furthermore, while there were more
troops up the line of the M. & O., it was highly likely that they

were well occupied—they would be if Blaney and his Second Iowa had done any good at all. And there was no possibility that any of these troops had passed each other, coming south and going north. So at the moment Bryce was satisfied he had nothing to worry about except the normal hazards of being at large in strange enemy territory.

There was still the pressing fact that most of them had not eaten for almost twenty-four hours. They had passed a couple of isolated farmsteads where they might have found some relief not long after they released the patrol, but Bryce hadn't wanted to linger this close to Macon. No use taking chances. But the problem was still there, in fact more so, and as the afternoon waned Bryce was acutely aware of it in the purely personal sense. There were few audible complaints from the men—nobody expected Captain Bryce to produce miracles—but they were still hungry. Now and then somebody made a casual remark, maybe like "Man, I'm hungrier than a bitch wolf with nine suckin' pups in a Kansas blizzard," but of course the remarks weren't directed specifically at *him*. Bryce shrugged inwardly and let it go.

Part of the afternoon, when the road veered abruptly away from paralleling the rail line and looked to keep going that way, Bryce had struck off across country. No use riding any farther than they had to. He had no glasses—the War Department didn't issue such luxuries to mere cavalry captains—but he had a most excellent German-made compass and didn't worry about being lost. In this geographical context lost was a rather meaningless word anyway. Near five o'clock they again emerged on a road of sorts and a half-hour later came rather unexpectedly—Bryce didn't remember it on Marlowe's map—to a village called Gillis. Perhaps, Bryce thought, for want of a better name. It was, in fact, hardly a village, merely a settlement, what in Illinois or Indiana would have been called a wide place in the road.

A company's entry didn't cause much of a visible stir—there were few people here to be stirred. A stooped man on a wagon seat behind a span of sleepy mules stared with mild interest but no excitement as the horsemen filed past. A pair of housewives paused in their talk at a decaying garden fence and watched silently. Three mongrel dogs ran yapping and snarling at the heels of the horses and one of them, mistakenly emboldened, leaped upward at a stirrup. Without a wasted motion the trooper leaned far down and lashed with a whistling quirt, and the dog departed, howling in short, frantic yipes, for parts unknown.

Bryce paused and beckoned to a ragged, barefooted Negro boy. The youth, tall and thin as a fence rail, looked both fascinated by the soldiery and scared half-speechless.

"Where's the main store in town here, boy?"

"De sto'?" A complicated question, to be sure.

"Yes, the store, damn it! The place where you'd go to buy a pair of shoes if you had any money."

"But Cap'n, Ah ain'— Oh, Ah reckon y'all mus' mean Mist' Lacey."

"I don't know whether I do or not, but where the hell is it?"

The youth pointed and they had to settle for that.

Lacey's store, such as it was, consisted of one large room which was part of a rambling one-story residence.

"See what you can turn up, Rogers," Bryce said to his first lieutenant, in fact A Company's only remaining lieutenant. "I'll handle the watering."

There was a rattling asthmatic pump and a trough that accommodated two horses at a time, and men and animals took their turns, the men replenishing their canteens while they were at it. The water tasted stale and flat and the captain crossed his fingers—sometimes strange well water turned a man's bowels almost inside out.

Rogers came back and handed Bryce a handful of dry cigars. "Don't blame me for these," Rogers said. "I just saw 'em and lifted 'em on general principles."

"Thanks. Any other luck?" He didn't expect too much but at the same time the needs of A Company were nothing like those of the brigade.

"Well, you won't mistake it for Christmas but it isn't so bad either. One ham, a couple of sides of fat bacon, a couple of potatoes around, enough corn meal for a regiment if we wanted to carry it. There were some weevily-looking black-eyed peas but I left 'em. Personally, I'd sooner eat hay and besides they take too long to cook for what you get out of 'em. Oh yes—half a bucket of scummy dill pickles."

"Any coffee?" Bryce's stomach cried out for solid food but even so he could almost taste the bitter but heartening taste of coffee, smell the good sharp aroma. Field-service coffee was usually hell's own brew but somehow a man developed a liking for it.

"No. The fellow claims he hasn't had a pound for almost a year—probably true, back here in the woods." Rogers grinned. "He sure ain't got any now. We took the place half apart lookin'. I got two quarts of whisky though. You better take care of it, Asa."

"All right," Bryce said indifferently. Personally, he liked liquor but now he wanted coffee. "It may come in handy. Get your stuff loaded. We've got a good hour of daylight yet."

The captain put two fingers in his mouth and whistled piercingly—a recall signal A Company recognized. He waited a few minutes, made a rapid mental count of noses, and said, "Where the devil are Cook and Dirks?"

Rogers looked around, shrugged, and said, "Blamed if I know. I sent 'em to try and scare up some horse feed."

They appeared after Bryce had whistled twice more, began to swear in a rising crescendo and began thinking of looking for them. They each had a fairly full grain sack behind the saddle and Dirks had another lumpy-looking tow sack across his legs.

"Took a little time, Cap'n," Dirks apologized.

"It must have. What's in that sack full of humps?"

Before Dirks could answer he shifted a leg and the sack emitted a chorus of frantic squawks. "It was just too good to pass up, Cap'n," Dirks explained. "We opened that shed door lookin' for corn or oats, see, and there was them six hens, settin'. All in a nice straight row. They was concentratin' on their work an' we just picked 'em off one at a time—they didn't even flag a wing."

"You pay for 'em?"

"Well, no sir. We was *lookin'* for somebody to pay—I was, that is—when Cook said you'd been whistlin', so naturally we had to go."

"All right," Bryce said curtly. He rubbed his face, the hand covering a grin. "Let's get on our way."

Riding again, he recalled with wry inward embarrassment his promise—threat?—to Marlowe that if he undertook this business he would let nothing stand in his way. The ludicrous things a man can say when his mouth is out of control! So far they had really cut a devastating swath—soundly defeated a three-man patrol and stolen six setting hens. Old Professor Bryce, the Avenging Sword, the Attila the Hun of east-central Mississippi! All the same, he reflected hungrily, stewed chicken would be all right; if they could manage to roast them, and they weren't *too* tough, so much the better.

He gave them two hours for supper—it took that long to cook the tough old hens halfway decently—and then drove them back into the saddles again. Their bellies full now, they went willingly, almost cheerfully. Not for nothing had he given them that three-hour bonus rest in the morning.

Midnight found them on the M. & O. right of way, about ten miles south of Macon, Bryce judged, although they had ridden a long thirty-mile loop to get here. Bryce wanted a bridge, the bigger the better, and they followed the line until they found one. The near-full moon was well into its downward arc but it would provide light of a sort for another hour. The bridge was only forty-odd feet long and the stream under it was shallow—one of the upper tributaries of the Pearl River, but the cut it ran through was a good twenty feet deep, enough to cause repairmen a worth-while amount of trouble. Most of them were old hands at this business and many of them carried short-handled axes, short enough to go in the saddlebags. Rails were torn out wherever they could find one loose enough to handle—these roads had had almost no maintenance since the start of the war. Telegraph poles were chopped off at the ground and dragged into piles on the tracks for burning. The wire was twisted into hopeless tangles, chopped into short lengths, and either flung into the stream or dragged off into the timber. The bridge timbers were too tough for their small tools but they had an answer to that: they scattered brush, dead limbs, and some of the tinder-dry telegraph poles the full length of the structure and set fire to it in the middle and at both ends. By the time they were ready to go the whole flaming mass had crashed into the stream-bed.

General Loring's troops had ridden from Meridian to Macon, but if they came back this way they were sure going to walk, at least for a few days.

Two o'clock and moonset found them asleep in an oak thicket five miles away. Bryce didn't bother to set a guard.

18

The "Enemy"

On the seventh day from La Grange—Marlowe recalled wryly that the Lord rested on that day—the brigade, with the obvious exceptions of A Company and the Second Iowa, had not laid eyes on a solitary uniformed Confederate. Which as a short-term gain was of course all to the good. In fact, considering that they had now covered between one hundred and sixty and one hundred and seventy miles, this was little short of miraculous. Blaney's diversion—and to a lesser extent Bryce's—should, or could, account for some of that, though Marlowe had no possible way of knowing.

All the same he was frankly worried over his good luck. It seemed to him pretty obvious that the longer it was postponed the more inevitable eventual collision became. Certainly the brigade was not invisible—when the roads dried again the cloud of dust they raised could be seen for miles—and just as certainly the

Rebels weren't blind or scared. It had been a very long time since anyone in this army had discounted the tenacious, even foolhardy, fighting ability of the Confederate military.

And this brought the colonel to another point, one which to him seemed more than passing strange. He had a feeling—no precise knowledge—that everybody else in this blasted country knew his whereabouts even if the Confederate commanders didn't. He was well aware that rumor of approaching disaster (and rumor of rumor) can and does travel in lightning if mysterious fashion. Still he couldn't help but marvel at the way the human mind reacted to what could have been no more than fantastic hearsay. To be sure the brigade was now laying hands on every horse and mule in its path, and also consuming a vast amount of other people's animal feed, but the main body had not touched a hair of a single inhabitant. And yet the country was being vacated, at any rate temporarily, almost as though in advance of the ravaging hordes of Genghis Khan. Not that he gave a damn personally.

The evidence was fleeting and circumstantial but it was there. A foraging detail would race for a barn, looking for animals and grain, and often enough finding one or both. Then when they turned their attention to the house for human provender it would likely as not be deserted, with every indication of a hasty departure. The foragers were irked because they had far less trouble finding food for horses than for men. Whether there was any or much personal "requisitioning" Marlowe didn't know—nor did the matter cause him any concern. He had issued the original covering order; he would assume it was being obeyed to the letter unless and until someone brought a specific charge. Actually there was almost no theft. Most of the brigade had neither time nor opportunity, and in many places valuable personal property had now been removed.

Here and there they recognized the signs of what might have been called nearly invisible panic. Nor was it confined to this particular highway, but appeared to extend variable distances in either direction. First there were the apparently deserted houses.

Then here and there, in a distant field or on side roads, they would occasionally glimpse wagons piled high with personal belongings. Often enough some frantic householder from off the direct route of the column, fleeing from he knew not what to he knew not where, would run smack into the brigade itself. Marlowe wondered what the inner reactions of these people were. Some of them, he supposed, would sheepishly realize what asses they had been, turn around and go home, and try to forget the whole thing. Others would remain convinced the rest of their lives that only this frantic, aimless dashing around had saved them from some forever-unseen but certainly horrible personal disaster. The brigade, after the pattern of soldiers everywhere, usually jeered these refugees mercilessly wherever they were encountered.

Marlowe and Lieutenant Davis were riding at the rear of the column when it turned abruptly left at an almost right-angled bend in the road.

"Come on, Jay," the colonel remarked. "I want to see Major Gray. Let's cut across lots. I'm a little tired of watching this damned endless road."

They kicked their horses into a canter and headed across a slightly rolling patch of country dotted with occasional clumps of trees and brush. Splashing through a shallow branch, they came out on faint wagon tracks which led over a low hill, presumably going to or from somewhere.

Marlowe exclaimed suddenly, "Say, wait a minute, Lieutenant. Let's see what the devil's going on over there."

Davis turned and saw a wagon and a sway-backed old horse. There was a small white boy on the wagon seat, and partially concealed by the wagon two nondescript Negroes were doing something.

The two reined in on either side of the surprised Negroes and Marlowe demanded peremptorily, "What the hell do you niggers think you're doing?" He could see, in a way, but still matters seemed a little confused.

The Negroes very willingly stopped digging and leaned on the shovels. One of them raked sweat with a forefinger.

"Why, Cap'n, suh, we takin' keer that propity o' Miz' Magruder." The man pointed toward the two bulky chests in the wagon.

"I see," Marlowe said. "The family jewels and bullion, I suppose?"

The man grinned whitely. "Naw suh, Ah reckon not much— jes' Miz' Magruder's propity. She allow she won't have de Yankees gittin' hit. She purty mad 'bout dat."

"Well, I don't blame her a bit." The colonel moved over beside the wagon and lifted a chest lid. "Let's have a look. Might be contraband, Davis."

The boy—he might have been eight years old—came suddenly to life and shrilled, "Don't y'all go messin' with my ma's things!"

"Hold your water, son," Davis said severely. "The colonel won't hurt the things."

Marlowe turned over the homely stuff casually but curiously. He was astonished—but no, that wasn't quite it either. Some heavy winter bedclothing probably not now in use, a man's worn civilian suit and shoes, a banjo with two broken strings, a made-in-Waterbury clock, several odd pieces of cheap pressed glass, an oil painting, very bad technically but no doubt a fair facsimile of *somebody*— He stopped looking and dropped the lid.

"I can see your ma wouldn't want the Yankees to steal that stuff," he said gravely.

"Say—that man called you colonel an' you got on swords. You a real sure 'nough army colonel, sir?"

"I suppose it's a matter of opinion." Marlowe smiled a little thinly.

The boy's eyes shone excitedly. "Well, say, I bet you're out after them dam' Yankees!"

"Why, more or less. We were just taking a short cut after them when we saw you and came over."

"I bet you get 'em!"

"Could be—anyway, we'd better."

"Golly! We musta just got our things out here in time. Say, my pa's a soldier," the lad volunteered proudly.

"That so? Where is he, son, do you know?"

"Yes *sir!* He's in Virginia. He's Battery B of Major Blake Abernathy's Meridian Light Artillery. The best dam' battery in General Lee's whole army!"

Marlowe laughed. "By George, I wouldn't doubt it for a minute. Here, buy yourself a railroad." Fishing in a pocket, he came up with a two-bit piece and flipped it to the boy. He turned to the two Negroes. "I'd advise you not to bury it too deep, boys— it won't be so hard to dig up."

As they trotted away Marlowe commented, "The eternally damned silly human race."

Davis shrugged. "It beats me, sir."

"Still," the colonel said thoughtfully, "what do you suppose the people in, say, Peoria would do if they suddenly heard that a few thousand cavalry under Forrest—it wouldn't have to be true —were heading their way? Not that I'm any Forrest. But don't lay any bets on what they might do."

Fragmentary Excerpt from the Columbus (Mississippi) *Republic.*

The past week has been an eventful one. The boldest and we may say one of the most successful raids of cavalry that has been known since the war began has been made (we say it with shame) through the very center of Mississippi, and at the time of this writing we fear have escaped without the loss of a man. We are almost inclined to believe the words of a correspondent, that the manhood of Mississippi had gone to the wars; women only were left, though some of them wore the garb of men. We do not know where the responsibility rests, but wherever it is, if it is not a fit and proper subject for court-martial, we are afraid there is none. It is reported that between four and five thousand

Federal cavalry started on this dastardly raid. They divided; some 1,500, or perhaps a few more, stopped and gave Colonel Barteau battle, while the remainder, 3,000 strong, marched directly south, scouring the country, from eight to ten miles wide, leaving the railroad, south of West Point, on their left. They encamped one night within twenty-five miles of this place. They destroyed the hospital at Okolona and a few other buildings, passing south through Houston, Siloam, and Starkville, to within one mile of Macon, and thence south to New . . .

19

The Light Touch

Breakfast for A Company, eaten shortly after daybreak in spite of their few short hours of sleep, was meager. Nobody had saved much from the night before—not that Bryce blamed anyone—much; he had been as hungry as anyone else.

This morning he held a short two-man council of war with Lieutenant Rogers.

"I don't see how we can chance hitting the railroad again," the captain explained. "They may have found the break already. Anyway, they will soon enough. It's going to take some fancy fixing but anyway they'll have men scattered all over the place. As I see it, our best bet now is to try and make it back to the column."

"Un-hunh. So?"

"It's not so damned simple and it's going to take a little doing. Here, let me show you." Bryce drew a crude diagram according to what he remembered of Marlowe's map. "Y'see, up here near Starkville, about where we took off from the column, the road we'd been on is only about ten miles from the M. & O. But from there on down the railroad angles farther east or the brigade's track farther west, howsomever you want to call it. It means partly that it's a damned sight farther for us going back than it was coming."

"Yeah, but that's not the only thing—"

"I know. I'm coming to that. We been gone since yesterday morning, so as of now the brigade is at least a full day farther south and still going. Say we went straight on back west from here, wherever the hell *here* is, by the time we reach the road over there again they will be *two* full days farther down the line ahead of us. It's a good twenty-five miles from here to the old road on a beeline. That's one hell of a head start, Dave."

"Figuring won't change it. All we can do is try. Jesus, Asa, there's no place else to go."

"I know. But I aim to cut off to the southwest as much as we can. That'll take us down the shorter hypotenuse of the triangle. It'll cut down the distance a good deal and ought to bring us out somewhere around Philadelphia. From there we see what we can find out and recalculate if we have to. All right with you?"

"I don't see much choice, Asa."

"All right—just so we're in agreement. I figure the boys have a right to know what we're tryin' to do. And if I break my neck it'll be up to you then."

The captain inserted fingers in his mouth and whistled.

Bryce wasn't worrying about roads just now. In fact, as of now he hadn't the slightest notion where the nearest road lay. They had approached the M. & O. across country, gone away from it in the same manner, and made camp in the dark. Moreover, it was unlikely that *any* road ran in the exact direction they wanted —the roads here had a natural tendency to run east-west and north-south, always allowing for the topography—except that some-times they seemed to double back on themselves.

None of the country they had covered in the past week could be called thickly settled—here it was even less so. For one thing it wasn't worth much as farm land, certainly not for cotton. It was rough going, perhaps not so bad as some they'd seen in Kentucky and Tennessee but rough enough. About all Bryce could do was get a compass fix on something resembling a landmark, reach it—or try to—and start over again. They waded streams where the horses could barely maintain a footing, worked and cursed their way through slashing thickets, and fought off or endured endless swarms of gnats.

Nobody talked much about eating, it was too hard on the nerves. All they had now was an ample supply of meal and salt.

Past midafternoon they emerged on the nearest thing to a road they had seen in hours and Bryce said grimly, "We'll take this at least for a while. Right now I personally don't give a damn if it leads straight into Richmond."

When Bryce spotted the Negro shack—of course it might *not* have been Negro but it was a safe bet—he was at once taken with an idea. There would be little here to feed a cavalry company, but all the same—

He raised an arm in signal and A Company moved raggedly upon the bare yard of the shack and reined in—or rather the animals came to an automatic halt. Bryce turned to say a word to Sergeant Brown, riding with him. As they came up the only signs of life had been a few listlessly pecking chickens in the weeds and a thin drift of smoke from the tired-looking pole-and-mud chimney. But when the captain swung around again there were two Negro boys standing in the open doorway. He started to say something—and then his vocal cords were suddenly paralyzed. So, for that matter, was the rest of A Company.

The two boys were perhaps three years old. Their skins were black as soft coal, their eyes rolled whitely upward toward the silent horsemen—and they were Adam naked. They were identical twins, each with a forefinger in his mouth, as alike as two peas—except for one astonishing feature. The one on Bryce's left seemed to be normally arranged, but the personal organ of the other was in a rampant state of erection, pointing defiantly upward at an angle of better than forty-five degrees. Thumbs in mouths, they stared up at Bryce in silent innocence.

A Company crowded forward in fascination, making a thick knot about the log doorstep.

A truly handsome yellow girl—she might have been seventeen or eighteen, obviously the boy's mother, appeared behind them in the doorway, wiping her hands nervously on a rag of some sort. Her face mirrored surprise, apprehension, a certain only half-concealed fear of what she didn't understand.

Bryce raised a hand and pointed with a stern forefinger. "What—" he demanded. He choked, found his voice again and said, "What's the matter with that boy there?"

Startled, the girl leaned far forward and looked down over the heads of her offspring. She wore only a ragged calico dress and when she bent over the captain could see somewhat south of normal. Ordinarily he would have been interested in the purely objective sense, but now he was just too tired to care. She was obviously a little bewildered at the sudden demand and mumbled, "Mattuh wid him, suh?"

"Certainly," Bryce barked sternly. "He surely wasn't born that way, was he?"

Company A almost held its collective breath.

The girl frowned, then her brow cleared and she grinned innocently, shyly. "Aw, you gemmens mus' be foolin'. Y'all knows dere ain't nothin' *wrong* wid him—nothin' 'ceptin' he size an' at he age he jes' natchally cain't he'p dat."

Somewhere in the knot of horsemen a voice exploded. "Oh, sweet Jesus! Nothin' wrong wid him but his size!" A dam burst and laughter rolled out in a great flood. They roared, they threw their heads back and howled, they pounded each other helplessly, they choked, recovered, and began all over again while weary horses shuffled nervously and no doubt wondered what it was about. Bryce slid to the ground, leaned his dirty forehead against the sweat-damp saddle skirt, and let the laughter gush until his empty belly began to hurt. This outpouring, he suddenly realized, was as good for them—well, almost—as a full meal.

When he looked up again the woman was still there, still grinning in innocent if apprehensive bewilderment. The boys, probably scared by this violent and inexplicable uproar, had retreated behind their mother's ragged skirt.

Bryce, finally controlling his merriment, said, "You—you've got some fire in there, I see. Can you make us up a batch of johnny-cake?"

Her brow cleared and she said cheerfully, "Why, yassuh, Ah reckons, 'ceptin' Ah wouldn' have 'nough meal foh all dese gemmen—"

"Don't worry about that," Bryce said. "We don't aim to take yours. Here, boys, pony up those meal sacks." He searched his pockets and came up with a shiny quarter. The girl eyed it hesitantly but hungrily, then almost snatched it.

"Ah got to get me some mo' fyuhwood—"

"You get busy inside," Bryce growled. "We'll fill your whole blasted yard with wood!"

"Yassuh!"

It would take time for the baking, of course, and Bryce cared not at all. Both horses and men needed rest and this would kill the proverbial two birds.

"This'll take an hour or so. The woman hasn't got pans enough to do any good with one batch. Get the saddles off and give the nags a breather," he ordered. "Better put a couple of men out there on the road, Rogers. Relieve 'em at the end of a half-hour—or rather have 'em pull out a couple of other men then."

Five minutes later Captain Bryce was sound asleep in the dirt at the foot of a chinaberry tree. Now and then his lean body twitched involuntarily from exhaustion and muscular tension, and two flies crawled unheeded over the dirt-encrusted stubble of his face. He didn't much resemble a sometime professor of history.

20

Night Ride

Near ten o'clock on this morning of the twenty-third, south of Louisville, the brigade pounded across the Pearl River bridge. Colonel Marlowe lingered behind to watch the rear guard burn the long wooden structure. The Pearl was by far the largest stream they had crossed up to now, and while they had been burning bridges now for two days most of them hadn't amounted to much and their destruction would not hold up determined pursuit for long. But Marlowe accounted the destruction useful if each one delayed pursuit for no more than an hour. The destruction of the Pearl bridge, however, would leave a real hole behind them.

They moved on southward and passed through the county seat of Philadelphia at three in the afternoon.

Marlowe would not have said he was either worried or apprehensive. Dissatisfied was perhaps the better word—though he wondered if that wasn't the normal condition of a conscientious field commander. He had never, even in his own mind, set an exact time when he intended to reach the Southern. Five days had been possible theoretically, six, no, seven, was far more likely. And yet this was already the tail end of the seventh day and they still had a long way to go.

South of Philadephia he rode with a leg thrown loosely over the saddle pommel, the worn map spread out for the hundredth time. He considered the basic arithmetic of the situation. They had passed Philadelphia but as usual in the latish afternoon they were slowing down. In normal procedure they would not cover a great deal more ground by suppertime. It was about thirty miles from Philadelphia to Decatur, a small part of which they would lop off by evening. It was another eight miles from Decatur to Newton and the Southern Railroad, his present combined target. Operating as they were now, with luck they would reach Newton about dark tomorrow night—and that was just about the worst possible time.

When he put the map away in an inside pocket his mind was made up. He sent Sergeant King to fetch Dick Gray and Secord, and when they were all together he put it to them bluntly.

"Bedding down for the night as usual, we'll be due to hit the Southern about dark tomorrow night. And that just won't do. For one thing, the Southern, through Meridian and Jackson, is *the* supply route into Vicksburg, and I'll make a small bet there are at least a few troops at Newton—maybe just going or coming. If there aren't, Meridian is only thirty miles straight east and there are bound to be troops there. How long, once the word is out, will it take them to get to Newton from Meridian? An hour? Two? Anyway, not long. All right. So we have the brigade largely dismounted, scattered to hell and gone up and down, working on the railroad. It'll be night, remember, and we don't know the ground. If force moved in on us in that condition, from either direction or maybe both—the minute we break the telegraph line Meridian and Jackson will guess that something's wrong—we wouldn't have a prayer. No, it just won't do."

"Well, in that case," Gray said, "I suppose we'll just have to lay over. That would rest horses and men and God knows they need it. That way they'd be fresher—"

"No!" Marlowe snapped impatiently. "You still miss the point, Dick. It'd still put us there at the wrong time of day. No, we're going on through, now, *tonight!* We'll give 'em an hour at suppertime, that's all. Better start passing the word that we won't unsaddle. Any comment?"

"You're the boss." Secord rubbed his chin in thought. "It's going to be hell on the horses. I'll miss my guess if we don't lose a few. Some of 'em are damned poorly off, Jack."

"For that I don't give a damn. That's what the horses are for— to get us there. We worry about other things afterwards. Barring something like an act of God, by noon tomorrow this job ought to be half done."

"Half?" Gray said curiously. "What's the other half?"

"Getting ourselves out of this hole once we've reached the bottom of it," Marlowe said calmly.

In an operation such as this, of all possible times dawn was the ideal. Uniformed sentries, if any, having gotten through the night unalarmed, would be yawning, fuzzy-minded, thinking mostly of their reliefs and breakfast and sleep. Ordinary citizens would be barely coming alive again, stretching, yawning uncertainly, wondering whether to get up, to turn over and sleep for just thirty seconds more—or in some cases of devoted wives and husbands, letting nature decide whether they occupy themselves otherwise. . . .

It was, in a way, requiring a good deal of the men. Marlowe knew that very well indeed. Never in their two years of service had they covered this much distance in a single move, and when they had made considerable moves it had always been through already conquered, or partially conquered, territory. The old clichés, "born and raised in the saddle" and "horse and man were as one," were just so much moonshine. Seven full days in the saddle, from daylight to dusk, foraging on the side, caring for the animals, going partly hungry, keeping formation of a sort, making and breaking their skeleton camps, and always with the chance, even the probability, that hell might break loose at the next bridge or bend in the road—it hardly added up to a pleasant excursion. They had not been attacked, to be sure, and the men had been lulled to some extent on that very account. But they weren't stupid, at least not in that sense, and they knew very well where they were. Many a man found himself casting a frequent furtive glance over a shoulder, just in case—

There was another side to it. The men would cuss blue murder at the prospect of an all-night ride, but it would be done. And there is always a certain lift, a relief, a spare surge of energy, when men come in sight of a specific goal, whatever it may be. They would, Marlowe knew only too well, be literally half-dead on their feet by midmorning tomorrow. But the extra needed driving power would also be there, provided by the very fact of finally doing what they set out to do, the knowledge that once done, done *now*, it would not have to be done again. And the day after tomorrow would be still another day. . . .

21

Havoc

They drove on through the town of Decatur, around two-thirty, in the darkness after moonset and before the first sign of dawn. No one in the sleeping town actually *saw* them, though a few light sleepers rose and came to front windows in somewhat nervous curiosity, roused by the steady tramp of hoofs. They saw little more than a dark blur of almost silent horsemen, indistinguishable as friend or foe and identified as cavalry only by the sound of hoofs and their numbers. The brigade now numbered less than a thousand men, and most of them passed through Decatur at a tired walk. But naturally the legend immediately took root that thousands of wild-riding horsemen had swept through the streets at breakneck speed. A few more imaginative souls hinted that they had seized weapons with the notion of opposing the invaders, and had only refrained because of the vast numbers.

Pursuant to his specific orders, when Sergeant Bullen and his men on point approached what they judged to be the outskirts of Newton, they retired at once to the head of the column. Also pursuant to previous orders, Captain Landry of D Company was waiting, or rather riding, with Marlowe. The colonel didn't distrust Sergeant Bullen. It was just that he wanted someone with a somewhat different, if not keener, mind than Bullen's to report the exact situation in Newton. Landry was elected. He took the sergeant back with him, to mind his horses, near the point where Bullen had stopped and turned back, while the captain went on in afoot.

In the meantime the column waited, men asleep or drowsing on animals which likewise seemed to be drowsing. Marlowe, Secord, Gray, and Lieutenant Colonel Fairlie were in a small group afoot, but Marlowe would not allow the men to relax on the ground now. He too much feared the weakness of the flesh.

"Nothing to do but wait it out," Marlowe said shortly. They were withdrawn a little from the main body of the column and the colonel fumbled in a saddlebag and came up with a bottle of whisky. He took a draught, handed the bottle to Secord in the semidarkness, and said, "Pass it around and finish it, gentlemen. You may need it by daylight."

Heedless of any example he might set, he dropped on the roadside grass and let his forehead fall forward on his drawn-up knees. Sometimes the briefest sleep was a help—

. . . In spite of the satiety of the night hours Marlowe had awakened at the first flush of dawn. Suddenly, quite unaccountably wide awake, he had stared at the ornate plaster ceiling of the St. Louis Hotel as the light through the open French doors on the balcony very gradually dispelled the intimate darkness of the room. It would be hot in a matter of hours but now the air was simply pleasant on his bare skin. Careful not to disturb the sleeping girl, he rose and moved to the open doorway on the iron-grilled balcony. Through the interstices of the lush-growing vines he could see (but not be seen by) part of Chartres Street below and, beyond the levee a few squares away, the great flow of the Mississippi. He took a deep, lung-filling breath and his nostrils caught the elusive odor of sweet olive mixed with the faintly fragrant stench of the New Orleans streets—no matter how elegant the immediate surroundings you could never quite escape *that*. In the tall, intricately carved bed behind him the naked girl stirred and he turned, moving back slightly into the deeper gloom just inside the doorway. Though she did not awaken he still stood there, watching her, savoring her with his mind rather than the senses. They had been married—yes, this would be the tenth day, the second of their wedding stay in New Orleans. Of course when a man marries he expects to discover *some* things about his wife that he did not know in the previous state of emotional suspension —often enough to his dismay. But he had very frankly been un- prepared for this whole new world of fleshly delight he had dis- covered in—or with—this demure, unworldly girl he had married back there in Illinois. To be sure her face was beautiful—so much was obvious, and while she had appeared comely enough other- wise the ordinary female dress did not afford too much specific information. He assumed she had no extraordinary bodily defects but again he had been unprepared for the sheer wanton perfection of her flesh—and most certainly not for the almost violent passion waiting there to be unloosed. He had hardly expected her to be cold —after all, courtship, even of the most respectable and accepted kind, had been more intimately revealing, or suggestive, than that —but neither had he expected this vehemence which he, even in his greater experience, could no more than cope with adequately. Rather than merely accept the basic male-female physical rela- tionship with properly modest willingness, she had plunged her- self into it as though to know and experience it completely in the shortest possible time. Women, he began dimly to perceive, under the surface artificialities, were actually the great realists. (It amused him to remember that they had first been introduced on the steps of the First Methodist Church.) As he watched she stretched in sleep, her full breasts lifted as though in offering, the long back arching into the flowing curves of hips and thighs in a movement of satisfied, if all unconscious, voluptuousness. She was his wife but that was no reason why he could not or should not, at least in this privacy, consider her objectively as isolated female. Did the fabled Greek hetaera, he wondered, appear like this? And what did they know of love through professional training and practice that she did not know by instinct? He thought fleetingly: a Methodist courtesan—and was amused at the inherent incongruity. Her body relaxed and a smile moved across her lips. She turned on her side and her arms moved, still in sleep, toward the place he had lately left empty. . . .

"Colonel!"

Someone was shaking his shoulder and he emerged from the dream with a mild start. The sky here also was perceptibly lighter now. A rooster crowed raucously in the distance, and not far off he could hear heavy liquid sound as a horse made water in the road. Somewhere to the east, to their left, there was the rumble of train wheels.

"Colonel!" It was Secord's voice, urgent. "God damn it, Colonel! Landry's back."

"All right, Frank," Marlowe said calmly. "Let's have it. I see it's getting light fast."

Landry was brief and to the point. There were troops, yes, how many precisely it was impossible to tell. There were four or five sentries along the tracks. There were a depot, a freight house of considerable size, a long cotton warehouse. Probably, Landry thought, the troops were quartered in one or both of the latter two buildings. There were none to be seen elsewhere and that should mean probably not more than two short companies. There was also a train, a dozen or so freight cars, standing but with steam up.

"Ah," said Marlowe, the sound of the other train even louder in his ears now. "On a passing track?"

"No, Colonel, on the main line, west of the cotton plant and also headed west. My guess is they've got a little trouble—maybe a hotbox."

"Hmm. I wonder what about this one from the east?"

"Hell, I hear it," Landry said. "It'll have to stop. No way to get by the other one without a lot of horsing around. There is a passing track, but the one in there now has run way past it."

"Ah," Marlowe said, "just like Christmas in April, Captain." Two freights westbound for Vicksburg, at any rate to Jackson, which amounted to the same thing. Well, everybody got lucky once in a while.

He gave it to them tersely, the ideas he had been waiting to let fall into place. Secord would take the Second and pass around to the other side of the town, taking a westward route to avoid the train coming in from the east—they could hear its brake shoes grinding and wailing now. Secord would have exactly a half-hour. He would dismount three companies and send them in afoot, the others to remain mounted in reserve. If there were many men in the buildings, and they didn't panic, from that concealment they could play merry hell with horsemen. The First would send in three dismounted companies from this side. From there on events would shape themselves.

"One other thing, Frank," Marlowe said as Secord climbed back into the saddle. "Detail a company to nail the crew of that westbound train, especially the enginemen. They may have some trouble, as Landry says, but it also may not be serious enough to keep them from pulling out in an emergency. But if it gets away I promise somebody'll sweat! Gray will take care of the other train. That's all, Frank." Almost as an afterthought he snapped open his watch face and said, "It's exactly five-fifteen. Luck."

The light was growing with each moment. More roosters joined in the chorus and a railroad engine whistled a signal of some sort. In the road, horses stamped and sneezed and here and there leather creaked loudly. The dawn stillness was so heavy that every smallest sound seemed magnified tenfold.

There would be no bugles this morning. The word went down the line file by file.

Marlowe looked at his watch one last time, snapped it shut, and said almost casually, "All right, Dick. Better get 'em moving—"

When they were under way again he had one sharp moment of near panic—no one knew what was in or on that train in from the east. Troops? It could be. But the time to worry was past. Secord was committed and thus so were they all.

The town of Newton, what there was of it, was hillier than Marlowe had expected; in fact, all of east central Mississippi was hillier than he had expected. His tattered, two-dimensional Colson map told him nothing of the local topography. Of course he was by now accustomed to the endless hills and hellishly tangled forests of the Tennessee-Mississippi line, but he had supposed that by now, this far down, Mississippi would begin to level off, somewhat in the manner of the boot of Louisiana; it hadn't—at least not yet, nor did it at Newton.

Of course all they had to do to find the line of the Southern was to follow this principal road into town—and keep going. It led them eventually down the sharp incline of the street (road?) which divided the primitive business area to the point at the foot where the railroad naturally sought the easiest east-west level through the town.

Fifty yards this side of the rail tracks—from here he could see both the passenger station and the freight house—the colonel suddenly stopped and dismounted. Sergeant King had the bridle reins before Marlowe even needed to nod at him. He glanced upward at a faded sign on a faded store front, which read: P. GASH, GEN. MERCH. He smiled faintly and said, "Take him around to the side of the building, Sergeant, out of the line of fire. I wouldn't want to be left here afoot."

"Yes sir!"

"You will please inform Major Gray and Colonel Secord that

until further notice this will be brigade headquarters—the establishment of P. Gash, to be exact."

"Right, sir."

Marlowe, standing, put a muddy-booted foot on the hitch rail
and thrust an unlighted cigar between his teeth. (The sky grew
a shade or two lighter.) He was a little tense, of course, but already his saddle muscles had relaxed—in fact his tenseness was
mental rather than physical. He felt also that exhilaration, brief
now to be sure because it was obscured by other matters crowding in upon him, of special accomplishment. This, against the odds,
was the place they had started for. And now they were here. That
was half the story. After a while the other half—would it be as
long?—would begin. Well you played each hand as the cards came
to you. How else?

. . . The firing began then, and a ball slapped into the faded
weatherboarding behind Marlowe, but he didn't turn his head—
you never heard the one that made the big difference.

Though they had much farther to go, the Second's carbine fire
erupted first. It was all right with Marlowe—it let him know that
Secord was in there where he was supposed to be.

The town was fairly open, particularly around the railroad
property. It provided the small garrison—it was obvious within
minutes that it was all concentrated in the long freight house—
with a convenient field of fire, but it wasn't going to do them
much good. Not in the long run. The brigade held all the trumps.

The dismounted men used every bit of available cover, and as
the colonel watched, almost dispassionately, the windows of the
freight house seemed literally to melt away—in the solid crash
of small-arms fire the falling glass made no audible sound. There
was almost no breeze this morning and at once the powder smoke
began to build into an acrid haze that irritated nostrils and eyes.
The Rebel sentries, save only one, were gone; the one remaining
lay face downward between the railroad tracks. From the corner
of one eye Marlowe saw a civilian emerge from a house. The man,
galluses dragging about his hips, took one startled look at this

naturally unbelievable scene, then set off down the street at a dead run. Marlowe didn't bother to look after him again.

The men in the freight house didn't have a prayer but as usual these people were selling high. Rifle fire poured steadily from the shattered window openings. Marlowe wasn't surprised; you always expected to be hit back; there seldom was an easy way to do these things. They would quit eventually, of course, when they had to—perhaps when they ran out of ammunition, but in the meantime they would get a snack while the brigade was getting a meal.

The ten or a dozen blue-coated troopers made a dash at an angle across the open space and the colonel instantly saw why (he perhaps should have seen it before)—there were no windows in the ends of the freight house. Once sheltered there they could— and apparently this was in their minds—set fire to the building— it was scheduled to go anyway as a part of the destructive pattern. Seven of the troopers made it, though one sprawled face downward on the ground after he reached shelter. The others lay scattered in the open ground and across the tracks. Unaware that he did so, the colonel sighed—you always paid something for everything.

Major Gray cantered up and dismounted on the run.

The colonel's thought shifted instantly and he demanded, "What about those train crews?"

"All under control. One fellow was a little overambitious and got himself shot—naturally. What do you think, Jack? I've still got four loose companies. The men here on the ground can handle that bunch in the freight house before long. Why not put the others to work on the railroad, get it started?"

"Yes, I think so. That other train—what was it?"

"Ten ramshackle freight cars of miscellaneous stuff."

"Might as well have at it then," Marlowe said almost casually. "But before they burn the cars have the freight checked. There ought to be some stuff we can use in at least one of the two trains. If there is, have it put aside so we can pick it up later." He

frowned thoughtfully, looking out across the miniature battle-
ground again. "Have you seen Keller anywhere?"

"Why, no, not specifically, but of course he doesn't belong
up here. Seems to me he said he'd picked a nice yard back there
a street or two—a place where he could handle the wounded and
it'd still be easy to get to. I'll see if you want me—"

"Never mind," Marlowe said impatiently. "Get on with your
business, Dick. I'll check on it pretty soon."

Specifically, the location and operation of the aid station were
not the personal responsibility of the brigadier. They were first
the business of the surgeon and, after that, the regimental commander. All the same the First had been his own and its over-all
welfare was almost a fetish with him. He knew he wouldn't rest
until he had satisfied himself. There was obviously no crisis im-
minent here; the situation was in hand; it would work out in a
matter of time. Having gotten the brigade this far, he had done
nothing except to make himself available. Surely he wouldn't be
missed for a mere ten minutes.

The word had been passed to the men. The fire from the freight
house had slackened considerably now and they were able to
pick up a wounded man here and there. Some of them were being
carried past Marlowe. He didn't bother to count them now—the
figures would be bad enough when he got the totals later. And
there would be an even more pressing problem: what the devil
to do with those too badly hurt to ride? Leaving them would mean
deliberately abandoning them to eventual imprisonment. He
shook his head in weary half-anger. But later, later, he told himself irritably. In the meantime—

He said, "Davis—hold the fort. I'll be back in ten minutes or
so at the most."

Leading his horse, he walked back down to the rutted cross
street, away from the noise and the pungent, drifting powder
smoke. It was full daylight now, and there was a big grassy yard,
with well-spaced trees. The wounded were being, had been, laid
out in a convenient row alongside a bank of riotously flowering

white and purple lilacs. As usual Marlowe half set his teeth—
you saw thousands of these bleeding men but somehow the sight
never quite became commonplace. But at least here there were
no artillery wounded—these men were still all of a piece. Artillery
fire was always the worst. Then, you usually didn't have men
but only what remained of men. He counted fourteen on the
new grass and two of them—even a layman could tell when they
were bad enough—were already beyond help. Keller was nowhere
to be seen but Marlowe recognized the spotted horse the taciturn
surgeon usually rode staked out now and happily grazing on the
spring grass. Corporal Dan Meigs, Keller's medical orderly and
all-round assistant, was kneeling beside a man who gasped violently for breath. Meigs was supporting the man's shoulders and
holding a canteen a few inches from his mouth, waiting patiently
for the gasping to cease.

Marlowe waited a moment and then touched the corporal on
the shoulder as he said, "Where the devil is Major Keller, Corporal?"

Meigs got to his feet, still holding the canteen, and abstractedly
scratched an ear with his free hand. He seemed uncertain, a little
flustered, as though somehow torn between two conflicting ap-
prehensions. "Well, Colonel, Sir," he said, "I kind of think it's like
this—"

"You kind of think!" Marlowe felt his boiling point begin to
rise. "What the hell kind of talk is that, man? More important—
where's Keller? Well, speak up!"

"Well, Colonel, you understand I got nothing to do with this—"

"God damn it!" Marlowe was suddenly furious. It was almost
always poor policy to display temper to an enlisted man, but
sometimes it also got results in a hurry. "Keller—what about him?
I want to know—and now!"

It was a story as simple and elemental as it was astonishing, as
much as Meigs really knew of it. This small boy, from the brick
house at the rear of this property, had come running down to the
street, naturally curious about all the apparent excitement. By a

wild mischance—Marlowe extracted this little by little—the boy's throat had been nicked by a stray ball. The scratch could hardly be called a wound but it had bled profusely, where the boy could see it, and he had become almost hysterical. Keller had dressed the scratch, quieted the lad, and led him back to the house. Then in a few minutes he had hurried back, picked up part of his kit, and returned to the house.

"What'd he say?" Marlowe demanded.

"Nothin', Colonel—well, I mean he was in a hurry an' just said he'd be back in a little bit—"

"Did you have any of our men here then?"

"No sir, nary a one, Colonel. Not until maybe fifteen, twenty minutes later. Then two fellows—"

"Well?" Marlowe said urgently, trying to hurry the man and still keep the story straight.

"I waited a little bit—he *said* he'd be back—and doin' what I could here, sir. Then I went up to the house." Meigs chewed his lower lip in thought. Marlowe here was the Old Man, the Ultimate Authority, yet Keller was his immediate superior, partial intimate, and sometime protector, and there was a certain loyalty— "He—I—well, I went up there and there was a nigger woman came to the door when I knocked an' she wouldn't let me in to see the major an' said she couldn't call him. I couldn't very well bust in the house, Colonel, sir—that's against every regulation. I'd have caught hell from someplace. This nigger woman just walled her eyes through the crack in the door an' said she'd tell the major, sir. That was all I could do. But I knowed what was goin' on. Some woman givin' birth—I know, sir, I heard that kind of yellin' an' carryin' on too many times before." The corporal turned docile and utterly honest eyes on the colonel.

Marlowe said harshly, "You haven't been back?"

Meigs shrugged eloquently. "Why, Christ alive, Colonel, I been plenty busy since! Just take a look. They started comin' in—an' *I* sure as hell can't make Major Keller do anything he don't intend to do—sir!"

Was there an implication in that *I?* No matter—the colonel didn't especially need it. Behind them on the new grass a man whimpered like a hurt, uncomprehending animal and another stronger voice muttered, "Hey, Corp, can you fix my collar? Seems like I'm half-chokin' to death—!"

As Marlowe strode—almost ran—toward the house he was half-blind with fury. It was a foolish state, of course, but at the moment he couldn't help himself. He couldn't imagine what Keller was up to and really he didn't care—he only knew there was a situation which had to be resolved, and now.

He slammed down the ornamental iron knocker with a force that literally shook the door in its frame. The Negro woman, presumably the same one Meigs had been talking about, opened the door a crack, a ferocious hostility showing in her dark eyes. "Mistuh," she said stolidly, "we jes' cain't—"

Her adamance, hostility, sense of loyalty, whatever it was, only infuriated him the more and he hadn't the least interest in what she might be saying. "Get out of my way!" he said with cold ferocity, and then he flung the door back with a violence that carried the black woman with it against the wall. Inside, he hesitated a moment to get his bearings—but the screaming came from behind the closed door immediately to his left—probably the front parlor. Without a second's hesitation he flung back the door and stepped into the room.

There was the tangled bed and the white, desperately writhing blur that was the woman. Surgeon Major Keller was leaning over her so that Marlowe could see little more than her lower limbs and an occasional glimpse of her face when her head moved from side to side in agony.

Faced with the fact, Marlowe was suddenly brought up short. Even a savage, in the presence of the basic mystery of birth—or death, for that matter—is instinctively reluctant to interrupt or intervene in the process. Marlowe held himself, within his admitted limitations, to be a man of good will and he understood perfectly Keller's being here. But his problem was Keller's *plus* a great many other complications—and he was still angry.

Keller paid no attention when Marlowe entered. Marlowe barked, "Keller!" He did not recoil at what he saw but neither did he have any desire to approach closer to the bed.

The surgeon straightened up, turned, and faced the colonel. He was in his shirt, his sleeves rolled far up, and his bare arms were bloody to above the elbows. He looked at and apparently through Marlowe and said abstractedly, "Well, what is it, Colonel?" His manner was that of a man whose mind was concentrated on something else entirely.

"What in God's name do you think you're doing, Keller?"

"Doing? It's obvious, I think. This woman will die if she doesn't get proper attention—maybe even then. You see, the cord—"

"*She'll* die!" Marlowe felt as though about to explode. "What the hell do you think is happening to those men out there in the yard?"

"One man can't do anything. Her need was first."

"It's no business of yours, Keller! Right now it's not your business if ten thousand Rebel brats are born or die!"

"I don't think you mean that, Colonel," Keller said calmly. "It's beside the point in any case. This is simply a matter of a human life. Perhaps two."

"And those ten, fifteen men out there are not?" Fury was building up inside Marlowe all over again.

"Wells will manage to handle it."

"Wells! He's probably got his own hands full, clear over on the other side of town. Hell, I don't even know where he is—it's not my especial business to know. God damn it, Keller! *You're* the surgeon of the First! And moreover you're an officer under oath, in case you'd forgotten."

Keller shrugged. "Possibly a question of which oath, Colonel, a matter of difference in words. In any case, I don't need a brigadier to point out my duty for me—"

The woman's animal scream rose in a slow crescendo and then ended in a sudden terrible gasping sound that left Marlowe shaken in spite of himself.

Still—with one sure motion he drew the heavy Navy Colt and pulled back the hammer.

"This is the end of the talk, Major Keller," he said coldly. "As of this moment you are under arrest. Pick up your gear and let's go!"

For an instant Keller's aplomb was jarred violently, but he recovered quickly enough, and went back to work, talking as he bent over the woman. "Why waste the histrionics, Colonel? I don't believe you'll use the pistol—not here and for this. What could you possibly gain, even from the point of view of what you call your duty?"

Well, what, to be sure? The scream was repeated again and its impression on the colonel was reflected in the faint trembling of the pistol barrel. But it still did not affect the iron in his will.

"No," he admitted, "I wouldn't gain much—but you're still under arrest. You have this much choice—bring your gear now and get to work. Otherwise, I send enough troopers up here to carry you."

For a long moment their wills clashed. Then Keller turned, shrugged, picked up his hat, tunic, and saddlebags, and moved toward the door. Marlowe made way for him and he did not look at the vast pain on the bed again.

In the hall the Negro woman glared at Marlowe with distilled hate. "Piss po' Yankee scum!" she muttered.

"Shut your filthy mouth!" Marlowe said with almost brutal indifference. "You'd do better taking care of your mistress, or better yet, finding another doctor for her."

At the foot of the veranda steps Keller hesitated, turned, and said, "I think you'll have this on your conscience, Marlowe—if you have one—for a long time."

"I have arithmetic on my side," Marlowe said almost mockingly. "Two back there in that bedroom—twelve or fifteen down there by the road."

"Not all those men down there, wounded badly or not, will die, Colonel, and you know it."

"No? But how many will die, Keller, because you weren't there? You're not God either, you know. In any case you are operating by regulations now, not sentiment. Come on, you're wasting still more time!"

Keller took a few more steps, hesitated, swallowed hard, and nodded slightly at the pistol Marlowe still held. "Really, that—uh, particular authority is hardly necessary, Colonel. The men—that is, I'm hardly in a position to run away."

Of course Marlowe knew precisely how Keller felt in this respect, but he did not care—the residue of his anger. Keller was no different from other men: no matter how righteous he felt his cause to be he still hated to be displayed in even symbolic handcuffs.

"I'd be derelict in another duty also if I gave you the slightest chance," Marlowe said stonily. "You're still under arrest."

The row of wounded had grown a little longer now but Marlowe had no concern about whether Keller would function properly here; he knew he would. Oddly (and yet why not?) he remembered the casual remark Keller had made to him: "Medicine is where you find it." Well, so it was, and so also was duty.

The men, those who were able to, stared at them in ill-concealed astonishment, then dropped their eyes under the colonel's hard stare. One man, white-faced and with a bloody leg, said, "For Christ's sake—" then shut his mouth abruptly. Meigs kept himself busy and avoided looking at Keller at all.

Two more troopers came up, between them supporting a sergeant with a leg wound. Marlowe waited until they had deposited their load then said, "You two men on some special duty?"

"Uh, no sir, not exactly," one of them answered. "We're just due to report back to Captain Brant, K Company."

"Very well. You've got a special detail now." Marlowe deliberately raised his voice so all could hear. Righteously or not, the anger still burned in him. "Surgeon Major Keller here is under arrest and in your charge. He is not to leave these grounds here without my specific permission. Is that clear?"

The prospective guards exchanged startled glances and one of them said, "*No* place, Colonel?"

"That's what I said. He is not to leave here and he is not to go to the house back there, and if he should attempt to leave you will take whatever steps may be necessary to detain him. Is that understood?"

"Yes sir," they answered in wooden duet.

Marlowe glanced at Keller, but the latter was already busy and paying no attention to the dialogue. He swung himself into the saddle and turned his horse. In the center of town a great and growing cloud of smoke was climbing slowly skyward. He was suddenly aware, surprisingly aware, that the firing had stopped entirely and now he could hear occasional distant shouts, men calling inquiries and information to each other. Secord caught sight of him, raised a hand in signal. Who, Marlowe thought with sad bitterness, was the God-damned idiot who had proclaimed that war brings to the fore man's noblest instincts? He rode on to meet Secord.

22

The Hero

Train Number Seven, westbound from Meridian to Vicksburg, via Jackson, had developed a hotbox somewhere east of Newton. One of the duty sentries had signaled the information to the train crew. They had stopped the train on the western edge of town and sent back a flagman to halt following train Number Ten. Considering the freight it was carrying, some of it, the last thing Seven's crew wanted was any kind of fire—directly behind the engine was a carload of loaded shells, and behind that a carload of artillery powder charges. It was a mighty poor way to organize a train carrying that kind of freight, but at Meridian they had been shorthanded and in a hurry.

The net result was that when the brigade swooped down on Newton, Numbers Seven and Ten were caught like sitting ducks. Long before the shooting ended Number Seven was in the hands of E Company of the Second, Captain Fitz Gordon. Pursuant to orders they had torn open car doors one by one, while Gordon made a mental note of the contents. Fitz had a personal method of dividing freight into two categories: goods the brigade needed and could carry away; everything else—which would be destroyed. The two cars of ammunition, however, posed a special problem. Captain Gordon called Sergeant Pixley, his second in command (E Company hadn't had a lieutenant on the roster for a year), into quick consultation.

"We can burn the damn' train where it stands," Fitz said cheerfully, "except for those two head cars. If we explode that stuff here at the edge of town and kill six or seven hundred Reb civilians, the Old Man will personally cut our throats."

Of course there weren't seven or even six hundred people in all Newton but Sergeant Pixley understood the figures well enough.

"Yeah, sure 'nough, Fitz." Pixley shifted his cud and looked thoughtful. "I been thinkin'—we got to get those two cars out of town before we touch off the rest of 'em anyway."

"You got an engineer handy?"

"Un-hunh. One that says he is. Tom Murphy. Worked for four years in the Chicago & Alton shops at Bloomington."

"Well, get him then."

Private Murphy was only too happy to leave off his bacon unloading and take part in more important matters.

"Sure, I kin run her," he assured Gordon. "I wasn't never no regular engineer, you unnerstand, but I used to run a yard hog an' I can sure git this tallowpot outta town. When we git some steam on her. It's way down, settin'."

Gordon and the sergeant rode in the cab with Murphy and six more men were on the woodpile in the tender. They rocked and bumped over the rough tracks for about a mile out of town and Gordon finally yelled in Murphy's ear, "This is plenty far enough!"

With only two cars behind him and at relatively slow speed, Murphy was able to stop the whole thing with the locomotive brakes—no need to use the brake wheels on the following cars. Through no special intent they came to a stop only a short distance from a wooden bridge, more accurately a trestle. The dry ravine it traversed wasn't very deep but the trestle was a good hundred and fifty feet long. Low down and with no superstructure, they hadn't seen it at a distance.

They canvassed the situation. Everybody walked around looking thoughtful but not vouchsafing any ideas as to how to procede from here.

"I dunno, Pix," Gordon said finally, doubtfully. "Orders are to wreck the engine beyond any repair but it's one hell of a chunk of iron."

"Wedge the safety valve," somebody said, "then stoke the supreme hell out of her an' let her blow herself up."

"How about that?" Fitz asked Railroader Murphy.

"Maybe." Murphy shook his head dubiously. "Maybe not, Cap'n. It all depends. You know how them things are—you don't want a boiler to blow, she'll blow to hell an' gone; you want her to blow, nothin' happens."

"But if the safety's locked, don't it have to blow up?" Fitz argued.

"Yeah, but it depends on what you mean by blow up. Somethin' has to give eventually but maybe it's just a plate or a row of rivets —your pressure goes out like a cyclone but she don't explode. There's no tellin'."

"Damn it!" Gordon said fervently. "We can set fire to the powder car but it may just burn like hell and brimstone and not explode either. I've seen it happen—no compression on loose powder. Then we still got the God-damned shells on our hands with no way to explode 'em. It's heavy stuff—I doubt that carbine and pistol fire would explode it. That's another thing you can't tell. And there's still the engine. Hell an' damnation!"

Pixley spat thoughtfully across a nameplate bolted to the engine cab—it was a carefully polished brass plaque which read PRIDE OF MERIDIAN.

"Well, we can burn the trestle and then run the whole works into the hole. That'd make a mess, I'll guarantee you."

"If we was sure it'd all blow. But supposin' it don't? Besides," Gordon objected, "it'd take too much time. That trestle's gonna take time to burn down to charcoal, Pix."

It was frustrating, to put the case mildly.

"Look, Sarge, I got kind of an idea," Murphy said almost apologetically, "if the Cap'n don't mind. Them shells in the head car?"

"That's right, Murph."

"I kin knock 'em off easy then," Murphy said confidently. "Bet a month's pay, Cap'n."

"We're all ears."

"Hunh? Oh—well, we run the two cars out in the middle of the trussle an' leave 'em, uncouple an' run the tallowpot on up ahead. I'll set her in reverse gear, put the Johnson bar in the corner—that's open the throttle wide open, Cap'n, see?—an' unload. When she hits I'll bet it'll put a hole in the ground like Pike's Peak upside down."

Pixley and Gordon looked at each other.

"It ought to at that," Gordon agreed. "But—well, you willing to take the chance?"

"Shucks, Cap'n," Murphy said in all modesty, "there's no chance. I'll take her down plenty far. The farther I take her the more time I got to unload—an' the faster she'll be travelin' when she hits."

"You got yourself a deal, Murphy! Get your rump back up there on the cushion."

"Yes sir! You all better get plenty far in the clear."

"How far, would you figure?" Fitz said.

"Jesus, Cap'n, you'd know more'n I do about that. But we got to walk back to town anyway—why'n't you just head back that way? I'll catch up with you when I'm done."

It seemed the obvious and logical thing to do.

"Well—watch yourself, Murph."

"Nothin' to it. Say, Cap'n, do me a small favor, will ya?"

"Sure, if I can, but hurry up."

"I got a pretty good watch—belonged to my old man." Murphy fished the timepiece from an inner pocket. "If I happen to roll when I jump I might bust it. You just hold it for me till I catch up with you—"

They ran the two cars carefully onto the trestle, pulled the coupling pin on the tender, and waved Murphy on. The eight men hustled back up the right of way, then by common consent moved a little away from the tracks. If they stayed on or near the track, in a direct line behind the cars, they would miss seeing three quarters of what happened—and nobody in his right mind would miss a free exhibition of a first-class train wreck.

Private Murphy toured slowly down the track, deliberately taking his time. He intended to make the most of this. Nothing approaching this in importance had fallen to his lot during the two practically anonymous years in E Company. This wouldn't make him a national hero but in the Second he would certainly be pointed out as the man who singlehandedly had staged the biggest train bust-up in the whole state of Mississippi.

At something over a thousand feet he set the throttle and eased to a stop. He hung out of the cab and looked back down the track—yes, this should give him plenty of room to maneuver in. Way behind him the boys were still hotfooting it up the track, casting occasional looks over their shoulders.

Murphy bailed more wood into the firebox and opened the ashpit door wide for all the draft she'd take. In the short distance involved the extra fire would gain little, but still, he was determined to leave nothing undone. Taking another look out the cab window, he saw that the boys had moved out a hundred yards or so from the trackside. Murphy grinned appreciatively. Trying to get a good look—and who wouldn't? Well, in a couple minutes he'd give them something to look at!

With the fire roaring like a blast furnace and smoke pouring from the funnel stack, he made a last careful check, then eased the reverse gear over. Then he broke the throttle a crack, making sure she was actually operating in reverse. She started to creep slowly. Well, now was the time. He slammed the throttle bar clear in and stepped back. For an instant the old engine shivered like an animal, the drivers caught for a split second, and then under the furious thrust started to spin, grinding whirling circles of fire off the rails. The engine still moved very slowly under the slippage, then the spinning drivers caught and she leaped like a bee-stung horse—and in that minute fraction of a second Murphy knew his mistake. He had instinctively braced himself for the tremendous jerk that was bound to come—but in the wrong direction, *as though the engine would move forward*, its normal direction. Off balance, in fact thrusting himself in the wrong direction, he was flung forward like a rag doll and his head slammed against the firebox. His arms had gone out instinctively and he screamed as his palms brought up against the almost red-hot iron. He rolled on the bucking iron deck, his mind a blur of pain and colored fire. But his sudden terror was also very great and he struggled to his knees, then with his elbows—his hands were useless now—managed to pull himself up alongside the engineer's seat—he would unload on this side. The seconds leaked away as he made it to his feet. The first great leap of the engine had sent an ash scoop slithering across the floor and in his dizziness Murphy didn't see it. As he took a step his toe hooked under the curve in the scoop handle and brought the infernal instrument crosswise between his ankles. As he floundered in a great fall, this time toward the gate of the tender, he knew this was the end of the line. His lips got only as far as "Hail Mary! full of grace—" but the rest was there in his mind.

At first the men in the field couldn't see Murphy in the engine cab because of the acute angle. But when they moved farther out in the field and the engine moved back a little they caught an occasional glimpse of him. When the engine leaped into furious life, their pulses started hammering. They were collectively almost willing Murphy to jump, waiting breathlessly for him to hurtle through the cab opening—and all they could see was the engine gathering speed like a juggernaut. They yelled, all unconsciously, as though he could heed their advice—

"Hey—!"

"Murph! You crazy bastard!"

"The crazy galoot—"

Then part of Hell rose up and out from its supposed abode in the nether regions and the sound, so near, was so vast that none of the eight could afterward swear they actually *heard* it—compression or no compression, the car of powder charges went up instantaneously with the rest. The eight were literally lifted from the earth and then slammed back, like pins struck by the ball in bowling.

There was no longer engine, trestle or cars, only smoke, raining debris and a silence so great it almost hurt the ears.

"He mighta unloaded from the other side an' we didn't see him," someone said hopefully but without conviction.

"No." Gordon shook his head. He fumbled around on the ground for his missing hat. "One of us would have seen if he had." Conscious of an unfamiliar weight in a pocket, he drew out the big silver watch and stared at it curiously, thoughtfully. "It's exactly twenty minutes to nine—he was a good soldier. Well, we better get the hell back to town."

23

The Human Situation

Nothing like this had ever happened in or to Newton; nothing like it would again. The inhabitants had, not unnaturally, been variously amazed, panicked, and frightened, when the brigade moved into action just after daybreak. But the excitement had waned with time, or at least altered its character—a high emotional pitch can be maintained only so long at a time. The emotion diminished most markedly when it became evident that the marauders intended no harm to civilians as long as they minded their own business. In fact, quite the contrary. For while riders patrolled the streets and the outskirts of the town, when embers from the burning freight house set fire to the porch of a nearby residence, a hard-swearing officer had ordered a bucket brigade of troopers into action and doused the fire within minutes.

Once the tension had relaxed somewhat the Newtonians, most

of them, decided they might as well enjoy the catastrophe which wasn't their responsibility. Almost anyone will take oath that he abhors catastrophe as opposed to the public interest, but at most the denial is only half-true—else how account for the hordes of avid spectators at hangings, murder trials, fires, and floods? A man enjoys disaster if only for the satisfaction of knowing it isn't happening to *him*. These mud-encrusted Yankees, to be sure, were laying waste to the Southern Railroad with furious enterprise, but then nobody owns a railroad. Oh, certainly, somebody, somewhere, the always mysterious "they," owned it, but not anyone in Newton, and in any case a railroad is not a personal thing like a cow, a buggy, or an old washtub. Of course much of Newton publicly bemoaned the damage to their railroad but there was nothing personal in it.

In a slightly different way that was also true of their feeling about their own surrendered troops. There were two companies of a Georgia regiment under a youthful Major Rawlings. Hopelessly outnumbered, with five dead and thirteen wounded, the tight-lipped young major quit. Lieutenant Colonel Fairlie, of the Second, took the surrender and along with it exacted the parole of some eighty-odd officers and men—their arms were smashed into junk and tossed into the burning freight house. (Afterward the young major realized that under the tension of the moment he had been cozzened. They could have successfully refused parole if he had played a little better poker. For along with taking prisoners is the problem of keeping them, and if there was anything the brigade didn't want it was prisoners to mount, feed, and convoy. But when the major realized this his word had been passed.) Newton took the Confederate wounded into their homes as they would have the victims of a train wreck. These men had been here only two days, none was from the neighborhood or even known here, and on top of that they were *Georgians*. Newton felt sorry for the boys, of course, but there was nothing personal involved here either.

It should be added that, in one of those queer turns of warfare, the Second Illinois had suffered only two men killed and four wounded. So when Fairlie took the Georgia major's parole he also promptly loaned him the services of Surgeon Major Wells of the Second.

. . . With dispassionate curiosity Marlowe watched—contemplated, perhaps, would be more accurate—the busy scene of destruction. He had often marveled, especially since becoming part of war himself, at the tremendous difference in the time required to build a thing—anything—and the time needed to destroy it. It seemed to him there ought to be a constructive principle of some kind there if it could be isolated. Just now he was watching the boys work on the cotton warehouse; he had given specific orders about it when he learned it contained some four hundred bales. Cotton in bales was stubborn and peculiar stuff. Highly inflammable in the raw state, it burned like fury, but in bales under pressure it burned layer by layer and took a long time. In a tightly piled stack the bales tended to protect and insulate each other, and left alone, a solid stack of bales might burn for hours, even days. But this one wouldn't. The men were dragging the bales apart, upending and rearranging them so that the draughts would go through, under, and around them like a blast furnace. With cotton and building both set ablaze the heat would be so intense no one could get close enough to put it out, even if the brigade had to leave before it was finished. It was about ready now, in fact, the boys were already firing it at one end and men were climbing to the roof with axes, to chop more ventilating holes.

A grimy-faced sergeant saluted haphazardly and said, "Beg pardon, Colonel—"

"Oh—hello, Charley. What's on your mind?"

"Man here says he has to speak to the commanding general—says it's urgent."

"All right," Marlowe said. "I'll see him, especially since he's promoted me."

Sergeant Barry grinned, waved a careless hand, and the man came forward hurriedly.

"General—" he began.

"Colonel," Marlowe interrupted. "Colonel John Marlowe, commanding the First Cavalry Brigade of the First Division, Sixteenth Army Corps. We might as well keep the record as correct as possible."

He eyed the man with mild curiosity, though he knew the type well enough. Sixty, perhaps sixty-five, the man wore a carefully trimmed but slightly tobacco-stained white Vandyke and thin blue veins showed on the pale skin of his hands and face. He was wearing a suit of fine but now somewhat frayed tussore silk, but in his haste he had forgotten collar and tie.

"My name is Hasford, Colonel. I'm the local manager for Forrester & Larkin."

"Oh?" Marlowe's tone was courteous but cool.

"That cotton warehouse your men are firing is my—our—property, Colonel." Mr. Hasford mopped his forehead with a thin hand that trembled slightly. "I must point out to you, sir, that we are only forwarding agents and the cotton is entirely private property."

"I would have assumed as much if I'd bothered to consider the matter at all," Marlowe acknowledged, still polite. "But why go to this trouble to remind me, Mr. Hasford?"

"Why, sir, it occurred to me—" Mr. Hasford's dilemma was almost painfully obvious and he was also obviously too intelligent not to be aware of its several sides. He knew that in the circumstances he couldn't possibly gain by bluster or threat if Marlowe's mind was made up, but for his conscience' sake he had to make an effort for his principles. "Well, you see, Colonel, I was told your people had made an especial effort to keep a private residence from burning." He cast an anguished eye at the cotton fire that was now really getting a start. "As you see, Colonel, that cotton is in precisely the same category—private property, that is. I supposed you weren't aware of that."

Marlowe smiled faintly but there was no warmth in it. "I'd be a fool if I didn't appreciate your personal position, sir, but that hardly means I'm going to do anything about it—in your favor, that is. You know and I know that cotton is contraband wherever it's found in Rebel territory—"

"A clearly illegal fiat, sir, a whim, in territory where you have no jurisdiction."

The colonel hooked his thumbs casually in his belt. "Come, come, Mr. Hasford. You're too much my senior for me to try and explain the facts of life—and that's one of the chief failings of you people, your failure to recognize reality. The Federal Government has jurisdiction here as of this moment precisely to the extent that I hold it. Cotton is Federal contraband and I'm a Federal officer. It's as simple as that, Mr. Hasford."

The man made a strong effort to cover his near-anguish. "But, Colonel Marlowe, just as one gentleman to another, it occurs to me—"

Marlowe's eyes hardened suddenly. "Whatever it was, Mr. Hasford," he said bleakly, "you're mistaken. Now if you'll excuse me—I'm busy."

Hasford started to say something else, saw how obviously useless it was, and turned away.

Marlowe watched him go, feeling a little sorry for him—up to a point. He would not deliberately insult a man half again his age, though the man himself had come close to it on his side. In any case, there was always the duty. He moved his glance back to the oily, choking smoke now blooming above and around the warehouse. Hmm. Let's see—about four hundred bales, the boys said. Raw cotton, any grade, was worth at least forty cents on the New York market—possibly more, he hadn't paid any attention to firm quotations for months. Say $200 for an average bale, a minimum of $80,000 burning there across the tracks. Well, they should have thought of that—

Major Gray rode up from somewhere and dismounted. He slapped his hat against a leg, knocking off the dust. He nodded at the waste and said, "Well, we're getting on with the business."

"Better, maybe, than we had a right to expect."

"I'm having the men work to the east along the tracks. With Meridian in that direction, if anything moves out from there they'll be stopped just that much shorter of Newton here."

"Yes. I'd thought—"

The sound of everything in the world, this immediate world at least, was momentarily drowned in the audible (and presently visible) but unpremeditated immolation of Private Thomas Murphy, Second Illinois Volunteer Cavalry. They felt the following shock wave under their feet and in a nearby building the window glass rattled like dice.

"Good God!" Marlowe said softly.

Gray had started noticeably, but he said, "Judas! That was Fitz Gordon with his ammunition. Well, that's two carloads that Vicksburg'll never use."

"I hope— Never mind. How far out are your boys now?"

"Mmm—little over a mile, I'd say—when I left to come in. That's the point. How much farther do you want 'em to go?"

Marlowe consulted his watch. "Quarter of nine now. Suppose we let 'em go for another hour, or say ten o'clock, and then decide whether to pull 'em back in."

"Fair enough. And say, Jack"—Gray hesitated momentarily—"what the devil's all this about Keller?"

"We don't have to go into that now. There're other things more important than one man." Of course this had been bound to come up. Marlowe was obviously disturbed but just as obviously determined.

"All right," Gray said evenly—but he could be stubborn too. "You're the boss, Jack—don't misunderstand anything. But it also happens the man is in my specific command and an officer to boot."

"I didn't know he was a friend of yours," Marlowe said unthinkingly.

"That's no answer, and you know it," Gray said levelly.

"Whether he's a friend of mine—which he isn't, particularly—has no bearing."

Well, it was true, of course. So Marlowe told him, thinking, why not? Now as well as any other time. Then he threw his cigar stub savagely to the ground. "Not that I'd change it, but —well, God damn it, Dick!—what would *you* have done?"

"I'm—not sure," Gray said soberly. "In the circumstances, probably exactly what you did—if I'd had the guts. I've got a wife myself—but never mind that. Are you going to press the charge officially?"

"Why, cer—that's beside the point. Nothing can be done about it here anyway."

"I know. That's what makes it the more complicated."

"I'll handle it, Dick!" the colonel said finally.

"Sure—and thanks for explaining. Hell, if it'd been any other time that he did it—"

"But it wasn't. What would you expect me to do if when you rode up here a while ago you'd been too drunk to get out of the saddle? Not that Keller was drunk. If he had been it would at least have been an excuse of a sort."

"Still, you have to admit the situation was damned unusual, Jack."

"You're wrong," Marlowe said coldly. "I don't *have* to admit anything of the sort. I'm in no way responsible for the fact that women give birth, and at peculiar times and places. I am responsible for the men in this command. So, for that matter, are you. Furthermore, Keller is your man and your responsibility. As I said, he's technically under guard now and I want him kept that way. He's not to get out of sight at any time and I want him aware of his situation."

Gray was about to remark that, in their present situation, no man in his right mind would *want* to get out of sight of his fellows, but sensing Marlowe's mood accurately he left it unsaid. Instead, he shrugged almost invisibly and said, "Well, I've still got work to do. I'll see you in about an hour."

Marlowe looked around for an unseen Sergeant King.

Sergeant Andy Bullen, temporarily relieved from his point duty, had been assigned the task of burning the passenger depot. He could have done the job alone without any great trouble, but of course, army fashion, he had four men to help him—or to watch. Either way, Andy didn't particularly care.

They methodically kicked in the four outside doors, then wandered around inside, not looking for anything in particular, just desultorily examining a place they hadn't seen before. There was nothing unusual about it—just a duplicate of a thousand other country railroad depots. They kicked in the door to the office and didn't find anything special there either—the usual ticket rack, the telegraph desk by the trackside windows, a couple of signal lanterns, a shelf of batteries to supply telegraph power, a square iron safe, a wall clock, three battered but still sturdy chairs, a shelf containing dusty railroad paper forms and records. The boys weren't especially bent on stealing anything for themselves. Still, if they came on any small personal trinket that appealed to them they would have lifted it rather than let it go to waste in the fire—even if they would throw it away later. But there just wasn't anything here worth bothering about.

Private Pete Barker, sitting on the telegraph counter, had picked up a piece of scrap board on his way in. Now he began peeling long shavings from the board with a barlow knife. With some of this hardwood office stuff a man needed a pretty good starter. "Pull down them calendars," he said to no one in particular, "an' them paper pads off the shelf. Crumple an' wad the stuff up."

In the gents' and ladies' waiting rooms the boys threw up windows—nothing like plenty of cross ventilation. Little Willy Frick, a hardened old soldier of seventeen, sang, with fine vocal flourishes:

> Just before the battle, Mother,
> I was drinkin' mountain dew,

> When I saw the Rebs acomin',
> To the rear I quickly flew.

"You gonna do any flyin' to the rear from this here Godfor-saken place," the sergeant said dryly, "you better have eagle wings. I'll bet there ain't another outfit in the whole damn' army as far from home as this one. Ain't nobody else this crazy."

"Well, Mississippi don't look much different to me than Tennessee, except it ain't so steep up an' down an' we ain't eatin' as regular."

"Maybe we will for a day or two, son." Bullen nodded outside, where the supply men were sorting provision boxes and barrels, breaking open some and discarding others. "If the Old Man will leave us stop long enough to eat it. I got an idea that directly we're gonna leave here like a bat outta hell."

"Yeah, I guess so," Willy said indifferently. "Say, Sarge, it'd been about as easy to bust these windas."

Willy sang:

> Our Halleck's bound for Dixie, for Dixie, with
> a million boys or two.
> He'll never give up Dixie till she's back in
> the Union true—

It was some fifteen minutes later, when they had the building well ablaze, that a fat man came running up to them. He was obviously wrought up over something but he was so out of breath it took him a full minute to get anything said.

"Which—o'—you—gents—is the boss in charge here?"

"I am," Bullen said a little belligerently. "So what about it, Mister?"

"I'm—Roy—Mackey—station agent for the road."

"Well, now, is that so? Then you're gonna have a nice little vacation. The company won't be needin' your services for a few days anyhow. Nice weather for fishin'."

"I—I got to git in that office, boys," the fat man wheezed—he was gradually getting back to normal.

"What for—you got a bottle stashed in there? Maybe we didn't look hard enough."

"I tell you this ain't no jokin' matter, Mister! There's a thousand dollars in cash in there an' I got to git it!"

"Great Godalmighty! A thousand dollars!" Andy exclaimed. "Why didn't you say so, man? Whereabouts is it?"

"In the safe, in the ticket office."

Andy whirled, ran to the wall of the office, and thrust his head into the smoke. Then he turned and yelled, "Come on, boys, c'mon! It's a little thick in there but we kin still make it!"

With that he went in over the window sill and the others followed as the children after the Hamelin piper. All but Mr. Mackey —he was too fat to go through the window opening.

Leaving aside the matter of motive, which was not a prime factor here in the beginning, it would appear that Sergeant Bullen and his men were functioning above and beyond the call of duty. They would have said so, had they thought about it at all, although their first reaction was brought about by something quite different.

Yet this whole rescue operation will bear some closer scrutiny. For consider. Bullen and company were at the moment engaged, cheerfully engaged, in destroying a building worth, with the furniture and telegraph equipment, some $5,000. A freight house worth perhaps $15,000 was already gone. So was rolling stock with a replacement value of more than $40,000. Their comrades in arms were busily tearing up track and telegraph line worth, conservatively, another $40,000. In a nutshell, the brigade was engaged in destroying at least $100,000 worth of railroad, not only without a single twinge of conscience—unthinkable, but with a fine feeling of duty well done. Nor had a single voice been raised in protest regarding the railroad proper. Not even Agent Mackey had questioned the destruction of the building where he had spent half his life. No, the mysterious, commonplace, magic word was *money*.

A man may stand by and watch the holy icons destroyed and he thinks: Well, regrettable, to be sure, but after all they can be replaced. But money? Ah!

So Bullen and the boys heaved, tugged, wrestled, kicked, jerked, pulled, and pushed, and otherwise managed with colossal effort to maneuver the iron safe out of the burning building. In the process they were burned and blistered, half-suffocated, their hair, eyebrows, and beards singed, their clothing scorched, and Willy Frick got a hand badly smashed between safe and doorjamb. Completely fagged, they hustled the iron box outside and in the clear of the now-blazing depot.

"By God, boys!" Andy panted triumphantly. "That was close! The iron sonofabitch is hot as a dollar pistol. Where's that fat slob of an agent?"

But Mackey was right there. He produced a big key and unlocked the box, and piled a mixture of Confederate currency, Federal greenbacks (the South was becoming more and more attached to the currency of its erstwhile enemies), and silver into a flour sack. The rescue squad looked on as proudly as though they'd just been elected to office.

"That sure was one close call an' I'm sure obliged to you boys, I shorely am. Five, ten minutes more an' the stuff might've been singed to a crisp. Well, I'd better be gettin' the stuff to a safe place," Mackey wheezed.

It was then that Sergeant Bullen came back to life. "Why, you damned shyster!" he roared. He rammed a Colt barrel into the startled agent's fat midriff. "Where the hell you think you goin' with that money?"

"Why, Mister, you know mighty well this's the propity of the Southern Railroad. As its duly an' properly authorized agent—"

"You Rebel jackass! Gimme that sack!"

Perhaps Mr. Mackey should have had credit for trying. But again maybe not—nobody gets credit for breathing instinctively. Being completely objective, and strictly on the evidence, it would appear that the rescue action was sheer idiocy—yet in an insane world the sane man is mad. When Sergeant Bullen dutifully and proudly handed the money over to his superior, Captain Landry, the latter said, "Damned nice work, Andy—mighty nice."

And when Landry handed the money on to Major Dick Gray, the major said, "By God! some of those boys of yours never miss a lick, Landry. Tell Sergeant Bullen I won't forget this."

So maybe there wasn't anything odd about it.

Mentally the colonel tallied the results of the morning's work: a $100,000 or so in the destroyed cotton warehouse, another $100,-000 or so in destroyed railroad property, destruction of badly needed Confederate supplies in an amount impossible to calculate. Moreover, the cost to the Confederacy could not actually be computed in dollars—even more important was the time and difficulty involved in replacement. Railroad iron and telegraph wire, for example, were next to impossible to obtain in the Confederate South at any price. So perhaps no one would ever accurately calculate the full military effect of this morning's destruction at Newton.

There was also the matter of casualties to the Georgia infantry and their subsequent parole, but Marlowe was aware that this was hardly important militarily. It would get into his report, supposing he was fortunate enough ever to get as far as a report, but it was hardly of earth-shaking consequence.

On the face of it he—they—had so far succeeded better than anyone, from Corps Headquarters down, had had any right to expect. Yet at the moment Marlowe had no especial feeling of elation, the supposedly normal emotion in the circumstances. Oh, to be sure he would rather have succeeded than failed, but he certainly had no feeling of great achievement. This might be a purely personal reaction but he suspected that other commanders, at least on occasion, felt this way. Well, this was no time for weighty reflections on what had already been done. As he had reminded Dick Gray, it was possible that this was the easiest half of this thing.

At least one problem had been disposed of, or at any rate dealt with—the wounded. They were going back north, to La Grange (Marlowe sincerely hoped) in wagons well cushioned with hay and blankets, with Captain Brant and K Company of the First as convoy. Left here, even in willing hands, they were certain to be prisoners in a matter of hours—that much was sure. In consideration of the rights of the majority he couldn't jeopardize the "safety" of the brigade with this added burden, and yet these men were entitled to no less than a chance to get out, whatever chance he was able to give them. A chance, for that matter, was all any of them had now.

He had put it to Captain Brant fairly as he saw it, trying not to exaggerate one way or another.

"You're in for no joy ride, but I think you've got at least an even chance to make it. You shouldn't have to worry about grub for a week—that's roughly the time it took us to get this far. With what may lay ahead of the rest of us I don't dare spare either Dr. Wells or Keller, but I'm going to give you Major Keller's medical orderly, Meigs."

"That'll be a help, sir. I know Meigs—he's all right. That'd worry me more'n any other part of the deal—looking after the hurt men, I mean."

The colonel sighed vaguely, looked thoughtful. "I know this is a tough assignment. I wouldn't relish it myself; nobody in his right mind would. But somebody has to do the job, Brant. I couldn't think of a better man."

"Well, thanks," Brant said with a certain woodenness. "As you say, somebody has to do it. I don't mind, honest." Captain Brant was a ripe old twenty-three.

"As I said," the colonel went on, "I really think you have at least an even chance to get through. Unless I miss my guess, all hell is apt to break loose around here before too long. Meridian and Jackson simply can't afford to ignore the mess we've made here. But if I was a Reb I wouldn't waste my time on a small convoy of wounded when I had the brigade to chase. It's an even bet they'll ignore you. The main thing, I think, is for you to get out of town and on your way as soon as you can."

"Just so they don't mistake me for the brigade—"

"They're not that stupid—I hope for your sake."

"Well—sir, suppose they *do* try to take me . . .?"

Marlowe sighed. "There's only one thing I can possibly tell you, Brant—use your own judgment."

"Very well, sir. One other thing—"

"Which one—out of many?"

"I was just thinking of that nice long bridge over the Pearl River, the one we burned."

"I know," Marlowe said shortly, "but it had to be done. It's trouble, yes, but not trouble we could very well foresee. If I were you I'd try to find another crossing farther west—to take you away from the line of the M. & O." The colonel consulted his watch a little impatiently and a little pointedly. "It's ten-fifteen, Brant. You'd better get moving. We'll be pulling out in about an hour. That will give you a little start. Not much, but some—make the most of it."

Brant saluted with a grimy hand. He had as active an imagination as the average man and right now he didn't expect much good of the immediate future. A few days ago (when was it, anyway? time seemed to have fallen apart), they had, most of them, mentally written off A Company. Was it K Company's turn now?

The local tavern was little more than a glorified boardinghouse but it did have a small liquor bar. Marlowe dropped a greenback on the counter. "Just leave the bottle here, Mister."

"My God!" Secord breathed wearily. "I'd sit down but I doubt that I'd ever get up again."

"Better not then," Marlowe said. "Your men all back in now?"

Both Gray and Secord nodded and Gray chuckled grimly. "The Rebs will be huntin' rails and telegraph wire from now on, Jack. I figure we tore up about four miles before we finally quit. Found a hundred-foot bridge just east of town too. But gentlemen, if you ask me, there's gonna be some mighty irritated people around here before long—and I don't mean civilians."

"I figure we've been borrowing time for two or maybe three hours already," Marlowe agreed.

The proprietor had been elaborately busy doing nothing but obviously keeping his ears open, and when Marlowe said, "You, there, Mister!" he came up with alacrity.

"Yes suh!"

"How far is it to Meridian?"

"Why, 'bout thutty mile, give or take a mite."

"Hmm. I see. Road runs directly there, I suppose?"

"Why, more or less, as the feller says. You follow right on out this street here, straight out. At the edge o' town she crosses over to the south o' the railroad but from there it mostly follows along it."

"About a six- or seven-hour ride," Marlowe observed almost carelessly, as though half-talking to himself. Then, sharply, "Many of you people's troops there in Meridian?"

The man shrugged and spread his hands. "Now, Gen'l, I jes' wouldn't know about that, for a fact. Personally, I ain't been there for a couple months an' we don't get much news like that here. Soldiers goin' an' comin' a good bit on the cars but we don't never know much about where they been or where they goin'."

"No, I suppose not," Marlowe agreed—it was probably true enough. "Well, it doesn't make much difference. We'll be joining up with another column around Meridian anyway."

This was, of course, the sheerest hogwash, meant only for the barman's ears. If the man wasn't taken in, why no harm would be done anyway.

"I see," Marlowe said again, apropos of nothing in particular. "Well, much obliged, Mister. Sorry we had to bust up your railroad, but then it's your war too."

"Well, I reckon so," the man agreed. "Leastwise we *got* it on our hands."

Hard to know how to take these fellas. These three were obviously officers and they were certainly running this foofaraw, but they were also three of the dirtiest, roughest, savage-looking characters he had ever seen in one place. The first word around was that they were bent on burning the entire town, and then it turned out that nothing remotely like that actually happened. And here they not only paid but overpaid for the liquor they drank and didn't even bother to take the bottle with them, when obviously they could have drunk his liquor for nothing had they chose. Certainly he had not been prepared to argue the point. It was all a little confusing.

They had a last round and returned to the street.

"I've been figuring up, in case anybody's interested," Secord said. "As of now it's just about thirty hours since anybody's had any sleep. Thirty hours, over fifty miles, and a lot of damned hard work. As usual I'm not trying to tell you your business, Jack, but the flesh can only take so much, mine included."

"It'll have to take a little more, just the same," Marlowe said, "including yours. Right now the thing we need most between us and Newton is distance, the more the better. The horses, most of them, thank God, have had some rest here—not enough of the right kind but still rest. Well, find a bugler and let's get on the road again. We'll take the Meridian road out of town for the sake of appearances, then we'll see. The day's young yet, gentlemen—and they'll ride because they have to!"

Five miles east of Newton they swung abruptly south, through Garlandville, and then somewhat to the southwest. At dusk they were still on their feet but literally staggering, with horses becoming more and more unwilling. Some men, perhaps the lucky ones, had slept in their saddles for hours. More had reached the state of exhaustion where jumping nerves made relaxation impossible. Marlowe himself dozed occasionally but his will always drove him awake again within moments. Calculating again from the tattered map, he was astonished to find that, when they passed through Garlandville, they had covered more than sixty-five miles since yesterday morning.

. . . In the fast-falling dusk Marlowe had been dozing, a slab of hard bread forgotten in his grimy fingers. He came to with a start, the pungent, familiar odor assailing his nostrils sharply. He blinked, getting Sergeant King in focus. The sergeant was hunched at his small cooking fire, nursing the two coffee pails—tin cans with improvised wire bails, his and the colonel's—which were a part of every trooper's equipment. The sergeant looked like a wolf tired from being chased all day by relays of hounds.

The colonel grinned faintly as he said, "All right, Sergeant, where'd you steal it?" There had been no coffee for three days now. "Not that I give a damn—I'm just curious."

"Now them's strong words, Colonel," the sergeant said in a mock-hurt tone. "This coffee is proper enemy supplies. It took some huntin' but I finally found it in a box marked General J. C. Pemberton, Jackson Headquarters, C.S.A., Personal an' Private Stores—"

THE PURSUIT

So great was the consternation created by this raid that it was impossible to obtain any reliable information of the enemy's movements, rumor placing him in various places at the same time.

> *From Lieutenant General J. C. Pemberton's*
> *official report of the Vicksburg Campaign.*

Confederate troops did descend on Newton from both east and west, Meridian and Jackson, in fact those from Meridian arrived little more than an hour after the brigade had turned south away from the railroad. But it was no more than the usual barn-locking gesture. They were only a small infantry force which of course had to detrain several miles east of town, where the good rail line ended, and they had no chance of catching a cavalry brigade, even had they known where to begin looking for it. Meridian had already been stripped of the bulk of its available troops—particularly those sent north on the M. & O. and tem-

porarily isolated at Macon by A Company. These troops under General Loring were still busily looking for the brigade where it was not.

For a time it was even believed in some responsible quarters that reports of the havoc at Newton were just another false alarm— every other alarm thus far had proved to be false.

From the Confederate point of view, especially that of the officers personally hunting the phantom brigade of horse, it would have been much better if General Pemberton had confined himself to the immediate defense of Vicksburg. For here on the ground the responsible officers were buffeted between what common sense dictated they do in order to intercept the brigade and what Pemberton, in natural anxiety and from a great distance, tele- graphed they must *do.*

In fact, Pemberton's orders flew like carnival confetti and with about as much lethal effect. It was true that he was a man sorely beset on all sides, but even so—

One of his more fanciful notions was that Marlowe somehow intended to seize and occupy Jackson, the state capital, and he exhorted Governor Pettus to call the citizenry there to arms. There is no record of what he thought Marlowe would possibly want with Jackson, even supposing he was able to take it. On the other hand, and in especial contradiction to the Jackson notion, Pemberton, like Hurlbut, assumed that Marlowe would try to re- turn more or less as he had come, through northern Mississippi. To head that off—after the surprise debacle at Newton the ap- prehension of the brigade also became a matter of saving personal face and allaying the fears of the civilian population—he ordered Chalmers and 1,500 cavalry, from Panola, on the Mississippi Cen- tral Railroad, all the way across to Okolona, on the line of the M. & O. (Fortunately for Colonel Blaney, by the time Chalmers got there the Second Iowa, crippled and battered as it was, was already thirty miles to the north and almost back to La Grange.) Tilghman was ordered from Canton eastward to Carthage, nearer to Marlowe's supposed return route; and Featherston's brigade was moved from Fort Pemberton on the Yazoo River to Granada for the same reason. One of the few things all this proved was Marlowe's original contention that, after the first few days, it would be easier for him to fly than move the brigade back the way they had come, or by way of northern Alabama either.

Far to the south, in the boot of Louisiana, just in case, Gardner on the twenty-fourth, the day Marlowe struck Newton, was ordered eastward from Port Hudson to Tangipahoa, on the New Orleans & Jackson Railroad; and from Ponchatoula, south almost to the shore of Lake Pontchartrain above New Orleans, Simonton was ordered north to join Gardner. Probably at no other time in this bitter four-year contest were so many set to catch so few— and with such poor luck. By the time he struck Newton the Confederate actually engaged in hunting Marlowe could have eaten the brigade's horses at one sitting.

Marlowe could never remember exactly when he had made the decision (on that long-ago night in Memphis, perhaps?), but he had known for a long time that wherever he was going, it wasn't back to northern Mississippi.

24

Bryce Again

Bryce, in the beginning, took for granted that A Company would overtake the column. It would hardly be as simple as a trip to the post office but it would be done. (Like Marlowe, Bryce was still surprised at the continued rough, rolling nature of the country—he too supposed that it would flatten out a little down here.) There was the inexorable arithmetic of distance, but of course Colonel Marlowe had been right when he pointed out that A Company, with thirty-odd men, was far more mobile than the brigade.

Being constituted as he was, Bryce believed in canvassing the prospects of every situation. Admittedly he might not come up with the right answer—there were almost always the unknown factors —but it wasn't because he rushed into things blindly. So now he was feeling his way, or, more accurately, thinking it ahead. The problem was not only to catch the brigade but themselves stay uncaught.

As for A Company, they did not regard Captain Bryce as an omniscient superman—they were hardly as unsophisticated as that. They didn't think General Grant was omniscient either, in fact they knew better. But had the question arisen, Asa Bryce would have been re-elected company commander without a dissenting vote. It is a commonplace that soldiers become accustomed to obedience to orders and discipline, but beyond obeying orders they also come to rely on them. So it was with A Company. They supposed, and had a right to suppose, that Captain Bryce knew more about the plans and intentions of the Old Man than they did. That's the way it should be. Well, Bryce did know more than A Company at large, but—a thing there was no reason to explain —that wasn't saying too much. Marlowe had said that, after Newton, he did not know exactly where the brigade would go; he wasn't certain of anything except that they wouldn't be turning back. If Bryce hadn't rejoined the brigade by Newton, then it would be up to him to find them. The brigade would not willingly leave for the Rebels any more trail than could be helped; neither would they leave one for A Company.

Within the limits of individual personality, veterans tend to become fatalists, the invisible powers always made the decisions anyway—thus A Company. They would follow Captain Bryce without question as long as he was in the saddle. But more than that, and without either of them being altogether aware of it, the captain would also carry them a little.

This area of Noxubee and Neshoba counties was one of the most sparsely settled in all Mississippi. Still moving cross country, probing for the open spaces in the sometimes almost impenetrable forest, and skirting the worst hills, after leaving the Negro shack where the woman had made them the johnnycake, they rode until dark without seeing another human being. Hungry though hardly starving (yet), they spent the night of April 23–24 camped in deep timber, far short of Philadelphia. With the rough and roundabout going they had covered less distance than Bryce had supposed. It was also farther from Macon to Philadelphia than he had guessed, relying only on his memory of Marlowe's map.

It was during these hours, of course, that the brigade outdistanced them still more, the result of its all-night ride through Decatur to Newton.

If Bryce's timing was a little off, his navigation was pretty good —they struck the brigade's trail a little above Philadelphia in midafternoon of the twenty-fourth. Bryce and Rogers talked it over and decided it was simple prudence to go around the town rather than through it—the passing of the brigade *might* have left the inhabitants in a mood that would do a lone company no good. Later this night they made a dark and hungry bivouac some miles below Philadelphia, at almost exactly the same moment the brigade was making an exhausted camp between Garlandville and Raleigh. If Bryce had known that some sixty-odd miles now separated A Company from the brigade, and that in between the line of the Southern now swarmed with Rebel troops—but he didn't know.

Before they bedded down and there was still a little light, Bryce got hold of Sergeant Nate Brown and said, "Got your repair stuff with you, Nate?"

"Sure, I always got it, Cap'n. What do you need?" Nate sounded a little as though he had a mouthful of hot mush but at the moment Bryce didn't remark the fact.

Besides being more or less official farrier for the First, Nate was general repairman for A Company. Naturally clever with his hands, he was called upon to fix everything from missing buttons and insignia to loose bootheels.

"I just noticed when I unsaddled that I've got a stirrup leather almost worn in two."

"Yeah," Nate agreed, examining the leather, "could have throwed you good. I'll lay a couple short splices on top and bottom an' double rivet 'em."

"I wouldn't bother you, Nate, except—"

"Shucks, that's all right, Cap'n. It's got to be fixed—dangerous. Could bust your neck—or somethin' more important if you dropped on 'em in the saddle."

Bryce realized then that Nate's voice was more personally miserable than merely weary, and that wasn't normal with the sergeant. Bryce frowned, peered more closely at him, and said suddenly, "Say, what's the matter with you, Nate?"

The sergeant turned so Bryce could see the other side of his face and said, "Aw, it's this sonofabitchin' toothache, Cap'n." His left jaw was swollen prodigiously, and that, together with the whiskers and dirt, made him look something like a lopsided gorilla.

Strangely, Bryce had an almost uncontrollable desire to laugh. Not at what was obviously a brutally ulcerated tooth, of course, but at the macabre humor of the larger situation—something like a man going into battle while worrying about whether his hat was on straight and his boots properly polished. Even then Bryce couldn't conceal a mild grin.

"I know how God-damn' funny it must look," the sergeant said doggedly, "but it don't feel that way."

"Oh, hell, Nate," Bryce said with instant contrition, "actually I was thinking of something else—of that little nigger kid in heat yesterday afternoon."

"Yeah—oh, Jesus, Cap'n, don't make me laugh—the damn' thing hurts worse'n ever when I do. I thought I'd bust too, for a fact. It was worth the price of a ticket. Still, I wouldn't 'a' come all the way to Mississippi just to see it. Fact is, right now I'd just as soon I'd passed up this war an' waited for the next one."

"Who doesn't? Well, I just happened to think—" Bryce rummaged in a saddlebag and came up with a half-filled flat pint of whisky. "See if that helps any—it's all I've got." He winked. "Medical supplies, naturally."

"Well, naturally." Nate drank from the bottle as though it held lemonade. "Aaaah! That sure helps *me* whether it does anything for the tooth or not."

"It's probably not the best whisky in the world," Asa said apologetically. "I'm not much of a judge."

"Well," Nate said judiciously, "there ain't any real bad whisky, you might say. It's just that some brands're better'n others."

"Finish it up, Nate. Not enough there to hurt anybody."

"Well, thanks, Cap'n! I was just thinkin'—I s'pose you figger to post a guard?"

"Actually I don't think it's really necessary, and I wish I didn't have to, Nate, but at the same time—?"

"All right. I'll take it—"

"It's not your turn—"

Nate shrugged. "I know. I ain't givin' anything away free, Cap'n, but hell, I'll never get any sleep with this jaw anyway. So—"

"Fair enough then." Bryce wouldn't haggle over it. He simply added, "I'll appreciate it. But if you get to the place where you think you can sleep, then put a couple of other men on it. They'll have had some rest by then anyway."

"There's one thing—I'll have to have a little fire for light enough to patch that strap."

"Well—use your own judgment, but keep it small and as much out of sight of the road as possible."

As a generality, Bryce reflected, men like these were hard to whip. The trouble was, there were just as many like them on the other side.

He couldn't sleep, not right away. That the ground under the blankets was hard was of no moment; it was just that he couldn't relax. They were off the road a short distance—unlike the brigade they couldn't afford to stand on their numerical strength, they hardly more than outnumbered a strong sheriff's posse. Another thing was that he kept hearing things which cold reason told him weren't there at all. . . .

There were others also unable to relax and let go. Sprawled on the ground with their eyes closed, they still rolled in the saddle, like sailors just ashore after a hundred-day winter Cape Horn passage. Somewhere in the darkness—it was full dark now—a mouth organ played softly and presently a not very good voice joined in:

> The years creep slowly by, Lorena,
> The snow is on the grass again;
> The sun's low down the sky, Lorena,
> The frost gleams where the flow'rs have been.

A voice—Bryce recognized it as Sergeant Brown's—said savagely, "Shut it off, you two! The God-damned Johnnies can hear that yowlin' a mile away!"

But Bryce noticed that the order hadn't come until the verse had ended.

Presently he slept, dreaming, drifting in that state of subconscious suspension where one dreams and simultaneously is aware of and observes the dreaming with a singular detachment. . . . Professor Asa Bryce, 10 A.M., Room 206, Farnsworth Hall, Monday, Wednesday, and Friday—he doesn't really see the faces of the class once it settles down and gives him its alleged attention—his chair swivels round and through the open windows, in that wonderful spring just before Sumter, there is the smell of first-cut grass, a squirrel chases another frantically in the branches of a towering New England elm in Illinois . . . the ancient words borrowed—well, all right, lifted bodily then, from the stately paragraphs of Thucydides . . . and the professor would shortly come to know that this was not merely the record of an ancient war, but the thing itself rendered into words: ". . . When the day dawned Nicias led forward his army, and the Syracusans and their allies assailed them on every side, hurling javelins and other missiles at them. The Athenians hurried on to the river Assinarus. They hoped to gain a little relief if they forded the river, for the mass of horsemen and other troops overwhelmed and crushed them; and they were worn out by fatigue and thirst. But no sooner did they reach the river than they lost all order and rushed in . . . the Peloponnesians came down the bank and slaughtered them, falling chiefly upon those who were in the river. Where-upon the water became foul, but was drunk all the same, although muddy and dyed with blood, and the soldiers fought for it . . . the rain came down like solid water and the only way the thunder could be distinguished from the slamming bah-*loom!* of the ten-inch Columbiads on the gunboats was by the colors in the watery sky. The lightning, of course, was a flashing electric blue while the lingering muzzle flashes were a pale orange. The steamboats, with fire blooming from the chimneytops and open firedoors, kept pulling in there at Pittsburgh Landing, and out again, and one wondered how the pilots (of course they were civilians, the best of their kind in the world) could see a hand before their faces, much less manage a landing in this watery blackness—though the lightning flashes helped a little. The infantry kept pouring off the boats and heading up that slippery trough of soupy mud which led to the top of the bluff. Now and then a man cursed wearily as he slipped and fell and the officers kept on snarling monotonously, "Close up! Close up!" of course quite without effect. "Buell's men," someone said. "Where in Christ's sweet name have they been?" Not that it made any difference now that they were here and Don Carlos Buell—if that wasn't a hell of a name for a Yankee general—but all the same he was all that saved our ass that second day at Shiloh even if he was late . . ." When the professor paused a bucktoothed country youth in the front row said politely, "Uh, beg pardon, Professor, but I'm—uh, taking notes and just now I'm a little confused about which war this is. It seems to me, sir—" And Professor Bryce said angrily: "*Which* war? Why, God damn your hopelessly ignorant soul! I'm talking about *the* war. What other war do you think there is?"

He came awake with a start that brought his torso half-erect and was dimly aware that his muscles had been taut as piano strings. A restless horse stamped and sneezed, the sharp odor of pine boughs was in his nostrils, and overhead a falling star shown whitely nine (ninety?) million miles down the dark backdrop of the southern sky. Then the captain turned over and slept like one of the million billion dead.

25

Private Schwartz' War

It was the day the brigade covered the shortest distance, a miserable nine miles. They had spent the night only fifteen miles below the line of the wrecked Southern. Marlowe chafed at that— it was too close by far—but nothing could be done about it. (They had also been camped within four miles of a place called, of all things, Lorena.) He could demand so much of the men and animals and then it was only common sense to end it abruptly, not try to wring a few hours more from a machine that was only too obviously running down. Since they had to have a letdown then let it be now and as complete as possible—against the day when he very likely would have to demand even more of them, quite probably for their own sake.

For a change there was again plenty of food on hand. They had been too exhausted to make much use of it the night before, but they made up for it the next morning, when it appeared actually true that the Old Man was going to give them a little time. So what with one thing and another it was near noon when they got under way—the longest rest anyone had had in eight days.

Marlowe's mind was made up now: it was to be Baton Rouge. The Rebels, at last meager report, still had posts as far down on the Mississippi as Port Hudson, and in south-central Louisiana–Mississippi as far south as the northern shore of Lake Ponchartrain. Federal forces had held New Orleans for almost a year but, except as far up the river as Baton Rouge, hadn't made much progress in extending their hold on the rest of Louisiana. Now for the brigade Marlowe had decided it would be Baton Rouge or nothing. Once here in southwestern Mississippi, which they were in fact, there was almost no place else they could go.

Sergeant Bullen, pleased with his work of the day before and the commendation it had brought, was back on the long point again—by choice.

Captain Landry had commented on this point to Major Gray. "It was and is a volunteer proposition and the Old Man agreed to rotate the job. But Andy don't want to be rotated. Personally, I think he's just bein' a brave man in capital letters—or maybe it's plain bullheadedness—something like his name. You know—give a man a temporary detail he don't like for any reason and you're a dirty bastard for pushing it off on him; if for some crazy reason he happens to like it then he thinks it's his by natural right. But I don't see that it makes any great difference here. Andy's done all right and I don't see any reason to pull him off if he wants to stay out there."

"All right then, neither do I," Gray agreed. "It's not worth wasting words over. If he wants to keep his neck stuck out, why then let him."

So Sergeant Bullen was again out on the long point, but this time with two new men. Private Dorsey, who had wanted to be relieved chiefly because the Old Man had said they would be, had gotten his wish, pressed down and running over. After a completely uneventful week on a duty deemed hazardous enough to warrant volunteers, Dorsey had been one of the first men killed instantly in the attack at Newton. Private Moore had withdrawn for personal reasons having nothing to do with pushing his luck. It was simply that a week was enough.

Now Sergeant Bullen was supported by Corporal Dan Frost, a taciturn but experienced noncom whom Andy took for granted as his personal peer, and a youth the sergeant had never paid much attention to.

Andy said a little dourly, as though expecting the worst, "What's your name, bud?"

"Private Bernhard Schwartz, sir."

"Aw, owl dung," Andy said inelegantly. "I know you been around long enough to know I don't rate that sir stuff. Fact is, I won't stand for it, bud. But Godalmighty damn! From here on in you're plain Dutch. How about that, Dan?"

Corporal Frost shrugged. He knew Andy's big mouth and didn't much care for it but still it didn't do any real harm. "If he don't care then I sure don't. Dutch or Mabel, what's the difference?"

"Mabel?—say, that's a good one. But anyhow, how the hell can you go around yellin' for somebody named Bernhard?" Andy argued, though obviously nobody was arguing with him.

"Aw, that's all right, Sarge," young Schwartz said. "Some of 'em call me Dutch all the time anyway. But you ast me my name an' I—"

"Yeah, yeah! Say, Dutch, you got a spare piece of eatin' tobacco on you?"

"Why, no, I ain't," Dutch said apologetically. "I ain't never used it."

At that Andy just grunted. Landry *would* send him a greenhorn like this.

As for Private Schwartz, he was very happy to be here but he had smartened up enough now not to show it in public. He had braved official wrath in order to make this trip at all and so far it had turned out to be nothing but hard riding without rest or sleep and either being half-hungry all the time or really hungry half the time. He wouldn't have minded all this if it had included some real soldiering. At the Battle of Newton—which of course would go into the records as a mere skirmish—he hadn't even had a chance to fire his carbine; older hands had seen to it that he was put with the horse detail. Now this was more like it. He was hardly winning the war on his own, he knew that well enough, but all the same this was something important. They didn't ask for volunteers for nothing. He sure wished he had some eating tobacco to offer the sergeant. Up home now Paw—Papa—had been violently opposed to the use of tobacco in any form, had forbidden it to the family in fact, chiefly on the all-important ground that it cost money.

. . . Here west and south of Newton the ground suddenly stopped rolling and became relatively flat, though the road still curved endlessly. The country was still heavily timbered, mostly with pine, with here and there an open stretch, and the earth changed from the flame red to what seemed to the men from Illinois a more natural earth color. Schwartz wondered where in this country you found the magnificent plantation establishments, with their hordes of slaves, that he'd heard so much about—certainly he could count those he had seen on his fingers and they weren't so fancy at that. . . .

The farm wasn't much of a place but it was the first they'd seen for an hour. Andy reined in at a little distance and looked the place over with a practiced eye—a nondescript unpainted house, a couple of lean-to sheds, a leaning barn which stood about sixty yards from the house. But there was a well between house and barn and Andy said, "Sure a piss-pore looking place but I reckon we may as well water while we got the chance. No tellin' how far it is to the next one."

Actually water, water fit to drink, was not too easily come by in this country. There were streams, to be sure, but they were usually either high and muddy or sluggish and muddy. There were clear springs in plenty but they were seldom at the roadside in plain view and were never easy for a stranger to find.

There was no fence along the road so they simply rode diagonally across the yard toward the well. Neither Bullen nor Frost was exactly sure of what happened next.

A man emerged from somewhere at the rear of the house and ran for the barn like a scared rabbit, at the same time yelling, "Joe! Harry! Hey, there—!"

Andy managed part of a "What the hell—?" when the rifle cracked at the barn. But Andy recognized the Confederate uniform, such as it was, and the cap, and so did Frost. The runner was apparently unarmed but to Andy the connection between the runner and the shot was only too clear—painfully so. Andy's horse sank slowly to its knees and then even as it rolled over Andy was off and dragging his carbine from the boot. The animal seemed to hesitate momentarily, then heaved a great breath and dropped woodenly on its side. Andy instinctively went to the ground behind his fallen horse but even as he did so he yelled, "Dutch! You damn' fool! Get down." He flipped a shot at the runner, almost to the barn now, thought the man staggered but he wasn't sure—he might only have stumbled. At any rate the man made the shelter of the barn door.

Corporal Frost jammed home his spurs savagely, whirled and made for the shelter of a house corner in a matter of seconds.

But Private Schwartz was caught in a sudden fog of indecision and inexperience. At that first rifle shot he had reached for his carbine, but when Andy yelled "Get down!" he had stayed his hand and instead started to dismount. In fact, he had risen in the saddle, his weight on his left leg in the stirrup, when the second shot exploded. Balanced in midair, his right leg just coming across the animal's hindquarters, a perfect target, the bullet literally knocked him clear of the saddle. There was no pain, just a thudding shock, as though someone had struck him in the chest with a vigorous but friendly fist. He slammed to the ground on his left side, but, strangely, he didn't much feel that either. Then he rolled over on his back and wondered, but only for a second out of eternity, why the blue spring sky had suddenly turned black.

Without taking his eyes from the barn Andy called, "You there, Dan?"

"Yeah, I made it. What the hell you reckon's goin' on here?"

"I dunno yet—whatever it is they ain't foolin'."

Frost said, "Damn!" as a bullet tore splinters from the corner of the house, but high.

His face pressed close to the hot hair of the horse's barrel, Andy took careful aim at a spot on the left side of the open door. Chips flew but he couldn't see that anything else happened. Up to now Andy hadn't had time to think, he had reacted instinctively out of long experience, but now he saw there was something mighty complicated here. He was sure the runner wore a Confederate uniform, and so presumably whoever else was in the barn with him was in the same category. But still, why this blasting away without any preliminaries? *They* were in civilian dress and couldn't have been identified otherwise at any distance, and it didn't make sense that soldiers would ambush their own civilian compatriots. They might have scouted the column and so knew that Bullen and the others were actually an advance, but that hardly made sense either. There were no horses in sight (of course they could be inside the barn), so how could they have scouted the column and still have arrived here ahead of the advance? And if they had merely wanted to stage an ambush they had passed up a dozen far better places in the last two miles of road. Mighty peculiar.

"I'm gonna work around to the back side of the house," Frost called cautiously—he was only about fifteen yards from Andy's barricade. "See if I can do any better from there."

Andy felt the bullet snatch hungrily at his jacket sleeve and saw smoke at a loft window. "Well," he called calmly, "see if you can handle that sonofabitch upstairs. He's above me an' that last one was too close. He's got the angle on me an' I can't get no closer to the ground without diggin' a hole."

"Keep your shirt on—I'm goin'."

Andy fired again at the darker bulk alongside the door and then grunted a satisfied "Uh-huh!" The man's body fell across the opening, against the opposite doorjamb, then slumped face down across the threshold.

Somewhere inside the house a child burst into terrified crying and Andy thought, "Well, by God! What next?" Another slug from the loft smacked into his barrier of flesh. Then somewhere to the left and behind him Frost's carbine cracked and splinters leaped from the frame of the loft window. Frost fired with steady concentration, laying a pattern around the window. At this range the heavy-calibered Sharps' slugs went through the old wood of the barn like cheese. (A good many of the men in the First carried the six-seven shot Spencer repeating carbines, even though the magazine had a dangerous habit of exploding. Those who preferred them carried the single-shot but more reliable Sharps'.) The rifle in the loft barked again, and this time Andy knew the man had shifted for a crack at Frost.

Odd how a man can get so wrapped up in his own immediate concerns—Andy had literally forgotten about the brigade. In fact, he didn't remember until the hoofs suddenly hammered in the road behind him—the head of the column had been less than ten minutes away—and B and C companies came storming up, Major Gray in the lead. Even as Gray snapped, "What the devil's coming off here, Andy?" a man, the runner, with a bloody leg now, emerged from the barn, his hands carefully in the air. He was limping badly.

"Search me, Major," the sergeant said in sudden exhaustion. "We just ain't had time to sort it out yet. It all happened too sudden."

"Well, is this the end of it?" Gray demanded. "Christ! The colonel's back there ready to put the brigade in battle order. That's what it sounded like to us."

Well, naturally. When firing suddenly erupted about where Bullen was presumed to be, the brigade took for granted that the law of averages had finally caught up with it.

In one way and another they finally got it straightened out, partly from the slightly wounded prisoner and partly from the frightened young woman with the crying child. The two dead men—Frost had gotten the one in the loft—and the remaining live one were, had been, simply Confederate deserters tired of the war for their own various personal reasons. The woman's husband was away for the day and—no, the men hadn't offered her any harm. They had simply wanted something to eat and that's what the man was doing at the house. Why had they opened fire on Sergeant Bullen's party? Well, three obviously heavily armed men rode into the yard after stopping and looking the place over carefully. They hadn't headed for the house directly, but for the barn—for a fact the well *was* in that direction. In the deserters' natural state of mind, all men of that mold were looking for them. What else? For the past week they had been dodging everything that resembled authority. It hadn't occurred to them that the riders could be anything else but civilian deputies, probably more dangerous to them than some of their former comrades in arms would have been. Civilian officials, safely out of battle territory, were apt to be mighty zealous in dealing with sneaking, back-sliding cowards and deserters—

Major Gray stared stonily at the sullen prisoner. "The simplest thing," Gray said, as though thinking aloud, "would be to stand you against the barn and use a firing squad on you."

The man looked up quickly, alertly. "No—y'all cain't do that!"

"Happens you're wrong, soldier," Gray said coldly. "We *can* stand you up there, but since we're not murdering bushwhacking sonsabitches we probably won't."

But the prisoner wasn't so dull as his appearance seemed to indicate, nor yet so subdued. "You can talk, Major, but I know a thing or two. In the first place I'm in uniform an' if I'm not with my regiment right this minute it ain't noways any o' *your* business. I'm still in the C.S.A. army till it's proved different. In the second place, your men was in civilian clothes, they still are. They can be hung for that if they're caught an' anyways we had a right to shoot 'em. There ain't any regulation says you have to give any Yank advance notice, Major."

"So," Gray said, "a fancy-mouthed camp lawyer, eh?"

The prisoner shrugged. "You can call it what you want to, Major, you got the top hold, but it's still the truth an' you know it."

Allowing for certain rough phrasing, and leaving out the finer points, the man was right and Gray did know it. The major cursed heartily but this time under his breath. He was beginning to think this foray was a little fantastic. One damned thing after another happened and none of it bore any relation to orthodox warfare. However, the major still had an answer.

"Well, just so you'll have something to look forward to, I'm going to turn you over to the first sheriff we come across and tell him what you are. Then it'll be up to you to think up a good fancy lie to explain how you're a hundred miles from your proper outfit without covering orders."

"No—" Whatever the man might have expected this wasn't it and his dislike, or fear of it, showed a little. "I'm entitled to be a proper prisoner, I surrendered. I ain't arguin' that with you, Major—"

"You're not arguing anything with me. You're entitled to whatever we give you and we're not taking prisoners this week," Gray said indifferently. As he turned away he said, "The surgeon can have a look at that leg when he gets here."

Major Keller arrived directly, accompanied as usual by his two silent and rather embarrassed guards. As a matter of routine he knelt and looked at the Schwartz lad, as quickly shrugged and got to his feet again.

Gray, in order to keep the narrow road from clogging, had ordered the First to move on again. But when Marlowe arrived, moments later, and had a quick résumé of the situation, he turned to Lieutenant Davis and said shortly, "Find a bugler and have him blow a Halt. Send a man up front to make sure they hear it. Pass the word that gear is *not* to be unloaded."

To Sergeant King he said: "Tell Captain Landry—this soldier belonged to his company—that he is to find a suitable spot and take care of the burial. Tell him I want this done but I don't want any time wasted."

For there are deaths and deaths. After battle men are buried like so much refuse and it is an impersonal thing. Likely as not the men who gathered and buried the dead had not even knowingly seen them before. Even yesterday at Newton, under the pressure and heat of the moment, they had buried their dead without ceremony and thought nothing of it. But this was somehow different and everybody knew it, even those in the regiment who had never paid any attention to the bashful and rather inarticulate Schwartz lad.

For the moment the colonel and Keller were left almost alone. The Old Man eyed the surgeon. Keller looked at the colonel without a visible sign of emotion. It was the first time they had been face to face since Keller's arrest.

"I suppose you recognized the boy?"

"Certainly—why not, Colonel?"

"Of course. I suppose you're thinking—I would in your shoes—that if I hadn't reversed your judgment in La Grange the boy would still be alive?"

Keller shrugged, his face still expressionless. "It had occurred to me, Colonel—but only along with other things. That sort of speculation is futile. You could just as well say that except for certain events at Fort Sumter none of us would be here."

"You might be thinking," Marlowe said as though to himself, "that because I have a certain feeling of responsibility I'm giving the boy as decent a burial as may be, but you'd be wrong. This is a good excuse to give the men a short rest they wouldn't get otherwise."

"You know your own mind, sir."

Marlowe looked at the sky, the horses and men in the road, and back to the surgeon. His shoulders slumped a little as he said, in an altogether different tone, the bite suddenly gone, "I didn't make the God-damned war, Keller."

The surgeon shook his head slightly. "No, Colonel, I know you didn't," he said softly. "But remember, I didn't either."

Marlowe turned silently on his heel and strode off in the direction of D Company's activities.

As silently Keller watched him go. And he thought: "The sonofabitch is all iron," but there was no bitterness in his mind. But on second thought, no, it wasn't all iron—there had to be something else—

26

The Sniper

Again as a matter of caution A Company skirted Decatur as they had Philadelphia. One result, relatively unimportant, was that they missed Captain Brant and the slow convoy of wounded by about three miles. While meeting might have been pleasant enough, or perhaps reassuring, it wouldn't have done either party any real good. Their objectives were diametrically opposed and the information Bryce needed most, the brigade's proposed route, Captain Brant didn't have.

Bryce led the company, literally, with Lieutenant Rogers taking care of the rear. As long as he led them—he didn't insist on formation, merely that they keep reasonably together—he could be sure they were making the best possible speed. If he let someone else set the pace he could not be certain. The men would curse him privately but they would keep up. They would not, at least not yet, admit that they had less stamina than the captain.

His one driving thought was to overtake the brigade, that and staying out of trouble in the process. He had to gain ground somewhere, and to do that he had to ride faster or longer, or both. Well, it was easy to *say—*

He knew little or nothing about Newton except that it was, had been, the colonel's target point on the Southern. It couldn't be much of a place. Even the important places down here didn't add up to much as towns, at least not in the opinion of A Company. Still, the population of almost any town outnumbered them. Bryce counted up on his fingers—this was Saturday and Newton would be at its busiest and most populous. No use courting trouble there either.

By-passing Decatur to the east, they continued to stay away from the main road south and came to the Southern right of way around noon. Out of sheer curiosity they moved eastward a little way along the ruined line. To anyone with a penchant for wrecked railroads, this was a work of art. As old hands themselves, A Company could only admire a really professional job.

With deadpan thoughtfulness someone said, "It would have been better if they'd tore up the ties too, but I s'pose they were a mite pushed for time."

Bryce agreed but he also had a different feeling of satisfaction. As of now they were squarely on the trail of the brigade. Of course he had known very well that the Old Man was heading for Newton, but a lot of things *might* have happened to the brigade since A Company parted company with it.

As they moved around a wooded bend the captain gave his piercing whistle and held up a warning arm. A half-mile or so down the ruined track there was an engine—probably with cars behind it, smoking but apparently at a halt, with a small swarm of men in front of it. Apparently that was the eastern limit of the damage. Rogers rode up, and Bryce said, "Repair crew, looks like—and man, they sure got their work cut out for them. End of the line for us. Let's cut back south again. You notice those clouds rolling up behind us?"

"Sure—looks like we're in for it again, Asa. Let's see—uh—four days or so since we run into that slosher. Well, spring season— hell, you have to expect so much rain here in this country."

"I know, but personally I doubt that I'll ever really appreciate God's rain again. Let's go."

They rode through a timber belt and presently emerged on the Meridian road. None of them were expert trackers but they didn't have to be to know that the brigade had passed this way. None of these rural roads were much traveled, so the hundreds of hoof-prints were plain, not to mention the trail of droppings that could have been left only by a large and recently passed column of horsemen. Bryce was momentarily puzzled by the fact that the trail led toward Meridian. It didn't make too much sense. Me-ridian had never been on the agenda, it was almost sure to be rather heavily garrisoned, and the Old Man was no reckless dare-devil; he had guts to spare but he wasn't crazy. In one way or another it would be almost sure suicide to attack Meridian. Be-sides, he had already accomplished as much as had been origi-nally expected of him.

A quarter mile farther on he had the answer. A second road forked to the right, toward the southeast and away from the di-rection of Meridian, and the brigade had obviously taken it. He experienced an actual physical feeling of relief. Offhand it seemed hardly possible to miss an entire brigade of cavalry, even a half-strength brigade; but if half the Rebel troops in Mississippi could overlook it, and apparently they had so far, then certainly one lone company could. The captain knew only to well, and the idea gave him no peace, that, in the absence of a dusty track, they could pass within a mile of the brigade and never know it—and they could go on wandering like one of the ten Lost Tribes. That is until Rebel cavalry caught up with them. Or more likely—and Bryce grinned sourly at the notion—when an irate citizenry cornered them while they were trying to steal some corn meal and bacon.

The rain caught them a half-hour beyond the road fork. It wasn't too bad, considering. Just a steady fall that washed the roadside foliage and brought the spring odor of growth to their nostrils. They got wet, naturally, and they rode with heads and shoulders bent, but the water actually flushed away some of the accumulated dirt and grime. Here and there men probably dozed but in the rear a dogged Lieutenant Rogers kept them from straggling.

The sound of a rifle shot was as suddenly shocking as a fire bell in church. As the declining *wheeee* sound followed, men flinched involuntarily—you forget that you don't hear the bad one.

Bryce set his startled horse almost back on its haunches. "Nate!" he snapped at Sergeant Brown, "take your platoon and see if you can find that bushwhacker! Fast—before the sonofabitch gets away!"

This was open country here, that is not solidly timbered but dotted with clumps of trees and brush. There was plenty of cover yet it didn't seem that a man could move very far without being seen by the circling horsemen. They wasted a valuable twenty minutes without finding the slightest indication of where the shot had come from. It didn't seem possible but there it was.

"I dunno, Cap'n," Nate said in a worried tone, "didn't find hide nor hair of a thing. Could've been some smart damn'-fool kid. I dunno what else."

"Well—let's hope it's not something worse," Bryce said. "I'd just about as soon be shot as scared half to death. Let's get the hell out of here!"

It was still raining, gently enough but steadily, what farmers consider the finest kind of rain—a solid, steady fall but one slow enough to soak in rather than run off and waste itself. The road was becoming a little slippery underfoot but hadn't softened very deeply yet.

Almost exactly a half-hour later the second *wheeee* jerked them out of the state into which they had gradually relaxed again. Bryce cursed bitterly and this time turned loose the entire company, including himself. But again they found absolutely nothing, though they circled far beyond normal rifle range. Some men swore; others simply shut their mouths a little more grimly.

Bryce faced the men. "Like Nate said, that first one could have been a stray, or some crazy kid, but that couldn't happen twice. Now, by God, keep your heads up and your eyes open. First platoon right, second left. When we get that bird he's going to be a dead duck. Now watch it!"

It was all he could do, obviously, but of course he had the helpless feeling that it wasn't enough. Within their normal limits as men A Company wasn't afraid of anything much that it could see, but this was something else. Bryce could sense the tension in the files behind him. Behind him? He could feel it even more in himself.

The mud splattered under the hoofs and the rain came down benignly.

When Nate thought he caught a smoke puff from the corner of an eye he checked his horse instinctively. The animal minced in the road and its rump swung into the leg of Private Stumm who, as usual, had been riding almost knee to knee with the sergeant. Nate, along with everybody else, heard this third report but it was only later that he realized there had been no going-away *wheeee* as before.

Eddy Stumm said, "Nate—Nate, I—!" and there was such a strange urgency in his voice that the sergeant, intent as he was on the landscape, instantly swung around in the saddle. The boy's eyes had an oddly intent look. He put out a hand as though to steady himself on some support that wasn't there, opened his mouth wide as though trying for an especially deep breath. Then the bright blood gushed from his mouth, down over the silky yellow beard and the faded tunic, and Nate caught him as he started to topple from the saddle. For an instant Nate too was frozen into immobility as the warm blood ran across one of his bare hands and down the saddle skirt.

Then Nate came to life and said passionately, "God damn it! Somebody help me hold him!"

Two troopers rode in and held the boy until Nate could dismount, then they let go when Nate said, "I got him," and let the body slide gently into his oaken arms.

When Bryce had finished calling orders to Lieutenant Rogers and Sergeant Baker about this third pursuit, he dismounted and led his horse over to the roadside. Nate had laid Stumm on the thick wet grass and was down beside him on one knee. For a long moment the captain said nothing. Perhaps more than anyone else he knew how tough Nate Brown had stood like a hard but gentle older brother to Stumm—bawling him out, ragging him, prodding him, and always with an invisible hand under his elbow.

Finally the captain said quietly, "Well?"

Nate stood up and shrugged wearily—a little hopelessly, Bryce thought. Nate's face was fixed like a clay mask, a mask streaked by dirty rivulets as the rain ran down—his hat was still on the ground where it had fallen. "Nothin', Cap'n. Lungs. You don't get up from one in there." He glanced down at the scarlet still on the back of his hand. "He was done for before I got him outta the saddle."

"Well—"

"We'll have to bury him, Cap'n."

"Well, naturally—"

"I mean bury him, Cap'n. I—we can't just stick the—him in the ground, Cap'n."

"All right, Nate," Bryce said heavily. "I'll see what we can do. Get his things out of his pockets and take care of them. And Nate?"

"Hunh?"

"Uh—take a look around and see if you can find a place—you'd better take care of that too. Get what help you need when the boys get back."

. . . Presently Nate found a spot a little way back from the road, a low knoll partly surrounded by white dogwood. He drew his saber and marked off a proper rectangle, then mowed off the ground growth with the blade. The rain was still falling and it was slow, dirty work with only the small entrenching shovels and the saber blades for tools, even after Hayes and Dormire joined him.

Once Hayes sat back on the muddy edge of the hole and said wearily, "Hell, Sarge, don't you figure this is deep enough?"

"Deeper, damn it!" the sergeant snarled savagely. "I'll get it done right, by God, if I have to stay here all night!"

They didn't say any more, just kept digging.

As with others so with young Stumm—there were deaths and deaths. Nate wrapped the boy's body in the blankets he wouldn't need now, all but his booted lower legs, and other hands helped him lower the body so it wouldn't fall.

A Company gathered silently, solemnly, men leading horses by the bridle reins. Someone removed his hat and the others, glancing at each other a little furtively, followed suit.

Bryce looked around the rough semicircle and cleared his throat.

"I'm afraid I'm not very good at this," he said, realizing how awkward he was sounding, "and in any case this isn't a regulation military affair. So if any of you men—?" He left the question hanging there.

Men looked at the ground, at the gray sky, at each other, but nobody said anything.

"You, Nate?"

"Naw, Cap'n. I could—I reckon it's up to you."

The captain sighed. Yes, it was up to him. He cudgeled his tired brain, trying to remember. It didn't have to be a classic, of course, but it had to be something.

"Very well then—

". . . Almighty God, I—we commit to Thy care the—the immortal soul of Private Edward Stumm, late of the First Illinois Volunteer Cavalry. He was a good soldier, Lord, and deserves well of Thee."

Again he searched his memory.

". . . 'The mighty God, even the Lord, has spoken, and called the earth from the rising of the sun unto the going down thereof.

". . . 'For as in Adam all die, even so in Christ shall all be made alive.

". . . 'Then cometh the end, when he shall have delivered up the kingdom to God, even the Father—

". . . 'The last enemy that shall be destroyed is death.

". . . 'O death, where is thy sting? O grave, where is thy victory?

". . . 'Therefore, my beloved brethren, be ye steadfast, immovable, always abounding in the word of the Lord, for—forasmuch as ye know that your labor is not in vain in the Lord.

"Uh—'Glory be to the Father, and to the Son, and to the Holy Ghost. As it was in the—in the beginning, is now, and ever shall be, world without end—' "

He hesitated, staring unseeingly at the wet grass.

"And may the Lord have mercy on us all. Amen."

He turned and looked at Nate. "I guess we could fire the salute, but—"

"Naw," the sergeant said—it would make a terrible racket and besides they would probably need the ammunition. "I—I was thinkin'—maybe Shorty could blow a taps on his mouth organ."

And so it was.

Bryce glanced at the open grave and said, "Have the boys—"

"I'll finish it up, Cap'n," Nate said quickly. "You all go ahead. I'll catch up with you."

"But—" Bryce began. Then he said shortly, "All right, but make it fast, Sergeant. I don't want to have to send back for you."

Three quarters of an hour later Nate splashed up alongside the captain.

"I'm much obliged, Cap'n. I know you went out o' your way."

"All right." Bryce didn't look at him. He couldn't recall a casualty quite so affecting. In fact, A Company, fortunately, hadn't had a single casualty since the previous December. That was at some place called Stony Creek in Tennessee, when all one after-noon they had fought a savage rear-guard action in a blinding snowstorm and left not only the dead behind them but the wounded as well. That was the one which had almost wrecked the company and reduced it to its present bottom strength.

"I guess I didn't think of it before," Nate said almost apologeti-cally. "The boys find anything?"

"No, nothing—not a God-damned sign of anything."

Nor did they ever. But there was no more phantom shooting.

27

The Lost Company

Bryce laid claim to no phenomenal memory, only average, and moreover he'd made no attempt to memorize Marlowe's map below the line of the Southern. Now he admitted, though so far only to himself, that he didn't know where he was. Oh sure, he was somewhere in southern Mississippi, presently approaching the line of the Mobile & Ohio below Meridian, but beyond that he was groping, and the knowledge was a little wearing. He told himself he wasn't lost. On the other hand, neither did he know where he was.

There was another thing pushing at the back of his mind. This time yesterday he'd been sure he was on the trail of the brigade. Now there was this small germ of doubt. After the rain set in the visible signs of the column had been obliterated, and after they became preoccupied in the matter of the phantom killer they had lost interest in signs of the brigade for the time being, himself included. The few inquiries he'd dared risk this morning had revealed no slightest trace of Marlowe or any other troops. Of course his informants (misinformants?) could have been lying, but he didn't think so. He had tried three times and each time got generally the same answers, and he thought he would have detected a lie or at least some visible hesitation or confusion in one of the three.

Even with the doubt growing he decided he could only go ahead until he reached some definite point of reference—what form it might take he had no idea.

The rain had stopped during the night and this was another fine day, almost hot to men accustomed to a northern climate. They topped a small rise and Bryce's eye caught the glint of sunlight on railroad iron. There below and ahead, in the trees along the railroad tracks, was Enterprise—he had the name of the town from one of the people he had bespoken this morning. He studied the landscape for a few minutes—again he wished he had a decent pair of glasses. The place seemed to have a strange air of idleness, of somnolence—until he remembered this was Sunday. Rogers rode forward and joined him.

"Pretty little place," Rogers said, "but aside from that what do you think?"

"Frankly, I don't know. The place looks as dead as a graveyard but you never can tell. Nate"—Bryce turned to the sergeant—"better have the boys lay their carbines at the ready."

Again they moved forward, wary, trying to watch everything at once. They were perhaps a hundred yards from the railroad line when the flutter of shots exploded, not many, four or five, and all they could see for certain was the drifting smoke.

But there was something about the fire which made Bryce swing around and throw up a warning arm. "No!" he barked. "Hold it! All of you!"

There was another thing—nobody in the company had been hurt, an improbability at this range.

"I guess," Rogers drawled casually, "this is the bear trap we been lookin' for, Asa."

"Maybe, but I don't think so," Bryce said tersely.

Perhaps it was an ultra sensitivity induced by the events of yesterday afternoon, at any rate Bryce at the moment was perfectly sure that this ragged fire hadn't been meant to hurt them. He didn't believe strongly in inspiration but neither could he account rationally for his actions now.

"Rogers, hold the company right here! Sergeant, ride up here with me—I'm going to try something."

"Hold on—" Rogers began.

But Rogers was too late. Bryce and Brown rode slowly on ahead.

"Cap'n," Nate said, "what are we suppo—"

"Just stay shut up, Nate. I'll do the talking—if we get a chance to do any."

Bryce knew in general where the shooting had originated—a row of low sheds adjoining a much larger building which bore the legend, ENTERPRISE GIN COMPANY. His saber rasped from the scabbard. He affixed a soiled white handkerchief to the point and raised it aloft.

"Easy, Sergeant," he said softly. "Give 'em a little time."

An eternity of dead silence—they could hear the trees rustling loudly—seemed to pass as they neared the railroad tracks.

Then, forty yards or so away, a lean noncom in a butternut uniform stepped out into the open. He carried his rifle in the crook of his left arm and raised his right hand even with a shoulder. "Hold up, Yank! What's yore business?"

"Federal party with a message for the officer commanding at Enterprise!" Bryce said without a moment's hesitation.

"Well—wait right thar an' I'll see."

They waited—and in the interval Bryce seemed to see a good deal of his past life, as it is said a man does in the process of drowning. And the longer they waited the more foolhardy this business appeared. He would have sold their chances for a torn Confederate shinplaster. Once the sergeant said, "Cap'n, I still don't—" and the captain hissed, "I told you to shut up!" He kept his hands folded on the saddle pommel—they were trembling so he didn't trust them free. . . .

The party—an officer and two less ornate noncoms—rode out from behind the gin building. Doing it proper, Bryce thought with grim humor—it would have been a lot simpler to walk that short distance but that would have left the officer in the supposedly inferior position of the man on foot. Form and protocol were important.

They rode to within twenty feet of the two dirty cavalrymen before they stopped. Bryce could scarcely believe his eyes but he had to—the evidence was right there before him. The officer was a venerable nineteen or perhaps twenty. He sat ramrod stiff in the saddle and his uniform was a vision in itself—a perfect spotless gray, black braid at cuffs and collar, double row of tunic buttons gleaming like newly minted gold, the scarlet silk sash perfectly draped. Bryce wondered vaguely if they had been delayed because the officer stopped to dress. The major's leaves on the boy's shoulders were as shining as the buttons. The whole thing might have just come from the tissue-paper wrappings of some swank Richmond outfitter, and the weary captain had visions of a gala military victory ball—or dress parade for the governor at V.M.I.

"Good afternoon, Captain," the boy said, with a gravity that was almost travesty. "To what do we owe the honor of this visit?"

"We're a party from the command of Major General Marlowe," Bryce said brusquely. "Our business, Major, is to demand the peaceable surrender of Enterprise and all Confederate troops in the area."

"I—I see." The major's soft mouth twitched ever so slightly and he swallowed hard. Bryce could even see the movement of his Adam's apple under the stiffly erect embroidered collar. "Could you—that is, will you be good enough to put the demand in writing, Captain?"

"Why, certainly, be glad to," Bryce said. "To whom should it be addressed?" He could be just as nonsensically correct as anybody else.

"To—er, Colonel Max Sheffield, commanding the post."

Bryce deliberately took his time—he was afraid that if he didn't he would fumble disastrously. He found a pencil and an old envelope in an inner pocket. He consulted his watch gravely. Then he wrote, ending with, "—one hour only for your consideration, after which further delay will be at your peril." He liked that "peril" especially.

The gleaming baby major read the lines carefully, almost as though memorizing them. "Only one hour, Captain? That's not much time."

"Certainly enough to make up your mind, I should think," Bryce said indifferently. "But I'm sorry—actually I haven't any discretion in that regard."

"Yes, of course, I understand. Well—that is, where will we find you at the end of the hour, sir?"

Where? Yes, where, Bryce? A fair question.

"Oh, we'll fall back on our main body and wait for your answer. We'll honor a flag, of course," Bryce added.

"Well, then—"

They exchanged stiffly correct salutes and as the captain swung his horse he said, "All right, Sergeant."

Presently Nate whistled softly, "*Whew-whew!* My Jesus! I was so damn' scared my toes are still diggin' holes in my boot soles."

"Huh! *You* were scared!"

When they reached the baffled A Company Bryce didn't waste time in explanations but simply motioned them behind him. The files wheeled, fell into line, and suited their leisurely pace to his. They ambled out of town as though in no hurry to get anywhere. Beyond the little rise where they had paused a half-hour before, Bryce turned and looked back for the first time. They seemed to be safely out of sight.

"Now!" he called tensely. "If you want to keep on living let's get ourselves the hell out of here."

He laid the quirt viciously on his startled horse, a rare gesture for him.

The road they had come in on ran at an angle from northwest to southeast, but about a mile out of town it had been joined by one which appeared to run straight east and west. They would, he decided, take the latter. They hadn't found the brigade where they'd been; they could only try somewhere else now.

Once the idea had entered Bryce's mind he couldn't banish it, and now since late afternoon he had been wrestling with it, trying to reach a decision. He was one of those who believed that rules, even army regulations, were made for men and not vice versa. He had never understood those who could say calmly, "Yes, of course I know it's *wrong*, but it's the law and nothing can be done about it—"

Trying to make up his mind, he had kept them plodding on long after dark—one way of trying to gain a little ground. There was little audible grumbling. Nate Brown had given a lively personal account of what had occurred in the parley at Enterprise, and they understood the necessity of putting ground between themselves and the railroad.

The decision to halt for the night, as seemed to be the case in many things, was made by the outward event. For an hour they had been riding with scarcely more than an occasional word passing between the bone-weary riders. Bryce was so used to Rogers's reiterated, "Close up, damn it, close up!" that he hardly heard it. Then there was an eruption of hard words that set the whole company in commotion. Pulling up, Bryce turned to see what was going on. Rogers's voice was weary and exasperated.

"What the devil's the matter, Sims?"

"I ain't just sure yet," a voice answered, "but it looks like I got a gone horse here."

Riders made way for Bryce as he went back. The moon was on the wane now but it still provided a usable amount of light this time of the evening. Rogers had dismounted and so had Private Sims. Also, Sims's horse was down on its knees in the road, its head drooping in dumb resignation.

As Sims had explained it, the animal had stumbled, faltered a couple of times, then simply quit and gone down.

"Get your gear off and lighten him up," Bryce said. "See what happens then. Time we knocked off anyway."

There was nothing else to be done about it, at least not now. A man may quit for any of a thousand reasons, but the quitting actually occurs when his complicated brain orders his muscles to quit. And it may be that he only *thinks* he is finished—under a different stimulus he could go on if the game was worth it. A horse, being in truth a dumb animal, quits when for physical reasons there is no alternative. And Bryce had never heard of a horse that responded to patriotic reasoning. They were lucky in that this was the first animal that had actually quit cold on them, but it could have happened in a better place.

"Get 'em off the road, Rogers," Bryce ordered. "Then I want to talk to you for a minute or two."

They talked earnestly, or rather Bryce talked and Rogers listened, while the men unsaddled, staked horses, got a fire going, attended a dozen other minor chores.

"You're the boss, Asa," Rogers said finally, a little unhappily. "But I say you're wrong. We haven't shot our bolt yet by a hell of a ways."

"I've thought about it for the last three hours," the captain said stubbornly. "They're entitled to a choice, now, while we're still in the clear. Not when they're looking down a couple of hundred musket barrels."

"Let's get it over with then," Rogers said almost in disgust. "Half of 'em will be asleep if we don't—me included."

They walked back into the firelighted area and Bryce said, "Everybody up here close enough so I don't have to yell." Men moved in a little closer, curiously, and he said, "You might as well make yourselves comfortable, boys. I'm not exactly going to make a speech but this will take a few minutes to say."

He waited for them to settle down. Here and there near the fire a man nodded in spite of himself. Beyond the fire some men were visible only as shadows topped vaguely with eyes and beards.

"I won't go into the details of the orders I had from Colonel Marlowe when we started on this wild-goose chase," he began. "But part of it was this—we were of course to rejoin the brigade, but if it turned out that for some reason we couldn't, then I was to act as I saw fit.

"When we made that sashay to Macon and back to the line of march to Newton, I figure we lost about two days. You know how fast the column was moving; you know how fast we've been moving, and I doubt that we've gained a single mile. In fact, I imagine that water haul to Enterprise cost us some more time to-day. Actually I never knew exactly where Colonel Marlowe was heading, after Newton, because he didn't know himself. Yesterday we all thought he was heading for Enterprise. But if the column had ever been near Enterprise that young squirt there today would have known it. They would have been there two days *ahead* of today and he'd never fallen for that dumb show of mine."

The captain paused and caught a deep breath.

"Well, boys, as matters stand now I don't know where the hell the brigade is or where it intends to be. For all I know the Rebs may have mopped them up completely. We may be chasing something that doesn't exist any longer. I just don't know. Furthermore, I don't know where *we* are. There it is, for better or worse.

"Now I think that somewhere between Newton and Enterprise the brigade switched direction and headed back west—mind you, that's a guess. But we're sure they didn't go east, they didn't go back north to the line of the Southern—we know that's loaded. My guess is that they turned and headed west. From here the nearest real Federal force is gathered around Vicksburg. My further guess is that they headed that way because it's about the only place they *could* try for. I'm going to move on that supposition.

But—and here's the important point of all this—some of you may think I'm wrong. If that's the case, then you are free from here on to act as free agents; I'll take the responsibility. I'll even put it in writing for you if you want it that way. From here on you can decide for yourselves, if you want to, and when you do that you'll be entirely on your own—"

"But, Cap'n—" said a voice from the shadows.

"Hold on—I'll be done in a minute or two. If some—any of you want to keep on with me—and with Lieutenant Rogers, of course —why, fine. If the rest of you want to go north, or *half* the rest of you north and the other half south, that's all right too. Even *one* of you. But—I'm not only giving you the choice, I'm giving an order to make it, and now. There'll be no future business of saying, 'If Bryce had let us go when we *wanted* to *this* or that wouldn't have happened.' It's up to you, men, and I don't know how to make it any fairer. Oh, one other thing," he added gravely. "Any of you that leave are welcome to your share of the rations— nothing from nothing leaves nothing."

For a long moment there was only thick silence, then an almost plaintive voice said, "But, Cap'n, do we *have* to bust up?"

Bryce swallowed a grim chuckle. "Better authority than I am has stated that all a man really *has* to do is die. This choice is a little simpler but it's still up to you. Rogers and I are going to take a little walk. Discuss it, cuss it, or each of you decide for yourself—I don't give a damn, but do it. I want to know now what we'll be doing at daylight. Come on, Lieutenant."

They walked off in the darkness and when they came to the spot where Bryce had left his gear he said, "Hold on a minute."

Then they went on until they came to the edge of the road, well out of company earshot, and Bryce said, "For God's sake, let's sit down—or lie down."

After a while there was a slow gurgling sound and Bryce said, "Aaaah! Here, be careful you don't drop the bottle."

"What is it ?" Rogers said unthinkingly.

Bryce gave a small throaty chuckle. "Why, naturally, one of

those two quarts of whisky you stole at that place—where was it?—Gillis."

"I don't know. With this empty belly—I'm afraid gas may form and I'll go up like one of these newfangled balloons you hear about. Still—like everybody else I have only one life to give for my country."

After listening to a respectable gurgle Bryce took back the bottle. "You know," he said thoughtfully, "that whisky is better than I expected it to be. Incidentally, did you ever consider the place names in Mississippi?"

"No," Rogers said without interest.

"Now, if you were in Spain, say," Bryce went on, paying no attention to him, "and you came to a place called Smithville, you simply wouldn't believe it—it wouldn't be possible. Or if, say, in Italy you found a place name of Great Neck."

"Hell, they simply use the same names but in their own proper language versions. Nothing complicated about that. Hand me the bottle."

"That's the interesting point. Over here we don't change the names. Here in Mississippi they have Corinth, Cato, and Macedonia which they stole from Greece, Granada from Spain, Buena Vista from Mexico, Sebastopol from Russia, Kosciusko from Poland, and a mess like Sucarnoochee from the helpless Cherokees. That last works out though. Just to keep everything even they stole the land from the Cherokees too. A hell of a country—I don't suppose the Indians would want it back now after what we've done to it. I wouldn't. You through with the bottle?"

"Here. Best name I ever heard of for a town was up in Indiana—a place called Whatfor? Couldn't hardly have been more appropriate."

For a little while they sat silent, listening to the crickets and occasionally exchanging the bottle.

Finally Bryce said, "You're not drunk, are you?"

"Well, I don't think so. I was more'n half-paralyzed anyway."

"Let's go then."

They went back to the firelight. The captain looked around thoughtfully and said, "Well, gentlemen?"

Sergeant Baker had been named to do the talking.

"Well, we mulled it around some, Cap'n—you might say there wasn't any argument to speak of. If it's all the same to you there ain't nobody goin' anywhere except with you an' the lieutenant. That's the way we started—we'll finish it the same way."

"All right—and thanks. I hope none of you has occasion to be sorry. Now get your sleep. Tomorrow we'll make a special try at one square meal."

THE PURSUIT

Bryce's was indeed an inspired bravura performance at Enterprise, a performance for which he couldn't account himself. But to be a success even an inspired performance requires a receptive audience, and the boyish major had done well in his own way. He had no means of knowing that A Company was not merely an advance party—he was in fact awaiting the arrival of this fabulous phantom division under General Marlowe. That was his latest intelligence.

The major—his name was Elkins—had himself arrived in Enterprise, from the south, with a detachment of the Thirty-Fifth Alabama Infantry less than two hours before the arrival of A Company. And he had not actually surrendered anything except the opportunity to immobilize A Company; he had merely accepted for transmission a demand which was more or less expected. Neither was his questioning of "General Marlowe's" time limit mere small talk. He knew that in an hour or so General Loring would be coming down from Meridian with the Seventh Kentucky and the Twelfth Louisiana—the same General Loring and the same troops that A Company had temporarily stranded at Macon, seventy-five miles to the north on the M. & O., by cutting railroad and telegraph lines four days before. (If the captain had known that at Enterprise he was only fifteen miles from Meridian, and that Loring had such a force in between, he would have been a good deal more perturbed than he was.) Moreover, neither Major Elkins nor anyone else had any notion of surrendering— Elkins had been playing almost the same game as Bryce, bluffing for time. When General Loring arrived, the whole force set out to deliver a personal answer to the supposed surrender demand. It wasn't their fault that the brigade had been represented only by the now-long-gone A Company.

28

The Soldier and the Lady

Bryce was actually not so far behind the brigade as his cal-
culations led him to believe; they had been fair enough but he did
not, dared not, allow for any lapses on the part of Colonel Marlowe. He knew that as long as the colonel had matters under
control there would be no lapses. Thus in spite of his wanderings
he had gained more ground than he supposed. A Company had
dallied nowhere—even the minor adventure at Enterprise and the
burial of Private Stumm had together consumed no more than an
hour and a half. The brigade had lost more than a long half-day in
the work at Newton, and the day they encountered the Rebel
deserters, the twenty-fifth, had been almost a total loss as far as
travel was concerned. In their late riding on the twenty-sixth, and
a before-dawn start on the twenty-seventh, they had picked up an
entire day, A Company that is, and hour for hour they covered
more ground than the brigade.

Again this morning Bryce had them on the road a little before daybreak. Aside from the ordinary calls of nature after sleep, all they had to do was saddle and ride. Today they didn't have the bothersome luxury of breakfast to delay them.

Bryce thought there was a noticeable difference in the way they took to the road this morning. Not that they had ever balked, or delayed deliberately, it was just that now the men seemed to have a more personal, individual sense of purpose. If that, Bryce thought, was an incidental result of last night's ultimatum, so much the better—he hoped it would last.

There was another thing bedeviling his mind a little now. Somewhere not too far ahead lay the Strong and Pearl rivers. He didn't know their exact location nor their relative size; he did know they were rivers of consequence and that if they didn't find a quick way across these streams—they were bound to be high because of the season—A Company was likely to find itself in another, and perhaps final, bad corner. Well, these were bridges to be crossed when they got there—in this case he could only hope the bridges would actually *be* there.

The road crossed a shallow river, ordinarily no more than a creek, and then turned right again along the bank. They came to a house a few hundred yards farther on. It stood on a nice little rise, at the end of a slightly curving lane, and the road ran between it and the river. The shrubs about the house and along the borders of the lane were uncared for and lush, even this early in the season, apparently beginning new growth where they had left off the previous autumn, without benefit of pruning. "House" seemed to describe the dwelling more accurately than mansion, but it was still the most imposing place they had seen for days. A wisp of smoke drifted from one of the chimneys but otherwise, from the road, they could see no other sign of life.

Bryce lifted a hand and the company stopped in its weary tracks. (Of course they had rested during the night but rest now was only a relative thing, for they stayed weary all the time and rest was merely respite, not refreshment.) For a long moment

Bryce sat contemplating the house, then slid stiffly to the ground. The spring morning was so quiet they could hear the gurgling sound of the shallow river a hundred yards to their right, and the sudden cawing of a crow was as startling as a bugle call.

"Place sure looks prosperous enough to feed one half-strength company," he said to Rogers, "and I promised we'd make a special effort today. This looks like too good a chance to pass up. Plenty of grass and water right here. Let the stock graze while I have a look at the situation up there."

"Better take a little help with you, just in case."

"I'm going to. Sergeant," Bryce called to Nate Brown, "bring Haney and Morris and let's take a walk up that lane."

They stumped up the drive, their weariness showing in their halting gait, past the cascading white spirea and half-a-dozen other shrubs Bryce couldn't even identify. The men waited while he went on up the broad steps and across the veranda to the pair of entrance doors. There was still an air of great quiet and Bryce thought, Well, I'll sure wake somebody—and he slammed the polished brass knocker almost viciously. The door opened almost instantly—he guessed the man had been waiting within reaching distance of the knob. The saffron-colored Negro looked at the captain with what seemed to be a mixture of curiosity, fright, and —could it be?—hostility.

"Yes suh?"

"Is your—" Bryce stopped. Somehow the word "master," even in this context, always gagged him a little. "Is the proprietor here?"

"Why, no suh. Not right now, but—"

"That will do, Jason. Please show the officer in. I'll speak to him."

The feminine voice was obviously not youthful—Bryce couldn't see the owner yet—but it had a wonderfully pleasing, bell-like quality, the sort of voice one automatically associated with what one thought of as a Lady. He reached automatically for his battered hat—he suddenly remembered that he hadn't spoken to a woman (aside from the Negro girl) for more than two weeks. It was an odd sensation.

The Negro turned slightly away from Bryce and said, "But, ma'am, you know Miss Ellen—"

"Nonsense, Jason. Show the gentleman into the blue parlor."

Bryce had a feeling that the Negro would still have barred him if he could. But there wasn't much he could do about it and Bryce didn't give him a chance anyway. He stepped into the hall and pushed the door all the way back in so doing. The butler dropped his eyes and seemed to shrug inwardly as he moved out of the way. Sun slanted on the polished floor as it streamed through a fanlight at the far end of the wide hall. Bryce felt a sudden acute sense of embarrassment—he was filthy from head to foot and one of his spurs had come loose and was dragging a little on the shining floor.

A few steps beyond the wide archway to the parlor the woman turned to face him. She was hardly ancient—fiftyish, he guessed. Her hair was very white, combed back severely and parted in the center, and was in startling contrast to her remarkably blue eyes. Her face was marked with myriad lines, especially about her mouth, but it was plain that once, perhaps not even so long ago, she had been a very beautiful woman. Now, in spite of the situation—the situation, that is, as Bryce naturally evaluated it—she seemed strangely self-possessed, perhaps serene was the better word.

Bryce shifted his hat from his right hand to his left and said, "I must apologize for the intrusion, ma'am. I'm Captain Bryce, of the First Illinois Cavalry—"

"Why, nonsense, Captain," she said brightly. "You're more than welcome. There, try that sofa; you look tired. Oh—I'm Mrs. Lawton, Mrs. *General* Lawton."

Temporarily numb with wonder, the captain sat. He settled back momentarily—he had almost forgotten the feel of fine furniture, or of any furniture. Of course he had often heard of families here in the deep South who were wholeheartedly Union, although he had not personally encountered any. Yet he had a strong feeling that that was not what applied here. Before he could re-form his thoughts she said, "May I offer you some refreshment? But what am I thinking? Jason!"

The man appeared in the doorway and again Bryce had the impression that he had been hovering.

"Ma'am?"

"Fetch the whisky for Captain Bryce, please—the *old* whisky, mind, Jason."

The man bowed slightly as though (Bryce thought) in disapproval and disappeared.

"Mrs. Lawton, as I said, I'm from the First Illinois and I wouldn't trouble you except that—"

"Yes, of course, so I understood. Naturally, I saw your men from the window. We are isolated here, you know, and news reaches us slowly. But it is a pleasure to welcome you to our country here. Frankly, I had not heard that Illinois had come into our glorious Confederacy, but I have always felt it was merely a matter of time. Quite a number of my mother's family—they were East Tennessee people—removed there. In the forties, I believe it was—"

Bryce swallowed hard, hunting for words. "Madam, I feel I owe you an explanation of my situation—"

"Of course. I'll be most interested—if you can spare the time. Oh, here's Jason."

The man put the tray on the parquetry-inlaid table within Bryce's reach and removed the stopper from the cut-glass decanter.

"Please help yourself, Captain," she said. "I know this is—what should I say?—not quite proper in the ordinary sense. But it is wartime, after all. So many of the usual amenities seem not to apply. But of course this is an occasion of sorts, at least for me."

The aroma of the spirits reached his nostrils and he suddenly wanted a drink badly—not an ordinary occurrence with him.

"Well, then—with your permission, Madam."

He tried to grasp the elusive something that was obviously here but his tired brain refused to deal with it.

"By all means. This unreasonable war, Captain, has been a difficult thing for me personally. I try not to complain, and of course I'm only one of many, but one may as well face the truth. My husband—he was General Miles Lawton—lost his life at that place called Pittsburgh Landing. He was on the staff of our General Albert Sidney Johnston. You didn't know him, my husband, I mean?"

"No," Bryce said. His collar seemed to be choking him almost to suffocation. "No, I'm afraid not, Madam. I was—there were a great many men involved there, you know. Er—may I?" He indicated the decanter. The whisky had proved to be smooth and velvety beyond belief.

"By all means, Captain. But you were there, at Pittsburgh Landing?"

"Yes," he said. Yes, God help him, he had been there and part of him always would be—or a part of Shiloh would always be with him.

"It was the more difficult for me," she went on quite calmly. "My son and my son-in-law were also killed there. Of course they did not hold the rank my husband did. Naturally. So much younger men—"

"I'm sorry," he managed, barely. Again he had the feeling of suffocation. The very room seemed oppressive beyond anything of the kind he had ever experienced.

"One learns how to go on, you know. One must. I'm afraid I was very foolish at first. In fact, I wrote several letters to General Johnston—I had met him at an affair in New Orleans some years ago. A charming man—charming. But I received no answer. Perhaps—in fact I'm sure now—I didn't quite realize how desperately the general's time is taken up with more important affairs than mine. He *is* our most important commander, is he not?"

He suddenly realized. God above! Johnston had died there in the shot-riddled timber at Shiloh, his jack boot running over with blood that would not stop flowing, exactly a year and—let's see—yes, a year and twenty days ago this afternoon. As with most men he had little experience of madness, he was in fact a little afraid of it if only because it was so seemingly inexplicable. It was something which he, at least, ordinarily associated with dark places, the night, the normally hidden. But here the bright sunlight streaming across the pattern of the carpet, the woman looking at him with interest, waiting for the polite answer to her last question—he could not imagine anything more macabre. At the same time he knew he could not, would not, do anything that would destroy this woman's fantasies. The problem now was how to get away from this daytime nightmare. And suddenly he felt a great wave of sorrow and regret. For himself? For her? For General Albert Sidney Johnston? No, he thought, not for any one but for all of us, God help us if He will.

"Madam, I am more sorry than I can say, believe me. If I had known—"

"Nonsense, young man. But you must have business to attend and here I've been dwelling on these purely private matters of the past. My daughter Ellen—Mrs. Pleasants—will be back shortly. She went this morning to pay a call on an ailing neighbor. She will very much want to meet you, I'm sure. But you'll be staying to dinner and I must see to the servants. I didn't realize—here it is after eleven now. Oh, your men are included, but of *course*."

"I'm afraid that's out of the question—"

But she had risen and he perforce rose with her.

"Jason!" she called, and again the butler appeared almost instantaneously. "Jason, please conduct Captain Bryce to the gentlemen's accommodation and see that he has what he needs. Then when Miss Ellen comes in tell her I want to see her immediately. I'll be in the kitchen for the next few minutes."

Well—well? It was a relief to have her gone, yet somehow it seemed to him that he couldn't simply walk out the front door, no matter how much he wanted to. And come hell or high water there was still A Company to be fed. He would have to think of something.

He followed the saffron Negro back into the hall and paused a moment by the open front door. One of the men, Haney, was fast asleep, sprawled across the steps. "Sergeant," he said quietly, and Nate looked up from his dozing. "Take it easy for a little longer. Send a man to tell Rogers this'll take awhile."

"Everything all right, Cap'n?"

"Pretty soon," Bryce said obliquely.

He followed the man Jason up the broad stairs and along the upper hall to a large, cool bedroom.

"I'll have watuh an' towels direc'ly, Cap'n. You want a razuh?"

"No—I won't have time for that."

He pushed the door almost shut, unbuckled and hung up his saber-pistol belt, and peeled off the almost stiff tunic. In the enclosed space his nostrils were suddenly assailed by his own acid effluvia and he was startled. My God!—it was like a goat ten days dead. But the shock he got when he looked in the mirror was even worse. His eyes were badly inflamed, his skin and beard were encrusted, literally, with dirt, and his lips were almost caked over.

The Negro came back quickly and silently, bearing towels and a pitcher of very hot water which he placed on the mahogany washstand.

Then the man, apparently summoning some secret courage, looked squarely at him and said, "Cap'n, you knows—'bout her, I mean?" He nodded slightly in the general direction of belowstairs.

"Certainly I know—now!" Bryce snapped. "Do I look like a damned fool? But I didn't know when I came to the door. How the hell would I?"

The Negro seemed to relax visibly. "Why, no suh—cose not," he said respectfully.

Bryce regarded the man thoughtfully. This was obviously no

dim-witted, transplanted field hand, and now the captain thought he understood a little of the man's loyalty to his mistress. It was hardly a thing to question or condemn, rather the contrary.

"I didn't come here to pay a social call either," the captain went on. "You're smart enough to know that. You saw the men outside and in the road. But we're not Yankee savages either, even if we do look like it."

"No *suh!*" Jason agreed earnestly.

"All right. But my men are hungry as dogs. That's my business here and I don't intend to forget that for *any* reason. You understand?"

"I—I reckon so, Cap'n, but maybe if'n you'd spell it out a little mo'—"

"Very well. You're the major-domo here, I take it. You know how much it takes to feed thirty-five men hungry enough to eat skunk. They'll need supper too. Now see that the stuff gets put on your kitchen gallery and I'll send a detail after it. In the circumstances I'd hate to have to send a bigger detail to work over your smokehouse and pantry in person, but I *could*. Do you follow me?"

"I'll manage, Cap'n," Jason said quietly.

"Good. Er—Mrs. Lawton naturally caught me a little unawares but I'll manage something when I go back downstairs. Now get moving!"

When the Negro had gone he stripped, took his time at the basin, and kicked himself for not requesting a razor. He grinned wryly at his face, bewhiskered but now relatively clean, in the mirror of the huge marble-topped dresser. He was sure he had the distinction of being the only man in A Company, if indeed not the whole brigade, who for ten days had had anything resembling a bath, or even a decent wash. The slug of brandy he took from the dresser decanter left him breathless for a moment—

But when he presently returned to the parlor the lady wasn't there—yet in a sense she was too, the Mrs. General Lawton of twenty-five years ago. The girl turned quickly at the sound of his footsteps in the hall and a hand went to her throat as he came toward her. Her hair was arranged the same as her mother's, except its color was a midnight black. Her eyes were the same wide electric blue and she was beautiful in spite of her look of worry, of inner retreat.

"Captain, please," she said swiftly, directly, "I have just come in and talked with my mother and I must explain—"

"No," he interrupted, "that's hardly necessary. I'm not altogether stupid and I talked to your man Jason. In fact, I made certain arrangements with him. I hope you will not dislike me too much"—why was he saying this last?—"because there is nothing you can or I will do about it."

"I'm afraid I don't understand, sir."

"It's very simple, Mrs. Pleasants. My men are hungry and this establishment is going to feed them. That was my sole reason for stopping here."

She started slightly at his use of her name. "I don't see—but really we have almost nothing to spare, sir. And surely you haven't any right—"

"Right has nothing to do with it," he said, suddenly harsh, "and I have no choice."

"I still don't quite understand," she said in a voice that seemed obviously puzzled, and honestly so. "I—I went to see some friends this morning and those Yankee soldiers hadn't molested them at all—"

"What? What the devil are you talking about?" In his sudden excitement he took a sudden, almost threatening step toward her, though he had no slightest thought of threat.

"Why, Mr. Gilmore said there were literally hundreds of Yankee riders went past his place and they didn't even stop except a couple of them to inquire about the road. He found out this morning that they took his only two horses but—"

"For Christ's sake!" he said, oblivious of the company. In his excitement he took another step toward her and seized her by the wrist, not thinking of her at all now in the personal sense.

She drew a startled breath as she snatched her arm away. "Why, you must be mad—" and then she bit her lip over the word she did not, would not, ordinarily use or even think.

"Where? Where was this?" he demanded harshly.

"Why, on the Cedar Springs road, about two miles north of us here—"

"Yes—yes, and when?"

"Yesterday evening, I think he said, some time just before dark. He knew they were Yankees—he could see that plain enough, but at least they didn't steal anything—well, nothing except the horses."

He made a small gesture toward her wrist. "I'm sorry," he said, "for that. This is terribly important to us. But as for stealing—we do what we have to in the circumstances and we didn't make those. At another time and place, Mrs. Pleasants, I'm sure meeting you would have been a most rewarding experience. Believe me, if I had known about your mother I would have done this differently. Well—"

"If you've finished, why don't you go?" she said steadily.

He bowed stiffly, turned on his heel, and strode out of the parlor. What else was there to do?

Down at the roadside Rogers rolled over on his back and said amiably, "Well, where in hell you been—making a private peace treaty with Jeff Davis?"

"None of your God-damned business," Bryce said with quiet savagery.

Rogers popped upright and exclaimed, "Well, I'll be teetotally damned! Now what've I done?"

"Forget it," Bryce said apologetically. "I've got some news that changes a number of things. Now listen—"

So it was Rogers who took a detail and picked up the forage from the rear gallery of the house—taking Captain Bryce at his word, Jason had performed handsomely. Evidently he figured he'd better. And while he was at it the lieutenant stole three fresh horses—or rather he traded their three worst nags for three fresh ones. Standard procedure.

Rogers wouldn't care, Bryce told himself. The house and its occupants meant nothing to him, just another relay stop on the road to wherever they were going. Perhaps, just then, he could not have explained his own feeling about the two women, but he would personally have starved before going back to the house.

"See anybody up there?" he asked when Rogers returned.

"Just a smart-looking nigger in a fancy striped weskit. He didn't say much, just looked like he might bite my leg off," Rogers said cheerfully. "You must have twisted somebody's arm clear up to his neck—or was it hers? Got three man-sized hams, to say nothing of a bushel of yams and a lot of other plunder. Say, not bad-looking horses, huh? Too bad there weren't more of 'em. You know, I been thinking, maybe after the war I'll take up horse stealin' as a regular trade. Fully experienced man."

"Let's move on a piece," Bryce said sourly. "I guess we have to steal people's grub but we don't have to insult them by eating it on their front lawn."

A half mile or so farther on they stopped again and worked havoc on the supplies from the Lawton ménage. Bryce, in spite of his own hunger, was anxious to get on but he allowed the men to make the most of the occasion. They would later travel the better for it.

Something over a mile to the north at the next crossroad they found the trail of the brigade. This time there was no mistaking it—a blind man could have found it with his hands—the deep dust of the road marked with hundreds of hoofprints, the kind of trail left only by a really sizable body of cavalry.

The captain knew what he had to do now. He leaned on his saddle pommel and looked them over man by man, trying to make a choice. He would have picked Sergeant Brown as a matter of course but didn't feel like sparing him. The sergeant was a man to have beside you when you needed a man. He said, "Sergeant Baker, Privates Monahan and Burke. Unload your gear and split it up among the rest of the boys to carry for you. Keep your pistols and if you don't have a few extra rounds, get them from somebody else. Switch your horse gear to the three horses Lieutenant Rogers just requisitioned at that last place we stopped—they look pretty good. The track of the column is right there in front of you. All you have to do is ride like hell until you catch the brigade —and don't spare the horses."

"Yes sir," Baker said eagerly. "What'll I tell the Old—I mean Colonel Marlowe or Major Gray?"

"Tell him we're on our way—oh, hell, he'll know that anyway. Just say this: 'Captain Bryce's compliments and he respectfully requests that A Company be allowed to burn its own bridges from here on.' He'll understand that."

"We're on our way, Captain!"

And within minutes they were. The rest of A Company gave them a cheer as the thick dust swirled under the hoofs.

From an objective view, Bryce thought wryly, if and when they rejoined the brigade—and that now seemed to be a probability rather than a vague possibility; how much better off would they be? About all you could say positively was that they'd have more company. But that was only part of his mind thinking. Over and beyond that was the gratifying knowledge that the brigade, at least as of last night, was still a free operating force. More than once, especially during the last couple of days, Bryce had suspected that such was not the case—the odds were all in the other direction. The notion had given him an almost overburdening feeling of vast loneliness. But furthermore, if their luck held, in a matter of hours he could report "Mission accomplished"—and damn Marlowe! He suspected that Marlowe had never actually expected A Company to rejoin the column. Well, Marlowe, the granite-minded sonofabitch, he could be shown too! He wondered whether, had he been in Marlowe's boots, he would have had the guts (that wasn't quite the word but at the moment he couldn't think of a better) to dispatch a lone company on a mission such as A Company had had. Would he?

As for the rest of A Company, the knowledge that the brigade was still intact and now only a relatively few hours ahead of them was like a collective injection of some potent drug.

29

The Prodigals

Colonel Marlowe silently cursed the unpredictable geography of rural Mississippi. As usual this failed to alter the tactical situation but it relieved his feelings.

Now in the back of his mind was the gradually growing fear—no, that was hardly the word for it yet—that his—their luck was due to run out any time. Already he'd had more than his share, more than he had any right to expect, and he knew it.

At the moment he saw and understood his tactical position precisely but it was one of those things he could not, for the time being, change one iota. He did not consider himself in a predicament yet but the situation had all the makings of one.

Somewhat against his better judgment he had once more divided his force, temporarily, of course—if I keep doing this, he reminded himself, I'll wind up as a one-man cavalry expedition.

Now he waited it out near the middle of the ten-mile stretch of road which connected the bridge over the Strong River and the ferry crossing at the far wider and deeper Pearl River. Approximately the remaining half of the First Illinois was strung out between this point and the Pearl to the west. Secord and the Second were some five miles behind him, at the Strong bridge. Exactly where Gray and the other half of the First were he could only guess—and hope.

The situation had developed in a way he might have foreseen but hadn't. But even if he had foreseen it he did not believe he could have done otherwise; this was simply one of those risks which had to be taken. Back there at the bridge the Strong flowed roughly from north to south. Ten miles west of the Strong bridge the larger Pearl also flowed roughly from north to south but it was not bridged—it could be negotiated here only by a lone horse-powered ferry. Then to really complicate matters further, a mile or so south of the Strong bridge, that is downstream, that river turned almost straight west to join the Pearl. One or two, perhaps even a few, strongly mounted horsemen might have made it across these streams, especially the smaller Strong, by swimming, but for the entire brigade to try it was out of the question. The colonel had to rely on the already provided crossings—anything else was too big a gamble.

This was terrible ground here but even so Marlowe could have swung to his left, southward, and followed around the south bank of the Strong without actually crossing it. That would still have brought him smack against the Pearl, with a possible crossing he knew not where. And cross the Pearl he must if he was to reach Hazlehurst and the New Orleans & Jackson Railroad. Originally these had been only possible, not even probable, objectives, but now that he had in fact come this way they were there and had to be negotiated.

Why not, then, simply plunge on across the Pearl and into Hazlehurst? Well, several reasons. For one thing, they knew there was Rebel force behind them and to the north, near the line of the Southern. How much they didn't know, but they knew it was there—Secord had two companies probing for it right now. This force had smartly stayed east of the Strong, outside the loop formed by the conjunction of the two streams. Elemental, of course, for Secord to destroy the Strong bridge and so leave the pursuing Rebel force outside the loop—except that that would leave the brigade on the inside of the loop with no place to go but ahead. So far Marlowe had gone straight ahead, not stopping once for reasons outside his own control, not even considering a possible line of retreat. This was different. For Hazlehurst ahead, on the N. O. & J., was hardly more than thirty miles below Jackson; any amount of troops could have been moved down there in less than two hours. For all Marlowe knew, up to now that is, Hazlehurst and the railroad might very well be swarming with Rebel force. They had the previous night, some of them, moved as far forward as the east bank of the Pearl but for good reasons could go no farther then—and if the brigade should be caught between the railroad and the bottleneck at the Pearl ferry, then a smart Rebel commander, one with sufficient force at his disposal, could make hash of the brigade. Or if he was caught with rivers on three sides of him, with Jackson and the Southern on the fourth side—particularly if he had destroyed the Strong bridge—then no miracle he could imagine would save him there either. Whether his invisible opponents were working toward this end the colonel could not know; he had to go on the theory that they might be.

Now much, perhaps everything, depended on what Dick Gray was doing, had done already this morning—and where the devil *was* Gray?

He lay back on the warm grass with his eyes closed but not even dozing now. His mind, tired as it was, was still too active for sleep. Then he came upright, looked around, and said sharply, "Davis!"

"Yes sir," the lieutenant answered wearily.

"How long now since there was any word from Secord?"

"Mmm. Two—no, nearer three hours, Colonel."

"Get a courier back there and see what the devil he's up to now. No, better go see for yourself."

"Yes sir," Davis said, wearier now than ever. He had just gotten soundly asleep for the first time in twenty-two hours.

. . . They had reached the Strong bridge last night some two hours after dark. Leaving the Second there, Marlowe had gone on ahead with Gray and part of the First. It had been almost three hours later when one of the men from the point came back and reported they had reached the Pearl.

"What's there?" Marlowe had asked impatiently.

"Mighty little you can see, sir. The road slopes right down into the river and o' course she's plenty high now. You can tell where the ferry comes in easy enough, but in this dark that's about all."

"Hmm. See anything on the other side?"

"Nary a thing, Colonel. Black as the back yard of hell on Halloween night."

Marlowe turned to the dark figure that was Major Gray. "Come on, Dick," he said. "Let's have a look for ourselves."

But, as the soldier had reported, there was little to be seen except the dark swift water and a vague line which might have been the far bank.

"God damn it!" Marlowe swore. "The ferry *would* be on the other bank. If we had it over here now—"

"In this black stuff, and on that water?" Gray said harshly. "I don't mind losing men in normal wear and tear, you expect that, but I wouldn't put a dog out there now and I'm not scared of water either. Get the ferry out of control just once and what've you got? You lose a boatload of men and animals and leave the brigade up the creek without a paddle to boot. Christ, Jack!"

"Well, all right," Marlowe conceded. Frequently Gray was right and this was just common sense anyway. "Until first light then—"

At daylight a thick, chilling mist hugged the water but did not obscure the opposite bank—the mist would burn off later with the sun. The three point men, still in the civilian dress and with no weapons showing, led their animals to the water's edge and began waving arms and yelling. After what seemed an age a man on the far bank emerged from the ferryhouse, yawned, stretched, and finally produced a team from a lean-to shed. At long last he led the team to the wooden ferry and placed them on the treadmill apparatus. The treadmill in turn was geared to a series of wooden friction pulleys which ran on the guide cable stretching from one bank to the other—in the darkness they hadn't seen the cable the night before. As a vehicle it was very nearly the water-borne version of the oxcart, almost as primitive, as awkward, and if possible even slower. It seemed to take forever to cross even after the ferryman got it under way.

Here on this side, at the ferry approach, it was quiet as a graveyard. There was plenty of cover and except for Bullen and his cohorts there were no horsemen in sight.

One of the three men spat in disgust and said wearily, "Jesus, you think the Second Coming's slow, take a look at that."

"I dunno," a second voice answered. "Army payday's got it beat all hollow for bein' slow."

The scow finally grounded on the muddy margin and the bewhiskered, one-gallused local Charon said cheerfully, "Mornin', gents. Out a mite early, ain't ye?"

"Some maybe," Sergeant Bullen agreed. "Got some business in Hazlehurst that won't wait too long."

"Un-hunh. Ain't seen nothin' of a big mess o' Yank calvary, have y'all?"

"Why, Godamighty, no!" Andy said innocently. "Is there supposed to be some around?"

"Yup—plenty. So they say anyhow. Feller come all the way out from Hazlehurst las' night'n said be on the lookout for 'em. Dang fool wanted me to cut the ferry line but I told'm he better bring hisself along plenty o' help any time he wanted that done. Why, hell's far, just about as soon cut m'own throat. I tol' him, I said, 'Man, I'll take keer o' any Yanks that shows up at *this* landin'—' "

"Well," Andy said agreeably, "now's your chance to get started, Mister, an' we're in a hellfire hurry." He brought the heavy Navy Colt around from behind him and jammed it so hard in the old man's thin belly that he lost his chew as he coughed and leaned forward to ease his midriff.

"Now, y'all looky here, Mister—"

"Shut up an' get back there and keep that team up an' comin'! We'll take charge of the boat from here on!"

The business of the pistol was of course pointless. The old man was as harmless as a new pup and as helpless. Not that the Sergeant meant him any personal harm. The pistol more than anything was a symbol of their utter weariness and tearing impatience of everything.

The ferrying turned out to be a study in slow motion and apparently nothing could be done to speed it up. Because of the high, swift current the boat, especially when loaded, was thrust hard against the guide cable and the primitive power plant had to overcome that friction as well as move the awkward craft forward. The leaky hull, even with dangerous crowding, held an absolute maximum of twenty men and horses. The trip across, loaded, required a full six minutes—Marlowe timed it carefully. The trip back empty was a little faster, but the little extra time was more than lost in loading and unloading. Marlowe did rapid mental arithmetic. Five round trips per hour, a maximum total of one hundred men and horses. With A Company still missing the strength of the column still stood at around nine hundred men and horses. He was a little shocked at what the figures added up to.

Marlowe and Gray had crossed in the first load and now the colonel was wearing a path on the far bank with his nervous pacing. He smoked furiously, pausing now and then to scowl angrily at the whole ferrying business. Presently he turned abruptly to Gray, who was leaning against a tree with his eyes closed, almost as though in pain.

"Dick!" he said sharply, "does anything strike you as peculiar about this ferrying process?"

"Several things," Gray said wearily, "but I'm no mind reader. Which one are you thinking about, Jack?"

"This crossing is one hell of a chore as such, Dick, but there's a worse side to it—time. At this rate it'll take better than four hours just to cross the First alone. Very well. It would take just exactly the same amount of time to haul 'em back the other way —if it turns out that way. If some real hell should turn up at Hazlehurst and the railroad, and we should have to back up to here, most of them simply won't get back across because there just will not be time. We'd be cornered in here like steers in a slaughter pen."

"You put these things so delicately, Jack," Gray said slowly. "But all right. I'm with you so far, but what then?"

Marlowe smiled sardonically at the tired major. "To avoid crossing them all back I'm not going to bring them all over in the first place."

The major frowned slightly. "You'll have to be plainer than that for me."

"It occurs to me that if you can't handle Hazlehurst with, say, two hundred men, then it might very well also be too hot for the whole brigade—what we have left of one. It could be one of those things where we might win on points but take such a hell of a chewing in the process that it wouldn't be worth it. If you have to come backing out in a hurry it'll be easier to get you back across the Pearl here than it would be the brigade, or even all the First. Do you follow me?"

"If *I* have to back out—" Gray said slowly, a little stiffly. He was wide awake again now. "Yes, I reckon I follow you all right, Jack. But you could be all wrong—about Hazlehurst, I mean."

"That's right—I could be. So that's why you'll go on to Hazlehurst and find out."

"All right. Two hundred men, did you say?"

"I'm willing to gamble that that's either enough or we don't have enough altogether. Anyhow, it's enough to try. Take the first two hundred men to come across."

"Very well. What, specifically, do you want done—supposing we're in a position to do anything?"

The colonel shrugged, almost as though dismissing the whole matter from his mind. "The usual thing—you know. See what you can learn in general. Tear up as much railroad as you can *if* you can. After all"—Marlowe grinned at Dick—"we haven't had a chance at a nice railroad since we left Newton and it seems a shame to pass up any opportunities. Oh, yes—take that damned Rebel deserter with you and get rid of him somewhere. Get rid of him if you have to shoot him. I'm tired of looking at him and feeding him."

When Gray and his force had gone the colonel—he assumed personal command of the remainder of the First now—posted a patrol about a half mile west of the Pearl, left another at the ferry landing on the west bank, and withdrew the ferryboat to the east side. Thus it was that the remaining larger half of the First became scattered along the road from the bank of the Pearl eastward—this was the way they had done most of their resting since leaving Newton, and at noon the colonel found himself fuming restlessly at a point midway between the Pearl and the Strong.

As it turned out, in all probability Major Gray would have had more trouble getting from the suburbs into downtown Chicago than he had getting into Hazlehurst. As was so often the case their chief antagonist was the inexorable arithmetic of time. It had taken from something before six to a little after eight to get his two hundred troopers over the Pearl. The ride to Hazlehurst took them up to eleven o'clock—or rather eleven found them about a mile outside the town while a patrol was sent on a routine reconnaissance of the place. This was simply ordinary procedure. By the time the patrol had returned and the main body moved forward again it was noon. These things require just so much time. There was the further fact that when they had started Dick Gray had been in no hurry. Oh, he hadn't held back, deliberately dawdled. But in a different frame of mind he could have made it into Hazlehurst far faster than he did. He was much too good an officer, in the purely routine military sense, to risk the safety of men on a mere personal whim of the moment. But now, after ten solid days of this, he was weary with a vast weariness that included his mind. He was well aware of this but it was something like a broken leg: until it improved of itself it could only be endured. He found that more and more he was asking men to repeat the simplest remarks; they just didn't always register the first time. The men were worn to the point of exhaustion also—and only naturally. But it was plain truth that he and Secord and Marlowe had carried the heaviest burden of wakefulness. You could count Blaney in that too, except that no one had the least notion of what had happened to him.

It would be unreasonable to suppose Gray *hoped* to find opposition at Hazlehurst, but he certainly expected to. It could, in his estimation, hardly be otherwise. Marlowe was guessing—or gambling—he *knew* no more about it than anyone else. It was true that the Old Man—damn him!—had been amazingly right so far. Right—or lucky? Either way he was so damnably sure, always, or so it seemed to Gray just now. Oh, Marlowe didn't parade it; he didn't have to; but it was always there. He would gamble his mother on his damned guesses. He would gamble the Second Iowa, the brigade, this half of the First Illinois, Major Dick Gray—

Damn his arrogant cocksureness! But if the Old Man would send four under-strength companies to do a brigade-sized job, then *he*, Major Richard Chase Gray, would damned well show him how to do it right. He did not, he told himself at the moment, give a good red damn if there were two thousand Reb troops waiting for him somewhere ahead! All this was the result of mental and physical fatigue, of course, for ordinarily Dick Gray was far more intelligent, but strange as the reasoning might be, right now it seemed to him to be perfectly logical. . . .

Actually there wasn't even a corporal's guard here to offer resistance. They simply rode into town without a hand being raised against them. Small boys and dogs followed their progress from the edge of town, their elders for the most part, unable to grasp so strange a development immediately, simply gaped in astonishment, assuming for the moment that these filthy, weary men and horses were some of their own. This was the local county seat but in size was little more than an overgrown village.

"I'd better get on down to the railroad," Gray told Landry of D Company. "Get down there yourself as soon as you can make it."

Landry nodded. "This shouldn't take too long."

They had worked this out on the way into town. D had in its charge the Rebel deserter-prisoner. From Captain Landry on down D Company, of which Private Schwartz had been a member, had its own notions concerning the hapless deserter. Left to themselves they would very likely have handled the situation much sooner—but of course there was always the Old Man. For his part, after two days of abuse and insults the bedeviled prisoner was ready to welcome almost any change short of immediate execution.

They rode up to the small wooden courthouse, the prisoner in their midst, looking a good deal like some of the posses not unknown hereabouts. Landry eyed the prisoner in disgust and said, "Unload, scum. You've stunk up a good honest horse long enough."

Perversely human, soldiers will often enough despise a deserter from the other side more than one of their own—perhaps because they can better understand the possible motivation of their own. In this instance there was, to be sure, something more than mere enemy desertion involved—they wouldn't have gone so far out of their way to kick a mere Rebel deserter as such.

"How about undoin' these, Cap'n?" The prisoner held up his bound wrists.

"Get down, I said!" Landry repeated. "Your legs aren't tied. Climb down before you get knocked down!"

The man managed awkwardly, fell heavily backward when his

left foot caught in the stirrup and he couldn't catch himself. They watched dispassionately as he got to his feet.

"Bullen, Crossman," Landry said. "Boot him up the steps and let's get this over with."

They entered the dim corridor, saw a door opening at the end labeled SHERIFF, and hustled the prisoner through it. A chunky red-faced man was reading a battered newspaper, his feet hoisted on the desk before him. He didn't appear to be armed but a heavy-calibered derringer lay on the littered desk top.

"You the sheriff?" Landry demanded without preamble.

"Why, no suh, I'm his head deputy. Sheriff's out *de*-liverin' a co't order. What can I do for you gents?"

The deputy had a pleasant enough manner. Then as he got to his feet he took a second quick, puzzled look. In all truth their uniforms were faded enough and now filmed with dust, as were their beards, hair, and hats, and at a glance it was hard for the layman to know what army they did belong to. A closer observer might have noticed the brass buckles stamped USA. But the deputy, whatever the cause, had already smelled a rat of some sort.

"Why say, y'all don't look to me—"

"Don't make any difference what we look like to you, Mister, but just so you don't worry over it I'll tell you right now we're out of the First Illinois Cavalry," Landry interrupted brusquely. As a routine precaution he picked the derringer from the desk and thrust it through his belt. "If the high sheriff's not around you'll do just as well. Got a prisoner here for you—this skunk of a Confederate army deserter. I understand your people pay a bounty on 'em but we won't insist on that. Well, you can handle him, can't you?"

"Well, now, I dunno about that. I don't know what authority y'all got bringin' him in here, fer instance—"

"Ah, hell," Landry said in vast disgust, "you don't need to know anything about any authority. We're making you a present of the murdering sonofabitch—it's as simple as that. You'll have to figure it out from there. There's this much more—chances are that if any of my men find him loose anywhere—and we'll be around a while—you'll have a dead deserter instead of a live one!"

Major Gray had made a beeline for the railroad station, taking with him Lieutenant Burr of B Company and a Corporal Sweet who was a telegrapher. There was always the chance that the station had already wired a warning somewhere but Gray doubted that. The majority of the men were still out of sight, there hadn't been time for the agent to be really sure of their identity and the station was some distance from the center of town, where he'd left Landry.

They walked into the empty station—apparently there was no train due in for at least a while. Gray stood unobtrusively at the ticket window, the others a little to one side. The operator was busy copying something and over a shoulder he said, "Just a minute, please."

Gray glanced inquiringly at Sweet, who had an ear cocked toward the chattering telegraph sounder. Sweet's lips silently formed the words "Train order" and the major nodded.

The operator tapped an acknowledgment, closed the key, and came over to the window. Intent on the train order still in his hand, he hardly looked up as he said, "Yes sir?"

"Could I have a telegraph blank, please?"

"Yes *sir*—right here you are."

"Thanks," Gray said. "By the way, this is official army business. I'm Major Gray, First Alabama Volunteers—" It was often astonishing how much you could get away with if you simply acted as though everything was perfectly normal. So far the agent hadn't given the slightest indication that he surmised anything out of order. "We're hunting the Yankee cavalry that's supposed to be loose around here somewhere. You heard anything about that?"

"Why, some, Major—not a lot. The wire's carried quite a lot of stuff for down below here but when it's not for me I don't pay too much attention if I'm busy. You know how it is. And none of it was for me here."

"Yes, I see. Incidentally, we're from over west, along the river, sort of strangers around here, you might say. Who's in command at Jackson now?"

"Well, o' course Gen'l Pemberton hisself was there for a while—don't know if he is now or not." The agent frowned in concentration. "Last time I had anything for him from here seems like there was some Colonel Russell. Had charge of the local troops there, I reckon."

"Thanks," Gray said; "that'll do well enough. All right, boys."

Burr opened the door and he and Sweet stepped into the office. The agent turned as he exclaimed, "Here, now y'all wait a minute. This is private—" but that's as far as he went. He'd never had a pair of Colts staring nakedly at him from point-blank range before. He started to raise his arms but Burr said amiably, "Never mind that, Mister. We don't need to make you uncomfortable. We just want to use your telegraph outfit for a little while before we wreck it for you. In fact, you can even sit down—no, over there in that corner."

Gray came in and looked around, paused, and examined a fancifully lithographed pictorial map of the New Orleans & Jackson system. "Well, well," he said, "this might come in handy." After looking carefully at the map for another long moment he took it down, folded it, and thrust it under his belt. Then he took the telegraph form and wrote rapidly. Once he turned to the operator and snapped, "What's your name?"

"Johnson." It came reluctantly.

"All of it!"

"Amos Johnson."

Gray finished the message and handed it to Sweet, saying, "That ought to do it if anything will."

Sweet said to the operator, "What's the Jackson call?"

"JN."

In less than half a minute the Jackson operator answered with a "Go ahead—JN."

Sweet fired it at them:

Colonel Russell,
Commanding CSA Forces,
Jackson

Heavy cavalry force under General Marlowe sighted heading rapidly northeast Strong River bridge direction Brandon or Morton on Southern ten this morning information just received this office.

Sgd., Amos Johnson, Agent N. O. & J.

"You'll never get away with this," the operator said in sudden defiance.

"It might be," Gray agreed, "and then again we might. But one thing's sure, you won't be able to contradict that for a while unless you do it on foot. You got any personal stuff around here?"

"A few odds and ends. Why? They ain't worth stealin'."

"Well, no, but you've got about two minutes to get it out of here before this place starts to burn. All right, Lieutenant. Better get the boys started to work. Break the telegraph line first. Have 'em start here and work to the north."

A half-hour later the telegraph line was down for a hundred yards and both passenger depot and freight house were well ablaze. From there on they worked methodically on tracks and wire. It was a repetition of Newton but on a small scale and they didn't catch any rolling stock on hand.

It was hot hard work but as usual the men, once they were at it, carried on enthusiastically. Gray was up and down the line, exhorting, giving an order here and there, mostly just keeping an eye on the whole operation. Every now and then he frowned in worried concentration. There was something—something that somehow persisted in eluding his tired mind. There was something he knew he had to do, ought to do, but now it just wasn't there.

His eyes felt as though they were loaded with cinders and he wondered a little vaguely if he was feverish. Well, at least he was showing Marlowe, damn him! He still wished he could recall this other thing.

In these things, as in battle, time both crawls and rushes away. As Gray lowered his canteen after a long drink he saw, through the drifting smoke, a mounted rider apparently talking to one of his own pickets. There was something familiar about the rider but in the haze and at this distance he couldn't quite recognize him. Even as he watched the man straightened in the saddle, set in his spurs, and tore off toward the east, in the direction of the Pearl crossing.

The major rode quickly over to the picket and said, "Who the devil was that, Keck?"

"Why, Lieutenant Davis, sir, the Old—Colonel Marlowe's aide. He wanted to know what time we got here and if we'd had any trouble, so naturally I told him. I said you was right around somewhere but he said never mind, he was in a hell of a hurry."

The knowledge of what he had done, or, more precisely, *not* done, struck the major's consciousness like a blow in the face. This was what he had tried to remember and somehow failed . . . he had known between eleven and twelve that Hazlehurst was wide open. A single rider pressing a good horse could have had the information, the thing Marlowe needed above all, to the Pearl ferry crossing something after one o'clock. Marlowe would have started the ferrying again and those first across would have been *here* by this time—it was three-thirty now. The Second, providing their patrols were in, would have long since fired the Strong bridge and themselves be in the ferrying process by now. Gray could see every detail of it in his mind. Marlowe, tired of waiting and sweating it out by the roadside, unable to comprehend, wondering futilely what in God's name could have prevented Gray from getting at least *one* man back, had sent Davis to see for himself, and Davis had to make the entire round trip.

The hours of silence would naturally have indicated to the colonel that something was mightily wrong—five full hours they couldn't afford to lose. And Marlowe wouldn't risk ferrying a single other man until Davis got back—that was the whole proposition. Christ's name! Five full hours lost into eternity because he, Dick Gray, was a damned fool who couldn't remember routine procedure. He had been cavorting around Hazlehurst, thinking he was cutting a heroic figure, while the simple truth was that he might, possibly, have put the whole brigade in a hole that even Marlowe's luck couldn't get them out of. There would be five more full hours during which he, Gray, would not dare pull out of Hazlehurst, either forward or back, while even now Rebel troops were probably moving both north and south along the N. O. & J. The whole brigade *could* have been into Hazlehurst and out again—except for the brilliant Major Dick Gray.

He suddenly knew what it was to be simultaneously ill both physically and emotionally.

The permanent colonelcy of the First had never been filled—it had been more or less taken for granted that he, Gray, would have it in the natural course of time. But now—well, the important thing now was his failure, his failure in what was perhaps the worst spot they had been in thus far. Marlowe would be ruthless; he hadn't the slightest doubt of that. Of course he had no fear of the colonel in the purely personal sense—it was this larger, more impersonal thing that Marlowe represented. The Old Man hadn't hesitated in the matter of Keller, and Keller's temporary defection had been as nothing compared with this.

All this he saw in a matter of seconds while he sat there in the saddle, looking at Corporal Keck but in fact not seeing him at all. As stiffly as a rheumatic old man he got to the ground and for a moment stood there clinging to a stirrup strap—he couldn't know how suddenly white his face had gone.

The picket, Keck, said anxiously, "Say, there—you all right, Major?"

"What? Oh, sure, I'm all right. Damned smoke got down my windpipe the wrong way, I guess."

"Yes sir," Keck said sympathetically. "It's a nuisance."

It was almost six-thirty and already the shadows were lengthening rapidly. Here in the bottom of this timber-walled road it was already early dusk. They were standing at the Strong bridgehead and Secord said hotly, "God damn it, Jack! We're lucky they got back at all, let alone late. It was you insisted we send Fairlie out in that damned brush. They rode twenty extra miles and lost six men while they tore up that damned nosy Rebel patrol, then you complain because they're not back when you think they ought to be. By God, I—"

"Forget it, Frank, forget it," Marlowe said wearily. "I'm sorry. We're all a little too close to the end of our tethers. But by God there was a while there a couple of hours ago when I think I could have strangled Gray with my bare hands—"

"Say," Secord said, mollified, "what happened up there anyway? I heard the word came back that Hazlehurst was all clear but—"

"That's the whole point. But never mind that now." Marlowe flipped the bridle reins over his horse's drooping neck. "We've got work to do. I wouldn't risk that ferry crossing in the dark but now we have to. Well, the men are more familiar with the ground now and we'll have to risk bank fires for light—"

He broke off as a shot exploded somewhere back down the road and the chorus of yells was set off. Marlowe turned back to Secord and frowned. "Now what the devil is coming off? It doesn't sound—"

In the narrow road men made way for the galloping horses, but the word went ahead faster and presently the two officers caught the gist of it.

"Hey, A—!"

"A Company—!"

"A Company's made it back!"

It rang down the line of the Second like a hallelujah.

A Company, of course, was not back, but most certainly a visible part of it was. Sergeant Baker swung down and saluted and Marlowe offered his hand.

"If I didn't see you myself I'm not sure I'd believe it," the colonel said. "But you're not all of it? I mean—"

"No sir, Colonel. We had three fresh horses and we been floggin' hell out of 'em ever since near noon. The Lord willing, the rest of 'em will be along directly."

"Captain Bryce?" Marlowe said quickly.

"Yes sir. He's all right, Colonel. I mean he's *sure* all right. He sent word—'Cap'n Bryce's compliments and he respectfully requests that A company be allowed to burn its own bridges from here on in.'"

Marlowe glanced at Secord in the fading light and chuckled wryly. "A nice touch. I appreciate the captain's feelings and I doubt that in his position I'd have been able to put it so diplomatically. Well, Sergeant, it's a good thing you made it when you did or he'd have been too late for this one."

The sergeant looked—he'd been in too much of a hurry before—and swallowed hard. The long wooden bridge was wide enough for only one normal-width vehicle and on half of that they had heaped dry brush from end to end, barely leaving room for two horses closely abreast.

Baker said, "Yes sir, I see."

The colonel sighed. "Well, how far behind would you say they are, Sergeant?"

"Well, not so far probably in miles, sir. It's just that with them wore-out horses they don't make any time."

"You'll have to wait for them, Frank," Marlowe said. "Anyway somebody will. There's no choice now."

"No, not with them this close," Secord agreed. "I'd hope somebody would do the same for me. All right—I'll leave two companies to wait for them and then fire the bridge behind them."

"Good enough," Marlowe said. "You might as well wait here with your men, Sergeant. Get a little rest. Hard to tell when you'll get another chance."

Marlowe moved off down the fast-darkening road, Sergeant King dozing twenty feet behind him.

Mentally the colonel damned Gray to hell. If Bryce had taken the majority when it was offered him this possibly, probably wouldn't have happened. Then he reined in his thought processes abruptly. There was no balancing these things in one's mind. If Gray *had* functioned properly then the Strong bridge would have been charred and useless embers at least two hours ago, and in that case A Company—

He shook his head angrily, almost like a bewildered animal. He thought he had been tired before but it had never been anything like this. And it would get worse before it got better. What would happen, he wondered, if he simply and finally fell out of the saddle and stayed out? Probably, among other things, the war would go on.

. . . Near two in the morning, somewhere on the road west of Hazlehurst, Sergeant King shook the colonel's shoulder again and then kicked the small fire into fresh life. For an instant the blaze flared up and the light outlined the sergeant's homely features.

"Let it go, Sergeant," Bryce said. "The hell with it. Let him sleep, now he's at it."

"No sir," King said stubbornly. "He said to wake him when you come in, so I wake him if it takes till sunup. 'Course if it does," he added, "I'll catch hell on that account too."

As though waiting for some special signal Marlowe rolled over and came to his feet in one continuous movement. "All right, Sergeant," he said through a stifled yawn. "You made it as usual." He held out a hand and said, "Well, welcome back, Bryce."

"Thanks, Colonel," the captain said dryly, "I appreciate the sentiment but I might add, welcome back to what?"

Marlowe pursed his lips slightly and then said mildly, "I was being strictly personal, Asa, no more."

"It's occurred to me often enough that you never really expected us back."

Well, the colonel thought, in the circumstances perhaps he's entitled to a little bitterness, but he said, "Oh, I don't know, Asa—I always thought the odds were better than even. Maybe I have more confidence in you than you have in yourself. Bad trip?"

Bryce shrugged wearily. "What could you expect?"

"About this whole business—do you know anything I don't know but ought to?"

Bryce shook his head. "I don't know what it would be. A hundred miles back and God knows how long ago I had a few things. They're worthless now. We've been concentrating on staying alive and finding the column."

"Lose any men?"

"One."

"Well, not bad, considering, not bad at all."

"As a statistic, no, but wherever the boy is, he won't appreciate that. It was a man lost to no purpose whatever."

It was Marlowe's turn to shrug indifferently. "How many do serve a purpose except in the over-all sense?" His tone was harsher now. "You think too much about that side of it, Asa. In this business you use the best means at hand. If you can't do that, then you don't belong in it in the first place."

For a moment Bryce was silent. There was never any point in fighting the colonel on this kind of ground. He said, "If that's all for tonight, Colonel—?"

"It's not, Bryce—not quite. I've got a point to make and it has to be done now. Sit down and take the weight off your feet."

Thinking, the colonel pushed the fire closer together with a bit of stick. There was a way to approach everything and everyone, including Bryce. He hoped he would find the right way the first time.

Watching Marlowe's heavy-lidded, mildly-brooding face, high-lighted now by the fire, Bryce thought: The ideal pro-consul, nineteenth-century fashion, holding himself to the main chance—or duty as he saw it—and devil take the hindmost.

"You had your chance at the majority," Marlowe said carefully, "and for your own reasons didn't take it. What would you say now if I offered you command of the First?"

"*What!*"

It wasn't a question, and Marlowe knew that. He merely said, "You heard me, Asa."

"But what happened to Gray? Did he—?"

"Nothing's happened to his corporeal body, not as far as I know. But I asked you a question that takes an answer."

"*Are* you offering it to me?" Bryce parried.

"Not as of this moment. I've been working something over in my mind and I wanted an answer to that part of it."

"On the basis of that alone then the answer is a plain and simple no—no, thanks, Colonel."

Marlowe sighed faintly. "That's about what I guessed it might be. Very well, then let me remind you of something else. Regulations provide that I operate this brigade in the best possible way, *according to my judgment*. So if the occasion arises, in my judgment, then you will damned well take the First because that will be an order!"

"And you expect something like that?" Bryce knew now that Marlowe wasn't, hadn't been, merely making conversation. But A Company had been away for six full days and almost five full nights and so at the moment knew nothing of the thousand things which might have happened to the brigade in that time.

"I have to provide for any possibility," Marlowe said shortly. "I thought you were entitled to at least a suggestion of what might happen. Better get what sleep you can and I'll see you to-morrow. And Asa—I meant it when I said I'm glad to see you back."

"Then we're even, Colonel. Good night."

Marlowe lay back down and closed his eyes instantly.

As Bryce walked away in the darkness he smiled a little sardonically. The colonel was not always brilliant but certainly he was seldom dull.

30

A Bad Day

As surely as he knew his name was Dick Gray he knew he was due to feel Marlowe's wrath. What form it might take was entirely unpredictable but it would come just as certainly as tomorrow's sunrise. There was Keller, for instance, whose transgression had been less than his own. If Keller was being hurt he didn't show it on the outside. At the same time Gray knew the man was not granite all the way through. Probably at least two thirds of the men did not know why Keller was under arrest, but he was, and markedly so. That fact all the men did know, and that alone was enough to make him suspect in their eyes, to undermine and unbalance his ordinary position in the over-all scheme of things, to render him neither fish nor fowl.

The price of error was one of the most uncertain things in this army. Like everyone else Gray knew of officers who had committed staggering errors and received not even a mild reprimand. For other far less disastrous defaults men were broken on the rack of official, by-the-book disapproval. The uncertainty itself was one of the worst parts of these things. For Gray that had begun around three-thirty yesterday afternoon, when he saw Lieutenant Davis head eastward on the Pearl River road. There had then been nothing he could do but begin waiting it out.

It had been some time after dark when the first elements of the second half of the First began to arrive in the town. Gray had with him Companies B, C, and D. When Companies E, F, and G arrived Gray found they were under the command of Captain Fred Ware, E Company. Ware found Gray at the general store-post office the latter had taken over as temporary headquarters.

"Go straight on across the railroad—what's left of it—for about three hundred yards and you'll find a good bivouac spot," Gray said, giving the order as a matter of everyday routine.

"Sorry, Major." Captain Ware appeared strangely apologetic. "It so happens we're not stopping. Orders from Colonel Marlowe. I was just to stop here and let you know."

"Oh? You mean you're going on ahead? What about the rest of the regiment—and the Second?"

"I wouldn't know about that last, Major. For that I reckon you'll have to wait on the Old Man. But we're not exactly going on ahead. I'm going south here, to around Byhala, to tear up some more railroad."

"Well, hell, we've torn it apart here already. What more does he want?" Gray, understandably, was becoming more bewildered by the moment.

Ware shrugged. "Don't ask me, Major. The colonel did say that if we went on west and south, as he figured, this would be our last chance to get in a lick at the railroads. Nothin' much between here and the Big River now."

"But you've got to get back—"

"Sure. We'll cut back west some time in the morning and pick up the column—I hope. I'd hate like hell to be another A Company, especially now that we've got this far."

Ware, of course, had left the bank of the Pearl ahead of the news of A Company's return.

"The colonel sent no word for me at all?"

"Not by me, Major—except for me to tell you where I'm going."

"Well," Gray said a little lamely, "watch yourself and good luck, Fred. I'll see you tomorrow—let's hope."

Standing on the strip of sagging wooden sidewalk outside the store, he watched the three companies turn the corner and plod southward in the night. He shrugged—and wondered. At this rate the First Illinois would shortly cease to exist as a regiment.

When Marlowe finally rode into Hazlehurst Gray didn't see him. He did not, in fact, know Marlowe was there until Lieutenant Davis sought him out to deliver a terse order.

"We're going to move on a ways yet tonight," Davis said. "The colonel is worried that with all this delay some force is likely to come down on us from up Jackson way. You are to let the Second go by and then move your men in behind them. There's a small detail still back at the Strong bridge but you needn't wait on them."

"*Behind* the Second, did you say?"

"That's right, Major."

"Very well." The First had led the column for more than ten days, ever since La Grange, but apparently not any longer. "Did the colonel want to see me?"

"Not that I know of," Davis said woodenly. "Leastwise he didn't say so to me."

Was there veiled contempt, animosity in Davis's voice, Gray wondered? It didn't sound like it exactly, but still . . . He wished a little desperately that he could ask Davis what Marlowe had said when Davis got back to the Pearl in the afternoon, but of course that was impossible. He said shortly, "Very well, Davis."

The sun this morning rose an angry red and the rain began around eight o'clock. To their good fortune, it was neither storm nor downpour, just a steady fall of medium light rain that appeared set for most of the day. In time the mud would slow the column; it would slow the pursuit as well.

Riding toward the rear of the column now, Gray again failed to see Marlowe until after the rain began. It was around nine o'clock when, a short distance ahead, he spotted King by the roadside, holding the reins of Marlowe's riderless horse. As Gray came nearer the colonel emerged from the roadside brush, putting his clothing back in order. He wiped the saddle seat with a dirty handkerchief and had just remounted when Gray pulled out of line and moved over beside him. Sergeant King, his shoulders hunched as though in disgust at the rain, went on slowly down the road.

"Morning, Dick," Marlowe said around his dead cigar. His tone might have been warm or cold but muffled by the cigar it was hard to tell.

Gray was determined to keep this as cool and unemotional as possible. He said, "Well, Jack, hadn't we just as well get it over with now as any time?"

(It occurred to Gray that, while the colonel had so far said nothing officially damning, he had said no word about the workmanlike job they had done on the N. O. & J. yesterday afternoon. Never effusive about these things, the colonel was also seldom without a brief "Well done" when it was deserved. That, in itself, to Gray was symptomatic.)

"What was that?" Marlowe said absently. He seemed interested in something on the rain-misted horizon now. "Oh, yes. Well, I wish we could, but I'm afraid it's going to take three or four days yet, even if our luck holds up. I had a vague notion of cutting off here and trying for our lines below Vicksburg, but it simply won't do. We just don't know enough about the situation thereabouts—"

"Damn it, Jack! You know that wasn't what I meant." To Gray it was only too obvious that Marlowe was deliberately dissembling.

"No?" the colonel said blandly. He turned in the saddle and regarded Gray impersonally, somewhat (or so Gray thought) as though examining a strange species of insect. "Well, what then, Dick?"

"You know only too well I'm talking about that damn' fool mistake I made yesterday at Hazlehurst!" If Marlowe was going to force him to spell it out, well, now that he had opened his mouth he would have to go on.

"Oh, yes, that," Marlowe said thoughtfully. He regarded his dead and sodden cigar with distaste, then tossed it aside. "Well, frankly, I haven't had time to give much thought to it. Too many other things on my mind. And you wouldn't want me to go off half-cocked about it, would you, Dick?"

"By God, I know you!" Try as he would Gray couldn't keep all the anger out of his voice.

"Do you?" The question sounded as though the colonel was really interested in an answer. "Do you? I wonder? But if that's true you shouldn't really be in much doubt, should you? Still, you'll have to wait on more pressing matters, Dick."

The discussion ended there because the Colonel deliberately slapped his bridle reins and rode off, leaving Gray glaring after him in anger and frustration. He had seen Marlowe play this game before, at other times in fact he had rather admired the technique, though hardly so now. In spite of Marlowe's noncommittal attitude (he had experienced that before too) he was not foolish enough to suppose, or even hope, that Marlowe would choose to ignore the whole business. His whole experience with the colonel could only make him believe otherwise. He reminded himself that the only trouble to come out of the delay, at least so far, was the delay itself, but that was small comfort—

At three in the afternoon it was still raining. No one was excited or even surprised when spasmodic rifle fire broke out on the brigade's front. Their ears had been alerted, albeit unconsciously, for that special sound for so long that it was almost a relief when it came. At least that gave you an idea where *they* were at the moment. With the horses coming almost automatically to a stop in the road as the orders went back along the line, many men kept right on sleeping in their saddles. If there was real fighting to be done the officers would awaken them in time—that was their business.

Believing the civilian-dressed point no longer especially useful —admittedly Sergeant Bullen had done a first-rate job as long as it was necessary—Marlowe had ordered them recalled. He had an idea that such a thin subterfuge would no longer take in anyone pursuing the brigade in earnest. He knew that if he were managing the pursuit he would fine comb everything that moved on these roads. So now Bishop's B Company of the Second was out in front.

Marlowe and Secord, near the head of the column, pulled into the thin shelter of a chinaberry tree.

"Sounds like somebody means it," Secord said. "Want to send somebody up to see?"

"It never sounds *good* to me," Marlowe retorted. "Maybe we'd— No, let it go. Bishop will report when he has something. Let the other side do the pushing."

They waited, their faces expressionless, each lost for the moment in his own thoughts. The sky kept on dripping mildly but steadily.

The firing continued in an odd fashion, spasmodic, scattered, almost as though both sides were reluctant—both officers could easily recognize the difference between Bishop's carbines and the muskets on the other side. Of course some of the worst things often started like this, in the beginning both sides merely probing, getting set for the real thing to come. Actually the firing had a kind of unimportant sound, something like an offstage sound effect —except that to the brigade any and all firing was important now.

Even Marlowe was becoming impatient by the time Captain Bishop himself came slashing back through the mud to report.

"It's cavalry, anyway some of it," Bishop said hurriedly.

"How much?" Secord snapped.

Bishop shook his head. "Can't say exactly yet, sir. Of course as soon as we sighted 'em we slowed down, practically stopped, gave 'em a chance to show their hands if they wanted to. I got the impression—"

"For God's sake, Bishop! We've got to have something more than an impression!"

"I know, sir," the captain said stolidly, "but up to now that's all I've got. I saw maybe two, three companies of horse but I don't know what maybe I didn't see. This rain ain't bad but all the same it cuts down the distance you can be sure of anything. If you say so, sir, I'll drive on in and try to flush 'em out in the open."

Secord and Marlowe looked at each other briefly. Secord said, as though talking to himself, "Infantry with a cavalry screen ahead of it, maybe?"

Marlowe shrugged. "It always could be, Frank. I'll tell you, Captain. Dismount your men and move the animals back a reasonable distance. Then put the men in a skirmish line and move up, but easy. Don't rush it—just keep moving until you come up against something solid. The Rebs will either have to back up or stand. If they stand, we'll move in and back you up. We can't afford to tangle with a division but, by God, I'm not going to be held up now by a bunch of militia on horseback!"

Militia? Secord thought; he doubted it. When the captain had gone he said, "What do you think?"

"Only that it's too early to tell—or to worry. Damn such a country to hell!" Secord knew what Marlowe meant—only now and then did the pine forest and undergrowth break away so you could see a reasonable distance ahead, then it would close in again.

The firing continued but neither increased nor decreased. Marlowe said, "That could be real force up there, but where the hell would it come from? This is the Natchez road and there's no reason to suppose there's any considerable force there. Why should there be?"

Secord looked at him in mild astonishment but Marlowe was paying no attention to him. "Why should there be? Don't ask me, Jack. Why should *we* be here with nine hundred men? It's just as good a question. Well, what do you want to do?"

"Leave the Second mounted but put 'em in a double skirmish line, close order. They'll have hell in this underbrush but I can't help that now. I'll have the First left in column but pull them in closer."

"What there is left of the First."

"I know, damn it! Ware ought to be back by now if he's coming back."

Again Secord looked at Marlowe in mild wonder. There were a hundred reasons why Ware couldn't have gotten back and Marlowe should have been the first to realize that. Well, Secord thought, he's as exhausted as everybody else, but he said, "He may have come up at the rear already."

"Maybe—I doubt it. Gray is supposed to let me know."

But Ware wasn't back from Byhala—not quite yet.

So now in the shape of a big, lopsided T the brigade moved forward, more slowly now, waiting for something to happen and feeling the tension mounting.

After what seemed an age Bishop was back. "They're not running," he said to Marlowe, "but they're sure backing up as fast as we move in. If there's any infantry strength up there it would likely have showed itself by now. Give me two more companies, Colonel, and I'll damned well settle it one way or another!"

Marlowe shook his head. "Not yet, Captain. Keep your pants on for a bit. There's a small town up ahead, I'd guess not much more than a wide spot in the road—Union Church. I don't want to chance breaking the column apart again—anyway not until Ware gets back."

"Just say the word."

"Don't worry, I will," Marlowe said grimly, "but not yet. You got any men hurt?"

"Nary a one unless it's happened since I've been back here now. So far the Johnnies don't seem to be shooting worth a damn. Kind of seems like they're not really trying."

"Good. Just keep pushing, Bishop. It's early yet."

Early in the game he meant, of course, not the hour of the day. Time rushed away and in this rain darkness would be coming on in an hour and a half.

Presently Secord rode in beside him again and Marlowe said, "What do you think, Frank?"

Secord shook his head. "I'm not. No use in both of us guessing. The way I feel right now it's easier just to agree with somebody."

It was the courier from Major Gray who brought Marlowe up standing. It was the first time today that the colonel really began to feel that this, at long last, might be the place where the whole thing ended.

"The rear guard got a good look, Colonel," the courier panted. "Four mounted companies, or thereabouts, and the sonsabitches got two guns with 'em!"

Now, Marlowe thought, is the time to come up with something really brilliant, but just how do you go about it?

"Major Gray says he needs orders," the courier said.

"Well," Marlowe said acidly, "to begin with he might try praying—"

"Beg pardon, sir?" said the startled noncom.

"Never mind, Corporal. I'll have to think of something better than that. In the meantime tell the major to tighten his files and keep coming. Let them have the first bite."

He had a fine mental picture of those two guns. They would of necessity be small bore, probably two-pounders, otherwise they probably couldn't have been moved this far in the mud; but if this

Rebel decided to lay shrapnel fire in that narrow road it was apt to be the end of the four present companies of the First. Shrapnel from even light guns, at what this range would be, could be hell on earth. Still, the visibility was poor and darkness not too far away.

It took no special genius to hazard a good guess as to where this second Confederate force had come from. At a road fork three hours earlier Marlowe had made a mental note. Another road entered this one, angling in from the northwest, and at the junction an almost illegible sign had read: Payton—Deerwester—Port Gibson. Marlowe hadn't the least doubt that this second force had come from Port Gibson; it could hardly be otherwise. His information so far, taken at face value and discounting the guns, indicated that even without Ware his own force well outnumbered these other two together. As in a checker game, the choice position was the one in the middle and he had it—up to now. He could go through either of these two forces if he so chose and if it came to that, but he was going to be clawed badly in the process. There was the further possibility that all these things were irrelevant details and the two forces in front of and behind him were only part of a far larger enveloping movement. According to the only information he'd had in the matter, the Confederate General Gardner at Port Hudson had 20,000 men at his disposal, 1,500 of them cavalry. True, Port Hudson was at least fifty miles to the southwest. But if the brigade could move more than four hundred miles southwest through central Mississippi, then most surely Gardner could move fifty miles in the opposite direction without straining himself in the least—he could if the Rebels wanted the brigade badly enough, and Marlowe thought they did. Maybe these two present forces were no more than decoys, waiting for the main show to put in its appearance. The colonel wondered if an animal, not quite dead, might feel something like this as it watched the buzzards gathering overhead.

The firing in his front had almost stopped—he was just now aware of that. And somehow he actually relaxed a little when the firing in the rear began—he had been unconsciously expecting it. He was instantly aware that there was something odd about this rear fire but at the moment he couldn't isolate the peculiarity. He whirled his horse and splashed toward the rear—Gray far more than Secord was likely to need advice now.

Gray and Captain Bryce, both mounted, were at the roadside when the colonel came flogging up in a small blizzard of mud—but they weren't anything like as far along the road as he'd expected them to be. Bryce belonged here, for here was where A Company was, but Gray—? What was he doing here, with the action of the moment obviously so far away? At this distance Gray couldn't possibly know what was going on, much less do anything to control it.

"God damn and blast it, Gray!" For once the colonel allowed his anger to have its own way. "What the hell are you doing back here, so far from the action you can hardly hear it? By God, sir! For the second time in two days—!"

"Hold it!" Gray said coldly. "Take another listen, Jack. None of that fire is coming from this part of the First."

Well, and so it wasn't. If the colonel hadn't been in such a blind, tearing hurry he might have seen that this section of the First was all here in the road. They were tense and waiting, ready, to be sure, but they weren't firing at anyone, not yet.

Gray and Bryce looked at the Old Man in mild astonishment as the colonel brought himself up short and then actually chuckled aloud.

"Oh, great Lord!" Marlowe said. "This is too rich. That's Ware tangling with that bunch back there. We ought to have a copy of Hardee's *Tactics* to tell us what to do next—this is a situation no one in his right mind could have invented."

"Could be," Bryce said soberly, "but from here it just doesn't look that funny to me."

"Don't you see? We're piled up here in the road like a damned four-layer cake—Rebels, us, more Rebels, Ware, or vice versa.

And I'd wager a month's pay neither of those two Rebel forces knows who or what the other one is."

But Marlowe sobered, thinking, his mind alert again. He could bring three or four companies of the Second back to help Gray, and if Ware had enough sense to understand what was happening they would smash this Rebel force to bits. Marlowe would have wagered more than a month's pay that he knew exactly what had happened. The force there in his front had obviously advanced eastward on the Natchez road, eventually meeting them head on. The other Rebel, coming down the Port Gibson road, had picked up their trail at the road fork—it could hardly be missed in this mud, and promptly followed the brigade back toward the west. Then Ware and *his* men, coming into this same Natchez road from the southeast, no doubt hurrying to catch the brigade, had moved in behind the Port Gibson Rebels, probably blissfully unaware that they in turn were following both fox and hounds.

Marlowe's black depression went away as fast as it had come. Now—he couldn't have said why—he was as sure as a man could be that they were going to get clear of this. He'd had that feeling momentarily after their initial success at Newton but it had gradually dwindled into his near-despair of a half-hour ago. Now the feeling of elation was back and he felt some of his sodden physical weariness pass away for the time being.

"Gray," he said briskly, "send a man—no, better make it two men, around this Rebel here and get in touch with Ware. Tell him, first, where we are, so he'll know exactly. Then tell him he's to drive straight in while we move back from this end. Tell him he's got nothing to worry about."

"I'll go, Colonel," Bryce offered.

"No, you won't, Bryce," Marlowe told him. "You've had your independent excursion. Get a couple of good men, Gray—and hurry. Don't move your own force back too fast—give the couriers a little margin to spare. I'll be back."

He set off down the rainy, slowly darkening road to find Secord and give him his orders. Along with everything else he was now worrying a little about ammunition, or more precisely the way it might now be distributed. They had all started with forty rounds but in the nature of things some men had scarcely fired a shot while others would have nearly empty cartridge boxes. This matter of distribution could make a difference.

A horseman loomed out of the rain ahead and Davis's voice called, "That you, Colonel?"

"Yes, certainly. What is it?"

"Captain Bishop reports back that he's right up to the edge of this place, Union Church, and has lost all contact with the other people. He thinks they've pulled out entirely while they had a chance, when they found out what they were up against. He needs instructions, sir."

"All right," Marlowe said briskly. "He'll get 'em, and soon!"

Union Church was only a hamlet and a small one to boot. Bishop's men found a meagerly stocked general store and promptly kicked in the front door. Captain Bishop had orders that the Old Man wanted a place where he could hold a staff conference to canvass the situation. They found only candles to provide light but the boys were lavish with them—the store proprietor was furnishing the candles even though he didn't know it yet. The perennial forager, Sergeant King had turned up a small store of peppermint-stick candy and passed it out as long as it lasted. The sergeant also hotted up the stove at the rear of the store and Marlowe, Gray, Secord, and Lieutenant Davis were enjoying the last of King's hoarded store of Vicksburg-bound coffee. Lieutenant Colonel Fairlie of the Second was here too, but he had stretched out on a wooden counter and gone quietly to sleep.

Marlowe had long since known that Captain Ware had the situation in their rear well under control, but it was an hour and a half after full dark when Ware himself arrived to report. The rain had stopped earlier but the captain still looked as though he'd been sleeping in a hog wallow—with the hogs for company. He also looked as exhausted as he was in fact.

"Well," Marlowe said almost too impatiently, "what happened back there?"

Ware sat wearily on an upturned keg and said, with infinite weariness, "You mean back there at Byhala or this afternoon, sir?"

"Well, both, but this afternoon particularly," he interrupted himself to say warmly, "I know you did well. Did you lose any men?"

"I think two or three, Colonel, but in the God-damned dark and rain and mud there wasn't a chance to make a sure check. Matter of fact, we haven't had a chance yet—the company officers are doing it now."

They were all silent for a moment. This was always one of the hard things. Those two or three men might have only been wounded but in this weather and darkness they could only have been found by accident, and with the situation as it was there could be no going back after them when daylight came again. Well—

"Much trouble besides that?" Marlowe said. As he talked he was trimming the skin from a cold boiled sweet potato and enjoying the inside in a way he would once, not so long ago, not have imagined possible. "Sergeant," he said, "please see if you can find me a little more salt. This yam wants a bit more flavor."

"Enough trouble to last me a long time, Colonel."

"I guess that's true. Everybody gets his share sooner or later. Sergeant, see if there's some of that alleged coffee left for the captain—"

"Well, we came into this Natchez road here about two miles east of the Port Gibson fork and in this mud the trail was plain as a goat's backside. Leastwise it was plain that cavalry had passed that way and there was no reason to suppose it wasn't all ours. The boys perked up a little and we figured we'd be back in the line in short order. Then the whole thing blew up in our faces. I figured at first some of our own rear guard was trigger jumpy and I was ready to take somebody apart—until I caught sight of those two guns they had. Believe me, Colonel, that scared the living hell out of me. The thing was, I didn't have any place to go but back and where would that get me?"

"But the couriers got to you?"

"Yes sir. Good men. If it hadn't been for them I'd never have known what was going on; how could I? Actually, it was them brought word the Rebs were pulling out, across country to the north, away from the road. It was getting dark and some of them almost ran over our two men before they got to us. We kept pushing, feeling them out to make sure they were actually getting away and not just sucking us into something. One of their guns got mired in a little creek and a squad out of F Company ran smack dab into 'em. I guess they came out about even."

"Even how?" someone asked.

Ware chuckled in spite of his weariness. "One side was scared as bad as the other. The Rebs yanked their two-bit gun of there by main strength and awkwardness and the squad got the hell out in the opposite direction. Is there any more coffee, Colonel?"

"What happened at Byhala?"

Ware shrugged, as though that was an old and often-repeated story. "The usual thing, Colonel. We put as big a hole in the railroad as time would allow and lost two men and some horses in the process: Mahaffey and Stillwell out of F. A bunch of these damned home-grown militia. They let go one good blast and then high tailed it for the woods. We stole enough horses to replace and got a couple extra for good measure. Say, we heard some racket up here in front—we figured there was more trouble."

"Not that amounted to anything," Marlowe said, "at least not yet."

Secord yawned vastly. "Well, comes the usual question—what now?"

Major Gray had been leaning against a molasses barrel, apparently more asleep than awake. Now he came suddenly erect and spoke directly to Marlowe, "I'd like to raise a point—if it's permitted, *sir*."

Marlowe's brows moved upward a trifle. It wasn't Gray's question which made him wonder, but the manner. They never stood on formality in these conferences, and in the circumstances the fact that subordinates were present wouldn't have mattered. "Well?" Marlowe said.

"How far do you make it to Vicksburg?" Gray said in a tight voice.

"Call it fifty miles."

"And how far to Natchez?"

"Say forty, give or take a little."

"And how much to Baton Rouge?"

"Hmm," Marlowe said, wondering, "call it twice as far as Vicksburg."

"Then I say either place is better than Baton Rouge!"

There was sudden tension in the room. Again it wasn't the major's words—they had often enough discussed these things loosely—but his manner. They all sensed that Gray wasn't really discussing or considering, but challenging.

Marlowe regarded him noncommittally for a moment, then he said, with deceptive mildness, "Your head isn't working, Dick. Natchez, supposing we could get there, would leave us with our backs to the Mississippi and half the Confederate army in front of us. Vicksburg is simply an unknown factor, not worth considering as long as we have any other choice. Our prime business now is to get the brigade out as nearly intact as possible. No—Baton Rouge is our best chance. It comes down to the longest way around being the shortest—"

"By God, Jack, you're guessing—as usual!"

Colonel Fairlie came awake with a start and swung his legs to the floor.

"Careful, Dick," Marlowe said evenly but coldly. "Call it what you like, it's got us this far. That covers it as far as I'm concerned."

He was certain he knew what was gnawing at Gray, and even if he sympathized a little he could only permit the major to go so far. He, Marlowe, had to keep this on an impersonal basis or he was lost. Tempers were already too short all the way around.

It was Fairlie who almost exploded the situation. For one thing he ranked Gray and for another he was a part of the Second, not Gray's command. These things made a difference in official relationships. In this army, for better or worse, it was the regiment around which all else was built, and while the officers of different regiments perforce cooperated they also felt, maintained, an almost bitter independence of each other.

So far Fairlie had said not one word—in fact, no one had paid any attention to him, and they were all rendered momentarily speechless when without preamble he took a half-step toward Gray and said tensely, "By Christ, Gray! Are you trying to tell Colonel Marlowe his business?"

The major stood his ground. "Maybe it's time some of us did! Maybe it's time—"

"God damn you!" Fairlie said bitterly. "After yesterday afternoon you shouldn't be allowed to give orders to a platoon—"

Secord moved. "Easy, easy," he said. For Gray he cared nothing, or almost nothing, but Fairlie was something else again. His own voice was suddenly angry but it was also surprised and a little bewildered. "What the hell is going on here anyway?"

"That'll do, gentlemen!" Marlowe's voice cut across the tension like the crack of a mule whip. More mildly he said, "I'll handle it, Frank."

"Well—" Secord began.

Gray's mouth twisted slightly and from a corner of his eye he saw Captain Ware looking at him curiously. The major suddenly felt tired beyond all enduring, and as though a well of hostility had closed around him—

"One moment, gentlemen." Marlowe's voice was even but glacier cold. "Major Gray has raised a point that it seems he didn't intend. Your suggestions are welcome but over and beyond that I will run this business according to my best judgment as long as I'm able to function. When I can't, then the responsibility will fall to Secord, but until then not to him or to anyone else! I won't put the question as to whether that's clear. It has to be because there is no alternative."

Giving them a chance to collect themselves, he momentarily turned slightly and said to Ware, "I'm obliged to you, Captain. Better get some rest—you've earned it and we'll be getting away early. Davis, suppose you see if that patrol has come back from the west yet—"

The candles flickered as Captain Bryce pushed the door open and paused at the threshold. "Excuse me—" he said, wondering if he was interrupting something.

"Come on in, Bryce," Marlowe said—a sudden thought in connection with Bryce had occurred to him. "Your A Company will be at the head of the line again in the morning, so you'd better be in on this." He paused for a moment, looked from one to the other of them. Satisfied, he said, "Now, here is the situation—

THE PURSUIT

It would be foolish to suggest that the eventual fall of Vicksburg was due to the work of Colonel John Marlowe and the First Brigade. For once General Pemberton had determined to stand there, and Grant in turn had determined to bring the full weight of his men and metal to bear, then Vicksburg fell victim of the logic of events. Nevertheless, the value of what the brigade accomplished could never be measured with real accuracy—certainly it went far beyond anything its original planners expected or even hoped. All General Hurlbut or anyone else had asked was that Marlowe break the Southern Railway–Vicksburg–Jackson supply line and then make his own escape if he could. No one foresaw the astonishing dislocation of Confederate forces all over Mississippi. No one could ever accurately estimate the amount of

Confederate force wasted at one time or another in some phase of the fruitless pursuit, but it was probably no less than 10,000 men—a force which, concentrated in the right place, very well might have prevented Grant from crossing the Mississippi and taking Grand Gulf, which became the anchor point of the Federals below Vicksburg.

General Pemberton's preoccupation with Marlowe's activities was beyond ordinary understanding. Sometimes he acted as though he knew—and after ten days he certainly should have even if the reports were conflicting—that the brigade was no more than an oversized raiding party. At other times he acted as though the brigade was the sole Union threat to the Western Confederacy, and Grant's legions as nothing. After the strike at Hazlehurst, for instance, it seems that Pemberton should have been able to estimate the brigade's strength within a few companies—and Gardner at Port Hudson to the southwest had enough force to swallow Marlowe's command. Yet on that same day Pemberton ordered the luckless Colonel Barteau—Blaney and the Second Iowa had long since escaped Barteau, after hurting him badly—all the way from northeastern Mississippi to Hazlehurst, a distance of more than 250 miles.

At the actual scene of operations—the scene as far as the brigade was concerned—it was Colonel Wirt Adams's cavalry from Port Gibson (and Natchez) which of all the Confederate pursuit first made actual contact with the brigade. Captain Cleveland's three companies, which advanced eastward from Natchez through Union Church, were actually a portion of Colonel Adams's Tenth Arkansas Cavalry, which, in turn, at Port Gibson, made up most of the cavalry defense of Grand Gulf nearby. Captain Cleveland, in the nature of things, never hoped to do more than delay the brigade on the Natchez road. The detachment of the Tenth Arkansas which was caught between Marlowe and Captain Ware was commanded by Colonel Adams himself—to his misfortune he'd had no way of knowing the brigade in his front was not intact, and he didn't find out until he was caught in the middle. Then there was nothing for him to do except pull out, which of course he did, making a flanking movement around the brigade at Union Church during the night and joining forces with Captain Cleveland beyond the village. Colonel Adams had things all planned. Before approaching the brigade from the rear he had sent five companies from his own force, the Tenth, to nearby Fayette, to set an ambush into which he confidently expected to drive the brigade. As a plan it was perhaps not too badly conceived (at least it was a definite plan), except that his force was too small and nothing went as he had expected. After joining forces with Captain Cleveland, Adams sat squarely across the road to Natchez —on this route and in this direction where else could the brigade go?—set for another and larger holding action. In view of all the furore set afoot by Pemberton, Adams didn't doubt that help would be along shortly.

Help was on the way. On this morning of the twenty ninth 500 cavalry under Colonel Bob Richardson arrived in Hazlehurst from Jackson to the north—about two days too late. After some difference of opinion as to which way the brigade had gone—a confusion brought about by the fact that the detachment under Captain Ware had actually gone south—Richardson guessed correctly and headed west for Union Church. He was aware that Adams and the Tenth Arkansas were somewhere to the west. The prospects of catching the brigade in a larger squeeze appeared excellent—except that Marlowe wasn't there to be caught. When Colonel Richardson finally made contact on the Natchez road it was with his own companion in arms, Colonel Adams.

In the meantime Confederate patience was wearing thinner and the trap they were preparing in the area of the Louisiana–Mississippi line grew ever wider and deeper. In addition to the various commands now closing in (supposedly) on the brigade from all sides, General Gardner sent Colonel Miles's Louisiana Legion— 2,300 men plus a battery of field guns—from Port Hudson to Clinton, squarely across the route the brigade must take to reach Baton Rouge.

But with all their planning, and their now vastly superior numbers, there was one factor, in the long run perhaps the most important of all, which the Confederate commands could not control: the continuing good fortune that rode with Marlowe and the brigade.

31

Fox and Hounds

At daybreak the colonel reversed the column almost in its tracks. Moving by back roads and across country, southeast from Union Church to Brookhaven, they came to the latter place late on the afternoon of the twenty-ninth. It had been another day of short rations and hard riding but they had seen nothing resembling a Confederate soldier.

(Colonel Richardson, having again picked up the trail where the column had reversed its tracks at Union Church, was following doggedly. But Richardson now was not a direct threat. He could travel no faster than Marlowe and the only way he could expect to overtake him was for the brigade to be stopped by something in its front.)

At Brookhaven they again made a big hole in the line of the N. O. & J.—someone remarked that they all now regarded railroads not as lines of transportation but something to be torn up as expeditiously as possible. Actually they hardly stopped at Brookhaven. They turned south again here and the physical assault upon the railroad was really no more than a part of the process of moving. This had the disadvantage of stretching the column precariously thin, but that too was a risk the colonel took deliberately. Perhaps, he told himself, it was a foolish thing to do. But there was always the possibility that they would not make it in the clear, and if that had to be—these things were always on the knees of the gods—then he would have sold for the highest possible price. Always the one thing had to be balanced against the other—it was one of the curses of command.

They worked their way still southward, from Brookhaven through Summit, and Marlowe pondered the matter of going on to Osyka. The word at Summit was that strong Rebel force was moving rapidly north along the railroad from as far south as Ponchatoula, in Louisiana, and Marlowe was willing to assume this was true because it *ought* to be.

It was surprising how, here in supposedly enemy territory, so much information was handed them gratis. Much of it was misinformation, probably some of it was deliberate misdirection—not much, for the civilians are few who will singlehandedly try to divert a cavalry column the size of this one, and a great deal of it was true. There was more sheer friendliness toward the brigade than anyone not experiencing it could have imagined. Yet after all families are peculiar, and what was this except a family quarrel on a national level?

In the end it was not Marlowe who made the real decision regarding Osyka. It was Colonel Secord—and Marlowe was secretly glad of it. At a bivouac below Summit, Secord sought him out and asked for a private word. Marlowe said, "Certainly, Frank. I wanted to talk to you anyway."

A red moon was just rising on the eastern horizon and they walked a little way from Marlowe's fire. When they stopped walking Secord said, "Have you decided whether to go on to Osyka tomorrow?"

"It's rattling around in my mind," Marlowe parried. "Why?"

Secord ignored the question and said, in what was apparently an abrupt change of subject, "Have you ever known me to question your judgment, Jack?"

"Why, no," Marlowe said in surprise. He smiled thinly. "At any rate not publicly—and since I've been in a position to give the orders."

"And you don't question the fact that I'd take the Second wherever you ordered me to—or anyway try?"

"Don't be a fool, Frank!"

"All right. Then I'm saying to forget Osyka. Let's get the hell away from this railroad and make for Baton Rouge—tomorrow morning."

For a long moment Marlowe was silent. Then he said quietly, "Any special reason, Frank?"

"One good enough for me. Simply and frankly, I've had enough. I think I'm not the only one. Gray—"

"God damn it, are you making excuses for Gray? Because if you are—!"

"No," Secord said calmly, "neither making excuses or anything else. One thing I'm saying is that a man has his limitations and he doesn't necessarily set them himself. He doesn't always know when he's reached them—or gone beyond. There's such a thing as quitting when you're even, too—and as of now we're way ahead."

"Frank, listen to me—"

"No," Secord said stubbornly. "This has been between you and me. If you say Osyka in the morning, then that's where we go. But I wanted you to know how I feel—I thought you ought to. Let's leave it at that."

"I—" Marlowe began, and then he stopped. For a very long moment the silence hung between them like a stone—until Marlowe said, "Very well, then, Frank. I guess we understand each other. It will be Baton Rouge in the morning."

. . . Finding himself again at the head of the column, along with Bryce and the returned A Company, it might have been supposed Gray should have felt relieved to be back in his usual place. Actually he felt no such thing. Perhaps it was simply a matter of natural human perversity. Having been wrongfully removed from his proper place—Gray's reasoning—he was likewise suspicious of the motives which restored him. When Marlowe deliberately switched him after his failure at Hazlehurst he'd assumed it was the Old Man's way of showing he no longer trusted him—*post hoc ergo propter hoc.* Marlowe hadn't said so, had chosen to be maddeningly noncommittal, but there it was. And now, with no word of explanation, he had been put back—and *that* was suspicious. (Actually the switch at Hazlehurst on Marlowe's part had been plain common sense. He wanted Secord out in front because the Second was intact under one command whereas the First was then split into three parts, A Company not having come up yet. At Union Church the First was intact again for the first time in ten days, and since Marlowe wanted to turn the column in its tracks, doing that automatically returned the First to the lead position. In the course of the weary march to Brookhaven the various companies had gradually shuffled themselves until they were in the normal A, B, C positions. It was as simple as that and involved no more thought on Marlowe's part.) Was Marlowe planning something in which he, Gray, would catch the first blow? Who, in the circumstances, could predict what Marlowe would do? And then, with his mind in this particular state of disarray, he recalled that the First hadn't been returned to the lead until after the arrival of Bryce and A Company. He was quite aware that Marlowe had a high opinion of Captain Bryce as an officer—so did he for that matter. He was also aware that Bryce had refused the majority before it was offered to him. Could it be that the colonel was now trusting him only under the guardian eye of Bryce? That too was galling to his mind. In his state of mind it was natural that he should overlook one further possibility, the only one that was actually true—none of these things existed save in Major Gray's tired imagination.

One by-product of all this was that Gray scarcely spoke to Bryce except in the briefest kind of way and when it was necessary in carrying out routine procedure. Bryce didn't mind, in fact he thought nothing of it. For this was generally true of the entire column now. All the way down the line the men had reached a state of fatigue beyond fatigue. There was no more lighthearted humor, no more horseplay, no more snatches of song. Men spoke to each other in monosyllables and then scarcely more than duty required. They performed routine chores almost as a matter of automatic reaction, one result of the long, dull, grueling hours of drill.

Watching them pass by him on the road southwest of Summit on this fresh May day morning, Marlowe wondered if they would be able to whip a first-rate Rebel company should the need arise. He felt suddenly old himself—perhaps Secord had been right. No, there was more to it than that—perhaps he had known this all along and it had needed Secord to make him face up to it.

As for fighting—he had no idea now just how soon he was going to find out.

Somewhere down this endlessly winding green tunnel of pines and white flowering magnolias lay the Tickfaw River. The Tickfaw, and the much larger Amite farther west, together with its tributary Comite, flowed perversely southward to empty into Lake Maurepas, the smaller sister of Lake Pontchartrain, rather than into the Mississippi—and this in spite of the fact that at one point the Amite came within fifteen miles of Baton Rouge. The word they had was that Tickfaw and Comite were fordable but Amite was not.

With Bryce and A Company in the advance—the Old Man had warned the captain not to get more than a half mile ahead but that was always a relative matter. The Old Man had also warned him against the Tickfaw bridge. Not that the bridge itself was important if the stream could be forded, but a bridge was always a logical blockade point. If there were Rebel troops in the area—and Marlowe did not see how there could not be now—the bridge would be the focal point of their activity. So now A Company moved cautiously. Bryce knew the crossing was up ahead; he did not know where it was in relation to his own position.

There was another thing. Although their route was now generally south-southwest, by an accident of topography they were approaching the Tickfaw from the west, moving straight east—these roads wound and twisted here in order to find the high places in this low, swampy country. Somewhere east of the bridge the road would turn south again. But at the point where they turned east, about ten o'clock this morning, another road entered from the west, forming a T intersection. They had halted there for a few minutes when they found Sergeant Nate Brown and Privates Stark and Burris, the point, which had again been established, waiting for them. The Sergeant dismounted, waved his arm from west to east along the road. "Have a look, Cap'n. Horse prints an' horse dung—an' damn' fresh. Cavalry—what else?—an' sure as hell not ours."

Bryce gave the trail only a cursory glance. Brown, having looked intimately at perhaps ten thousand horse hoofs, could read the impressions they made almost better than he could read print. That, among other good reasons, was why Bryce had him out as point.

Bryce nodded and said briefly, "Can you say how many?"

Nate shook his head. "Not too close—at a guess I'd say a couple hundred, but it's a guess, Cap'n."

"All right. Keep going, Nate, but make it single file and keep as far over on one side of the road as you can."

They waited to give Nate a little head start, and Bryce sent a man back to alert the column.

. . . The sergeant moved cautiously but steadily forward, keeping well over to the edge of the road. It was perhaps a half-hour later when he glimpsed a plantation house off to his left, gleaming white in the center of its park of magnolias and acacias; it was several hundred yards from the road. The point moved on, even more cautious and alert now. At a place just beyond the house the road turned abruptly left. And a hundred yards on down the road there were three horsemen. The animals were tethered under a tree. Two of the men sat on a fallen log and the third lay on his back on the ground, his hat pulled down over his face—probably asleep, Nate thought. The two men on the log glanced in the point's direction but neither of them moved. Three rifles were stacked carelessly against the log.

"Easy now," Nate said softly. "I'll handle it to begin with but be ready for whatever we have to do."

They moved on at a walk, riding loosely, as though in no hurry to get anywhere.

A dozen feet from the log Nate halted and said easily, "Howdy, gents. Y'all on picket?"

"Yeah, an' damn' tired of it too," one of the men said. He yawned. The man on the ground didn't stir.

"Huntin' them slippery Yanks, I reckon?"

"Not huntin' exactly. We're headin' for Osyka. The word is they're headin' down there an' we aim to cut 'em off. Plenty o' help comin' from north an' south along the railroad," the butternut said indifferently. "But they say this Gen'l Marlowe is slippery as a greased eel." The man got up and stretched.

Nate warned Stark and Burris with his eyes and knew they got it. "That's what we heard too," Nate said. "What outfit you boys from?"

"Major De Beaun's Ninth Loosiana Rangers." The butternut's eyes suddenly narrowed. "Say . . . !"

The heavy Colt snaked out of Nate's holster and he barked, "Make one move, Reb, an' this'll cut you in two!"

The other man on the log made the mistake of starting to get up. Stark set his spurs brutally and his horse's chest struck the man squarely, catapulting him backward for ten feet. Burris was on the ground, and as the man who had apparently been asleep started to rise Burris put a boot against his rump and shoved. Even as the man's face went into the dirt Burris swept up the three rifles where they stood against the log. Nate too was on the ground now. He lowered his pistol as Stark and Burris covered the others with theirs.

"Where the hell is this Ranger outfit?" Nate said.

"Go to hell, you Yank bastard!"

Nate was perfectly aware of the rules regarding the interrogation of prisoners, such as they were. But he was bitterly tired, hungry, nerve drawn, and in a hurry. The pistol barrel snaked out and smashed the man across the stubbled jaw—not hard enough to stun him or knock him down, just enough to make him reel for an instant and to hurt cruelly.

"I said, where are they?" Nate repeated harshly.

Sullenly, as the man held his jaw with one hand, "Down at the river crossing."

"The bridge?"

"Yeah, I reckon."

"How many of you? Talk up, God damn it! We're in a hurry!" Nate of course knew A Company would be rounding the sharp bend any moment now. He wanted to hand over the prisoners and get on down the road.

"Three companies. Couple hundred men."

"All right. What're you doin' back here?"

"Rear picket. The major wanted to water an' rest a little. They're gonna send to call us in when they're ready to move."

"Not today they won't," Nate said grimly. "Any more o' you around anywhere?"

"Four. They'll be back. An' when they are they'll fix you Yank sonsabitches for keeps."

Whatever Nate was going to say next was lost in the sound of the gunfire which erupted around the bend behind them. Oh, Christ! Nate thought. Now they've warned the whole damn' Reb outfit at the bridge! He could guess what had happened—A Company had run into the other four pickets. The gravel lane which led to the plantation house lay back around the bend.

. . . Bryce, Nate, and Lieutenant Rogers conferred briefly. It had been as Nate guessed. The other men of the picket had emerged from the lane and run straight into A Company in the road. Now two of the unwary pickets were dead and Sergeant Baker had a charge of buckshot in one thigh.

"The God-damn' shooting's warned everybody in the county," Nate said.

"How could it be helped?" Bryce retorted. "Take your boys and feel on down the road a piece but don't start anything. Fall back on us. We'll be right behind you."

Once more Nate and his boys moved on down the road, tense, every sense alert. It was perhaps a quarter mile farther down that they saw the other horsemen. They were standing in the road, as though waiting and listening for something. As they came closer Nate could see, in the brilliant near-noon sunlight, the twin gold bars on the collar of the taller of the two riders; the bars twinkled in the brilliant light as the man's horse moved slightly. Nate motioned with a hand for the others to move more slowly.

The officer rose in his stirrups and shouted, "What the hell is going on back there?"

Nate cupped his hands and yelled back, "I can't hear you!"

From here it appeared that the officer was armed only with a pistol, the other trooper only with a carbine or musket on a shoulder sling.

Nate said, "Burris, when we get within jumpin' distance of 'em you cut out the private and keep him covered. Don't fool. If he makes a bad move let him have it. Stark, you an' me'll ride in on the fancy officer an' take him. You go in on his left side and nail his pistol. I'll go in on his right an' get *him*."

Even as the pickets back up the road these two suspected nothing and it went like clockwork. Burris seized the reins of the private's horse and covered him with his pistol. Nate and Stark moved in on the startled officer knee to knee, and as the man's hand shot toward the holster flap Stark seized his wrist in an iron grip and with his other hand yanked the pistol free. Nate moved to grasp the man's right arm but the officer twisted free and attempted to strike at him. Nate shifted his tactics. His oaklike right arm went around the man's neck—of course both he and Stark were facing the man, literally lifted and dragged him up and out of the saddle and over the horse's rump, let go, and let the officer crash into the dust of the road. They sat their horses and watched passively as the man scrambled to his feet, alternately pale and livid with rage.

"What the hell is the meaning of this? Can't you God-damned stupid conscript hunters see that I'm an army officer? God damn you! I'm Captain Pierre Darbois of the Ninth Louisiana—"

Nate grinned as he interrupted Darbois. "I know, Captain. But you're mistaken—we ain't huntin' conscripts. We're huntin' real live mean Rebel sonsabitches, the rougher the better, an' we'll take 'em alive or dead, it don't matter—"

When Darbois started to say something Nate again interrupted. "Happens you two are prisoners, Captain. This is a detachment out of the First Illinois, Gen'l Marlowe's First Brigade—you found us sooner than you expected, I reckon. Burris, take that private's old iron and heave it into the brush. Then you herd these two back up the road. Tell Bryce we'll wait here for them—an' for God's sake for them to keep it quiet. I caught a sight of the bridge up ahead." He looked quizzically at Captain Darbois as he said to him, "You can get back on an' ride, they won't be takin' the horses away from you till you get back to the brigade."

When the company came up Nate said to Bryce, "The bridge is there, a little to the left where the road bends a mite again. Me, I say we've rode far enough."

Bryce nodded. "I think so. We'll make it afoot from here on."

They left the horses, drawn into the brush at one side of the road, and went on, one platoon on either side of the road Indian file, taking cover and moving as stealthily as might be. Bryce had the men on the right, Rogers the other. Except for the katydids and the croaking of frogs in the low ground it was so quiet that once, when he twisted under a muscadine, Bryce could actually hear his belt leather creak.

It wasn't much of a bridge, something more than fifty feet long and perhaps six feet above the present water level. As Bryce and Nate peered cautiously through the screen of brush they could read the story clearly enough. De Beaun's men had obviously wanted to render the bridge useless once they were all across but they hadn't wanted to burn it—in the Confederacy heavy planking, like railroad iron, was hard to come by. Already they had taken down the siding and it was piled carelessly at either end of the bridge, but the floor planking was still intact—as with practically all these bridges it was only wide enough for one vehicle or two horses abreast.

Bryce could see nothing but he knew only too well *they* were there, in the thinner timber and brush on the other side. In a lush magnolia nearby a mockingbird sang with sudden piercing sweetness. The captain's throat contracted—so much beauty, so much useless blood spilled and to be spilled. Behind them now in the road there was the growing thunder of hoofs, faint at first and then growing in volume. Gray would be along now. He'd dropped back earlier on business with B Company.

"God damn Gray!" Bryce said with quiet savagery—there was little need for caution now. He and Nate were now perhaps a hundred feet from the bridgehead. Bryce caught a metallic glint in the brush on the other side of the little river. He stepped into the road as the major slid his horse to a halt.

"What's going on here anyway?" Gray demanded, almost as though everything was about to end in violent disaster and it was all the captain's fault.

Farther down the road, too far, Bryce could see the colonel on the outside of the column, passing the files, pounding toward them here.

"We haven't had time to find out yet," Bryce said coolly. "It's dead certain that brush across there is sure death for somebody. If you'll just hold on—"

"Hell!" Gray exploded. "The only way to get across the damned bridge is to cross!"

Without thinking, meaning nothing at all, an ordinary instinctively friendly gesture really, Bryce raised a hand and grasped the bit ring of Gray's horse. At that same moment one of De Beaun's Creoles, probably tense with the waiting *they* were doing, let go a single shot.

Gray snarled, "Get your damned hand off that bridle!" At the same time he swung his horse so that the ring was jerked from Bryce's hand and snapped at the bugler, "The Charge!"

The man's short-coupled calvary bugle came up in instantaneous reaction to the order, and the shrill call shattered the momentary stillness.

"No!" Bryce cried out even as he leaped out of the way. "For Christ's sake, Dick, wait—!"

Nobody but Gray then or ever would know what went through the man's mind at that moment. He sank spurs in his horse and was on the bridge in seconds, yards ahead of the first files behind him—

Bryce shouted, hoping he could be heard above the hammering hoofs, "Nate! Rogers! Get your men up to the bank and see if you can give them some help. On the double!"

Gray got perhaps twenty feet onto the bridge proper. Running toward the riverbank, pistol in hand, Bryce saw the whole thing. It was a cinch that the men on the opposite bank were looking straight down their rifle barrels when the bugle sounded. It seemed to Bryce, and it was highly probable, that Gray and his mount were hit at the same time. The horse stumbled and went down, slithered across the bridge planking—there was no longer a rail even to break the motion—and went off into the river on the downstream side. As near as the captain could tell Gray never came out of the saddle.

The lead files had been yards behind the major but once started, and with the pressure building up behind them, they couldn't possibly stop.

Marlowe, riding outside the column, had almost reached Bryce and Gray when the bugle sounded—but not quite. Someone, seeing Marlowe reel in the saddle, cried, "Oh, Jesus! They got the Old Man—" and then the owner of the voice was swept onward.

Being outside the column, Marlowe hadn't been able to get on the bridge because it was already filled with riders. The blow—that's exactly what it felt like, caught the colonel high on the left breast. He bent backward in the saddle but instinctively clung to the reins to keep from falling. The horse, hurt sorely when the bit was yanked suddenly upward in its mouth, reared in an effort to relieve the pressure. Marlowe, when the animal reared, was thrown abruptly forward again before he could catch himself. One foot came out of the stirrup and he slid sidewise along the horse's neck. Past the center of gravity and unable to recover now, he freed his other boot and slid slowly to the horse's thick mane. He staggered, still clinging to a rein, choking and unable to get his breath for a moment. He took for granted that he was hit and so did Bryce, who was at his side in a matter of seconds.

Hell was loose on the other side of the river but at the moment there was nothing Bryce could do about that.

Involuntarily the colonel's hand went to his breast, where the pain was beginning to form, but strangely, after a few hard gasps, he began to breathe easier and his legs seemed perfectly all right—and there wasn't a drop of blood anywhere.

"Better get off your feet, Colonel," Bryce said with rough urgency. "Here, let me—"

"Just hold on a minute," Marlowe said in an odd voice. He had jerked open his tunic and Bryce could see there was a small hole in the cloth—it might have been no more than a small tear. The colonel reached for his shirt pocket and extracted the watch—his forefinger could feel the deep dent in the soft gold of the back. As Bryce watched in astonishment Marlowe pressed the stem release and flipped open the hunter cover on the front—smashed bits of crystal and small brass parts cascaded over his fingers and fell to the ground.

It had been a beautiful watch, of course, and anyone would hate to have it ruined, but even so Bryce was a little amazed at the look of anguish in Marlowe's face as he stared at the small wreckage in his hand. Marlowe muttered something Bryce didn't catch but he thought, He should be congratulating himself instead of fretting over a watch.

In his sudden relief Bryce said, in an attempt at humor, "Too bad it wasn't a Bible, Colonel. Then you could testify to the usual personal miracle——"

"God damn y—," Marlowe started to say. Then, "No, I'm sorry, Asa—but you'd never guess what kind of a miracle it actually was. Was that Gray on the bridge?"

"Yes," Bryce said soberly, back to the reality of the moment, "yes, it was. He seemed—oh, hell, I don't know."

. . . The melee on the far bank had been almost as short as it was ferocious. For once Marlowe had misjudged his men badly. In his mind the question had not been, Would they fight? but, Could they? They were weary beyond all description, yes, but they had also played the role of the hunted for so long that when the chance came to strike back it was like a tremendous emotional release. They had come this far, it would take a great deal to keep them from going the rest of the way. For the Ninth Louisiana this was a routine operation, but for the brigade it was their only way out. They had struck De Beaun's Creoles like a small thunderbolt.

"Well," Marlowe said harshly, "whatever he thought, and did, it's done now. So now you're elected to the First. You'll take it now because there is no choice, Bryce."

The captain swung around. "No—!"

"You heard me and I shouldn't have to repeat it. As of now you're in command of the First."

"Why, hell, Colonel. Fairlie ranks me and—"

Almost unnoticed by either of them Secord had ridden up and

dismounted. "What about Fairlie?" Secord said heavily. "I didn't suppose you'd heard over here yet."

"You mean finished?" Marlowe said quickly.

Secord shook his head. "No, not yet. But he got it bad, damn it! Keller's working on him now, along with the rest, the rest of the First, I mean. Wells is taking care of my people, naturally, but Fairlie happened to be where Keller could get at him easier than Wells."

The colonel looked at Bryce and said, "Well, now, Asa?"

The captain took a deep breath and said, "Very well then—so be it, Colonel."

"Then I suggest you get across the river and get about organizing your command. We'll be moving out again as soon as things can be straightened out over there."

As he watched him go—A Company's horses had been brought up now—the colonel thought, Well, it's that kind of army—the First in command of a captain; the Second with a full colonel but without either a major or lieutenant colonel. It was the old refrain—a hell of a way to run a war; but it still held good.

Thus it was that Bryce came to the Tickfaw bridge a company commander and crossed it as an acting colonel of regiment.

As a matter of routine Bryce sent three companies of the First after the departed Rangers. Bryce didn't want to catch them, he merely wanted to make sure they didn't decide to stage another ambush, even though this one had been more or less thrust upon De Beaun.

In the meantime, for Marlowe, there was once more the problem of the casualties. He made his way to Keller's erstwhile field hospital—to give it a courtesy title.

"What, precisely, is the situation, Keller?" the colonel asked tersely.

"We have four outright dead from the First, all of them from B Company, I think—they were right behind Major Gray," Keller said with wooden correctness. "There are two more wounded men who probably won't last out the day—"

"Would having more medical supplies make any difference?" Marlowe interrupted.

Keller shook his head. "No—it's just that they haven't quite gone over the edge yet—a matter of hours, more or less. There are four men hurt but who can still ride if they have the guts and want to get out badly enough. They won't be any good militarily but riding won't make them any worse—at least not until they can get more medical attention later on—and of course there's Wells of the Second. There are two more wounded. They couldn't ride under any circumstances but with medical care, even without the proper drugs, they'd have a better than even chance of making it."

"Does that include Fairlie?"

"It does, Colonel."

Marlowe rubbed his forehead wearily. Not much went on in the brigade that he didn't know about in one way or another. And one of the things he knew was that Keller, regardless of his coventry since Newton, had never for a moment shirked his medical duties. They had not been great, to be sure—one broken arm, a trooper with a mashed foot that a horse had stepped on in the dark, saddle boils, the usual bowel trouble from bad water and food, but Keller, when well he might have, had never equivocated.

The colonel looked around, saw the two wooden-faced privates, in this instance Hall and Burch out of G Company, who were serving as Keller's secondary shadows. "You men are dismissed from your present duty as of now," he said wearily. "Report to your company commander and tell him not to send any replacements."

"Yes *sir!*" they answered as though with one voice.

Keller's lips twitched a little sardonically. "Is that supposed to mean something special, Colonel?"

"As far as I'm concerned it means that as of now your status is exactly what it was when we left La Grange."

"I take it that means you're withdrawing any charges against me?"

"If you want to put it that way. Officially, of course, there never were any—or perhaps I should say formally rather than officially, if you like the distinction."

"I'm much obliged to you, Colonel."

"No," Marlowe said. He sighed faintly. "No, Major, there is no reason to thank me, sir. On the other hand, I have no apologies to make. Suppose we leave it at that."

"As you wish, Colonel," Keller said with a slight bow.

"Now there's the matter of Fairlie and this other man—"

"Sergeant Francis."

"—Yes. Well, do you have any suggestions?"

"Yes, Colonel. They'll have to have professional care in order to make it at all. With your permission I'll stay and give it to them."

"You'd do that, Major?"

Keller shrugged. "Who else is there? Wells can take care of anything between here and Baton Rouge."

"If you do this," Marlowe said slowly, "you know it's a hundred to one you'll end up in a prison camp."

"I suppose so, but that would be a secondary consideration, Colonel. I think I told you once that medicine is where you find it. Let's leave it at that. Before you go I'd appreciate some help in having these men moved back to that plantation house we passed on the other side of the river. Whatever kind of people they are, they can hardly refuse shelter to men as badly hurt as these—I'll handle it. I would appreciate the help of at least one sound man —of course that's asking a great deal."

"Yes," Marlowe said, "it is, but I think you'll get it. Now you'd best get about your business while I get about mine."

The colonel ordered a team and wagon found and it was—he never bothered to ask how or where. But a sound man to stay behind with Keller—you could ask a man to volunteer for a risk that might make him a hero but how ask a man to volunteer for the sure hell of a Rebel prison camp? Still, he had promised Keller, at least by implication; he would have to try because he could do no less. It was then that Private Burch found him.

"Permission to speak to the colonel?" Burch said stiffly.

"Certainly, but do it fast!"

"I understand Major Keller is staying behind with the wounded, sir. I been—well, with the major three days now. If he stays he'll need some help. With the colonel's permission, I'd like to stay."

The colonel's manner softened imperceptibly as he said, "What's your name?"

"Private Steven Burch, sir, G Company."

"That would be Captain Bracey. Does he know about this?"

"Yes sir. I had his permission to ask you, sir."

"I see. Are you sure you know what you're letting yourself in for?"

"Yes sir, I'm sure," Burch said steadily.

The colonel looked at his open blue eyes and rather solemn face and thought, Well, if he's not he'll find out soon enough. "Very well, Burch—and I won't forget this. Get your horse and gear and report to Major Keller immediately. And Burch—"

"Yes sir?"

"Good luck, son."

Marlowe stood beside the road near the east end of the bridge. Keller had his wagon loaded and was ready to move even as the bugles were sounding the Fall In. Marlowe said, "I'm giving you an escort as far as the house, Major, just in case. They can catch up with us."

"I doubt we'll need it, but thanks. By the way, I turned my horse over to Captain Bryce—good man there—he'll need him worse than I do now."

"I—er." For once the colonel seemed somewhat at a loss for words. "I just want to say that if it's humanly possible I'll get a party back here to you from Baton Rouge. But you know—" the colonel's voice drifted away.

Keller smiled faintly. "I know. Don't make any promises you can't keep, Colonel. I never expect miracles."

"I said *if*, sir. That's the best anybody could do."

"I guess we understand each other."

"I wonder," Marlowe said almost musingly, "I wonder. Will you shake hands, Major? I'll wish you luck."

The bugles were more urgent now—Secord and Bryce would be driving the men.

"Why not, Colonel? And luck to you."

32

The Last Long Ride

The word was that this would be the final drive for Baton Rouge. Aside from the usual breaks to water men and horses and attend the calls of nature the brigade would not stop again unless it was stopped. There were no threats that anyone would be abandoned if he failed to keep up. It was assumed that one man was as able as another—the riding wounded, of course, were an exception—and no one expected to be carried.

Later, in both time and space, and as men will, many who were there would recall the ride from Tickfaw bridge to Baton Rouge as an all-out, hell-for-leather rush for the safety of the Union lines, with the enemy practically breathing down the backs of their filthy necks—time is a mirror which has a way of distorting these things. They traveled more nearly at a crawl than a rush. Men straggled, really through little fault of their own. Animals went lame and had to be beaten and spurred cruelly. For those who made it this ride was memorable enough in itself and without embellishment.

Sometime during the late afternoon they left Mississippi for Louisiana, though no one knew exactly when—there was no "line" as such and the semitropical scenery didn't change. This was delta country here, not remotely central or northern Mississippi. Actually this territory north and east of Baton Rouge, in the military sense, was much like that in Mississippi south of La Grange. Union troops held Baton Rouge firmly and had for a long time, but beyond was a sort of no-man's land which the Federals merely patrolled for an indeterminate distance to make sure the Confederates weren't moving in. Likewise Rebel patrols probed toward the city to make certain no extraordinary movement was coming out of Baton Rouge. The wandering patrols were here only to observe and communicate and they constituted no great force in themselves.

This being delta country, and the first day of May, the temperature rose to the mid eighties and, to men totally unaccustomed to it, the accompanying high humidity was worse than mere discomfort. Near physical exhaustion already, the heat and humidity sapped their strength still further. The dust rolled up by the shuffling hoofs was inescapable, they couldn't outrun it, there were always too many men who had to be behind. The dust powdered and coated skin, beards, uniforms, horses, equipment; it settled in every skin crack and crease and their copious sweat made these as raw as broken blisters. There was no escape for anyone. Few men prefer mud as a condition and they had suffered their share in the past two weeks, but right now a *little* mud would have been welcome. In these two driving, grueling weeks few of them had had off more than hats, boots, and tunics, and these only on occasion. They had been subjected to rain, mud, dust, heat, swamp and river water, wood and gunpowder smoke, and now, individually and collectively, they stank to heaven. There was no other word for it—they stank.

Well, having taken so much, they could take a little more.

As usual the weight on Marlowe was heavy—in his mind he carried *all* the knowledge that the others, officers included, only had piecemeal. From information gathered bit by bit, for instance, he knew that Colonel Miles's 2,400-man Louisiana Legion was—had been—at Clinton, Louisiana. Sometime this evening the brigade, on this route—and for them there was no other now—would pass through Greensburg, and Greensburg was no more than ten miles from Clinton. What did Miles know? And knowing it, what would he do? Some sixteen miles beyond Greensburg was Williams's bridge over the Amite. Every information said the Amite was unfordable and this bridge was thus the last gateway to escape. What if Miles was waiting for them at the bridge—or somewhere in between? What if some corporal's guard had already burned the bridge? What, what, what?

Except for what he could snatch in the saddle this would be one more sleepless night—his eyes felt now as though they were full of hot cinders. Physically he felt all right otherwise, in fact right now he felt strangely buoyant. Sheer exhaustion would overtake him eventually, he knew, and he would go out like a snuffed candle, but that was a luxury he and the brigade could not afford yet, not yet.

They plodded into Greensburg after dark and slowed only long enough, one company at a time, to water men and horses. Men were as usual detailed to make the routine inquiries—there were always people ready to talk whether they knew anything or not. But here no one knew anything about the Louisiana Legion except that there had been a lot of soldiers in and around Clinton for several days. Of course this at best was negative information. The Legion might very well have gone southeast to Williams's Bridge without anyone in Clinton having the least knowledge of the move.

(The Marlowe luck was still in. On hearing of the fight at Tickfaw bridge Colonel Miles had immediately moved his Legion in that general direction, but his luck—or judgment—was bad. As the brigade passed southward through Greensburg the Legion, some five miles to the north, was turning into this road over which the brigade had just come, but turning north, toward Osyka, and *away* from the brigade. Whatever the reason, Miles had dawdled in Clinton too long—he could have divided his forces

—half of them would have been more than a match for the exhausted brigade, and covered both the Clinton and Greensburg roads. Instead, he had missed his last, best chance by a hairbreadth as distance. At Osyka, in the meantime, Richardson and De Beaun had met and compared errors of judgment, joined their two forces of 500 and 300 cavalry and again started doggedly southwest. They both knew now, whether or not they admitted it to each other, that the game was about over, but in any case they would play it out to the end. Their only real hope was that the Louisiana Legion would head the brigade this side of the Amite and they would come up from the rear for the finale.)

Now after dark, from the colonel's point of view and that of the other officers as well, the worst thing was the terrible straggling. During the day the men helped each other. If you dozed and awakened to find your file man was gone you could look around and find him. But now in the dark you dozed, awakened, and found yourself riding among dark shapes you didn't recognize. As someone remarked, they were scattered all over hell and half of Louisiana. It was a good thing, Marlowe thought grimly, that they had a road to channel them or they would have been over half of Mississippi as well.

After dark the heat abated considerably but the rolling dust was there the same as ever, adding gray fog to the inky darkness. Later there would be a moon, but it would be late.

Roving up and down the line, Marlowe traveled half again as far as the others. He kept his quirt so busy that after a while the flesh of his wrist was nearly raw. He exhorted company commanders, snarled and swore at them—and wondered if it did any good at all. He was certain that by morning, in spite of all that could be done, he would have lost more men. All they could do was try to keep the number down. Men—their animals rather—staggered, slouched, limped, drifted, meandered, moved in fits and starts, singly and in bunches, in everything except regulation formation. But they moved.

"God damn it, Colonel!" a nameless company commander exploded in exasperation. "We can't carry the sonsabitches on our backs!"

"I know, but it's up to you to move 'em one way or another. Remember they're riding, not walking. Get a club and bear down on the horses. If the horse moves, the man has to."

If it was hard on the animals then the answer was that horses were more expendable than men. Men slept in every conceivable position. Some had their friends tie their ankles to the saddle cinches to keep from falling. It was a dangerous and foolish business but officers gave up trying to stop it. Some of the men would remember this as the longest night of their lives; others remembered it only in dark patches or not at all.

. . . The yellow moon was up, at least full above the horizon, and Marlowe had the feeling it was late—he no longer had a personal means of knowing the time. He heard Sergeant Brown of A Company inquiring along the line for him.

"Here, Sergeant—what is it?"

"Cap'n Bryce thinks we're up to the Amite, Colonel. Must be from the size of it. He'd like you to have a look."

"Right away, Sergeant."

They rode down on the outside of the standing files; almost every man was now asleep.

To the waiting Bryce Marlowe said, "You been up there, Asa?"

"No sir, I was waiting for you. Nate was up there—he had the point."

From here, with the thick growth of willows and other stuff pressing in on the road, the river couldn't be seen.

"How far is it, Sergeant?"

"Call it two hundred yards, sir. There's a little kink in the road just ahead. There's a fire on the other bank. Seems to be maybe three hundred feet upstream from the bridge itself."

"All right, Asa," Marlowe said. "Come on. We'll walk—I want to get the kinks out of my legs."

As they stood in the shadows near the very entrance to the bridge Bryce could hear Marlowe's almost passionate sigh.

The moon wasn't high enough to light the river brilliantly, but there was enough light for them to see the Amite—the bridge was about six hundred feet long—rolling swiftly and bank full, and the long, dark line of the bridge itself. As Nate had said, there was a fire of some sort upstream on the opposite bank, and still a little farther upstream a light as though in a dwelling of some sort. In the deep night quiet they heard a man shout something on the far bank but they couldn't distinguish the words.

"I think, Asa," Marlowe said slowly, "that if I manage to live a very long time I'll never see a more beautiful or more welcome sight than that. You know what it means."

"Yes," Bryce said soberly, "I know what it means, Colonel. Once across that strip of timber—and it looks as open as a baby's face—we've made it. My congratulations, Colonel!"

"Suppose we leave that until later, if ever," Marlowe said dryly. "Right now we have to decide what to do here and now. Now see what you think of this idea—"

Even as they had watched a man had left the area of the fire and walked toward the bridge. Within minutes another man arrived at the fire *from* the direction of the bridge.

"I'm going to gamble that there's actually only one man at the bridge," Marlowe said. "My guess is that that's a picket fire and the guard has just changed. Send three mounted men across the bridge. They're to act as though they're in no hurry—let 'em walk. When they're challenged they'll say they're couriers for Port Hudson. That should get them within jumping distance of the picket. After that it will be up to them. When they've secured the guard they will signal and you'll take the rest of A Company across as fast as you can make it. After that we'll see what happens. Or have you got a better idea?"

"That's good enough to try," Bryce said laconically, "except that I suggest you start the rest of the column across directly behind us. If we need help over there that will get it to us. If we don't—well, you'll be that much farther on your way."

"Good enough. Who do you want to send?"

"Lieutenant Rogers, Nate, somebody else they pick themselves."

"All right, let's get back then."

It went almost too well. A quarter-hour later the broken cadenced hoofs of the brigade were thudding on the bridge planks. An aide of Secord hurried up to inquire whether the rear guard should fire the bridge when they were across.

"Tell Colonel Secord no," Marlowe said shortly. "I don't want to waste the time now. Besides, that's a lot of bridge to have to replace and our own people coming up from Baton Rouge may want to use it one of these days."

The colonel technically was not the last man across the bridge, but he waited at the southern end until the last man was across. As the rear guard, K Company of the Second, came across he called, "Is that everybody?"

The company commander, a Lieutenant Dixon, recognized Marlowe's voice and said respectfully, "Yes sir, as far as I can tell. We've been trying to stay about a quarter mile behind the column and when we closed up at the bridge we were careful to gather everybody in. In this dark we may have missed somebody but we tried not to."

"That's all anybody could do," Marlowe said. "Get on with it, Lieutenant."

He never knew when he went to sleep, how long he slept, or what finally brought him awake again. But when he did awaken he knew instantly that he was utterly alone. The horse was cropping grass at the roadside, apparently contented and oblivious of its limp rider. Coming out of the unawareness of sleep the darkness seemed the more intense—there were stars but a reef of cloud had drifted across the moon. He was aware of insect sounds, the faint creak of his saddle when he moved, the sound of the horse's hoofs as it changed position in the tall grass. His senses came alive as though released by a spring, and when the release came he experienced a wave of sheer terror that was actually physical—he could feel it in his whole body, blind, wholly unreasoning, and wholly gripping, for the moment drowning every other emotion. He might have awakened and found himself alone and adrift on an ocean without limits.

It is somehow assumed that a man is either brave or not brave, that this is a condition which either does or does not obtain, always and everywhere. But this is not so. Like almost everything else bravery is a relative thing—a man may defy all tigers and still flee a specific mouse. So at this time and place Colonel Jack Marlowe was afraid. He did not understand it or try to—one does not analyze fear when it is so acute it blots out every other thought.

The emotion remained though much of the paralysis passed after that first sickening moment. In an almost helpless reaction he lashed savagely at the neck of the wholly innocent animal under him, jerked its head upright, and in blind, conditioned obedience the horse shuffled off down the road.

Gradually, with the physical movement, the terrible feeling drained away and his normal faculties began to take over again. He even relaxed enough to grin mockingly at himself—he was the hard-shelled drill sergeant who, showing a recruit the manual of arms, manages to shoot himself in the foot.

Then, suddenly, he reined to a stop. The sound had been there before but only now did it reach his conscious mind. Guns! At a very considerable distance, to be sure, but certainly guns, and very heavy ones. There was no mistaking the sound once you knew it. Columbiads, or very heavy mortars. These could only mean gunboats, and gunboats could only mean the Mississippi. Port Hudson? Most likely, in fact it had to be—it was now the southernmost Confederate position on the river, not far above Baton Rouge—and in the great closing movement around Vicksburg Grant would be covering every possibility. The point was, this sound should mean something to him—his tired mind told him that much but no more.

And then—great God, yes!—he had the answer: this fire came from his left. *From his left!* Asleep for he knew not how long, he had then blindly lashed the horse into motion—and now he was moving dead in the opposite direction from the brigade, back the way they had come! He could feel his body ooze sweat and the terror moved in him again, but only for a moment. He dismounted, moved over to the side of the road and then beside it for perhaps twenty yards. His eyes became more accustomed to the darkness and he managed to avoid obstacles and pitfalls. He felt in a pocket and found two sulphur matches—just two! He knelt at the edge of the road and, nursing the match to sputtering flame behind the shield of his hand, he almost held his breath. The flame flared, smoked, died down, then moved into steady life, and in the deep dust he could see the melange of countless overlapping hoofprints, all pointing directly opposite the direction he'd been traveling. His sigh of relief was almost a sob.

It was near the edge of dawn when he came in sight of the ghostly figures of the rear guard—rear guard in name only now. No one challenged him—no one so much as made a greeting of any kind. He might have been General Lee for all anybody cared. Those who were half-awake regarded him with about the same interest they would have shown another fence post. Those who were sound asleep in their saddles kept right on sleeping, dead men on almost dead horses.

Riding on up to find Secord, he again found Sergeant Brown looking for him. "Cap'n Bryce's compliments, sir. We're at what seems to be the Comite. We've checked it careful—no bridge of course. They'll get their asses wet but we can make it easy enough. Cap'n Bryce wants instructions."

"Then tell him just to get on with it as he sees fit, Sergeant."

The eminently correct young lieutenant inevitably reminded Bryce of the equally correct and youthful Confederate major at Enterprise. This one, however, wore Massachusetts insignia on his stiff clean uniform collar, his accent was pure unadulterated Back Bay, and he had behind him a patrol of some twenty men. His face, at sight of the hairy, filthy, junk-laden horsemen filling the road as far as he could see, was about evenly divided between astonishment, embarrassment, and distaste.

"I'm Lieutenant Barry, Captain—staff of General Wayne, commanding at Baton Rouge," the youth said stiffly.

Bryce grinned in appreciation. "Captain Bryce, lieutenant, commanding the First Illinois Cavalry, First Brigade, First Division, Sixteenth Army Corps." Keep the record straight, he thought. This was where order began again.

"Command—?" The lieutenant looked his well-bred unbelief. "Did you say *commanding?*"

"That's exactly what I said," Bryce said shortly. "What can we do for you, Lieutenant?"

"Did you—er, say First *Illinois?*"

"That's what I said—from La Grange, Tennessee, by way of Newton, Jackson, Hazlehurst, and God knows what points between in Mississippi—and right now we've got business in Baton Rouge that we don't aim to put off. We've been on the road now for something over twenty-eight hours and fought one right smart engagement on the way. Our men are a little beat, Lieutenant."

"Well—" The lieutenant was looking more and more uncomfortable. "We had reports that some unauthorized force was operating in this area. My instructions are to hold you—any such force—until I can report the facts to General Wayne's headquarters."

"Well, I'll be— Did you say *hold?*"

"Er—in a manner of speaking, of course. Since we have no information of any Federal troops operating here, why, naturally we—"

"How far is it into town?" Bryce interrupted abruptly.

"Why, about five miles."

"That close? You'd have been in a mighty peculiar predicament if we'd turned out to be a bunch of those red-necked sonsabitches of Forrest's."

"That's not the question, Captain."

"Well, no," Bryce conceded gravely, "you've got a point there.

But I'll tell you, Lieutenant—I daresay my boys would just as soon sleep here as anywhere, but—"

Lieutenant Barry looked down the files of A Company and was startled to see that at least half of them *were* asleep and the rest seemed to be in a kind of doubtful state.

"—However, I'm only in command of this regiment, not the brigade. That's Colonel John Marlowe and he very likely will have a different view."

"You might have said so, Captain," stiffly. "Naturally I didn't know—"

"Well, you didn't ask me," Bryce said solemnly. "Let me give you some friendly advice, Lieutenant. This Colonel Marlowe is a salty sonofabitch. He's brought this brigade about six hundred miles without being stopped by all the Rebels in Mississippi. He'll likely take a very dim view of being stopped here by a few feet of headquarters red tape. Nate," he said to the sergeant, "get on down the line and tell the colonel he's wanted."

"I—well, naturally I have my orders," Barry said even more uncertainly—he couldn't recall any regulation which covered this exact situation. He had come to the deep South by way of New Orleans and General Ben Butler's occupation troops (which of course wasn't his fault) and this was the first real contact he'd had with these shaggy and irreverent Westerners. They might not be complete barbarians but from the looks of things they didn't come up to—well, maybe conform was the better word—the standards of New England troops. This Captain Bryce and the way he spoke of his brigade commander—while they waited the captain sat, or lounged, with one leg thrown over the saddle pommel, resting, and even when the colonel appeared he didn't move an inch. Bryce simply jerked head and thumb in the lieutenant's direction and said indifferently, "Fellow here wants a word with you, Colonel." The lieutenant knew better—he saluted.

Marlowe hadn't been far away. In fact, he had made his way forward as soon as the road began to clog up and had met Nate on the way. He listened to Barry courteously, then turned to Bryce and snapped, "How long have you been stopped here, Captain?"

"Oh, ten minutes, give or take a little."

"Then that's ten minutes too long. Now, Lieutenant, I'm not advising you, I'm telling you. The best thing you can do is to high tail it back to your headquarters and tell General Wayne we're coming in and any kind of official permission is irrelevant."

"I—am I to report you verbatim, sir?"

"Suit yourself. You will also tell him that I need camp space and first-class rations for nine hundred men and horses. Your horses are fresher than ours, Lieutenant. Even so I suggest that if you don't get the hell out of here we'll be there ahead of you, because we're moving now."

The lieutenant got out of there in a fast-moving cloud of dust.

Even so they came into the outskirts of Baton Rouge and halted. It was only common sense—after all they had no idea where they'd be going now. As a matter of routine procedure Marlowe, with Davis and King, went on ahead to General Wayne's headquarters.

What Lieutenant Barry told the general the colonel never knew nor cared. But it so happened that the general was a perceptive man with both imagination and a sense of humor, and once in possession of a few odd facts, both from Barry and Marlowe, he knew he had something unusual on his hands. Whatever the whole truth might prove to be, a brigade, even one as under strength as this, didn't materialize out of thin air. If no more than half of this were true then the general was witnessing the finale of a small miracle.

Baton Rouge was no city in the New Orleans sense, but neither was it a mere country town. It had been the state capital until the Federal capture and occupation and its people had a certain Latin feeling for drama. Since they couldn't get rid of the Federal garrison it was only common sense to get along with it, and like New Orleans the place was partial to public parades and diversions. The entry of the battered First Brigade, what was left of it, was hardly triumphal in the ordinary sense—it was both something less and more. This was Saturday afternoon and the word went round that something unusual was happening. So Baton Rouge turned out en masse to watch and cheer, for these were brave men and it did not matter that for the moment they were on the other side.

The shiny-booted major in command of the honor guard saluted Bryce and Secord and said formally, "If you gentlemen are ready we'll be glad to conduct you through town to your camp grounds."

"Quite a turnout you've got there, Major," Secord said dryly. "It wouldn't have taken all that to get us through town."

"General Wayne's orders, Colonel. I—personally I'd like to say it's an honor."

It *was* quite a turnout for such short notice. The flags of the cavalry squadron snapped in the breeze and its horses were sleek and shining. And behind the honor guard was the crack band of the Fifty-fifth New York. Saddle sore, filthy, dead beat, their horses lame, streaked with sweat where they weren't coated with caked dust, the brigade got itself into formation of a sort. Baton Rouge never saw anything quite like it before or since. Here and there men rode with bloodstained bandages, no more than able to stay in the saddle. Here a trooper rode with one foot out of the stirrup, a boot sole flapping loosely. There was a man with one tunic sleeve ripped from shoulder to wrist.

. . . The general set out cigars, a bottle and glasses, and within five minutes became an enthusiastic audience of one. Of necessity Marlowe had to explain matters up to a point, and presently Wayne was exclaiming, "Well, by God, sir, this is simply astonishing—astonishing!" The general also had a sense of occasion, and twice he left the office to issue hurried orders of his own.

"I'm sorry, sir," Marlowe said finally—he had tried to make it fast but even so it had been an hour since he'd left the brigade and he'd found a far more amiable and expansive welcome than he'd expected. "If you'll excuse me—personally I'm at your service at any time but I owe the men their rest. God knows they've earned it. The least I can do—"

"Certainly, certainly, Colonel! I sit here jabbering as though you'd just come from a canter in the park."

As they got to their feet Marlowe swayed and staggered a half-step, steadied himself with a hand on a table top.

"Man!" Wayne exclaimed contritely and grasped Marlowe's arm. "You're half-dead and I don't wonder. Plenty of time to talk later and in the meantime I'll get telegrams off to Memphis. I can't get directly to Grant at Vicksburg but he'll hear eventually. Come along, my boy."

Still holding Marlowe's arm, the general conducted him down the corridor and out onto the broad stone steps of the building. At the edge of the street Sergeant King was still holding his, Marlowe's, horse. The general nodded to someone. The drums rolled off and the band swung into the stirring brilliant "Sword of Chapultepec."

In the street Lieutenant Rogers, now in command of A Company, barked above the brass, "Eyes left, God damn it, and the saber salute at the order!"

"Hell, General," Marlowe said a little sheepishly, "this was hardly necessary—we're not used to it."

"Nonsense, Colonel! I'm only sorry we didn't have time to do it up properly."

"Well, for the sake of the men—"

As he watched the First go by, file after file of sabers flashing in the hot sunlight, he suddenly remembered that last dew-fresh morning at La Grange, so far away and long ago, felt that same lift of the heart which had nothing to do with the larger issues of the war—and a very great but quite unselfish pride which few men are privileged to know more than once and most men not at all.

Far down the tree-bordered street the drums crashed and the band shifted into the warm, lilting melody of "Listen to the Mockingbird." The colonel's throat hurt a little and again he was having trouble seeing clearly. Dust and lack of sleep, he thought.

33

Epilogue

Bryce had finished his letter, addressed to the Reverend Jonathan Bryce, Congregational Rectory, Dover, Illinois. He let the sheets lie on the table under the orange light of the field lantern as he relighted his dead cigar.

Strange, he thought, how he should remember his father in this particular way at this moment. He had, since the beginning of his war service, been home on leave three different times, but now he was remembering the night in May, two years ago this time, when he was to go into the service for the first time. The old man (though Bryce did not think of him as old), thin and rather frail-looking, his wispy hair very white, his manner uncompromisingly gentle, had stood there by the desk in the study, and Bryce had thought, for the first time in his life, this is *my* father—my *father*. The thought, or rather the way it presented itself, was a little shocking. A curious thing. Of course Jonathan Bryce had *always* been his father, and that was just the point. One took a father more or less for granted, not in the sense of being indifferent, but in the very nature of things. And this was the first time Bryce had thought specifically: this man is my father, this man and no other, and without him I would neither be nor be what I am. So long as he is here I am, in a sense and whether I prefer it that way or not, but an extension of his shadow. And thinking this way he had seen his father in an entirely new light, felt for him a regard, a compassion—in the meaning of a fellowship of feeling, a tenderness that was, and for the first time, intensely personal. . . . Bryce let his eyes drift over some of the lines he had just written.

"—A difficult, in a way foolish operation, but it was carried out with remarkable success, as success in these things is measured. There was, to be sure, a fantastic amount of luck involved, otherwise this would be written, if at all, from some Rebel prison camp . . . but above all there was the brigade commander, the Colonel Marlowe I have written you so much about. It is now, however, and properly, Brigadier General Marlowe, though I think that is a matter of no moment to him . . . if they had given him an army corps the Union cause would be that much better served . . . We have been told, by people who set store by such matters, that ours was the longest military march within a given time on record, and this to say nothing of what we accomplished on the way . . . to keep the record straight I should tell you that my proper title is now lieutenant colonel . . . more responsibility, naturally . . . always so in a regiment of cavalry, for unlike men, horses, valuable as property, can't be dismissed and left to shift for themselves . . . had refused the promotion before but accepted it now through force of circumstances. I find it difficult to explain—"

A shadow fell across the corner of the table and a slightly drunken voice, a cautious mixture of jocularity and due respect, said, "Am I interruptin' anything, Major?"

Ninety per cent of the brigade, particularly the enlisted men, had not a cent in their pockets when they arrived in Baton Rouge. But in their first flush of enthusiasm the Creole tavernkeepers had been lavish with both hospitality and credit. And wisely, that first Saturday night and Sunday after their arrival, the provost looked the other way unless they were molesting some of the local citizenry or breaking up private property.

"Not a thing, Nate," Bryce said. "I'm all through. Come on in."

Sergeant Brown looked curiously around at the inside of the tent, though it was precisely like ten thousand others. It did have an entirely impersonal appearance—Bryce hadn't been here long enough to give it any mark of himself. The sergeant looked as though he had expected to find something special about it.

"I take it this is now official regimental headquarters of the First," Nate said with monumental gravity.

"Well, temporarily at least, though frankly I hadn't given it much thought, Nate."

"Un-hunh. Well, naturally I been uptown speculatin' around but I heard the word. I reckon congratulations are in order— Major."

"If you feel that way, then thanks, Nate. But—as long as we're on the subject we might as well keep the record straight—it's lieutenant colonel, not major."

"The hell you—er, well—uh, congratulations anyway."

Bryce chuckled. "All right—I get the point."

Nate said, "You know, Cap'n, you an' me have soldiered a long ways together—" He hesitated.

"A long ways, Nate," Bryce agreed. He hadn't missed that deliberate "Cap'n." He knew from wide experience that Nate wasn't that drunk.

"Un-hunh. Well, from now on we won't be seein' each other quite so much, I reckon—"

"Oh, I don't know." Bryce intended to make Nate his personal orderly, but decided now was not the time to bring up the subject.

"Well, I know, Cap'n," Nate said owlishly. "So while I'm drunk enough I want to tell you this story—I probably won't have a chance again. No offense, nothin' personal, you understand? Well, anyhow, it seems like this fellow's uncle died an' left him a barrel o' money, and all his friends said, 'Y'know, inheritin' all that money ain't gone to ol' George's head a bit—he's the same no-good sonofabitch he always was!' "

Bryce's laughter bubbled and choked around his cigar until he took it from his teeth. He started to say something, then stopped when their ears caught the first faint, faraway notes of Tattoo, the preliminary to the Lights Out to follow. It was a call almost never used by the buglers of the First Brigade, nor had they played a Taps since the night before they rode out of La Grange. But here in Baton Rouge General Wayne was running a spit-and-polish garrison post and they had all the trimmings. Now, as soldiers will, they waited and listened, each lost for the moment in his own thoughts, until the last long trumpet note died away.

Set in Linotype Janson
Format by Edwin H. Kaplin
Manufactured by Geo. McKibbin & Son, Inc.
Published by HARPER & BROTHERS, *New York*

TENNESSEE
ARKANSAS
MISSISSIPPI
MISSISSIPPI
MEMPHIS & CHARLESTON R.R.
MISSISSIPPI CENTRAL R.R.
MOBILE & OHIO
RIVER
PEARL RIVER
La Grange
Corinth
Iuka
Ripley
New Albany
Pontotoc
Houston
Tupelo
Verona
Okolona
West Point
Starkville
Macon
Louisville
Philadelphia
Grenada
Durant
1ST DAY
2ND DAY
3RD DAY
4TH DAY
5TH DAY
6TH DAY
7TH DAY